It's Not Your Mother's Bridge Club

It's Not Your Mother's Bridge Club

Michele VanOrt Cozzens

McKenna Publishing Group

San Luis Obispo, California

It's Not Your Mother's Bridge Club

ISBN: 978-1-932172-30-0

LCCN: 2008933140

Cover design by Leslie A. Parker

First Edition
10 9 8 7 6 5 4 3 2 1
Printed in the United States of America

Visit us on the Web at: www.mckennapubgrp.com

For All My Sisters:

Wombmates, Roomates

And of the Sledge Variety

Also By Michele VanOrt Cozzens

NONFICTION
I'm Living Your Dream Life:
The Story of a Northwoods Resort Owner

The Things I Wish I'd Said

FICTION
A Line Between Friends

The Snake Eyes Dice Club

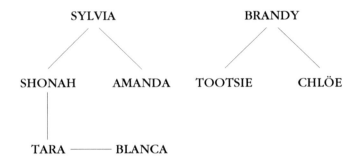

Prologue:

I know one woman who plays mahjong, and a couple who play bridge. But I know about a hundred women who play bunko. What is bunko? First of all it has nothing to do with cards. Imagine the game of Yahtzee married to the game of craps. Bunko, a dice game played throughout suburban enclaves of twenty-first century America, is the innocuous scion of this union. And a dice club or bunko group isn't about the game. It's about the women who play it.

The Dice Club is a fun, girl's night in, and a once-a-month chance to get out of the dinner, homework and clean-up routine and spend time with friends. It costs a five-dollar ante, requires a little imagination when providing either a gift or, in some cases, a costume for the theme. In terms of intellectual stimulation, it's a bit like a book club without having to read a book.

The game of bunko is played in pairs with four to a table. Some groups, like ours, have eight. Some have twelve or even sixteen. Players begin by rolling three dice for ones. Each one rolled counts as a point and rolling continues. Should no ones come up on a roll, the dice are passed left. The object is to reach twenty-one points. Three ones in a single roll is a bunko, and it automatically scores twenty-one.

The Top Table has the bell and controls the game. The first pair to reach twenty-one at this table rings the bell and play stops. Winners stay for the next round and losers move to the Bottom Table. When play for twos, threes, fours, fives and sixes ensues, new pairs are formed and the dice continue to roll. By the end of play, odds are good that players have teamed up with each member of the club, and bonds of friendship accrue more quickly than points.

—Shonah Bartlett
From her column, *The Dice Club Chronicles*

Chapter 1
September

Shonah

I'm forty-five, a journalist soccer mom. That's the six-word life story I came up with while listening to NPR the other day. It was a challenge using only six words because my life includes so much more and, well, words are my life. My name is Shonah Bartlett, and I'm also a wife, a sister, a girlfriend, a daughter. I am a twenty-first century American woman, who is unaccustomed to limits since I've always been told I can have it all. Recently, though, I've learned that having it all actually means doing it all. And so I do my best.

Tonight I'm doing my best to prepare my house for a party. I'm hosting The Snake Eyes Dice Club. We are eight women who gather regularly to play bunko and during the school year we meet once a month. Or at least we try. In the last two years our meetings have had all the regularity of a menopausal menstrual cycle. So, it's probably better to say we meet when we can, once a month if possible, and never in the summer. This is the Rattlesnake Valley, after all, a desert community in southern Arizona. Temperate in December, and as my fellow Dice Club member Tootsie Fennimore the Alabama Belle would say, hotter than a red-assed bee in July.

I volunteered to host the Dice Club to kick off our fifth season to get my hosting responsibilities out of the way, and have been preparing for two days. We just returned from our summer cabin in Telluride and it usually takes weeks to get the stale smell of desert out of my furniture, and the collective of dried, crunchy crickets and spiders vacuumed up. I've got my sons, Sammy and Jonas, enlisted in a cleaning frenzy. Jonas, who is ten, thinks it's great fun collecting critters. Sammy, on the other hand, my bright boy who is best described as a middle school mélange of hormones, is currently not participating. He's either in the shower or in the mirror.

"Awesome!" cries Jonas. I set down a Windex bottle on my kitchen counter and look toward the television armoire to see denim pockets swinging in samba dance fashion. I watch as he slowly turns, and before his wide, crooked grin, he displays a leggy bug that looks like something I made with my Creeper Crawler machine in 1965. It's six inches long and the color of snot. "It's a scorpion! Can we keep it? Please?"

"Keep it?" My shoulders shimmy the heebie-jeebies. "Are you out of your mind?"

"DAD?"

Dan, my all-boy husband, overrules my decision with a nod of his head, and the dead, snot-colored scorpion is added to the collection of creepy crawlers residing in our garage freezer. Jonas stores it next to the frosty boxes of fund-raiser foods I know we'll never eat.

Bless his heart, Dan has veto power on anything resembling snakes, snails or puppy dog tails. The minute he brought home an Arizona Cardinals football helmet and an infant-sized jersey for Sammy, I put him in charge of all things testosterone. I grew up with three sisters, learning very little about things that make young boys pant with delight—particularly the creatures that grow and roam in the desert. For whatever reason, I thought scorpions were red. God knows I didn't see any growing up in the Pacific Northwest. I must have equated scorpions with lobsters.

It's just after six. Dan has shuffled the boys out the door taking them to dinner, which means the house is suddenly quiet. The air is full of anticipation. Mine. Any moment my kitchen will be filled with the high-pitched, long-time-no-see squeals of eight women. Sylvia will be first. The ever efficient and capable Sylvia Ostrander will sashay through the front door, hips first, without bothering to ring, and we'll give each other the same double-cheeked air-kiss we've been exchanging since fifth grade. I love having her to myself—even if it's only for five minutes. Nobody can make me laugh the way Sylvia does, and in that brief time before the desert mirage world that is the Rattlesnake Valley world steps in again, we'll revert to the girls we were over thirty years ago while growing up together in Oregon—Lake Oswego, Oregon, our home town. That's the place where I thought we'd experienced all life's changes.

I couldn't have been more wrong. Sometimes I don't recognize the woman looking back at me in the mirror. And that didn't happen until I moved to the Rattlesnake Valley. This life—filled with relentlessly sunny skies and overfilled calendar squares—is *not* the life I had dreamed for myself. I attended a hippie college in the Pacific Northwest, where there wasn't a sorority, fraternity, or Republican on campus. And there was very little sunshine. Upon graduation, I believed I'd climb the writing rungs of that career and find my way to New York City. Instead, I landed in the desert with the snakes and scorpions, and nary a Democrat in sight. It seems I spend half my time driving around the Rattlesnake Valley with a car full of kids singing off-key to their iPods, and the other half folding laundry. The only writing I do is for a weekly column, which pays me a hundred bucks a pop. And my sole social outing for the month? The Dice Club.

I'd never considered joining a bunko group or a dice club. Book clubs I knew. But bunko? The first time I'd heard of it I thought it had something to do with cards—like poker—but I was wrong. There's no strategy, pure luck, and unless you're hosting the party, there's no preparation or thought involved other than what you're going to wear. Really, it's just a chance to get out and have fun with friends. And what middle-aged mother couldn't use a night out?

Sylvia Ostrander formed the club and I'm in it because of her. She hasn't changed much since our days in Oregon. All I have to do is squint my eyes and I can still picture Silly Sylvia in 1972 with tight dishwater blonde braids, wearing a crocheted vest and platform shoes. Now, however, her foiled tresses are expertly coiffed and her forehead has been stabbed free of corrugated wrinkles with regular Botox injections, (which she thinks no one knows about). Her designer clothes look as though they've been purchased off New York runway models. Silly doesn't describe her at all. She fits into Rattlesnake Valley society as though she designed the town. She and her high-powered attorney husband introduced me to Dan Bartlett, a real estate developer. He's the Donald Trump of Southern Arizona—with much better hair—and the man for whom I happily gave away all my journalistic ambitions and married.

Sylvia, along with her sorority sister Brandy Lynn—a quick-witted and foul-mouthed cowgirl—handpicked the original members of our Dice Club. They are the key deciders of not only who gets to join this spicy Southwestern salsa of a group when someone drops out, but also who gets to sub when someone doesn't show. They have strict yet simple rules: Members must be fun, discreet, and must be able to say the f-word without reserve. I'm still working on that. There was a time when I let that f-bomb fly freely; however, ever since I heard my son repeat this word from his car seat after a rude driver on the freeway had just cut us off, I've used an internal editor to have that "f" stand for "flip" or "fudge."

Other rules of the Dice Club are: No men. No kids. No drink counters.

I've got two tables ready, each with four chairs. In the dining room is the designated top table. It's the table that controls the game. I'm expecting Sylvia and Brandy Lynn, Tootsie the Alabama Belle, and Chlöe the Canadian. Okay, so that's four. Let's see …who else?

I move to the table in our kitchen and put three dice and four pencils on the bottom table. Counting on my fingers, "Blanca Midnight." That's her artist's name. Her regular name is Blanca Fernglen, but she's probably the most artistic woman I've ever met. And with her rich brown skin tone and delphinium blue eyes, the most exotically beautiful as well. Okay then, I'm up to five. "Three more." Biting my thumbnail, I come up with the last names: Tara—she's my next door neighbor—me, of course, and …I scratch my head.

"Aha!" It comes to me. Amanda Prince. My lip curls when I picture the sour expression of Amanda Prince. What kind of mood will *she* be in tonight?

Sylvia brought Amanda Prince into the Dice Club last year. She's the assistant to Sylvia's high-powered attorney husband. Inviting her to the Dice Club seemed like a good idea since Sylvia was trying to save her from an emotional tailspin after her young son died. I don't know all the details because Amanda doesn't talk about it, and I don't feel I know her well enough to ask. At best, I'd say our conversations have been cordial but empty. I understand her son was sickly. He had asthma and was often in the hospital. Then one day, he just stopped breathing.

It's too horrible to think about. Amanda can be as crabby as she needs to be.

An overwhelming sense of dread shoots through me. Is my house ready for all this personality? Brandy Lynn alone is a hurricane of energy. She's someone whose bad side I don't ever want to see aimed at me.

Brandy posed most of The Snake Eyes Dice Club rules and I've always been a rule follower. Between Sylvia and Brandy, Brandy's definitely the more outspoken of the two. Aside from ending up in the same sorority, I still don't know how they became friends. Brandy is 4-H, and Sylvia is Junior League. Brandy wears Wrangler jeans and cowboy boots, and Sylvia wears Armani suits and Prada shoes. Sylvia's makeup is always perfect and never smeared, while Brandy's eyelashes and eyebrows are so blonde you can't even tell they're there. Brandy Lynn is strong and athletic; I once saw her pick up the very delicate Sylvia Ostrander and spin her over her head. It was her way of winning an argument. And on the last twirl, they both collapsed to the floor and laughed like little girls.

Never underestimate the power of a sense of humor.

It's six-fifteen. Chica, my chihuahua, is following me everywhere. She knows something's up and is trying to get on my good side because she senses she'll soon be crated at the back of the house, a place as far away from the front door as possible. Whenever the doorbell rings, her high-pitched yapping cuts right through my temples. I'd keep the front door open, but it's a hundred degrees.

I uncork a Kendall Jackson, reach for a wine glass and pour. Half full? I glance at Chica, her cinnamon eyes staring at me, full non-judgmental love. I keep pouring. Okay, three quarters. I take a reassuring sip, set down the glass and scoop up my dog. She licks the hand cream off my hand as I carry her to my bedroom. I push open the door and she scurries from my arms and hops upon the bed, immediately burying herself in the vast collection of pillows.

A quick check in the full-length mirror, I rub my fingers through straight, dark bangs, and then turn to the side and suck in my stomach. I'm wearing a new bra that's made an astounding difference to my profile, and this lacy bustier-type thing is really showing off the girls. Cupping them in my hands, I think of the old, accented woman at the bra boutique where I recently spent over four hundred bucks on new undergarments. She told me to burn the failure of a bra I'd previously chosen at Victoria's Secret. She wasn't kidding. This was just after she taught me the true secret of choosing the right size brassiere. "Vut is happening here?" she had asked me as she stuck a sharp, enameled nail into the right side of my cleavage, which had a pronounced bra line and excess boob spilling from it. "Theese is not goot!"

No doubt my chest will be the first thing everyone notices. Tara Shephard, the thirty-nine year old Texas beauty queen and my next door neighbor, will definitely notice. Tara's whole world is about boobs. I guess that's what happens when you shell out the coin it takes to go from a B cup to a double D cup. It works for her. Tara Shephard is gorgeous. If she's walking down the street with her pre-Raphaelite, apricot tresses flowing in the breeze, car horns honk and drivers slow down and greet her.

No doubt, she'll be the last to arrive, even though she lives the closest to me. It takes her hours to get ready, and she'll be half in the bag. The other thing about Tara is that she drinks. A lot. But I'll leave it at that, because my rule-following mentality tells me not to count. Did I mention she was gorgeous?

Chlöe the Canadian could stand to take some beauty lessons from Tara. Chlöe Forrest, part-time nurse, part-time blonde, does her own hair with Nice 'n Easy number ninety-seven. I'm not sure how she found her way into this collection of women, but I think it was through an acquaintance of Brandy's. Chlöe's a lovely person. Really she is. She's a hard worker, an amazing volunteer, and she certainly adds life to any room she enters. But my God, she's a schedule-spewer! Every one-sided conversation is about how busy she is running her severely gifted children all over town. When she talks to me I feel my neck go slack, and my eyes roll back into my head as though I'm dozing off during a boring movie on television.

Looking around, I'm satisfied. The tables are set and the house smells of baking bread. There are three minutes left on my Betty Crocker crescent rolls. Where did I leave my wine? I scan the kitchen, lit up with every available light, and see the sweating glass on the talavera-tiled counter next to the oven. Stashed. Oh my, have I become my mother? My mom always has a glass going. Usually it's tucked next to the blender or the toaster—back in a corner and not in plain sight while she spends her afternoons baking. I pick up the crystal vessel, hold it to the light and slowly spin, examining the glass—not the wine. I'm relieved to see it's fingerprint free. Mom's glass always has butter or flour marks.

Might as well fill it again. I'm not driving anywhere tonight. I'm glad Tara won't be driving tonight either, but even so, I worry about her walking between our two houses. The snakes are still out ...or she could easily walk into a cactus.

The heat of the oven pours into the kitchen as I lower the oven door, and now twelve golden crescent rolls wait along with me for my guests to arrive. There's no need to make more than a dozen. At any given time, carbs are off the menu for these women. I never know what to expect when I see them after our summer break. Last year they all turned anorexic on me. I think it had something to do with the television show *Desperate Housewives*.

The front door opens.

"Smells delicious!" Sylvia drops her Kate Spade bag and a neatly wrapped bunko gift on a chair in the foyer. "Have you been baking all day, little Susie Homemaker?"

We exchange cheek kisses. Her hair has grown longer over the summer, and the golden highlights are perfect. "I've become my mother. Didn't I swear in 1970-something that this would never happen?"

Sylvia flashes a whitened smile and heads straight for the bar. She looks over the liquor supply before mixing herself a vodka martini. "I always think of those little pizzas your mother used to make us for lunch. They're one of my most vivid childhood memories!" She laughs and slices a lime in half. "Figures it's about food. Look at my rear end! Have you ever seen me so heavy?"

Her rear end is clad in ecru linen Capri pants. It looks perfect, and stirs a bit of envy in me. "You're kidding, right?"

"Oh! I almost forgot." Sylvia rushes to where she had placed her purse. "Look what I brought you. I was going to bring you an apple—you know, like an apple for the teacher—since the bunko theme is 'Back to School.' But I've got a case of this and decided to bring a bottle to each of this year's hostesses." She sets down a bottle of wine on my kitchen island. It's dark, clearly a red wine, and has a pale pink label.

"Bitch, 2005," I say, a smile forming. "Your own label?"

"Perfect, don't ya think? Read the back."

I roll the bottle and see the word "bitch" repeated eight times in eight columns on the back label. Then I read the last line: "Bitch, bitch, bitch and bitch some more. Well! Nothing like a bottle of bitch."

We laugh and the doorbell rings. Brandy Lynn walks in, her silky blonde hair flowing behind her like a veil. "I'm early but don't ask me to help you with anything," she says. "Everyone in my house is driving me crazy and I just need to sit down and relax."

Sylvia rolls her eyes. "That's a nice way to greet your hostess, Brandy. At least ask Shonah how her summer was!"

I reach behind Brandy and squeeze her waist. She's all muscle underneath her skimpy black shirt. I had heard she went back to work as a physical therapist over the summer. Feels like she's been doing a lot of physical therapy on herself. "Brandy doesn't care about how my summer was."

"You're right. I don't." Brandy throws back her head and laughs. Then she zeroes in on my cleavage and furrows her brow. "I remember those," she says, referring, of course, to my breasts. She picks up a crescent roll, examines it momentarily and tosses it back into the breadbasket. "You expect me to eat this crap?"

"Certainly not." I point to the bottle of Bitch wine. "But I've got a bottle of red with your name on it. You are a red drinker, aren't you?"

"Yeah, yeah. Ha, ha. Not interested. I have to work in the morning. Who's coming tonight? Everyone?"

"I think so," Sylvia and I answer in unison.

The doorbell rings. "Come in," we shout.

It rings again. And then again.

"It's gotta be the high-powered attorney's assistant," says Brandy.

Sylvia sighs and sets down her triangle glass. "Amanda Prince." She walks toward the front door and whispers over her shoulder, "I don't think she knows how to walk into someone's house without the door being opened for her."

Sylvia opens the door and her voice sounds like it's climbing a small hill: "a -MAN-da!" she says. I wink at Brandy and walk toward the door to watch Sylvia leaning in for the double-cheeked air-kiss, but Amanda turns her head and brushes past her boss' wife. It was more like a slap on the cheek greeting than a kiss on the cheek greeting.

Can't Amanda at least fake her animosity toward Sylvia?

Amanda is dressed in a red Arizona tank top, long khaki shorts and dirty white flip-flops. She definitely didn't turn anorexic over the summer. Absently, I pick up my wine glass and gulp. I think she's given up, and I can't say I blame her. She had one child. One. And he's gone. God, what that must do to a person! That woman is just plain lost inside her grief.

As I had predicted, Tara Shephard was the last to arrive at seven o'clock, and she came in five minutes after Tootsie Fennimore. Tootsie, our Alabama Belle and former touring golf pro, is often late. I think it's because she spends so much time fussing over the gift-wrap for the present. We were all hovered over Tootsie's bunko gift, admiring it as we always do for the brilliant wrapping job, when Tara stumbled through the front door. Her trademark blue goblet—filled with who knows what—was in her right hand, and a plastic Safeway grocery bag was in her left. It contained her hastily wrapped bunko gift, which is usually something she pulls from her studio at the last minute. She wore a floor-length dress, Kelly green, which matched her eyes. Tonight they glowed like lanterns. She went for the smoky eye look, and surrounded them with as much kohl eyeliner as an Afghani bride. Drunk or sober, Tara never fails to take away my breath.

The theme for September: Back to School. We thought it was appropriate since most of the country thinks of September as the time when the new school year begins. Our kids, however, are practically at mid-term. Why our school district opts to take the kids out of the pools and into the classrooms in early August is beyond me. They might as well start in July for how it cuts into summer vacations.

We played two full rounds, which means there were a total of twelve games. The theme doesn't change the way the game is played. It's merely reflected in the prizes. We give money away for the most losses, the most wins, and the most "baby bunkos." Babies are when a player rolls three of a kind of the number we're not shooting for at the time. Say we're rolling for sixes, and someone rolls three fours. That's a baby.

"I've got triplets," says Sylvia.

"Not good enough," Tootsie Fennimore says triumphantly. "Seven sweet lil babies for me."

"If these are the only kinds of babies you can produce, Tootsie, you should consider yourself lucky," says Brandy.

Sylvia throws her an elbow. "What!" hisses Brandy. A scowl colors her face.

Tootsie is the only one in the club who hasn't had a baby. She's been married for a year and rumor is, she's trying. But she's forty. There could be fertility issues. "Yes," she says. "Well, these do seem to be the only kind of babies I can have." Tootsie's languid Southern drawl is softer than usual.

No one says anything. In the collective hush that's taken over the room, the rhythmic squeak of the ceiling fan is the only sound. I nervously move the bangs from my forehead and get up. Music. We need music. I push on the CD player, not knowing what I've got cued up, and am relieved when Neil Young's guitar begins strumming.

As I walk back to the amassing pile of scorecards thrown together for tallying, out of the corner of my eye I see Tootsie folding her scorecard into a paper airplane. She admires it for a second, and then shoots it at Brandy. Like a dart hitting its target, the tip nails Brandy square in the nose. "Hole in one!" Tootsie shouts.

The room erupts with laughter, and Brandy, for once, is speechless.

Some of the women are still seated at the game tables, some are gathering in the living room where we'll soon announce all the winners. The smoker, Amanda, is probably outside, and Tara, of course, is at the bar.

Chlöe Forrest, the Canadian schedule-spewer, is tonight's big winner. She moves to an oversized chair with flowered upholstery and prepares to hold court. A picked over dessert tray is on the coffee table in front of her, and she's surrounded by colorful gifts. It's like a bridal shower with a bunch of middle-aged women dressed in halter-tops and spaghetti straps, who failed to tell the bride that her one-inch black roots might not photograph well on her wedding day. Chlöe isn't the only one who is unkempt by now. Because it's late and far too warm in spite of my thermostats set at temperatures cold enough to hang meat, lipstick has faded and some of the mascara looks like Tara's eyeliner. Martini and wine glasses, cups of coffee, and bottles of Arrowhead water are half-full or empty.

I reach into an antique kitchen desk and grab a notepad. The pencil I used to tally points all evening is still behind my ear. Parking myself on a stool next to Chlöe, I plan to take notes on the contents of the bunko bag. I always do this. It's like I'm the designated maid of honor at the shower. I keep track of the gifts each month in response to the theme. If they're clever—and they usually are—I might mention them in my newspaper column.

"Where are Tara and Amanda?" asks Sylvia.

I glance at the bar and Tara's not there.

"Amanda's probably having a smoke," Brandy says.

"I'll get her." I get up and poke my head out the back door, and am greeted by the warm air of the desert night. Behind the amber glow of two lit cigarettes is the silhouette of craggy, saguaro-studded mountains. The ebony sky is filled with sparkling diamonds, and the air smells tangy, like creosote. A big, coyote moon rises in the east. Amanda is there, of course, and I'm surprised to see Tara with her. She must have started smoking again over the summer. "C'mon you two. Chlöe wants to open her gifts."

"She won again?" Tara flicks her cigarette butt into the kiva fireplace.

"She cheats," Amanda croaks.

Tara punches her shoulder and tiptoes toward me. "Who would cheat at dice?"

Amanda exhales a cloud of smoke. "Bunko artists."

So, Amanda has a sense of humor after all. I laugh and step back inside. Amanda and Tara follow me. Chlöe is already ripping through the first package. "A twelve-pack of... "

"Beer?" shouts Brandy Lynn. Brandy always has a punch line loaded and ready to fire.

"Beer? In this small package?" Chlöe laughs. She drops the package between her knees and stretches out her hands. Her skin is chapped, her nails not manicured. "It would have to be *aboot* this big to be beer, eh?" Chlöe's Canadian accent always grows stronger as the end of the evening draws near.

"I brought that," says Tootsie. "The wrap job is worth more than the gift."

"What I want to know is when you're actually going to enter the Gift Wrapping Olympics," says Brandy.

Tootsie's face turns a soft pink. "Maybe if the next fertility treatment doesn't take."

I catch Tootsie's eye and offer a half smile, then shrug my shoulders and write "pencils" on the gift list. Chlöe shows the room the six-pack of Dixon-Ticonderoga, Number Two lead pencils. "My kids can really use these. They go through them in the gifted program like crazy."

"There she goes again bragging *aboot* her gifted children," says Brandy.

I underline the word "pencils" twice.

"Hey Chlöe, you have such pretty blonde hair. Why do you dye the roots black?" Brandy's on a roll. Chlöe's accent may get stronger, but Brandy's jokes get meaner.

Sylvia Ostrander reaches past Tootsie and places her bejeweled hand on Brandy's toned upper arm and shoves her. "Enough of you and that mouth, Brandy Lynn," she says under her breath. Brandy just rolls her eyes, unfazed.

I hand Chlöe the next gift. It's a Starbucks gift card from Amanda.

"That'll go with the coffee cup I made," says Tara. "It's from my fall collection. Over there in that plastic bag. Sorry 'bout the wrap job. I was in a hurry."

The next gift is a "Get Organized!" package, contributed by Brandy Lynn. Everything out of Brandy is a command.

"This one's from me, *mi'ja*," says Blanca Midnight Fernglen, handing Chlöe an envelope. "It's a gift certificate for a pedicure. She's just up the street and she'll massage all that dead-mommy skin right off of your little footsies." Blanca, a divorced mother of three, flashes her famous smile—always brilliant—between full lips coated in Clinique's Angel Red lipstick. We regularly see that smile in television commercials and magazine ads when she's modeling exotic clothes for a local retail chain called "Sonoran Nights."

"You know, I've never had a pedicure before," remarks Chlöe.

The room erupts.

"You've got to be kidding me!" says Sylvia.

"*Mi'ja*, you haven't lived!" says Blanca.

"Doesn't surprise me," Brandy whispers behind her hand to no one.

"Don't they have pedicures in Canada?"

"C'mon Chlöe, keep going."

"Yeah. Some of us have to work in the morning," says Amanda Prince. She flashes a scornful, gray-eyed look in Sylvia's direction, and everyone sees it but Sylvia.

"No one has a busier schedule than yours truly," Chlöe says. "Shonah, hand me the next one."

"That *Soap Opera Digest* and box of bon-bons is from me," says Sylvia. "I don't know about any of you, but I've been enjoying my afternoon soaps without commentary from my daughter that I'm, like, so lame to watch them."

"Is that it?" Chlöe is still excited about being the big winner.

"No," I say handing her my gift, a box of "thank you" notes. "You can never have enough."

"Thank you, Shonah," Chlöe says. "And here's the one I brought. Winners do give their gifts to the hostess, right?"

I open Chlöe's package, smile, and show the room a three-pack of +1.5 reading glasses. "Nothing says back to school like a set of reading glasses!"

"I thought someone could use them for checking the kids' homework," says Chlöe. "I spend half my nights reading term papers and going over math problems, and I swear my eyes are really starting to go. I've never had to wear glasses until recently, but I found these at K-Mart, and so I bought a set for tonight and one for myself too. Oh! I'm glad it's someone who has kids." She glances at Tootsie.

"That's okay, Darlin'," says Tootsie. "You don't need to have kids to have middle-aged blindness set in. My husband's been wearing them for years."

I'd like to try on a pair, but I can't penetrate the thick plastic of the Blisterpak. "Thanks, Chlöe. It's even the right magnification for my particular set of middle-aged eyes."

"Cheaters!" cries Brandy. "You're such an old lady, Shonah."

Chlöe wads a collection of wrapping paper into a giant ball. "Here Brandy," she says, aiming to pitch. "You're the big athlete. Catch this!" Brandy bumps the wad like a volleyball, her blonde hair flipping to one side. Paper scraps separate and spew around the room.

"Don't worry Shonah," says Blanca. "I'll help you clean up the mess." She immediately stands up and gathers the strewn wrapping papers, while Tootsie collects empty bottles, glasses, napkins and paper plates from the main serving table.

Meanwhile, Tara Shephard, the thirty-nine-year-old former Texas beauty queen and commercially-successful potter, staggers back to the bar—her fake tits spilling from the Kelly green bodice of her dress—and she drinks directly from the 1.75 liter bottle of Absolut. After three heavy swallows, her head snaps forward, and lustrous apricot tendrils spill into her face. She blinks her eyes as though battling a harsh light and then laughs through her nose. "Hey ya'll, where we goin' dancin'?"

I exchange a look with Sylvia and whisper, "I'll be sure she gets home safely."

The party has a distinct feeling of being over. Some of the women grab bottles of water, some help gather the ruins of the evening. Others collect pencils, scorecards and dice. I spot Amanda Prince sneaking out the door. She doesn't say good night to anyone. Not even me.

Still staring at the front door and feeling offended, I hear a crash. I turn, walk into the kitchen, and find blue ceramic shards sprayed across my newly tiled floor. Standing amid them is Tara. She stares down at her broken goblet and slumps against the counter like a blow-up doll that's just been punctured.

I look at Sylvia and there's nothing keeping me from saying one word right out loud.

"Fuck."

Chapter 2
October

Remember when drinking used to be fun? When you could go out for happy hour and put away a few Long Island Ice Tea specials, dance the night away, flirt with guys and laugh so hard your cheeks hurt? Or you could grab a group of friends, head out to the quarter-beer bar and get pleasantly tipsy on less than five bucks? Then you'd sleep it off, get through the next day with little if any impact, and go out and do it again. It was called a weekend.

Today it's called time for rehab. Clearly, when some of us hit our forties, the party's over.

—Shonah Bartlett
From her column, *The Dice Club Chronicles*

Brandy

When Sylvia Ostrander and I started The Snake Eyes Dice Club, the first thing out of her mouth was "no men, no kids." I quickly added, "no drink counters." But that didn't mean we planned to form a drinking club. And now here I am at Costco, pushing a cart filled with booze toward the check-out counter, and I'm not sure it'll be enough to satisfy these asps. I'm sure the irony of this month's theme, "Betty Ford Bunko," will not be lost on the group. Well, maybe Chlöe the Canadian won't get it, and as for Princess Tara Shephard, well, if anyone *should* get it, it's her. We may have to make this meeting an intervention after all. That was Shonah's original idea when she suggested the theme. She was pretty pissed after cutting her hand on Tara's blue goblet daggers shot all over her travertine tile at the last Dice Club gathering.

Shonah takes everything so seriously.

I've seen three patients today and am taking the afternoon off to get ready for the Dice Club. Late last spring I went back to work three days a week. I'm a physical therapist and my patient list is getting bigger than I'd planned. I'm popular because I'm mean, and my patients truly believe in the concept, no pain, no gain. At least I think they do.

A forklift beeps in the aisle next to me. I hate this fucking warehouse of a store. I swear to God it's inbred and elderly shopping day today. People are pushing around flats as big as semis, filled with a year's supply of paper towels and five-gallon vats of salsa.

Please don't let me run into anyone I know.

Fat chance of that wish coming true. I've been in this town nearly all my life—came here when my twin brother, Sandy, and I were only five years old. I can't go anywhere without bumping into someone. It's like everyday is some kind of class reunion. Sometimes I think I should've moved away, but after living the roving gypsy life of a military brat, I don't have any serious plans to move again for the rest of my life.

Our dad, a retired Navy Admiral, brought us here from San Diego. He said Mom was sick of the sea and always wanted to live on a ranch in the desert and raise horses. She got what she wanted—at least for a little while—when we moved to a fourteen acre property in the shadow of the Tincan mountains. Our Uncle Joe sold us the land, and we rode horses every day with our cousins, Emma and Evan. There were a few really excellent years—that is, until breast cancer got the best of us. Mom died when we were twelve. Our two older sisters, June and Marlene, who were eighteen and twenty at the time, were already off to college, one in Austin, Texas, the other at UCLA. They didn't know what to do when our dad went into a state of permanent mourning.

He ended up leaving Sandy and me with our Uncle Joe and Aunt Madge—Mom's younger sister—in the Rattlesnake Valley, and went back to Long Beach to live on a houseboat. He's still there for most of the year, no doubt drinking Jack Daniels with fellow vets and talking about what's wrong with this country. "God damn hippies!" he always says. I think he means to say "liberals," but his mind rarely gets out of the 1940s let alone the 1960s.

I can't stand the liberals either …haven't gone as far as putting an "Annoy a Liberal" bumper sticker on my car, but I've given it some thought. I do sport a pink ribbon, though, and race for the cure each year. This season I'd like to get the ladies to participate in Bunko for Breast Cancer. I heard they've raised half a million to date. Sure wish all this awareness and fundraising had been around for *my* mother.

Anyway, after she died Dad eventually gave the ranch to Sandy and me. I live in the main house with my husband, Levi, who is a fifth generation Arizona rancher, his two kids from a previous marriage, and three of our own. Yes, that's right. Five kids. No one ever questions me about my quick temper once they learn that. Plus, my twin brother, who might as well be my sixth kid, lives in the guesthouse and doesn't pay any of the bills it takes to keep this place running. Don't even get me started on Sandy.

"Having a party?" A male voice calls from behind me.

I turn and see a familiar face. Wait, who is it? I recognize the face. Damn! How do I know him? Is he a baseball parent? Someone from 4-H? The clinic? "Hey ...uh, *you!*"

"Looks like you've got somethin' going on," he says, nodding at the contents of my cart. He's cute. Mexican? Italian? Definitely tall and dark. Wait, is that a fake tan? I follow his gorgeous eyes into my cart. They're a brilliant turquoise color. Yum. Oh crap, look at all this booze. Since I have virtually no alcohol in the house, I've collected a case of wine, a bottle of Patrón, six-packs of Corona and M.G.D., a tall box of Grey Goose, and a brown bottle of Kahlua. We're both still staring at all of it when it dawns on me that I've forgotten the mixers. I look back up at the cute, familiar face, still unsure of our connection. He uses his hand to stroke day-old whiskers on his chin. Who is this guy? He's actually *really* cute. I want him to say something else. Give me a clue.

"Big party?" he finally says.

"Yep, big party." If it weren't for the no men rule, I might ask him to join us. I look at my watch to indicate time is short, and turn my cart to head back for the mixers.

"So now I know what you girls do at your Dice Club parties."

Abrupt stop. What did he say? I turn around and look him in the turquoise eyes.

"Blanca told me that's where she was going tonight. I always get stuck with the kids on bunko night. At least when I'm in town."

It hits me. "David Fernglen." The name churns from my gut. It feels like a belch. I don't remember the last time I saw Blanca's asswipe of an ex-husband. And there's no way he had that skin color. Or those eyes. I know they were blue, like his half-breed kids, but not like that. He must be wearing contacts. Regardless, I should have recognized him. I just can't believe he's actually in the Rattlesnake Valley. This dick has basically abandoned Blanca and their three sons. When they were still married he bought them a big house in Sylvia Ostrander's exclusive, gated community and then left to take on one humanitarian role after the next in third world countries—between playing bit-part roles in feature films. He's some kind of trust fund kid who married a woman of color, Blanca, just to piss off his parents.

I glance around the little cart island we've formed next to the wall of athletic socks and notice everyone who passes us stares at David with the same where-do-I-know-that-guy-from look I must have had on my face too. When it comes to famous residents of the Rattlesnake Valley, I guess he tops the list. Pathetic.

I look in his cart. It's filled with giant boxes of Cheerios and granola bars, gallons of milk, and flats of grapes and strawberries. Well, at least he's feeding his kids.

"Blanca could use a fun night out," is all I manage to say.

Poor Blanca. She works her ass off both as a model for a local clothing store and working at Tara's uptown gallery. She's a pretty talented artist herself and Tara lets her show her paintings there. If anything, Blanca's the club sweetheart and I must say, that big smile of hers is infectious. We met when our kids were in a roping class together, and when I found out she lived near Sylvia, we started spending more time together. The Dice Club is the only night of the month she goes out, and when she does, she's like the college freshman gone wild after too much time in an austere, parochial home. Once she starts dancing, everyone's rhythm improves.

Blanca never has anything good to say about David. I purse my lips and move away. Funny thing is, I don't usually have anything nice to say about my husband, Levi, either. It would serve him right if I divorced him. He practically lives out in the guesthouse with my brother already. The kids wouldn't even notice.

Mixers. Mixers. Hmm, mixers. I'm surrounded by bright colors, great walls of choice. Mother of God! Why does everything in this store have to be the size of a hay bale? Which reminds me, I have a hay delivery coming this afternoon. I hope someone's there to pay the guy if he shows up before I can get home. In addition to my five kids and my lazy brother, I've got six horses to feed. And I should have just enough time to do it and then prepare for this party.

I choose cranberry juice, margarita mix, pineapple juice and three bottles of tonic. That should be enough. If I run out, I'm sure Tara will have a supply in her car bar. Shonah's going to make her drive tonight as an attempt to get her not to drink. Sounds like a bad idea to me. But far be it for Shonah Bartlett to listen to anything I say.

Moving my cart back toward the check out area, I think if I wheel fast enough and keep my head down, I can avoid bumping into anyone else. Hopefully David Fernglen is in the frozen food section in the back corner of the store, picking out stuff to get his family through the winter. Bastard.

Ooh, there's an open register. Rare. Out of the corner of my eye I see another woman aiming for it as well. I can beat this bitch. Look out! With one hand on the cart and the other reaching for a bottle of tonic, I edge out my competition and set the bottle on the conveyor belt. *I win!* I don't make eye contact with her, but the sneer of her upper lip is unmistakable. Ha! Sore loser.

The young, red-vested clerk reaches for my membership card, then grabs the tonic and scans it. Then he scans the second bottle, and the third. "Having a party?"

He's cute too. I wonder how old he is. Twenty-one? Twenty-two? Young enough to be my son? Maybe a nephew. Another backing forklift beeps along with the price scanner.

"Ma'am?"

"What? No." I hate when people call me ma'am. "No party. This should get my husband and me through the evening." I give him a wink, but the look on his face tells me he doesn't realize I'm kidding. Too young.

The booze comes to $306.26. Shit. There goes this week's paycheck. "Put it on my Costco American Express."

I sign the sales slip and head for the exit, then hand my receipt to the red-vested sentry, who is always stationed there with a chartreuse highlighter pen. With his black, Fab Four haircut and Mark Spitz mustache, he looks just like a guy I once dated in college. I don't believe he ever does a thorough comparison between what's in the cart and what's on the receipt. It's all just show.

"Afternoon," he says, not looking at me. He takes the receipt and glances in the cart. His eyes go from shifty slits to cat's eye marbles. Everyone's a judge when it comes to alcohol.

"I tried AA, Mr. Spitz, but it really ruined my drinking." I wink at him too.

No response. He makes a chartreuse hash mark on the receipt and hands it back to me. "Have a nice day."

Walking to my truck in the parking lot, I wonder, what am I going to do with all this booze if the Dice Club doesn't drink it?

10:05 p.m.

Returning from a quick trip to her car bar, Tara, with her arms loaded, uses her Jimmy fucking Choo "heal" to kick closed my front door. She's holding a bottle of cranberry juice, a can of pineapple juice, a fifth of

Absolut, and a bottle of something, I can't tell what. "My name is Tara Shephard," she says, "and I'm a Bunko Artist."

"Hi, Tara," we chime in response. And I was worried for about thirty seconds that this coven of eight wouldn't drink my Costco booze. No one's touched the beer or wine. Everyone's drinking "big girl drinks" tonight, and sure enough, we had to resort to Tara's car bar.

Frank Sinatra, taken from my dad's abandoned record collection, croons through surround-sound speakers. Sinatra's probably the appropriate era for Betty Ford, right? Everyone toasts the air with delicate, triangle martini glasses. Tara places her stash on the bar, turns, and surveys the room. She throws back another gulp of her drink, giggles, and a small stream of cosmopolitan escapes from her mouth. She's going to break something again. I just know it.

It feels later than it is. It's Amanda Prince's fault. She was pissed off from the moment she arrived. And now she's making another scene. She's all bent out of shape that we only played two rounds of bunko instead of three. Again. Why on earth didn't Sylvia explain to her that being a part of The Snake Eyes Dice Club isn't about bunko, for cry-eye? There've been times when we've only played one round. Two years ago at the Cinco de Mayo Dice Club, it took us so long to get started, we gave the bag of gifts to the first person to roll three fives! I mean, who's actually here to play for the money?

On second thought, maybe Chlöe the Canuck fills that bill. She could use an extra buck or two. If anything, it could help her afford to buy a new box of Clairol.

"I can't believe you people change the rules whenever you want with no regard for the rest of us. Pretty bush league if you ask me," Amanda says, still going on about it. She stomps around the room checking everyone's scores. "I didn't win anything. All this way for nothing. You guys do realize I don't live here in the Valley. I'm all the way across town." She gathers her things and leaves. As usual she says good night to no one and gives no thanks to me. I feel like spitting.

Instead I call out to the closed door. "Talk about bush league. Jesus!"

Blanca crosses herself.

"Brandy!" scolds Sylvia. "Amanda probably heard that." She jumps to her feet and dutifully runs after Amanda. Because Amanda works for her high-powered attorney husband, Sylvia thinks it's her responsibility to take care of her. I shake my head and look around the room. Everyone's head shakes back-and-forth too. It's like a room full of bobble-head dolls.

I think it's time to vote Amanda off the island.

After five minutes outside, Sylvia returns. Now her head is shaking back-and-forth. She falls into the sofa. It's a cowhide sofa, not something you can exactly sink into, and the firmness of it surprises her.

"Sylvia, what's wrong with Amanda this time?" asks Blanca. A gold cross hangs around her neck. It glistens like a neon light on her dark skin.

Sylvia shrugs. "Amanda has her good days and she has her bad days."

Aargh! I hate when Sylvia says that. "I'm sure she does. I just wish she didn't have to have one of her bad days in *my* house. I took the afternoon off to prepare for this party."

Sylvia glares at me. I know that expression quite well.

"Is she getting any counseling yet?" Blanca asks.

Sylvia shrugs. "Not that I know of. It just seems silly to get so angry about bunko."

"Clearly it's not about bunko," says Shonah.

No shit, Shonah. It's about life. And guess what? I'm sorry her kid died. Really, I am. But life goes on. That girl needs to talk to someone and find a way to channel her anger. Does she think she's got the market cornered on grief? No, I haven't lost a child …but I *was* a child when my mom died, and my dad may as well have died right along with her. I KNOW about loss and the five stages of grief. Maybe if she got some therapy, she could work through the stages instead of wavering all over the map and hanging out far too long in the angry stage.

"My former bunko group would never allow the game to be cut from three rounds to two. Especially two months in a row," says Chlöe Forrest, whose black roots are now greater than an inch on each side of her center part. "You have to stick to the rules or it's not fair to anyone. I'd be mad about it too."

I can't help but imitate Chlöe's Canadian accent. "This isn't *aboot* fairness or rules. She could have at least said 'thank you.' Or even 'fuck you.' A simple goodbye would be nice."

"Well, if anyone has to leave early it's me," Chlöe retorts. "I have a huge day tomorrow. I have a double shift at the clinic and before I go I have to administer fluoride treatments at the school. Looks like I have to be the substitute nurse again. Then I have to meet with the gifted teacher and at some point, I have to take the kids shoe shopping, do my grocery list for the weekend, and defrost the freezer in the garage because one of our patients is giving us a moose or something from his latest hunting trip. I don't know how I'm going to get everything done. I think I've had the most wins. Can we do the most wins first? I could sure use that twenty bucks."

See? I *knew* she needed the money.

10:20 p.m.

Indeed, with ten wins and two losses, Chlöe the Canuck has the most wins. Determining this, she plucks her twenty-dollar prize from my hands, calls "good night" to everyone, and leaves.

There's a collective sigh from the room.

"My name is Chlöe Forrest and I am a schedule-spewer-oholic," says Shonah.

"Goodbye Chlöe," sings the group.

"Sylvia," Blanca says in a low voice, "Is everything okay with Amanda at work?"

Sylvia holds up her hand in a stop position. "Don't know, don't want to know. I hate to say I'm running out of compassion, but I can't keep answering for her. Say, who wins the bag tonight?"

"Tootsie!"

"Again?"

Tootsie Fennimore, who is unusually quiet tonight, sits alone in the corner. I wonder what's wrong with her. She hasn't asked me to play golf with her in a long time. I stack the wrapped gifts at her feet, while Shonah whips out her steno pad and takes notes.

I had better watch what I say around that Shonah Bartlett. Some day, I know it's going to end up in her newspaper column.

The Betty Ford Bunko bag: A box of chocolates and a gift certificate to Baskin-Robbins; a six pack of O'Douls non-alcoholic beer; a bottle of sparkling cider; a ball cap with Betty Ford Clinic embroidery; a fifth of vodka with a sticky note attached to it reading "Vodka is odorless;" a campaign button reading "Ford and Dole in '76;" a tank-top reading "Rehab is for Quitters;" a hardbound copy of *Bill W. The Story of Bill Wilson, Co-Founder of Alcoholics Anonymous.*

Tara is back at the bar. I make eye contact with Shonah and whisper, "Take her keys." I'm not going to be responsible for the javelina she hits on the way home.

Tara

It's ten forty-five. I've had four drinks—okay, five if I count the glass of wine I drank at home while getting ready. Or did I pour myself a second? I can't remember. It doesn't matter. I don't feel drunk. My vision is clear, my speech isn't slurred. If I had to walk a straight line, I could. I'm getting pretty good at this drinking thing. I must have developed a tolerance or something.

Lordy, Brandy's house is huge. It looks like a rodeo hotel. Who on earth is her decorator? She's got colorful serapes and ropes hanging everywhere. Is that a saddle in the corner? I wonder if I can sit on it—ride it like a mechanical bull. I was pretty good at that back in Texas. Debra Winger had nothin' on me.

There's Sylvia looking all perfect across the room. How does she stay so slim? I'll bet she's taking something—or throwing up. Hmmm. She's got a glass in her hand. She's still drinking. Shonah's glass still has something left in it too. Tootsie just has a bottle of water. Oh well. She never drinks. I wonder why she even comes to these things.

How long has Blanca been next to me? What was I saying? Something about the gallery?

"I don't usually work with metals …my caldron …oh, what? I already told you about my pot being used on the set of *Friends*? Sorry. Gollie, it was so long ago. I was just getting started. Gee whiz, love your necklace …What? I said that too?"

Was I talking with Blanca? Sylvia? Wait a minute. I better stop. Where's the bottled water? Dang! Why did I agree to drive? Better check Brandy's Breathalyzer. "Brandy, where's the Breathalyzer?"

Brandy grabs something that looks like a cell phone from the wagon wheel coffee table, and tosses it to me. "Blow me, baby," she says.

Crass. Why does she have to throw everything all the time? What's with her? She has the mouth of a sailor. Doesn't she have a college degree?

I'm not sure how to work this thing. Do I put my mouth on this straw-like thinga-ma-bob? Is it even sterile? Whatever. Might as well give it my best shot. Placing the tube in my mouth, I blow. It makes me stumble back a bit. "Phew! Did I do it right?" I pull it away and look at the digital display. Squinting, I'm having a hard time reading the results. "Is this thing working? What's the legal number anyway?"

"Pour some water into it and blow again," says Brandy. "That'll give you the result you're looking for." She rolls her eyes and walks away. I declare, that girl rolls her eyes more than my twelve-year-old.

I hear Shonah say she'll drive me home.

"I'm fine. Really Shonah. It's not necessary. I'm fine. Fine. Ian will be waiting up for me. And he's gonna wanna get himself some 'a this!" I pretend to ride the mechanical bull. Yeah baby, I've still got the moves.

Brandy slaps her knee and waves an imaginary lasso above her head. "We know what you're going home to. Ride 'em cowgirl."

I throw the Breathalyzer back at her, and it bounces off her tacky coffee table. Good. That Brandy has always had her eye on Ian. She should pay more attention to her own man.

Putting my hand to my head, I steady the sway I feel climbing through my body. The truth is, riding my husband is the last thing I want to do. Yow! I may have just thrown out my back. You know what I need? Sleep. I can't even remember the last time I had a good night's sleep.

11:10 p.m.

Shonah pulls into my driveway. I'm not sure I remember walking to the car from Brandy's house. "I've never driven a Mercedes before," she says. "Makes me feel…"

"Rich?"

"Uh, no. I was going to say 'old.' "

"Ouch."

Shonah laughs. "I don't mean *you're* old. You're not even forty yet. Still just a little beauty queen!"

"Ha! Hardly. I feel old as the hills." My head is heavy and my stomach rumbles.

I think Shonah says something about only old people driving Mercedes—or something about Oregon. Whatever. She unlatches her seat belt and puts her hand on my shoulder. "Is everything okay, Tara?"

"Okay? Sure, everything's okay. Why do you ask?"

She takes a deep breath, and then looks away.

"What is it?" I ask her.

"It's just that you seem to be drinking an awful lot lately. And this car smells like smoke."

"Shonah, I hardly drank anything tonight." The nerve of her! Didn't we have a no drink counters rule in this club? "Maybe you should concentrate on your own intake and stop worrying about mine. You were drinking too. I saw you!"

"Okay, Tara," she says. "Whatever you say. Here's your keys. I'll walk home from here."

Whatever. I don't know what she's getting so huffy about. She's such a know-it-all.

I pull myself out of the car. It takes effort. This car is too low to the ground. Maybe I should get a bigger model. E Class. Where did Shonah go? She was here just a minute ago. What were we talking about anyway? Hmmm. I push the garage door button, and the big door labors to a close. It's squeaky. Ian should oil it or something.

Light seeps from the crack below our bedroom door. He's waited up. The rest of the house is dark, and the smell of Windex fills the air. I flip on the kitchen light and the granite countertops sparkle. They've cleaned up. It's a miracle.

In the living room, however, there's junk everywhere. Books, glasses, dirty socks. I pick up a small, white anklet with a red ring around the top. The heel is gray with sweat and dirt. "I HATE dirty socks!" No one is in the room to hear my complaint. Do all girls leave their dirty socks scattered around the house? I thought only boys did that. The matching sock has grass stains. Clearly Ian let them run around outside again without their shoes.

Ugh. My stomach aches. This house is such a beast. There's a glass with water and another with orange juice sitting on the glass coffee table. Unlike Brandy's coffee table, it's tasteful—tasteful like everything in my perfectly-appointed home. I keep thinking I should host a *feng shui* Dice Club, and teach these women how to decorate.

Tempted to flop onto the sofa and admire the dim light and the décor, I think better of it and instead collect the glasses and spill the remains into the sink. Flipping a switch, the garbage disposal roars. Oops. I meant to turn on the light above the sink. The noise awakens our old dog, a black lab named Alamo, who jingles his tags in a remote corner. He slowly works his way over to me and licks my kneecap. "Oh, hi baby." I pat his head. His dramatic yawn makes a small squeak. After a few seconds, he moseys back to his corner.

I open the fridge. My eyes go straight for the lower left drawer, and I see there's less than an inch left in the bottle of chardonnay I opened while getting ready to go out. Heavens to Betsy! Did I really drink that much before going to Brandy's? Ian must have had some with dinner. Quickly, I pull the bottle, tug at the cork and polish it off. Wiping my lips, I walk toward the garage. I had better stash this in the regular trash instead of the recycling bin. The neighbors might start noticing the number of bottles out there. Sometimes there are so many, I hear the clamor they make spilling into the recycling truck all the way from my studio.

I tiptoe back inside, sneering at the remaining piles in the living room—unfolded laundry, newspapers, school books—then fill a glass of water from the cooler and turn off the main light. The light above the sink still glows. One of these days I need to make a point of figuring out once and for all which switch is for the light and which is for the disposal.

11:25 p.m.

Ian is on the bed looking messy and incongruent with the Laura Ashley sheets. He's wearing pale green hospital pants cut off just above the knees and his toes wiggle when he sees me. He's like a dog wagging his tail.

An open book, *Confessions of a Street Addict*, lay across his chest, and his round, dark eyes match the brutish, penetrating leer of the author on the book jacket. The lights are bright—too bright for the time of night—and the stares of these two men rattle me. I take a sip of water. "Good book?"

"Another workaholic," he says, sitting up a little. "Went to Harvard. I don't think I could work the market the way he did. At least not right away. I think I'll stick to some day trading on the Internet. What do you think?"

"Workaholic, huh? Well, I'm an alcoholic." Holy man. Did I really just say that out loud? I sit next to him on the bed and his hand is immediately around my waist. Oh geez, he'll feel my fat rolls. "I just came from the Betty Ford Clinic."

"Are you sober?"

"Relatively. But I'm definitely clean. I showered before I left the house this evening. Here, smell my hair."

Ian buries his nose in my hair and takes a deep breath. I hope it doesn't smell like smoke. "I like it when you drink," he says. He closes the book with his free hand and the snap seems too loud. He returns it to the pile of unread or halfway read books on his nightstand. I wonder what other books he's got there. He's sure doing a lot of reading lately. I think he spends more time reading about potential occupations than looking for carpentry work.

"When you have a few drinks, it means I get some," he says.

"Why Ian Shephard! You think so, do you?" I get up and walk to my side of the bed. "Hey, do you think you can look at the garage door? It's awfully squeaky."

"I know one door I'd like to take a look at right now."

"Ian, you're such a sex maniac!"

"Nonsense," he says. "Take off your clothes."

"Did you say nonsense?" I set down the glass on my nightstand.

"I did."

"Okay, nonsense. Listen, I'm going to check on the girls. Okay?"

"They're fine. Come to bed."

"I'm sure they're fine. I just like to look at them when they're asleep. I'd rather go to bed with their peaceful faces on my mind instead of their dirty socks."

"I can put something else on your mind," he says, stroking his crotch.

Oh, please. A throbbing pain is starting at the back of my head.

I switch off the overhead light, open the door and ...*whoops!* "Shoot!" Where did this ugly blue throw rug come from? I nearly broke my neck on this bunched up thing. Was it there when I walked into the room?

1: 15 a.m.

How did I get naked? My pillows are smashed against the headboard and the sheet is kicked to the bottom of the bed. The down comforter isn't properly fitted inside the duvet cover, and I've got all cover and no duvet. What time is it? I have to squint to make out the amber stick figures on the DVD player across the room. I think I need glasses. Have I slept for an hour? Two hours? What time did I get home? Did I drive?

The room is filled with moon and Ian snores softly. Three small furrows knit his brow. I love the gray hairs at his temples. Why do men look good when they go gray? Damn if I'm going to let any gray hairs remain on this head. Gosh, he's handsome. If only he weren't always on me.

I'm parched. It takes only three swallows to finish the water in my glass. I need more. Oh, let me just lay here a minute. Maybe I'll fall back asleep. I hope the kids studied their spelling words. My stomach aches. Do I have to pee? Where are my pajamas? It's freezing in this room. Too cold for October. The heat had better be on at the other end of the house. Was I okay at Dice Club? Did I remember to thank Brandy? Amanda sure was a downer tonight. She needs some therapy. Or something. I should take her to lunch. But she'd probably smoke. And then I'd smoke. I've really got to give up the cigarettes. Man, it was probably the secondhand smoke that perpetuated her son's asthma. Yikes, I hope I didn't say anything like that in front of her tonight. What *did* I say tonight?

I hope the girls don't mind when I go out. I wonder if they notice when I drink.

Dang, it's cold. I don't need the kids getting sick again. I don't know what I'd do if something happened to one of them. Like poor little JonBenet Ramsey. Thank goodness I took the girls out of those pageants. I'd had enough of that life back in Texas. But at least it got me my scholarship and the chance to work under Sancho Frugolo. If it weren't for him, I wouldn't have learned the traditional Navajo coil method that made me famous. Yes, I am famous …Aah, yeah. Okay. Now I feel more relaxed. I take in a deep breath. Good golly, poor Amanda. She deserves to be teed off.

Dice Club just isn't as fun as it used to be. Maybe I should stop going…

I've got to get up. Bathroom. Yes, get up. "Dang it! Ian!" Why did he leave the exercise equipment there? He knows this is my path to the bathroom. Yow, that hurt my toe. Now I'm wide-awake, and he's over there all sound asleep. My head aches. Where are the Advil?

Wait, what was I doing?

I look around the room. Advil. Where are they? Hunt, hunt, hunt. I can't see anything. I'm tiptoeing. The arches of my feet are trained—I could be on point right now, tee-hee. Oh, yeah, ADVIL, where ARE you? Maybe they're in my studio. I could go out there. I KNOW I've got a pint of Absolut in the studio fridge. They're never far apart. It's like they're in alphabetical order: AB: Absolut; AD: Advil.

Aha! There they are. Of course, on his side of the bed. Can I shake out three or four pills without waking him? I'm tiptoeing again. Sweet Jesus it was the cosmopolitans. The sugar is surging through my veins. I feel like a kid who ate too many treats at a birthday party. I've got to cut back on that kind of drink. Just stick to wine.

I pop the pills onto my tongue. Bitter. Quickly, I grab my water glass and head to the kitchen to refill it. Yuck! The taste of these things! I force them back and finish the entire glass of water. "Ah!" It's a heavy exhale, just like the girls after they've taken an enormous sip of something.

I feel foggy. Heavy. I know this feeling—the feeling of an uninvited guest or a topic I don't want to discuss. It's the middle-of-the-night hangover. My hair hurts. I should cut it.

Pausing on the return trip to the bedroom, I flip open the hallway shutters and see the almost full moon. Is it waxing or waning? Which one is which? The gnarly mesquite trees cast shadows against the courtyard. It looks like Halloween. Boy, do I remember those crisp, magical Halloween nights in Texas when I was first allowed to be out after dark. I went trick-or-treating for part of the night, and then later met boys with beers at the corner. I had to chew massive quantities of Milky Ways and Mars Almond Bars to hide the beer on my breath before venturing home. And it was always a trick to sneak into the trailer without waking Mama. She was usually asleep in front of the television with Johnny Carson or the late movie casting eerie light into the room like a strobe. What a sad life she led.

Mama was alone for as long as I can remember and is still living in a trailer in East Texas. I tried to get her to move to the Rattlesnake Valley, but I think she's waiting for my daddy to return from the off shore oil rig he went to work at in 1974. Right. When pigs fly! The only other thing I know about this roughneck besides that he abandoned us was that he liked his Johnny Walker Red. I used to think that was his name: Johnny Walker. He sure as heckfire walked out the door. That's when Mama went to work as a bookkeeper in a real estate agency. She was always good with numbers. At night she waitressed at a nearby tavern where Johnny Walker used to drink, and saved all her tips to pay for frilly costumes, voice and dance lessons for me. It was her idea to put me in pageants after hearing from everyone what a little looker I was. Boy she made me work! And it wasn't just working on my dance steps for the next performance. From the time I was old enough to fake my age on a job application, I worked as everything from an aerobics instructor at the local community center to a clothing store sales consultant and a shelf-stocker at the grocer. I quit each job whenever I had to travel to another pageant. It was worth it, I tell ya.

Through the pageant circuit I ultimately won a scholarship to Texas State University where I majored in business and marketing—I got good with numbers too. Must have inherited that from Mama. But it was the minor in art that made me what I am today. I came to Arizona as an aspiring sculptress and studied under a renowned, traditional Native American potter, Sancho Frugolo. He took me under his wing because of my red hair, which he said was a symbol of life and strength of spirit. He said I was a divine messenger, and sometimes called me "Kachina." Even though he was this ancient creature with skin like leather, I think I fell in love with him. That is, until Ian Shephard came along and swept me right up. After meeting Ian, I gathered my own clay and mastered the art of hand-forming pots using the traditional coil method, and developed into a rare artisan among an exclusive group of Native American potters.

These days my work is on display in my own gallery and many galleries throughout the West. Because of the marketing plan I came up with six years ago, I dare say there's hardly a soul in the Valley who doesn't know the distinctive look of a Tara Shephard pot, platter or tile. My work often finds its way onto popular television shows—in sitcom kitchens and trendy apartments. Even Brandy has one of my bowls on her ugly coffee table. And she hates everyone and everything.

Sigh. The clamor of the Dice Club women cuts inside my head like the sound of dice splaying across a glass table. I'm glad I had the good sense to stop drinking. This hangover could be much worse. I need more sleep. I should go back to bed. Why am I still standing here? I can't make a decision. Should I return to the water cooler to refill it before falling back asleep? I'd rest easier knowing the water was next to me.

It's probably pushing two o'clock. I can still get four hours if I fall asleep right now. I wish I didn't have to get up in the morning. Why can't there just be one day to sleep in late?

Stepping back into the bedroom, I find Ian is awake. "You okay?"

"I'm fine. Go back to sleep."

"Can you get me some water too?"

1:45 a.m.

I bring Ian the water, but even though I'm only gone for five seconds, he's fast asleep, snoring. He switches from wakefulness to sleep as easily as I flip light switches. It's so unfair. I set down his water and then close the shutters, stifling the moonlight.

Is Nicole's book report due tomorrow? I think Gabrielle was supposed to memorize a poem. Did I fire that last load of platters? I can't remember if I signed the purchase orders for the Chamber. Sure wish the Advil would kick in. I know I left that last load in the dryer. Tomorrow the clothes will be all wrinkled. There's no way I'm going to iron anything in the morning. But can I really send my girls to school wrinkled?

I can't catch my breath.

The oversized amber stick figures of the clock are mocking me from across the room. I squint my eyes, trying to read them. Is it too late to call my mother? This stinks. I've got to stop drinking. I'll stop tomorrow. I won't even have a glass of wine with dinner. Dang it, we're having dinner with the Bartletts tomorrow night. Can I do it without ordering anything? Maybe I should cancel the babysitter and stay home with the girls. Is Nicole old enough to let them stay home alone? I hope there's nothing on the calendar for Saturday night. I wonder what time the first soccer game is that morning. Please don't let it be an early one. I really need a morning to sleep in. Oh, crud! We're the snack parents. I hope I can find oranges in this town tomorrow. Last week someone brought Ding Dongs as a snack. Ding Dongs! I didn't even like that garbage when I was a kid. Maybe I can make something healthy. Start a new trend. I should bring a pitcher of margaritas for the parents. Now there's an idea.

Gosh, I've got to stop drinking. Please let me fall asleep.

9:00 a.m.

"What!?" Huh? What was that noise? I'm sitting up in my bed, panting like a hound dog that's just run a mile. Good heavens, I'm soaking wet. The sheets around me are wet, wet, wet. Did I spill something? The blinds are open and daylight streams into the room. I am, for some reason, filled with an overwhelming sense of dread. Where's Ian? Are the girls here? I can't make out the numbers on the clock. They're too blurry. Holy man. What day is it?

I swing my legs to the side of the bed. Ooh, I'm dizzy. My head feels cloudy. What happened to me?

Ian walks in. "There she is," he says brightly. "Finally get some sleep?"

"I suppose so." My hair's all tangled. I can't even get my fingers through it. "What happened?"

"You were out. Completely. I didn't have the heart to wake you, so I got Nicki and Gabby ready. I don't have anything going on today."

Humph. When do you ever have anything going on? I yawn. And I hate when he uses nicknames for the girls. They have beautiful names, Nicole and Gabrielle. "Did they study for their spelling tests?"

"Everything's fine. Don't worry."

I grab my head. "I feel like I got hit by a truck."

"Did you take something last night?"

"Yeah. There was some Advil on your nightstand."

"Advil," he says skeptically. Ian walks to the nightstand and picks up the round, white bottle. He replaces the lid. Then he spins the bottle in his hand like he's about to roll bunko dice and laughs. "Is this the Advil you took?"

Turning my head feels like I'm dragging it. I look at the bottle in his hand, and do a double take. "Excedrin PM?" Wait a minute. The pills I took. They were round, had a bitter taste. Advil pills are usually oblong capsules and have no taste. But it was two in the morning, what did I care? I was trying to squash a premature hangover.

"How many did you take?"

"Apparently enough to knock me out cold. What an idiot!" I fall back into my pillow.

"You better be careful, Honey. That can be dangerous." He puts the bottle in his shirt pocket as if to store them for safekeeping—away from me. He comes to me, strokes my cheek and sits down. I don't want him to feel the wet sheets. "I should be careful, too, cause I sure do like it when you drink." He winks and then licks his lips. Then he kisses my forehead, gets up, and leaves the room.

What did he mean by that? Did we have sex last night? I stare after him for a moment, and then feel my breasts. Hard as rocks. I grasp my inner thighs. There's gotta be a sign. Some sign—any sign—we'd made love. Oh, my head is pounding. I can't remember what I did after I switched off the light. There was something about the moon. Yeah, the moon. And dirty socks.

Oh my Lord, I've got to stop drinking. I gotta get up.

I move in slow motion toward the bathroom. The room's too bright. I grab the edge of the sink to steady myself and turn toward the mirror. Oh! Horrors! There are bed linen creases on my face. I touch them, first with my left hand, then with my right, trying in vain to smooth out the creases. The night has aged me. Cripes! I look like death warmed over. Keeping one hand on my face, I reach out and put the other on the mirror, on a reflection of a face I hardly recognize. And then I take a step back and stand there, staring at my alien image for nearly a minute.

"My name is Tara Shephard," I hear myself say. "And I'm an alcoholic."

Chapter 3
November

I hate my butt. All the running, all the weights and all the sweat aren't doing a thing to battle the maximus of my glutamous. I blame it on my pregnancies. God knows my body hasn't been the same since those alien invasions. But I've seen plenty of women who've had more kids than I who manage to maintain phenomenal figures. I wonder, do they eat?

—Shonah Bartlett
From her column, *The Dice Club Chronicles*

Blanca

I decided months ago that my Dice Club theme would have something to do with lingerie. I have drawers full of it. When my boys are with their father, I wear it around the house just to please myself. I wear lingerie to bed, to breakfast, and even during my workout of sit-ups and weights. Later in the day, I even wear it to yoga. It drives my mother crazy.

"¡*Mi'ja!*" she yells while looking at my shapely brown legs protruding from a silky, magenta teddy, the color of prickly pear fruit. "*Por Dios*, put some clothes on."

"I like what I'm wearing, Mama." I pour coffee into a mug made by my boss and gallery mate, Tara Shephard. "Wearing this around the house helps me feel more comfortable when I model it for Sonoran Nights."

"Now they've asked you to model underwear?" My mother is aghast.

"Calm yourself, Mama. I love the way it feels on my skin." I caress my backside and flash a mischievous smile.

She crosses herself. *"Eso bien que lo se."*

"You know *everything* about me too well."

"Sí, mi'ja," she says. "Even as a baby, you always wanted the softest things around you. But I also know you hate the limelight. So why you choose to flaunt yourself in television and magazine ads *es incredible. Es de no creer."*

"It helps me. I get wonderful feedback from the people who've seen my commercials. It makes it easier to get publicity for my paintings."

"¿Que quieres decir?"

"I'm saying you're right. I hate the limelight. God knows I'd rather hibernate all day in my art studio; but if I want to be commercially successful with my paintings—and keep this *techo grande* over all our heads—I have to get publicity. The Sonoran Nights ads are just one way to put me out there in a positive light. People like the way I look on TV. It may lead to them liking the way my paintings look. *¿Entiendes?"*

"I understand you, *mi'ja. Entiendo."* Mama sips her coffee.

"Well, I bet you don't know this. There's a saying in the white people's world that says you can never be too rich or too thin. I like to add that you can never have too much lingerie. That's why I've asked all my *amigas* to bring underwear tonight. It's going to be a great party."

My petite mother is covered from head to toe in black. It's the costume of a pious widow. She crosses herself and goes out the back door toward the maid's *casita* to take her coffee.

"Don't forget to remind Lupita about the shopping!" I call after her.

I turn sideways to examine myself in the mirror next to the back door. Pressing my hand to my tummy, I suck in hard, pushing my breasts as high as they can go. I can't help but frown and release my breath. "The holidays are going to be murder on my figure." I swear, the quest to stay thin is unending.

I head to my workout room, an annex off the bedroom. I managed to wrest custody of the weight machine after the divorce in spite of my ex-husband's arguments. Sitting down on the machine, the ritual begins. With each abdominal crunch, I contemplate a long list of chores I need to accomplish before the Dice Club girls arrive at six o'clock.

My maid, Lupita, will be gone most of the morning doing the grocery shopping, which means I'll be forced to clean the bathrooms and do the vacuuming. Cleaning is my least favorite chore. I rarely clean my studio and since I won't allow Lupita or my mother inside, it remains cluttered and chaotic. Cooking, on the other hand, is my favorite part of entertaining. I planned the menu as though creating one of my oil paintings—by mixing my cultures. Mother and Lupita will help prepare Mexican hors d'oeuvres—*chimichangas, flautas,* and *quesadillas*—which I consider safe food items already incorporated into most of my friends' diets. I think I might even ask my mother to prepare some *flan* and *sopa pillas* for dessert. For the main course, I'm planning to fix my paternal grandmother's African Beef Bobotie recipe. And to honor my O'odham culture, I'll prepare beans. If before tonight the Dice Club didn't know that the O'odham were once called the Papago, and papago translates into "bean eaters," they'll certainly know it in the morning when they digest all the spices I intend to use. These women need a little imagination in the kitchen. If I have to face one more carrot, broccoli, cauliflower and celery stick relish tray on Dice Club night, I might just vomit into the ranch dressing bowl in the center.

Moving onto the weights I use to keep my upper arms in shape, I think about my own contribution to the bag. Since I don't plan to leave the house all day, I'll have to pull something from my personal stash.

Momentarily releasing the weights, I get up, go to my bedroom, and to the top drawer of my chiffonier. I have to rummage through a few bags until I find a pink and white striped Victoria's Secret bag. Inside there's a variety of thong panties—red, pink, teal, navy, purple, forest green, and very rare in my wardrobe, white. "Ha! This will be perfect. Like a white sale. *¡La Venta Blanca!*"

The price tag reads fourteen dollars. I purse my lips. They feel dry. We're supposed to spend ten dollars on our contribution to the bag.

"So what!" I toss them onto my pillow. I don't think anyone's spent only ten dollars on a gift since we started the club.

It's true. The bags have become more and more elaborate—and therefore, more and more prized. The women have grown competitive in the last few months and someone even suggested that each "bunko" or "baby bunko" rolled should have witness initials next to it on the score sheet. Sylvia Ostrander has her suspicions that some of the women are cheating. She would. She can be one of those uptight, tight-ass white bitches who narrows her eyes at everyone and judges. I know I'm not suspected—I've never won a thing—and I can't believe that any of these women would cheat just to get an extra twenty dollars or a bag full of *mierda*. Some of them get too drunk to count, maybe, but none of them would intentionally mismark their scorecards. Would they?

Tonight's bag will probably be the best ever. At least it would be for me since I already know I can't have enough lingerie. "Let the cats fight over it!" I laugh as I return to the workout room, and reach for the overhead bar on the weight machine.

"Seven …eight …nine …ten. Whew!" Sweat is dripping down my face. Last reps. Let's go. I miss the push of my personal trainer. I haven't been able to afford him since the divorce. There's a lot I can no longer afford. But I have enough. More than enough. *Está bien.* It was worth it just to get away from that jerk I was married to. He used to push me too, but I didn't like the direction. I've learned to push myself. Push. Push. Push. And pull. Pull. Pull. I feel my pulse rate surging. Large drops of sweat plunge from my scalp to my collarbone. *Yes!*

Just as I pull down the bar for my last rep, a startling, Latin beat fills the air. It's my cell phone, and this particular ring means one thing. My ex. David never keeps track of my schedule. Wiping the moisture from my brow with the back of my hand, I reach for the phone. "Hello?"

"I'm going out of town again," says the familiar voice. "You have to take the boys tonight."

"Oh no you don't." I reach for a towel. My heart is pumping. "I told you weeks ago that this is my night to host Dice Club. You said you didn't have a movie until after the first of the year, and there's no way you can pull this on me at the last minute."

"You don't understand, Blanca," he says. "I have to go to Kenya in the morning and I'll be there for ten days. The U.N called. That's the United Nations in case you forgot. My agent called and already has my short-term visa. You *know* this is something I've been wanting to do for a long time."

"Excuse me? What did you say?" I look in the mirror. Sometimes I feel like I need a witness to the conversations I have with him. He pulls so much crap, no one would believe me.

"I'm leaving just after midnight. The redeye to New York. I have a meeting there before taking a late morning flight to Paris and then to Nairobi. I'll make a copy of my itinerary and I'll be back just after Thanksgiving."

I can't help it. I have to scream. *"¡Hijo de puta!* You've had enough time to have your visa arranged and you're just getting around to telling me now? Have you told the boys?"

"I told you there was a chance I'd be headed overseas as an ambassador before the end of the year. But I wasn't certain the publicity and everything would be in place. I wanted to be sure before I told you. But yes, I told the boys last night. They could care less."

"Oh, you think so." I turn from the mirror and pace the room.

"Believe me, Blanca," he says, "you've managed to turn them into boring little people who accept all of life as mediocre. Ever since you pulled them out of the French immersion school, they've just learned to settle for whatever is put before them. They'll do so much better with three languages rather than two. So, congratulations. They're going to turn out just like you, Blanca *Midnight*."

I bite my lip, remembering how much he once supported and encouraged the use of the name Midnight when I signed my paintings. But just like most things between us, what we once thought we loved, we now despise in one another. "Obviously, David, you don't give a fig about the La Crosse tournament this weekend. And I still haven't seen a dime out of you for the team fees. In spite of how you feel about me and my *mediocre* life, our agreement was…"

"I knew you'd give me a hard time about this, Blanca," he interrupts. "You think your Dice Club is more important than the plight of East African refugees? I don't know what this bunko game thing is you've got going besides a night of heavy partying, but you're going to have to clean it up and find a way to do it with the boys around."

"No one has their kids around on Dice Club night. It's one of the rules. No husbands. No kids."

"No husbands, no kids? How perfect for you."

"David…"

"I don't have time for this. I'm leaving and that's the end of the story. Just put them out in the guesthouse with your mother and Lupita. They'll be fine," he says. "Look, I've already spent too much time on this call. I have a ton of things to do before I leave. Also, I need you to pick them up from school this afternoon, and then stop at my place to get their things. Okay? I really don't have time."

"David! Wait before you hang up on me again."

"What is it?"

"I have one question for you." I feel the bile well up in my throat. My heart is still racing. "You like to believe you're the extraordinary language specialist, right?"

"Yeah? So?"

"Right. So then, how do you say 'fuck you' in Swahili?"

I don't wait for a response.

Tootsie

The black and white checkerboard tiles of my foyer are making me dizzy. I think I've paced by this doorway sixty times. It's not going to make him come home any sooner. "Michael Bartholomew Fennimore, where on God's green earth are you?"

My terriers, Trixie and Teddy, scamper toward me when they hear my voice. Now they pace with me. "So help me Michael Fennimore, if you don't get here soon I'm going to burst!"

I look at my watch, even though I am keenly aware that it's now exactly thirty-eight hours since the ovulation kit told me my LH levels would be as ripe as a juicy red cherry that needs to be plucked. Maybe I should answer the door naked.

The thought of it makes my face feel hot. What would my mama think of that?

Taking Trixie in my hands while Teddy nips at my ankles, I tell her, "Tootsie Thompson Fennimore is no longer her mother's daughter. That's for sure!"

It doesn't even bother me to buy ovulation kits and pregnancy tests at the local Walgreens anymore. At first I placed them on the check out counter, as humiliated as the day I first became a woman, and each time since then when I had to put up tampons or panty-liners for the clerk to scan. I always knew my face turned red and I truly believed everyone in the store considered the possibility that Tootsie Thompson had something going on "down there."

I must be made of mercury.

That's what happens to girls who are raised in a proper Southern home. My mother, Veronica Vermillion Thompson, "Ronnie," saw to it that her one and only daughter was raised a lady. Not only was I taught to never act up in public, Mama insisted I execute only the most proper, white-glove behavior at all times. As a result, I, Tootsie Thompson, had an impeccable reputation on the LPGA golf circuit, right down to my white-gloved hands. I addressed every woman as "Ma'am," every man as "Sir." My competitors were not merely Betsy and Juli, but Miss Betsy and Miss Juli. Even Annika Sorenstam, five years my junior, was Miss Annika. Cynical television commentators sometimes wondered if it were an act, particularly when the camera focused on Mama in the gallery with purple parasol in hand and politely clapping for her daughter's fine play. The press called her "quaint." She about had a kitten when she read that.

Mama came to accept my foray into professional golf, but she would never allow me to do commercial endorsements. She wasn't a fan of television, primarily because it astounded her that ads for feminine hygiene products were featured "all-the-live-long-day." She believed it wasn't the least bit ladylike to discuss such indecent topics as menstruation and, Lord above, sexual intercourse. Veronica Vermillion Thompson may have prepared me for the cotillion, but certainly never armed me for the sexual revolution. That's something I definitely missed. Now when my friends talk about sex, I only have a vague idea what they're talking about. Just what is this "reverse cowgirl" thing Brandy Lynn's always talking about anyway? I declare, I don't get half her jokes.

In high school I focused on my long game, and then on my short game during college. Who had time for boyfriends? Once I hit the pro circuit, fellow southerners on the tour often said that when it came to matters of the heart, Tootsie Thompson was like a nun on a honeymoon.

It was true. At least until I met Michael Fennimore.

I'm pretty sure I know all I need to know by now. Except for how to get pregnant. This will be the—I count on my fingers—one-two-three-four-five-sixth month, now. Why can't I get pregnant? "I am going to wear him out if he ever gets home!"

The terriers yelp. I place my hands on my flat tummy and try with all my power to imagine the egg—a tiny golf ball—slowly traveling the perfect path down my fallopian tube. I've always been goal oriented and have had great success. This will work this time. I know it. The doctors said we were normal. Sure, we're a little older than most people going for a baby for the first time, but lots of women are having babies in their 40s now.

It's going to be a beautiful baby. If it's a boy, I'll name him Michael. Mama would approve. It's a good and proper thing to name a son after his daddy.

I am beyond late for Dice Club, and I'd really hate to miss Blanca Midnight's cooking. That woman sure knows how to throw all her ethnicity into a pot. She's part Mexican and part African American, with a few other spices mixed in for good measure. Someone or something gave her those blue eyes. I'm not sure what ethnic clan she relates to most. She just laughs, exposes huge white teeth between painted red lips and happily calls herself a "black bean." Yes indeed, her meals are always spectacular. But I can't let this ovulation opportunity slip by. Mama would be hoppin' mad if she knew I skipped out on an opportunity to produce her first grandchild to go throw dice with a bunch of foul-mouthed women. "Ha!" Surely, Mama would have a full-grown cat if she ever set foot into one of our wild Dice Club parties!

Punching Michael's cell number for the fourth time in fifteen minutes, it doesn't ring. Instead, it goes immediately to voice mail. "You have reached the…" says his recorded baritone voice. He's either on the line, or his battery is dead. Probably a dead battery. He never remembers to recharge that *thang*!

"Great balls of fire!" I push the off button on my portable phone. "Where the devil are you?" When I stamp my foot the dogs yap. Maybe I should sit down. I'll never get pregnant if I can't relax. And if it doesn't work this time, I declare, we're going for the harvest. I almost wish they'd told us it was a low sperm count or something like, God forbid, endometriosis. This unexplained, non-specific infertility is more frustrating than an afternoon round of high winds when the morning competitors had perfect conditions.

I toss the phone into a chair and go into my special room, the trophy room. Well, that's what Michael called it when he surprised me with it as a Christmas present last year. For weeks he hadn't allowed me access to the room that had been the den, and then on Christmas morning he gave me a giant scissors. He got it from one of his many construction sites—probably the Casino—where a congressman and a tribal leader held both ends of the scissors to cut a red ribbon at the dedication. Ceremoniously, Michael asked me to cut the gold ribbon stretched across the door, and snapped my photo while I did it. He then covered my eyes with his hand and escorted me into my gift.

With the constant flow of carpenters and interior decorators parading in and out of my home for six weeks, I spent hours fantasizing about what was going on in that room. Sometimes I dreamed of a state-of-the-art gift-wrapping room. There'd be a big, island table in the middle of the room, tape and ribbon dispensers, and rolls of colorful gift paper comparing to any department store wrapping facility.

Other times, when I allowed myself to think about it, I visualized the perfect nursery. Painted lemon yellow and white, clean and bright, the room for my imaginary baby defined sunshine. I hoped for a white, iron crib with a lacy skirt, and pure white bumpers. A rocking horse—hell, a collection of rocking horses—would sit next to the white, wooden rocking chair where each night I would nurse my precious child and read ABC books and stories about using the potty.

Yet when the day arrived and the room was revealed, I entered and came face-to-face not with a rocking horse collection or shimmering ribbons and colorful rolls of paper, but with a collection of photos of Tootsie Thompson, golfer. It was Michael Fennimore's version of the LPGA Hall of Fame, a little corner of the world dedicated solely to me.

I didn't know what to say, so I walked into the center of the room and stared at the walls with my mouth hanging open like I had a broken hinge or something. One wall held my first set of golf clubs. Irons and woods—real woods—were lined up horizontally, evenly spaced like rifles in a gun rack. Another wall featured golf balls significant to my career, encased in specially designed Plexiglas cubes—the same kind used to contain a collector's set of autographed baseballs. The balls included my one and only tournament hole-in-one; the one I had sunk for a birdie on the eighteenth to take the title of my first major; and the one presented to me by Miss Nancy Lopez when I won my first amateur event. Trophies of all sizes and shapes—made of wood, glass, copper, and bronze—filled a third wall.

I was flattered, of course, but my first thought was that it was like some kind of a shrine. It was creepy. Michael stood at my side, awaiting praise like a child who had just brought home a straight-A report card, but I was too overwhelmed to speak. "Well?" he finally said. "What do you think?"

"This is a hoot!" It was all I could think of to say.

I slowly walk around the room, and once again look at each element of my lucrative yet unfulfilling career. It was the career that has cost me my baby! I still don't feel comfortable in here. With so many images of me on the walls, it's a bit like looking through a kaleidoscope—fly eyes.

I've got to learn to take pride in my accomplishments. It may be all I end up with.

Relaxing into a plush, mauve sofa, I lift my feet to the glass-topped coffee table, and then pull them off as fast as if I'd stepped in hot coals. Sharp edges! It'll have to be replaced when the baby comes.

Again I look at my watch. Might as well go to Blanca's for Dice Club. The theme is "Leather and Lace." Maybe if I win, some new lingerie will do the trick. Or if I get a leather whip, I can crack it over Michael's behind for standing me up at ovulation hour! I pull out my cell phone again, but this time I press the send key for Blanca Midnight Fernglen.

Blanca

With the exception of Tootsie, late again, my Dice Club ladies arrive right on time and devour the food. No one realizes I've got my kids stashed out in Lupita's *casita*. Because of the theme, all the talk is about underwear. Brandy tries to convince everyone they should be wearing thongs.

"I don't know how you wear those things," cries Tootsie. "How can you possibly concentrate on a golf putt when you've got a thong wedged up your butt?"

Brandy laughs and uses her index finger to pull up the waistband of her thong underwear. She bends over and twists her athletic frame, so that red elastic arches above her low-slung jeans. It looks like a derisive, lipstick smile. "Once you go thong, you cannot go wrong," she sings.

"Hey!" says Sylvia. "That would make a great bumper sticker."

"I'd buy it," says Tara. "And I'd stick it right on my bumper." She pats her bottom and strikes a Paris Hilton pose. She could be a good model for Sonoran Nights, but she's already photographed a lot for her gallery ads. She's dressed in tight black slacks and a lace top that shows her lavender bra. "I never leave the house without a thong these days. V.P.L. is just so 1970s."

"Weren't you born in the 1970s?" asks Brandy.

"V.P.L?" Tootsie asks. "Am I, like, completely out of it?"

"Visible Panty Line," say Brandy. "You probably sported them on television back during your LPGA days and didn't even know it. Turn around. Let me see your ass."

Tootsie obeys the command and bends at the waist, showing off her *nalgas buenas* clad in tight-fitting, navy capri pants. The lines are smooth. She looks good!

Brandy reaches out and smacks Tootsie's bottom. "That's one fine ass you've got there, Tootsie Roll. I bet mine would still be that tight if I didn't have kids."

Tootsie straightens and blushes. Her usually pale skin bursts into such vivid color that it could probably light a cigarette across the room. She takes a sip of water. "Maybe we should play bunko," she says.

"Oh yes, bunko." I laugh. "That's why I had you all over here."

"Yeah," says Sylvia. "I kind of forgot why we were here, too. Something feels different."

"Well," says Shonah, "maybe it's because of this beautiful house and the amazing meal she just fed us? I feel like I'm at a dinner party. Not Dice Club night."

"Your home really is beautiful," says Sylvia. "The colors are so rich. There's so much …so much …texture!"

I'm flattered. "Thank you." She may be uptight, but she does have good taste.

"I told you she's an amazing artist," says Tara. She puts her arm around my waist and gives me a squeeze. I watch her eyebrows shoot up. I squeeze her back and figure out why. All that booze she's drinking is finding its way to her middle.

I choose a CD and the room fills with the reggae rhythms of Bob Marley. Stretching out my arms, I sashay to the middle of the sunken seating area, and move my hips in a circular motion. Everyone watches me dance and I feel beautiful.

David Fernglen doesn't know what he's missing!

I feel proud showing off my house. The room is Santa Fe style. The floors are a burnt-red concrete and the tall ceilings are beamed with full pine logs and thick, plank paneling. A mesquite and *piñon* fire roars in the kiva fireplace and fills the air with alluring incense. It's the smell of winter in the desert. We went right from summer to winter. No autumn. The fire gives off the perfect, warm glow, complementing my décor. I love to decorate as much as I love to cook. I haunt the galleries near the one where I work, where Tara allows me to share space without charge, but also regularly scout flea markets, antique stores and estate sales, looking for funky lamps, brocade tapestries, oversized pillows and unusual folk art. The fourteen-foot walls are covered with my colorful paintings of desert scenes and Native American gatherings. They're cubist in nature. Abstract. The colors are so vivid they practically sing.

Brandy, who has no interest in art or dancing, heads to the bar and uncorks a bottle of cabernet. Filling her glass to the rim, she sniffs the wine and unintentionally dunks the tip of her nose. "Now that's a new form of wine tasting," she says. "Hey Blanca, which one is the top table?"

"Wherever you park that saddle of yours," I tell her. Brandy always likes to be in charge.

The women move to the tables, my regular dining room table and a card table I set up next to it. It's already eight-fifteen and no one is much in the mood to toss dice. Our bellies are full of my delicious cuisine and the music has drowned out our voices. All the ladies have some kind of drink, with Tootsie and a noticeably quiet Tara both clinging to plastic bottles of Arrowhead water.

"We're missing someone," says Shonah. "There's an empty chair."

"I told you Amanda wasn't coming," says Sylvia. "We have to play with a ghost."

"Well then we're missing two people," says Brandy.

We all look around, our eyes silently counting.

"Oh my God!" laughs Shonah. "Chlöe isn't here!"

"How could we have missed her?" asks Tara.

"She probably got hung up on one of her many chores," Brandy says. "Lord knows she's busier than all of us combined."

"No wonder it feels different," says Sylvia, as she writes her name on her scorecard. "Dice Club hasn't had such an easy going feel since, uh…".

"Since before Amanda joined?" says Tootsie. She immediately brings her hand to her mouth and raises her shoulders. A guilty look flashes across her face. It was as though she had no control over her mouth.

The room erupts with laugher. "Didn't know you had it in ya, Miss Tootsie!" says Brandy.

Tootsie stammers. "I didn't…it's just that…".

"It's just that she adds so much tension," says Shonah.

"No kidding," Brandy says. "Whom can I piss off tonight if both Amanda and Chlöe aren't here?"

"Well I brought something really hot for the bag," says Sylvia. "I know you're going to fight over this one!"

"Is it leather or lace?" asks Brandy.

Sylvia shakes her head. "I'll never tell."

I sit at the top table with Brandy and Sylvia. Shonah, Tootsie and Tara sit at the card table.

"Bring it on," says Brandy. She picks up the brass bell and rings it to begin the round. "Here we go. Rolling for ones." Three dice splay onto the table. "One," she counts, and rolls again. "Two, three…I think I can handle leather, but I don't know what I'd do with a bunch of lacy lingerie. Levi might have a heart attack if I come to bed wearing something sexy." She tosses the dice.

"Would he even notice?" asks Sylvia.

"Ooh! Low blow," says Brandy with a laugh. "Four, five." Her hand moves quickly as she tallies her scorecard, scoops up the dice, and rolls again. "Three fours. Baby! That's five more. Are you getting this Sylvia?"

"Oh, I thought you were playing with the ghost," says Sylvia. "But I'll take your points and Blanca can have the ghost this round. We're up to ten so far. Almost halfway to twenty-one and a win!"

A burst of screams comes from the other. "Bunko!" shouts Tootsie.

"Shit," says Brandy. "I've got some catching up to do already."

We played six games for a total of one round. Since Chlöe Forrest isn't here to scold us for cutting short the competition, and Amanda isn't here to cause a scene, we all agree it's enough. With two bunkos, Tootsie's the big winner, again, and she's destined to receive the bag of leather and lace. *Buenos suerte.*

We fill our glasses one more time and relax in the plush leather furnishings of the sunken living room. I had better go and check on my boys in the *casita.*

Tootsie

We're waiting for Blanca to return. She said she had to check on something in her guesthouse and has been gone for nearly half an hour. Sylvia is keeping the music going and we hardly notice we're waiting, even though I'm eager to open the gifts. I have to say, this has been the best Dice Club night in months. I am truly on a roll! Winning two months in a row is unprecedented. Maybe this is a sign of good things to come.

Blanca rushes in with an armload of mesquite logs. She drops them into a copper bucket as the glowing embers emit a pulsating glow from the corner of the room. Standing back for a moment, she wipes her brow and catches her breath, and then adds a log to the fire. It ignites at once, and crackles like popping popcorn.

Shonah sits to my left with her notepad in hand, and Sylvia sits to my right. She hands me the packages, which I can't help but size up before opening. Some of the wrap jobs are decent, but others have had absolutely no thought. "I should have you all over for a wrapping seminar one of these days."

"Make it the theme for your next party," says Shonah. "Gift Wrap Bunko."

"Yeah," says Brandy. "You can call it Bundles and Bows Bunko or something like that."

"I'll think about it." From the first package, I pull out a gorgeous, teal nightgown. It has spaghetti straps, a low cut neckline and a deep back that will no doubt cut all the way down to my butt crack. "Wow," is all I can say. I stand and hold it against my compact frame. The satin fabric shimmers in the firelight.

"That's from me," says Sylvia. "Told you it would be a hit."

"It's too long on you, Tootsie," comments Brandy. "I think that was made for me. Not you. Even my neglected ass would look good in that number!"

"Eat your heart out, Brandy Lynn. This nightie is all mine, Sister Sledge."

"That ought to get your husband's sperm count up," says Brandy.

Big sigh. If only that were the problem. "What's next, Sylvia?"

"That little leather satchel is from me," says Shonah. "There's a lace sashay inside. I couldn't decide between leather or lace, so I just got them both."

I nod at her and smile. "Thank you, Miss Shonah."

Sylvia hands me a Victoria's Secret bag. "Ooh!" cries Blanca Midnight. "That's mine. I can't wait to see you open it. But I'm imposing a 'hostess rule' on this one. And you have to follow it."

"That depends. What's the rule?"

"You have to model it," Blanca says with a wry smile. She stands up, prances across the room, strikes a model's pose, turns and high-steps back to her chair. "You know it, *mi'ja*!"

I rummage through the hot pink tissue paper and after four layers, finally fish out a skimpy white thong. "Oh, my." Holding it up, I wave it in the air like a white flag of surrender. "No way! There's no way in HELL I'm letting ya'll see me in this thing. In your DREAMS!"

All the women shout at once.

"Oh come on!"

"What are you afraid of?"

"You have a fantastic figure!"

"I'd do it."

"So would I."

"I wouldn't be caught dead modeling that in front of the likes of this crowd," Sylvia whispers to Shonah.

"C'mon Tootsie," says Shonah. "You can do it."

"Do it," says Tara. "It'll be good for you."

"Once you go thong, you cannot go wrong," sings Brandy.

I feel my face heating up again and my heart starts to beat faster. I do have a beautiful, strong body. It's nothing to be ashamed of. These women may have all had their children and lost their tight tummies and their battle with backend cellulite, but I'm in the same good shape I've maintained throughout my professional golf career. "Oh what the hey. Keep your pants on ladies. I'll go in the other room and take off mine."

I get up, spin the thong on my index finger and walk toward an open doorway leading to Blanca's bedroom. "Try to contain yourself in the meantime. And keep your paws off my bag of gifts! Especially you Brandy Lynn."

Peeking from Blanca's bedroom door, I see Brandy snatch the teal nightgown and stuff it into her purse. She puts her finger to her lips and says, *"Shhhh!"*

"You're bad," says Shonah.

"Honey, you have no idea," Brandy says with a wink.

"I saw that!"

Blanca's bedroom is as gorgeous as her sunken living room. There's a lush patchwork quilt of rich colors on her king-sized bed. What a shame she has to sleep in it alone each night. That bed must seem like the size of an entire country.

I miss Michael. How I wish he would've made it home in time tonight.

I take off my pants and my plain white, schoolgirl briefs, and place them on the foot of the bed. I can't help but lose myself in the thought of making love atop the beautiful quilt before me. Next, I remove my white blouse and bra. Oh, to make love without it having anything to do with trying to conceive.

Touching myself ever so gently, I recall those mornings when I first met Michael Fennimore. I knew he had his eye on me from the first time he saw me play at the local LPGA event. He followed Wendy Ward and me for all eighteen holes. At first I thought he might be one of those weird, stalker guys, but there was something so charming in the way he applauded and kept his distance. He was a fan, yes, and I later learned he plays a decent game. But he has his own money—old money—where streets and buildings around the Valley are named after his family. I knew my mama, Veronica Vermillion Thompson, would surely approve.

When I next spotted him following me in Scottsdale, I wondered when he'd finally ask me out. Thank the good Lord he did. And he forever changed my life.

I lick my fingers and allow them to tease their way inside me. *Mmmm.*

Mornings with Michael. They extended to afternoons, and then to nights filled with passion and lust, and constant, constant ...uh! *Oh!* We couldn't get our clothes off fast enough.

I fall to the bed and place my hand over my soft, pubic mound. I lay there, panting ...longing for more. Oh, so much more!

Where has all the passion gone?

Another big sigh. I better get up. They'll wonder what's keeping me and I don't want anyone to come in and try to help me put on this silly piece of cloth. I glance in the full-length mirror across the room at my naked self. My tea cup-sized breasts are pert and crowned with albino-pink nipples, my skin smooth and alabaster. I turn from side to side and hesitantly smile.

Not bad. Not bad for a forty year old woman.

"Let me see how this works." I examine the thong panties—turn them every which way to figure out how they should be worn. Lordy, maybe I *will* need help. Finally, I find a tag, spread the elastic band and step into them, one leg at a time. The silky fabric triangle barely covers me. I try to poke the hairs inside, as I often do when wearing a bathing suit out of season, but there's just not enough fabric! How much does Victoria's Secret charge for this little slingshot anyway? Lifting the narrow straps above my hips, I feel the string of the thong cut through my butt cheeks. It's a definite self-inflicted "wedgie," and makes me want to giggle! I turn to examine my backside in the mirror.

"Good grief. My butt is just eating this thing!"

Just then, one of the French doors leading to the backyard flies open. Blanca Midnight's twelve-year old son—a beautiful boy with dark skin and blue eyes—bursts into the room like a paint ball. He spies me immediately and his blue eyes bulge from his face.

"Oh my God!" we say together.

I don't know what to do other than grab and cover my breasts. I cross my legs and try to hide my nakedness.

"I'm sor ...sor ...sorry," he stammers. "I didn't know anyone was in here."

"Heavens to Betsy! Go away. Shoo! Get out. Get *out*! Go back where you came from this instant!" My breasts spill from my hands as I wildly gesticulate for him to go back outside.

The boy stands in place, unable to move.

"Good Christ, what's wrong with you?"

"I ...I," he says. He puts his hands to his eyes and trips out the door. It remains open, and the crisp, November wind pulls the navy velvet curtains into the night.

I exhale heavily and grab my blouse from the bed. "Damn it to hell." Buttoning as I march back into the living room, I'm met with resounding applause.

"Shut up!" I scream at them. "All of you just shut up."

The room goes silent. "Damn it, Blanca. When you made the new rule saying I had to model the underwear you didn't tell me you discarded the old rule of having no kids present at bunko."

"Díos mio," says Blanca, crossing herself. "What happened?"

"What happened is that I'm afraid your youngest son may be scarred for life."

Blanca's bright red lips tighten into an angry line. "David!" she hisses.

"Is that his name?" I ask. "I thought it was..."

"No, not my son. My wretched ex-husband. ¡*Mamahuevo!*" She stamps her foot and swallows what's left of the wine in her glass.

"Mamahuevo?" asks Brandy. "What the hell does that mean? Mama's eggs?"

"Please Brandy, not now," says Blanca. "It's David's fault. He was supposed to have the kids. Today he called and said he was leaving for Kenya and I had to take them. I didn't think they'd come in the house."

"Kenya?" asks Sylvia. "As in Africa?"

"Didn't he, like, quit the Peace Corps about twenty years ago?" asks Shonah.

Blanca shakes her head. "He's doing it for the publicity. He now cares more about some refugee group than he does his own sons. Why do you think I left him?"

"Who does he think he is?" asks Brandy. "Brad fucking Pitt?"

"Brandy!" scolds Sylvia.

Brandy frowns at Sylvia. "He's a freak."

"What happened, Tootsie?" Tara asks. "Did he just see you in that thong?"

"That's not so bad," says Shonah. "You can't really see anything with your blouse hanging down."

I fall into an overstuffed chair, and like a slow boiling pot, my body quakes. I let out a small chuckle, and slowly, it builds to a hearty laugh. "Oh good golly, what a hoot! I'm afraid it was all me, and one little thong. You should have seen his face!"

"Oh my," someone says.

I hear a lot of snickering. "I'm sorry Blanca, but he may be having Mrs. Robinson fantasies for a few nights. Better check the bed sheets."

As everyone laughs, the front door opens and in walks Chlöe Forrest. "Hi there," she says, taking off her jacket. "Sorry I'm so late. I had to finish about fifteen loads of laundry, take my oldest to soccer practice across town since he's playing on that prestigious traveling team now. My daughter is going to the state finals for the spelling bee and I had to quiz her. My driver's license expired and . . ." She stops mid-schedule and looks at us all laughing. "What are you all doing? Are you taking a break between rounds? Did I miss something?"

I stand up, lift my blouse and flash my backside at Chlöe. "No, Chlöe, darlin'. You didn't miss a *thong*."

Chapter 4
December

Thank you for all the cards and calls after my mother's passing on Thanksgiving Day. They help. They truly do. I'm surprised by how many of you have written things like, "My mother's been dead for eight years, and I still miss her every day." Maybe I was hoping you'd say something more like "Don't worry, the pain will go away." But you've assured me, it doesn't. Not really.

I guess realizing this is the first step to accepting that death is a permanent state, and that I must learn to go on in spite of it. In fact, I think that's death's biggest lesson. When we lose someone we love, it becomes our responsibility to not only continue living, but also to continuing living well.

Our loved ones don't want us to die with them. They just want to be remembered.

—Shonah Bartlett
From her column, *The Dice Club Chronicles*

Amanda

I'm drenched with sweat. The room is dark, the air stale. Alas, the dream is over. Heat fills my chest and, oh Christ, here come the tears. Why did I have to wake up?

His last portrait, a fourth grade class photo, is the focal point of my bedroom. My eyes reach for it, my gaze—a weary and broken umbilical cord—is tethered to his familiar features. It's been nearly six weeks since he came to me in a dream. This one seemed so real, like he was in the house walking around, slamming doors, and drinking milk from the container. And then he left. Again.

In the last seventeen months, I've relived Sean's death a thousand times. Even when I unconsciously push it aside for a minute—sometimes ten minutes—it always comes back with a potent force.

I pull the blanket to my chin, wanting desperately to sink back into my dream. A fateful bargain, I promise I'll never again scold him for not putting milk in a glass—if only I could have him back. That kid loved milk. "Red cap," he called it. Nothing but full strength, whole milk for Sean. "Do you think Santa likes red cap?" he joked one Christmas. "It would make sense 'cause he wears a red cap. Get it? *RED* cap?" He repeated his clever joke to anyone who'd listen, and from that point forward it was stored in the family archives along with the holiday decorations.

Getting out of bed means facing the second Christmas season without him. Christmas means family and my family has been destroyed— taken away from me as though every Christmas present I'd ever received has been replaced with coal.

I sit up and stare at his photo, still trying to focus. It's like looking through a picture window on a rainy day. Spying my red and green reading glasses on top of a paperback novel on the nightstand, I place them on my nose. I love his haircut in this photo. It's so boyish. He still had the gap in his front teeth. Shortly after that photo was taken, I paid three hundred dollars to the dentist for a frenectomy to correct that gap. I only agreed to the simple surgical procedure because I secretly hoped it would help his labored breathing.

It didn't.

My pack of Marlboro Lights is half empty. I grab one, tap it on the dresser and light up. Releasing the smoke, it hovers in front of me like a gray storm cloud. Sean looks just like Manny. "Looked? Had looked?" I ask the air. "Whatever." I still can't get my past and present tenses straight where he's concerned. Will I ever have it clear?

I take another pull from the cigarette, and it triggers a severe cough. A rush of tears follows.

"Stop it! Stop crying." I sniff, jab the cigarette into an ashtray balancing on the edge of the nightstand, and wipe my eyes with the pale pink linen of the bed sheet. Half-moon mascara stains immediately look back at me. They are like damaged clown eyes.

I've gotta get up. Start this day. I stand and direct my mind to a safer place—a place that does not relive the days of asthma attacks, steroid treatments, and long nights at the hospital. "Don't think about him," I tell myself, shaking my head. One day will come when Sean is not the first thing I think of when I wake up. One day. "Let's see. What's hap-

pening today?" I reach for another cigarette and hold it between my lips unlit, and pull pillowcases from the plump bed pillows. A checklist appears in my mind's eye:
- Make a lunch.
- Mail letters on the way to work.
- Stop at Starbucks if the line isn't too long.
- Collect the last of this weekend's football betting pool.
- Retype the damn "Turner Interrogatory."

I set down the cigarette and bite my thumbnail. A vision of my boss, the powerful Richard Ostrander, Esquire, fills my mind. There's an ongoing murder trial obsessing everyone in the office. Everyone but me.

The yellow page of my imaginary checklist crumbles into a tight ball.

"Screw you, Esquire Ostrander and your spoiled little wife too." I pull the stained top sheet from the bed. I'm angry now. Fine. Familiar territory. It's better than the tears. I lift the corners of the fitted sheet, and along with the pillowcases, throw them to the floor. "I'd like to see Sylvia Ostrander have a day in my patent leather pumps. Just one day." Does she even realize what sort of creeps her husband defends? Edward "Eddie-Get-Yer-Gun" Turner is as guilty as a black-hatted bandit.

I know Sylvia has no idea how much I do for her husband. I go well beyond my job description. I'm a trained paralegal—and yet, he always has me doing menial secretarial chores. Dinner reservations. Trips to the post office. Staying late to wait for the UPS delivery. The list is endless. It's like I'm the only competent worker in the office and he, the rich son-of-a-bitch, takes advantage of me. "I don't trust the others as much as I trust you," he always says. But does he pay me any overtime? Hell no.

"Fuck them." The words spit from my tongue. "Fuck the fucking Ostranders and all their fucking money." I'm sick of performing for them. I'm tired of smiling, pretending I'm fine, and acting the way *they* think I should act.

I sit down hard on my stripped bed and light my cig. Smoke fills my lungs. Another comfortable, familiar feeling. There's an old bloodstain marring the mattress pad. Do I have "Spray and Wash" for the stains? I use far less of it since Sean...

I never expected to miss grass stains in the knees of his blue jeans.

Manny's pillow, a contoured island of pale pink, remains on the bed. Rolling over, I press my face to my husband's scent—a mixture of tobacco, musk and Scope. I drink it in, savor it like a glass of morning orange juice, then roll over and pull from my cigarette. Blowing the smoke upward in a thick, steady stream, I wonder, why can't I have Manny's strength?

Glancing at the clock on his nightstand, I calculate he's been gone for at least an hour. Manny's on the job by six, checking termite stations in the new Northwest developments, where transplanted residents are overly paranoid of scorpions and snakes, tarantulas, ants, centipedes and gila monsters. Many have their homes sprayed once a month. That's way too much if you ask me, but the non-stop development and influx of Easterners and Midwesterners is good for business—not that he reaps many financial benefits. Why couldn't I have married into money like Sylvia—and those Dice Club women over in the Valley? My life could have been so different.

With the burning cigarette between my teeth, I gather the linens and carry them to the laundry room. Taking one last drag, I pull it from my mouth and run the lit end under the faucet of the washtub. I like the sizzling sound of water hitting the fiery ember. Coughing, I spit into the sink, and then throw the butt into the trash atop discarded Bounce sheets and lint balls.

I return to my bedroom and my mental checklist. It's Thursday. Dice Club night. "Great. Just the people I want to see." Brandy sent around an email about the December schedule conflicts and asked us to vote on a date change. I voted to have Dice Club the previous week, but naturally, the vote didn't go in *my* favor. So what if that show-offy Tara Shephard was taking her bratty children to Disneyland? I wonder if she'd still be so chirpy if one of them had an asthma attack and stopped breathing. Adding to the list:

• Buy a Dice Club gift

The theme for Christmas Dice Club is to buy a gift you might give as a Christmas present to a friend or a sister. The budget is fifty dollars. Richard Ostrander, the high-powered attorney, only gave me a five hundred dollar Christmas bonus. Chump change for him. Maybe the rest of them can afford such extravagances, but if they knew how hard I have to work for my skimpy paychecks, they might have lowered the dollar amount.

But who thinks of me? Who cares about Amanda Prince's opinions?

Brandy and Shonah, Sylvia's cohorts. *Hrumph*! Screw them too. Imagine either one of them trying to do my job. Ha! Brandy with all her blonde hair flying around and her toilet mouth. Arrogant Shonah, always thinking she's the smartest one in the room just because she writes a newspaper column. And then there's Tara Shephard. "I'm so sure." All those Dice Club bitches and their perfect lives. Tara drinks like a gutter drunk. What the hell is she trying to escape from? She's got everything! Two healthy kids, a good-looking husband, a successful career, and boobs till next Tuesday. If any of them lost a child, I'd like to see *them* try to handle it. They're all so quick to give advice. To judge. If one more person sends me a list of psychologist's names or literature on the group Compassionate Friends, I'll probably drive my stupid Dodge Stratus into a light pole.

Why don't they realize how empty their comments are? Full of platitudes, they keep telling me how to grieve. What do they know about it? Nothing can bring back my son and no one can understand the torment I face on a daily basis. I can't help it. I'm consumed with his death and I just want to deal with it in my own way. Not in a way that others—especially Sylvia—expects. I'm so tired of Sylvia's watchful eye—her thinly veiled concern. I don't want to share my feelings with her or anyone. Not even Manny.

Where our grieving is concerned, we're in two different places.

Looking at Sean's photo again, the pain in my chest—the tight, dull ache of a broken heart—travels to my temples. It's only been seventeen months. I'm not ready to bring it all up again with some stupid, freaking therapist. I can't relive it.

I need another cig. Grabbing one, I place it between my lips without lighting it. Do I have one burning already? Where did I set it?

Time is running out and I don't want to be late for work. Being on time is important. I hate when people are late. It's always the same individuals with the same excuses. Some people just don't know how to respect time. Like Tara. Or Tootsie Fennimore. What's her excuse? She doesn't work. She doesn't even have kids.

In the mirror I brush the thin, graying bangs from my forehead. My hair is clean enough. A little concealer under my eyes will hide the puffiness. Can I get away with not showering? Lowering my nose to my armpit, I sniff. Not bad. I can put on a double dose of deodorant and no one will notice.

In my closet, I run my fingers along the hanging blouses and reject each. "I'm sick of these clothes." I'm not like Sylvia and the others who never wear the same thing twice. Do they spend all their free time in the mall? "Oh, to hell with them. What do they know about life?"

This pinstriped blouse will have to do.

Brandy

I'm the last to arrive at the Golf Club restaurant for lunch. I haven't even combed my hair. Turning the corner, I see both Sylvia and Tara's cars in the parking lot. Shonah and Tara must have driven together. Shonah's still a little shaky after her mother died of a stroke. She says it's the hardest when she's alone driving in her car. My mother's been dead for so long I don't even remember the grief as being something different in my world. And now I've got my goddamn father to deal with. "Shit!" My heart is still pumping from the phone conversation I just had with my sister. I can't believe she's sending him to stay with me.

A wicked winter wind makes the door hard to open. My hair blows all around me. I must look like a scarecrow. There they are in the back, not hard to spot. They're by far the youngest women in the restaurant, with no one else but a foursome of blue hairs shuffling the spots off a deck of cards. I wonder if that's what we'll look like with our bunko dice one day.

I fall into the only remaining chair at the round, corner table, and tuck my cell phone into my purse. "I've had the day from hell."

"And it's only half over," says Shonah.

"What's the matter?" Sylvia asks.

"I'll tell you as soon as I swallow something. Make it a merlot," she calls over her shoulder to the waitress.

Sylvia and Shonah have already sucked down half of a foot-tall iced tea, while Tara licks the salt off the rim of her margarita glass. She ought to be in fine form by Dice Club this evening.

I feel like a snake shedding its skin as I shimmy out of my black leather jacket, then hang it on the back of my chair. Using a black, coated rubber band from around my wrist, I pull my hair into a ponytail and sip from a glass of ice water. I put it back down on the table so hard, that several drops splash onto the white, linen tablecloth. Where's the napkin?

"Okay, spill it," says Shonah. She's obviously bounced back. Good. I'm glad we don't have to talk about her dead mother or the funeral or anything. She and I are the only ones at the table to have lost our mothers and unless you're in that club, you just don't get it. There's a time and a place and I'm glad this is neither. This is a girls' lunch where we get together to bitch about our lives and right now, I've just got to bitch about mine.

"First of all, Levi's—I mean, *our*—darling son tells me on the way out the door that he needs a gift for his Secret Santa exchange. He's known for *how* long and I just hear about it today? Then our daughter gets mad at me because I told her I had this lunch date. She expected me to take her out to lunch and do some Christmas shopping. So, they both leave the house pissed off. I'm not even sure what day Levi's eldest is coming home from school because neither of them ever tell me anything. Then I go to drive the little ones to school and I get in the car and Rush Limbaugh screams at me from the radio turned up full volume. I'm backing up while trying to turn down the radio, which I don't know how to work since it's a brand new car and it's as big as a condominium for chrissakes, and damn it if I don't scrape the entire right side against the garage. I didn't even notice I was doing it until the flippin' rearview mirror snapped off like a dry tree branch."

"You listen to Rush Limbaugh?" Shonah asks.

"Of course." I practically bark the words. "Don't start with me, Shonah."

"I thought he went deaf," says Sylvia.

"Yeah, from all that screaming," Shonah says. "I can't believe you listen to someone who refers to women as feminazis. You of all people!"

"Listen, I shave my pits and I like men. Okay? Just not my husband. And certainly not my father. Come to think of it, I hate my twin brother too. Hmmm." I sip the water again. Where's that wine? "Last night Levi took my new car to some kind of meeting where his pickup truck was inappropriate. He's the one who's clearly going deaf if he's got to listen to the radio at that volume. Levi always messes with my radio. The kids know not to do it, but he doesn't. He also leaves the toilet seat up. Like he gives a crap if I sit down and fall in."

"Oh, he gives a crap all right," says Tara.

"Get separate toilets," says Sylvia. "That's our solution. Richard won't go near my toilet."

"My boys bug me when I *don't* put the toilet seat up," says Shonah. "And they're nuts right now too. It's like they've completely gotten over the fact that their grandmother just died. Bring on the figgy pudding!"

"They're all nuts," says Tara. "It's all the Christmas candy and cookies and the garbage they give them at school."

"Did either of you get a phone call from Chlöe-the-rabid-room-mother about baking cookies for the fifth grade party today?" asks Shonah.

"I told her to fuck off," says Tara.

Wait a minute. Did Tara just use the f-word? I don't think I've ever heard that come out of her...

"No you didn't, Tara," says Shonah. "Did you?"

"No, I just told her to call someone else for a change. Just because she plays bunko with us, she thinks we're the only people she can call to make and bake and volunteer for all these stupid class parties. I can't believe she asked you, Shonah. Doesn't she know about your mom?"

"My mom was a baker. I made her favorite cookies. It was an honor."

I sip my water again and shake my head. "Well she didn't call me. I think she's afraid of me."

"We're *all* afraid of you, Brandy," says Sylvia. Sylvia reaches out and squeezes Shonah's hand. She went up to Oregon for the funeral. Sylvia's a good friend. I'm a terrible friend.

"Where does Chlöe Forrest find the time to work as a nurse and micromanage every aspect of her kids' lives? Do you think she sleeps?" Shonah asks.

I have to laugh. "I bet she recites her daily schedule in her sleep."

"I think Christmas has everyone freaked out," says Tara. "Do you think the kids sense our stress?"

"No," we all answer as if a programmed response. Sylvia and I nod our heads up and down as we say it. We used to do that at the sorority house all the time too.

The waitress brings my wine and takes our lunch orders. We're all chilled by the December wind, so decide on soup, and within minutes, four bowls of thick, tortilla soup arrive. Everyone but me begins eating. Instead I polish off the wine and ask for another.

"Slow down Brandy," says Sylvia. "This isn't like you. Come to think of it, I don't think I've ever seen you have a glass of wine with lunch. What's going on?"

"You want to know what's going on? I'll tell you what's going on. Dear old Dad is coming for Christmas. My sister's dumping him on us. And I mean dumping. On Christmas day. I'm so angry I could explode."

I spent the entire morning driving my scraped up condominium-on-wheels through town. I bought Secret Santa gifts for my kids and my gift for tonight's Christmas party. I dropped off boxes of used clothing at a local charity, *Casa de los Niños,* and stopped at the physical therapy clinic to deliver gifts to the office staff. I had a list of chores long enough to compete with any day in the life of Chlöe the Canuck Forrest.

Just as I headed toward the Valle Verde Golf Club to meet Sylvia, Shonah and Tara, my cell phone rang. Recognizing my sister June's phone number, I sang hello and hoped to have a nice pre-lunch chat. Since our frail and widowed eighty-five year old father was staying with her in Dallas, we spoke often, calling our chats "commiseration calls."

Our other sister, Marlene, who lives in Palm Springs, began the seasonal caretaking in October, and after the old man wore out his welcome there, he flew to Dallas. We've all learned that our father's company follows the law of diminishing returns. The longer he's away from his retirement community in Long Beach, the more ornery he becomes.

"When can you take him?" asked June.

I laughed. "Is it that bad?"

My sister launched into a lot of sighing and reasoning, and when her voice bent into an annoying Texas twang, I stopped listening, and just thought about my father. The last time I'd seen him, he'd shrunk to my height. Chocolate colored, amoeba-shaped bruises spotted his hands and forearms. The rest of his body was emaciated. His white hair had thinned and his face seemed pinched. His clothing was so old and tattered, that he looked like a pauper. He had stayed in my spare bedroom for nearly six weeks, sleeping until noon like a teenager home from college. Then after a breakfast of instant coffee and powdered doughnuts, he spent the afternoon reading the newspaper and watching television shows like *Judge Judy* and *Jeopardy!*, declaring all the participants "niggers and morons." I could have clobbered him. I had to shield my kids from his bigotry, and broke into a song and dance routine while trying to change the subject. My father will never understand how much the world has changed.

You know, I can put anyone in his or her place. Except for my father.

I prepared huge, ranch-style meals each evening, and my father sat at the head of the table, where he rambled on one of two topics: His days at sea, or how his family scrimped and saved during the Depression. His stories were the same ones we sat through in our youth when Mom was still alive. My kids were no different in their reactions. They yawned and rolled their eyes, pushed food around on their plates as a means of distraction, until finally, Levi flashed the lights and declared it time for homework. They bolted from the table as if a fire drill were underway, and my father hardly noticed. He kept talking—holding court at the table like some kind of king—while I cleared the table, put away food and washed the dishes. Each time he sat waiting for dessert, I fantasized about dumping it in his lap.

"So," said my sister, "you've got to take him immediately."

"Why the sudden rush?"

"Didn't you hear me? I said, he *slapped* Rudy."

"He slapped your son? What?"

"I've got to get him out of here, Brandy. He's so mean to my kids I can't take it anymore."

"Wait. Back up. Why did he slap him?"

"Does it matter? Listen, you and Sandy have to take him. Can you have Levi take care of the ticket?"

"No," I said. "Levi and I are both sick of making arrangements for Dad. And we can't take him. Levi's aunt and uncle are coming for Christmas, and his mom says they can't stay with her. I can't take Dad until they leave."

"I've already made the flight reservation," said June. "He has to be picked up at the airport at four-thirty on Christmas Day. And don't get all bent out of shape. I found a companion ticket and it only cost ninety bucks. Like you'd notice ninety bucks."

"What?" I was incredulous. That's when I turned my damaged vehicle into the Club parking lot and pulled over. "I'm not picking him up on Christmas Day. I'm cooking. And don't talk to me about ninety friggin' bucks." I slammed the gearshift into park as if adding an exclamation point.

"Have Sandy pay for it."

"Have Sandy do *all* of it," I told her. "Why is it always just the girls dealing with Dad?"

"A daughter's a daughter for the rest of her life. A son, well, I guess that doesn't apply to Sandy because he doesn't have a wife. He lives with you."

"I've gotta go," I said. "I'm stealing an hour with my girlfriends, and all morning I've felt like a criminal because of it."

"Brandy, if I had your life I would never complain," said June. "You work just two days a week, and only because you want to. You get a brand new car every other year and you actually get to have lunch with your friends?"

"I work THREE days a week. And yeah, that's right. My life is perfect and I have no right to complain. Thanks for dumping Dad on me. You could have asked me first." I pulled the cell phone from my ear, poked the END button with my thumbnail and pulled out to look for a place to park. When I turned off the car ignition, the engine hiccoughed twice before dying. "This car is cursed!" I shouted to the parking attendant. My voice was carried away in the wind.

My soup has grown cold. "I wished the wind would have carried me away too. All the way to flipping Mexico. Alone."

"Oh calm down, Brandy," says Sylvia. "It'll be okay."

I stir my soup. "Shonah, I'm sorry about your mother. I'm a terrible friend going on like this. And I'm a terrible mother, and a terrible daughter. And for the way I feel about my siblings right now, I'm not such a great sister either."

"You know that's not true," says Sylvia. "You're a wonderful mother. My God, you've got five kids, Brandy. It's not your fault that some of them choose to give you a hard time on the same day."

"If my sister made arrangements like that for Christmas day I'd be upset with her too," Tara says. "I might even let the old man rot at the airport."

"You don't have a sister," says Shonah.

"Or a father," says Sylvia.

"You guys don't understand. When my dad's around I feel like I've got yet another child in the house. And this one is the worst because he drinks bourbon, talks about Harry Truman and uses the n-word."

"So don't give him any booze," says Shonah.

"It's not that easy," I say. "He's sneaky. Sylvia, remember when he called you last year to bring over a bottle of Jack Daniels? He may even call a cab to take him to the liquor store."

"The cab driver wouldn't be able to find your ranch," says Sylvia. "Don't worry, I won't bring him anything if he calls."

"Brandy, you're a victim of the 'sandwich generation,' " says Shonah. "I wrote an article about it last summer."

"Yup," says Tara. "You're taking care of kids and taking care of a parent. You're the meat in the middle."

"Thanks a lot."

"And let's not forget about your brother sponging off your hospitality." Shonah says. "He must be the mustard."

The thought of Sandy makes me laugh. "Not spicy enough. He's more like the mayo."

"Does he even pay rent for your guesthouse?" asks Tara.

"Are you kidding me?" I take a gulp from the glass of ice water and cough. It doesn't clear and I cough again. "Wrong pipe." Holding my hand to my chest, I release another cough and then wipe a tear from my eye. "Looks like I just have to get comfortable in the role of mean mommy." I point to a deep, vertical line between my eyes. I know it's there and getting deeper by the minute. "See this line? It's my mean mommy line."

"I've got one, too," says Shonah.

"Me too," says Tara.

Sylvia places her index finger between her eyes, feeling for a nonexistent line. For what she spends in Botox there had better not be any lines.

"I just don't know what I'll do if he slaps one of my kids," I say.

"Slap him back," Tara says. "That ought to give him a good scare."

"You could answer one of the ads in my newspaper where they actually look for people to spank," says Shonah.

"Or write one," says Sylvia. "MM—Mean Mommy, in search of PP—pain pleasure."

I take a long sip of my second merlot. "Mean mommy and pain pleasure. That's a good one." Setting down the glass, it pains me to realize that I might be just like my old man. And he had been one mean daddy. Imagine abandoning your twelve year-old twins! What the hell kind of parent does that? Particularly after they've just lost their mother?

Polishing off the wine, I abruptly get up. I can't let down my kids. I've got to go. "Sorry to be the last to arrive and the first to leave, but duty calls." I grab my jacket and purse and head for the door. "You've got this, don't you Sylvia?"

"Always," she responds. Sylvia's high-powered attorney husband has a membership at the club and she takes us to lunch regularly to use up her restaurant allotment.

"Give 'em hell," calls Tara.

"What she said," Shonah says. "See you tonight."

I better get home before the wine kicks in.

Sylvia

I feel a little unsteady on this ladder. How serious is this "not a step" warning?

Oh what the hell! I take the last step and crown our fourteen-foot Christmas tree with the solemn-faced angel my husband refers to as "the old Polish woman." According to Richard, the high-powered attorney I married, the angel I chose for our first tree as husband and wife resembled his family's housekeeper. "She was a wonderful old Polish woman named Janina," he had said. "We were supposed to pronounce it 'Ya-neena'; however, my Dad called her 'Janina,' so we all did. That angel looks just like her." From that day forward, we have called the tree angel, "The old Polish woman."

The room smells of pine. It isn't from the artificial tree, but from the candles I've been burning for three days trying to get my enormous house to smell like Christmas in Oregon—actually, to smell like Oregon at any time of year. Each time I go back, I can't get over the natural scent of pine. Gosh, is this me missing home?

I slowly begin my descent down the ladder, glad I gave up buying real trees years ago. It's silly to spend a fortune on imported trees, only to have them drop needles all over my Persian rug. And then it took only two or three days of holding ornaments in the dry, desert climate before the live trees no longer showed any signs of life.

I close the ladder, pull it away from the tree, and lean it against a wall. Turning around, I admire the sparkling white lights of the tree.

"Beautiful."

I just love my house, but I tell you, keeping up appearances is exhausting! If anyone had heard the huge battle between Richard and I that filled this room not ten minutes ago, they'd never see the room as beautiful. I'm surprised the plants didn't wilt! He was furious because he had to take our daughter to dinner tonight so I could host Dice Club. I swear if I hear one more word about that Turner trial, I'm going to go out of my mind.

Surveying the common areas, I see everything's in place. Oh, I wish I had someone around to haul this ladder back to the storage room. I'm just not built for this kind of work. Richard could at least have stayed long enough to move it. Or he could have had José, the landscaper, do it. But no!

I stop half way to the garage to rest the ladder on the floor. The gate buzzer sounds. Please, don't let it be Amanda. Given her angry mood lately, spending fifteen minutes alone with her would be sheer torture. Worse, her tobacco aroma mingling with the pine will poison the atmosphere I've spent days trying to create. Last month's Dice Club was so much more fun without her. Tootsie and her thong! I wish I'd had my camera.

Finally, I make it to the garage with the ladder and store it, then race back to the kitchen to double check the spread. I see blonde hair. Brandy. Thank God.

"Merry Bunko," she says. "I brought clam dip. Made it fresh after I took a nap. Two glasses of wine at lunch just about did me in."

"Thank heavens it's you. I thought it might be Amanda."

"Nope. Just me," says Brandy. "What's up with her? Same old, same old, I imagine?"

"Richard says she's been a 'bitch-on-wheels' at the office lately. The rest of the office staff is complaining. They can't work with her. I think they've stopped feeling sorry for her and now compassion has turned into revulsion."

"Well, wasn't she pretty much a bitch *before* her son died?"

"I suppose so. I don't know. I just feel ...bad!"

"It reminds me of how I feel about my father. I still can't believe he's going to be at my house in a matter of days."

"Families and employees can be a curse. Let's not talk about them."

"Fine. But I'm not going to stand here and let you beat yourself up. You've been nothing but kind and supportive of Amanda. So, what can I do to help with this party?"

"Thank you Brandy. See, you *are* a good friend! Okay. I think the tables still need scorecards and pencils. Other than that, I'm ready. Are you okay? The way you threw back that wine at lunch today had me worried."

"I'm fine. The nap definitely helped and nothing registered on the Breathalyzer. Let me get the scorecards and pencils for you. Oops, there's the buzzer. I'll get it."

Shonah and Chlöe arrive together. Each puts her gift under the Christmas tree. Within minutes, Blanca Midnight shows up, and the kitchen fills with high-pitched laughter. Brandy appoints herself the designated bartender and pushes the eggnog, which no one seems to want. "It's low-cal," she says, waving the ladle like a fan with a banner in a football stadium. Soon Tootsie Fennimore arrives, and everyone rushes to see her package. She always has the most fabulously deco-rated packages, and this one, which is shaped like a fireplace stocking and lined with fuzzy green fur, is no exception. "Isn't it a hoot?" she says proudly.

I tell everyone to eat while it's hot. "I spent all day cooking and I don't want any leftovers. Who's not here yet?"

"Tara," shouts Blanca.

"Of course," says Shonah. "I was going to give her a ride, but she wasn't ready. It's a big night for her. Christmas means a special en-semble. Just you watch."

"She won't mind if we eat without her," I decide. "Grab plates. Eat!" I stand back while the women line up at the serving counter and fill their plates. I ate enough while cooking that I'm not hungry, and since my pants are already feeling a bit snug, I don't think I'll eat anything else. "Who left only an inch in the chardonnay?"

"I did," Shonah says, holding up her glass. "This is my allotment. I'm driving."

Taking a sip of Shonah's chardonnay dregs, it dawns on me that Amanda hasn't yet arrived. "Where's Amanda?" I ask. "It's not like her to be late."

"Did she call?" asks Tootsie.

"I don't think so." I reach for the phone and search the caller ID log. I don't see Amanda's name, or even Richard's office number. Nor are there any messages waiting on voice mail. "That's odd. This woman is never late for anything. I hope she's okay."

"If anyone should have been late tonight it's me," says Chlöe. "You wouldn't believe everything I had to do this afternoon. First it was the dry cleaners who said they didn't have these pants ready and then they took forever to locate them. Then I had to run to Big Lots, and from there to the school to drop all the..."

"Poor Amanda," says Tootsie, cutting off Chlöe. "She seems to be going in a tailspin lately."

"Really!" says Brandy. "Remember my Dice Club? She was so crabby. I was glad when she left because she was bringing everyone down. I didn't want my party to be a bummer."

"I never know what to say to her anymore," Tootsie says quietly.

"The holidays are hard," says Blanca Midnight. "Whenever my kids are with their dad—as rare as that is—it's the worst. I can't imagine what she goes through at Christmas."

"Don't you celebrate Kwanza or something, Blanca?" asks Brandy.

"You know it, *mi'ja*," laughs Blanca Midnight. "I celebrate everything."

"Shonah, this might be a hard Christmas for you," says Tootsie. "You okay?"

"I'm sure I'll associate Thanksgiving more with my mom than Christmas," Shonah says. She grabs a shrimp and dips it in sauce.

The front door swings open and in steps Tara Shephard with all the fanfare of Santa Claus. She's wearing a red, satin pants suit, and a sateen Santa cap. Her hair is in braids, and her eyes are as glazed as miniature ice rinks. She shakes her shoulders and the sound of jingle bells fills the room. Good God. I exchange knowing looks with Shonah and Brandy.

"I'll keep my eye on her," whispers Shonah.

Elvis sings *Blue Christmas* in the background while we eat, drink, and catch up with everyone's holiday plans. An hour has passed and Amanda still hasn't arrived. Now I'm really worried. She's not even answering her cell. Damn this nagging guilt I feel for thinking ill thoughts toward her. I've got to try to be more understanding. After all, no one can truly know the extent of her suffering. I practically have heart palpitations when my daughter gets an ear infection!

Everyone is finished eating. The plates are stacked in my sink. "We should get these dice rolling," I decide. "Amanda can just join whichever table has the ghost when she gets here. Someone start a card for her!"

"Let's go over the rules," says Tara. "Who's idea was it how to work this?"

"It was Chlöe's," says Shonah. "Remember she brought it from her Canadian group?"

"That's right," says Chlöe. "But it was Ohio, not Canada. Regardless, It's my idea, so I should explain it."

"Your hair looks nice tonight, Chlöe," says Brandy, who steps on Shonah's toe as she said it.

"Nice 'N Easy number ninety-seven," Chlöe says, tossing her head like she's Heather Locklear or something. "Thanks. Now. Everyone has her gift under the tree, right? Right. Even though we did this last year and you all should remember, for those who are more brain wave challenged, and God knows with the day I've had, if anyone is brain wave challenged it's me. The dry cleaning fiasco alone took forever! Anyway, this is how it works. When you roll a 'baby bunko,' you get to pick a wrapped gift from the tree. You can't make the trip unless you get a 'baby.' If you roll another, you can opt to keep the gift you have or you can take someone else's. You can't open a new one but you can steal. Everything else is the same. Okay?"

"We're going to dole out money too?" asks Tootsie. "Why don't we donate it to a charity—like *Casa de los Niños* or something? There's always Big Brothers, Big Sisters too."

"Let's donate it to our liquor fund," says Tara.

"I've donated enough clothing to *Casa de los Niños* this season to dress an entire Mexican pueblo," says Brandy. "Our forty bucks won't make a difference. Keep whatever money you win and consider it a stocking stuffer."

"Or a bra stuffer," says Tara with a shimmy.

"It was simply a suggestion," says Tootsie, pulling out a chair at the bottom table. "Whatever."

Each player finds a seat and Brandy has the bell in hand, rings it, and throws the dice. "One!" she shouts. She gathers the dice and shakes, is about to release them, and the front door opens. Amanda steps inside. She pauses in the doorway and everyone looks up.

It feels like all the air has been sucked out of the room. No one says a word. I know she has the gate code, but usually I hear the buzzer. Elvis must have drowned it out. And she never enters anyone's house without ringing first. All my instincts tell me something's wrong. I set down my wine glass and rush to the entryway. "Amanda! There you are." I reach to take her coat and smell the cigarette aroma that is Amanda. Her eyes hold a familiar and frightening expression. It's that of a loaded crossbow. "Merry Christmas. We were worried about you."

"Why?" she snorts. The notch deepens between her brows.

"Why?" I repeat, and look at my watch. "You're nearly an hour late. That's not like you."

"Well, some of us have to work, Mrs. Ostrander," she says. She takes off her coat, drapes it over her arm and breezes past me.

I'm absolutely stunned.

"I see you started without me," she says as she walks to the Christmas tree and drops her gift to the floor.

"I guess that wasn't breakable," says Brandy.

"Bad day at the office Amanda?" Shonah asks.

"What would you know about working in an office, Shonah?"

Shonah's mouth drops open.

"Here we go again," Tootsie says under her breath to Blanca, who sits next to her at the bottom table.

Oh please don't let anyone say anything to make it worse. I feel my heart pound heavily in my chest. I clap my hands together. "We haven't really started rolling yet." My voice is higher pitched than normal. I look at Brandy to make sure she isn't still rolling the dice. "Amanda, since we didn't know what time you'd show—or if you were coming at all—we just thought we'd get started and use a ghost scorecard for you. You're welcome to get yourself a drink of something—there's eggnog—and have some food."

"Or you can be our waitress for the first round since we actually did start," says Brandy.

Damn it, Brandy. I hiss at her. "Zip it!"

"Fine," says Amanda. "I'll be your little slave. Fitting don't you think? I work for your husband all day and then come here and work for you?"

"It's not like that Amanda," says Tootsie—always the peacemaker. "We'll wait for you. Really, the bell only rang about thirty seconds ago. Look at my scorecard. Completely blank!"

"No, no," says Amanda. "I'll be the waitress. I just want to know, though, how many rounds you all intend to play so I don't get ripped off again this month."

"Twelve," everyone shouts.

"Got it Amanda?" says Brandy. "Now get to work because I need a drink before I start rolling again. Tara's got a platter under that tree with my name on it. It may or may not have been on the set of *The Sopranos*. And since I don't want to hire a hit man to go after any of your family members, I'm warning all you girls right now that it's going home with me."

"What, you *don't-a* believe me that *thing-a was-a* used by *The Sopranos* for a spaghetti dinner?" says Tara with a terrible, slurring version of an Italian accent.

Amanda turns on her heel and walks out of sight, presumably toward the bar. I could kill Brandy. I return to the table, take a sip of wine, and have to whisper. "Brandy, I know you were just trying to lighten up the situation, but you don't know her the way I do. Some days she just can't take a joke."

Brandy picks up the bell. "She can never take a joke and I'm sick of it. I'm ringing this to get things started again. Pick up where you left off, ladies."

The brass bunko bell rings, rolling for ones continues, albeit reluctantly, and before the fourth player at the top table, Shonah, takes a turn at the dice, Amanda returns to the room with a glass of red wine. She walks right up to Brandy, stands next to her for a moment, and then dumps the entire contents into her lap.

"Jesus Christ!" shouts Brandy.

Blanca Midnight crosses herself.

Brandy throws her hands in the air and stands up. A blackened patch stains the front of her jeans, and she looks like a child who has just wet her pants.

"What's the matter, Brandy?" chuckles Amanda. "Can't take a joke?"

"What the...?" Brandy is barely able to breathe.

"Want to know what it's like to have a hit man come in and destroy your family? Or a disease that feels like a hit man take away all your hopes and dreams? Your happiness?"

Brandy stutters. "I didn't mean it like..."

"You ought to get a filter for that tongue," says Amanda.

The other women look on in disbelief. Oh my God, I knew it! I close my mouth and try to recover from the shock of seeing that wine spill in slow motion. I push back my chair and hurry toward the butler's pantry for a rag. Meanwhile, Shonah races to Brandy's side and puts her hand on her shoulder. "Are you okay?" she asks.

"No!" shouts Brandy. "Talk about not being able to take a joke. *Fuck!*"

Tootsie gets up and grabs Amanda by the arm and pulls her toward the powder room. "Come with me, Sweetheart," she says. "Let's talk over here."

"I don't want to talk," she shouts as Tootsie tugs on her arm. "Everyone wants me to talk about it. I don't want to talk!"

"It's okay, Sweetie. Really, I understand," says Tootsie. "No one is going to make you talk about a thing. Just come in here with me."

The bathroom door closes behind them with a thud, and I'm standing there watching everything with a damp rag in my hand. Everyone is looking at me with beseeching eyes. I want to cry. "I'm sorry. I don't know what to say other than what I always say. She's going through a difficult time."

Tears streak down Shonah's face. She uses her cocktail napkin to wipe her eyes and goes to the kitchen. Blanca bites her painted red lip. Tara shakes her head and her braids dance back-and-forth as she clucks her tongue. She polishes off her drink.

"Shouldn't we keep rolling?" asks Chlöe. "I don't have all night here. I've got to wrap presents when I get home and make my grocery list for a full day of holiday food shopping, and I'm sure my husband hasn't done the dishes tonight and..."

Blanca reaches over to the top table and rings the bell. "Let's take a break," she says.

I try to blot Brandy's pants, but Brandy stops me by taking the rag. "I think you should be more concerned about your carpet," she says.

"I'm not worried about the damn carpet. Believe me, it's not the first glass of wine this poor Persian has sucked up."

Brandy puts one hand on my shoulder and with the other, sets down the rag. "I'm sorry," she says. "It was my fault. I shouldn't have made the hit man comment. It was insensitive."

"I can't believe she did that to you. Especially because I'm the one she's mad at. Or at least the one she seems to be mad at."

"Honey, that girl is mad at the world," says Blanca Midnight. "I don't know when I've ever met an angrier person than Amanda Prince. I'm going to go check on Shonah." She heads toward the kitchen.

"Brandy's right. It was the hit man comment," says Chlöe. "It pissed her off."

"She was pissed when she got here," says Tara.

"That's true," Brandy says. "But I shouldn't have said it."

"Just keep walking on those egg shells," says Chlöe. "It's an impossible situation. No one can say or do the right thing around her. It's not your fault, Brandy. Nor is it yours', Sylvia. If you ask me, she owes you both an apology."

"I think she owes everyone an apology," says Shonah, returning to the room with Blanca. "She's going through a very angry stage of her grief. I recognize it. Don't you think I'm mad that I lost my mother on Thanksgiving? It's easy to be angry. To be angry at God, angry at the world, angry at anyone who looks at you the wrong way? But she's wearing it like a security blanket and she's only taking it out on us because she either thinks she can get away with it, or she believes we'll forgive her."

"It's a horrible thing that happened in her life," adds Tara.

"But that doesn't give her the right to treat any of us like shit," says Shonah. "Especially you, Sylvia."

Tootsie returns from the powder room and she's crying. We all stare at her as if she has the answers.

"Do any of you know how much I want to have a baby?" she asks. "I just can't imagine having one and then …and then…" She sniffs.

I sit back down at the top table. "Oh, for crying out loud." I pick up my scorecard and tear it in half. "Merry flipping Bunko everyone. This party is obviously a bust. What do you chicks say we just forget the dice, give all the gifts to charity and finish off the food and drink? Who's in?"

"Fine with me," says Tara. She polishes off what's left of her drink and picks up someone else's from the top table.

"Me too," say several others.

"I'm sorry," Tootsie says, "I didn't mean to . . ."

"You didn't," Shonah says. "Playing bunko doesn't feel right now."

"Well, I'm not sure that's fair, eh?" says Chlöe. "I mean, we just went over all the rules and I think…"

"Chlöe," says Brandy, "no one cares what you think."

Chlöe bites her lip, and then smiles at Brandy. She may be a woman who wastes far too much breath reciting her daily schedule, but she knows how to take a joke.

This is a good idea. "Okay, let's just stop the madness," I say.

"The madness must stop!" chant Shonah, Brandy and Tara, as though it were a programmed response. Tootsie and Blanca Midnight slap a high five.

"All I care about is Tara's platter," says Brandy. "We're not giving that away, are we?"

"That's the first thing we're giving away," says Tara. She thrusts her martini glass into the air. "Brandy, I'll get you another one that's been licked by Tony Soprano himself." A wave of liquid falls to the floor. Tara's eyes move to the spot it creates on the carpet. "Oops," she says. She places her hand on her hip, arches her back, and swallows what's left. "Sylvia," she sings, "I need a refill. And someone had better toss me that rag."

"Don't worry," says Shonah with a sniffle. "I'll drive her home."

Chapter 5
January

Do you remember the first time you got drunk? I do. I was sixteen. It was at Brenda Peterson's house in Lake Oswego, Oregon, and it was the day before I began my junior year of high school. It was one of the best days of my life.

It was a great day not because I got drunk, but rather, because of the reason I got drunk. It was the day my braces were removed, and it was better than anything that had ever happened to me. It was better than the day I got my ears pierced. Or the day I learned to ride a two-wheeler. It was better than the day I got dropped off at the movies for the first time without an adult. Or the day I was the only freshman to make the varsity basketball team.

The day my teeth were freed from the bondage of those nasty, silver "railroad track" bands, an unattractive accessory I'd lived with for my entire high school career, ranks right up there with my wedding day and the days my children were born. I knew the minute I slid my eager tongue back-and-forth across the buttery-soft smoothness of my newly straightened teeth that a celebration was in order.

The first person I called was Brenda. She was my best friend. And, more importantly, she had a car. She picked me up from the orthodontist's office in her rusty, white Corvair and the first thing she did when she saw me was roll down the window and whistle. I took that as a good sign.

"Get in," she said. "My parents left for Acapulco this morning. We're having screwdrivers for lunch."

"Screwdrivers?"

"Not the tools, you idiot. Vodka and orange juice. I raided their liquor cabinet."

—Shonah Bartlett
From her column, *The Dice Club Chronicles*

Shonah

"I love the smell of creosote in the morning," says Tara through a swirl of warm breath. "It reminds me of 7-up."

My breath is coming out in puffs. "I don't think I've had a 7-up since Sprite came on the market."

"I haven't drunk one since I had my first beer."

We jog at a steady pace along the wet asphalt road, a long black river meandering through scrappy desert outcroppings. Our feet hit the pavement in a synchronized stride like a metronome keeping time. With glowing pink cheeks and red noses, we don't usually speak much during the initial pain and exhilaration of our workout. Instead we focus on the dramatic landscape to the east of our neighborhood, where some mornings after our children board the school bus, we make time for ourselves. It's been over three weeks since our last run and we haven't spoken since Christmas Dice Club.

I've missed these runs. Three weeks is more than long enough to feel totally out of shape. I'm relieved the holidays are over and the kids are back in school. It's time to rekindle our routine. A healthy routine.

We're the only people on the road. Side by side, I'm a head taller than Tara. I have black hair and black leggings. A tall pepper mill. Tara's more like cinnamon than salt, with her red hair and stop-traffic figure. There hasn't been a single car—only a yellow school bus has passed us as it doubled back from the stop near our subdivision after picking up the remainder of its load. I feel calm and concentrate on my breathing. I'm trying to clear my mind of worries about my upcoming deadline.

I glance over at Tara. She's usually edgy and hawk-like, and scans the landscape for signs of newness or trouble. She's always the first to spot a sleeping snake, a coyote about to cross the road in front of us, or an out of place, faded black watch cap hanging from a tree branch. Today, however, she seems serene. Happy.

"Aah, this is great," Tara says. "There's just no such thing as a bad rainy day in the desert."

"You're in a good mood this morning. What's up?"

"I didn't drink yesterday."

"Oh?" This surprises me. "At all?"

"Really. I didn't. I'm making a concerted effort to cut back. It might even be my new year's resolution. Think I can go the entire month of January without drinking?"

"It's a good time to stop now that the holidays are over."

"I don't know. I can't imagine it. Do you think I'll be any fun?"

"Be any fun? Are you crazy?" I reach into my pocket for a tissue and blow my nose.

Tara stops abruptly. "I mean it Shonah," she says to my back. "Will y'all still love me if I stop drinking?"

I stop and turn around. Jogging in place for a moment, I ball up my tissue and stuff it back in my pocket. I grab Tara by the wrists. "Of course, we'll *all* still love you, Tara. If this is something you've decided to do, then I'll support you."

"The Club sure didn't seem very supportive of Amanda. I never even saw her come out of the bathroom that night."

Tara *did* see Amanda emerge from Sylvia's powder room that night. She just doesn't remember it. How many times have I had to piece together an evening for Tara? I drop her hands and run ahead.

Tara follows me. "Has anyone talked to her? Amanda?"

"She sent Sylvia an email. That's all I heard."

"Was it an apology?"

"Not exactly. Sylvia said it contained two words." I hold up one finger at a time. "One: 'I.' Two: 'QUIT!' "

"Wow," says Tara. She lets out a heavy exhale. "I'm going to assume she meant the Dice Club and not her job."

"Just the Dice Club. And I don't blame her. I wouldn't want to show my face again after what she did. Sylvia said we should probably take a break and not meet for a month or two, to give everyone time to forget about what happened."

"I guess my mind zoned out when it got ugly."

"Ah, the convenience of blackout."

"I'll pretend I didn't hear that," says Tara.

I pick up the pace.

"No one understands Amanda's pain," Tara says to my back.

"She doesn't *want* anyone to understand. Do you think she's got the market cornered on what it means to grieve? You think I don't cry everyday when I think about my mother?" Talking is making me slow down. "If you ask me, I think anger is a lazy form of grief."

"What?"

I want to run faster. "C'mon Tara. Keep up. Let's get back to the regular pace."

We race ahead, turning left onto a dirt road.

"I think she just needs a good haircut and a wardrobe update," says Tara. "Maybe some laser surgery to fix her eyes so she doesn't have to wear those strange glasses. I should take her shopping. I really like her."

"You think surgery is the answer? Seriously?"

"Geez, Shonah. I don't know."

"It's great that you like her, Tara. But instead of getting better, she's getting worse. She refuses to get counseling and wants to believe she's fine." I sniff and again reach into my pocket for another tissue. "She's clearly *not* fine, and she's taking her pain out on us. We know she's hurting, but it doesn't give her the right to be so nasty."

"She's not nasty."

"Tara, she poured a glass of red wine in Brandy's lap. And that was after she berated Sylvia in front of everyone—again."

"You have a point," sighs Tara. "Like I said, I really don't remember how it all went down. How long was she in the bathroom?"

"Forty-five minutes. Most people left by then."

"Did you?"

"No. God, don't you remember *anything*?"

Tara doesn't respond.

"Blanca and I stayed and helped Sylvia clean up. I felt sorry for Sylvia. She really went all out for the party. And then I drove your car home with you in it. Dan drove me back in the morning to get my car."

"Oh."

We run in silence for several minutes.

"It was Brandy's fault," Tara says suddenly. "I remember the comment about killing off her family members or something. I would have poured a drink on her too."

I slow down and nearly stop. "You've got to be kidding me. Come on, Tara. You thought Brandy's comment about getting your platter was pretty funny at the time."

Tara stops. "The truth is, I don't really remember much of anything from that night."

Annoyed, I push out a deep breath and stop too. Are we working out? I turn around and look right into Tara's green eyes. She's so beautiful. Framed by the mountains, she's engulfed in haze as steamy clouds of exhaled breath surround her. I step toward her. My heart is pounding heavily in my chest. I don't want to say it. But I must.

"Well then clearly, Amanda's not the only one who can benefit from some therapy."

Tara blinks. "What are you saying?"

"I think you're ready for a program, don't you?"

"But I feel good this morning," she says quickly. "I haven't felt this good in a long time."

I put my hands on her shoulders and have to blow the bangs from my eyes. "That's reason enough alone, isn't it? You could wake up feeling this good every morning."

"Do you mean A.A.? Please! Where could I go? I'm not anonymous in this town."

"People know your pottery. Not your face."

"I don't think you know how much publicity I do!"

I think of her ads. Yes, I've seen them and had to concede. "But it shouldn't matter. Really, Tara. People are much too tied up in their own lives to care about whether or not another wealthy, artsy-fartsy type goes into rehab."

"Right. Don't you remember all the gossip about Diana Ross when she was busted drunk driving the wrong way on Bellisimo Boulevard a few years back?"

"Tara, I love you. But you are *not* one of the Supremes."

Once again, we merge into a rhythmic stride, reach the end of the dirt road, touch a chain link fence with a sign reading "Rattlesnake Valley Water Treatment Facility," and turn around, heading back to the asphalt road. The January deep frost has left the mesquite trees barren and black. Only weeks earlier they were filled with fine, feathery green plumage. Their shedding has cleared the way for a more open view of the majestic mountains emerging behind the craggy foothills. After a night of heavy rain, the mountains own a deeper, more powerful presence. They demand attention. Snowcapped and grand, they protrude from the valley like powerful fists, raised in conquering glory.

Each hill we climb opens up three hundred sixty-degree views, exposing more and more of the valley. The active sky changes with every stride. It moves with us, pulling us forward like a vortex, while soft rain sprinkles ball up on our jackets. The textured clouds illustrate an alternative brush in each direction. To the north it looks like a field of cotton, and to the east, hazy remnants of a nearby fire. In the west, smoke signals spell more rain to come, and in the south, pale patches of blue and slanted sun streaks burst from the sky. They are reminders that such massive cloud cover is only temporary.

"You know, Tara, I almost hate to tell you this, but I understand your fear. I had a boss back in Portland who went into A.A., and we thought we'd never hear the end of his slogans. It got so none of us felt comfortable drinking around him at office parties."

"That's exactly my biggest fear," says Tara. "Who will want to be around me?"

"He was our boss. It was different. Listen, if you ask me to not drink around you, I won't. Okay?"

Tara stops again. "Give me a break, Shonah," she says. "We both know that our Dice Club nights aren't much more than an excuse to drink. 'Drunko Bunko.' That's what people say about our Dice Club you know."

Reluctantly, I stop running. "What people?"

"People. I don't know, just people. Someone's talking."

I grab Tara by the arm and pull her forward. "Who cares?"

"I care," she says. "I don't need this information getting back to my daughters. They're starting to notice things. Nicole actually filled my wine glass the other night, and she's never done that before. I feel like I've got to start sneaking my drinks."

"Tara, I…"

"I'm glad we're taking a break with the Dice Club. I've been thinking I should probably quit the Club."

"You *can't* quit the Club!"

"Now you sound like Ian—my husband, the enabler. He actually brings a merlot to my workshop each afternoon. It used to be five o'clock. But now sometimes it's as early as three-thirty."

"No wonder your kids are serving you. They're just imitating their daddy."

"And, of course, I keep going back to the bottle until it's gone. I'm just like my father, Johnny Walker Red. What stinks is that I didn't even know the guy."

"Well, they say it's hereditary. Like breast cancer. But if you catch it early, it's treatable before it can ruin your life."

"Or kill you," sighs Tara. "I just don't get it. I used to be able to drink without a problem. I don't know what's happened to me lately."

"Just keep jogging with me. We'll take it slow for the last mile."

"I'm too pooped. Let's walk."

"Okay." I'm tired too. After weeks without any exercise, I'm out of shape and winded. "Did I ever tell you about the woman named 'Doctor Vodka?' "

"Don't think so."

"I did an article on her back in Portland. She was a doctor and an alcoholic, and she wrote a book about recovery." I paused, trying to think of the name of the book. "What the heck was it called?"

"A few brain cells ago, was it?"

"Exactly. See? You can still be funny without the booze."

"Wait up a second," says Tara. She stops, squats, and takes off her Nike. "I have a pebble." Tara shakes her shoe and small stones spray to the ground.

"This doctor was married. She had a child late in life because of her medical career, and I think she said it was shortly after her fortieth birthday when things started to slip away. She had a million excuses to drink."

"Like what?"

"Oh man, there were lots of things. She was named in a lawsuit. Her husband, a high-profile attorney along the lines of Richard Ostrander was having a high-profile affair. Her office manager was ripping her off. Blah blah blah. She said she came home each night and went straight for the wine cellar. She wanted to dull her senses so she didn't need to think about her problems."

"That sounds familiar," says Tara. "Ooh, Shonah! Watch out for that branch!"

I duck just in time. "Thanks. It almost nailed me. Hey, wait a minute. What do you mean about the doctor's story sounding familiar? Ian would never cheat on you. I'll bet half the women in the Valley wish their husbands would look at them the way he looks at you."

"But that doesn't mean I don't feel cheated. I feel totally ripped off in having to be the sole provider. And he spends money—my money—like a spoiled brat."

"You're his enabler on that front."

"Ian tries to come up with ideas to make money, but that's part of the problem. Every time he reports a new idea or elaborate scheme, I pour myself a drink. And when I'm pouring, it *ain't* wine, my friend."

"Soon it wasn't wine for the doctor either." My foot skids on a few stray pebbles. "Whoa!"

"You okay?"

"Sure." I return to my stride. "The doctor said when she discovered vodka, it was the beginning of a love affair. She loved it because it quickened the buzz and didn't trace on her breath."

"That's the truth," says Tara. "I brought the vodka to Betty Ford Bunko with the message 'vodka is odorless.' "

"I figured that was you." We round the last corner and head toward our homes. "I'll get the name of her book. I may even have it in a box somewhere."

"I'm not much of a reader, Shonah."

"Yeah, but I think you'll relate to this. There's a chapter about bargaining. Things like saying you'll give up the hard stuff and only have a glass of wine with dinner or something like that. But there's another topic she covers, and that's about women's health issues changing after the age of forty. You're about to turn forty, right?"

"Don't remind me. Ugh!"

"She said right around the time you turn forty, your hormones get wiggy. They can change the way your body reacts to alcohol. That and you need to go to Wal-Mart and buy a pair of 'cheaters.' "

"I will *never* wear those Wal-Mart glasses," says Tara. "I won't even step into that Wal-Mart. Have you been in there lately? The aisles are like overcrowded streets where people drive without maps. I've never had more cart crashes in my life. No one even says 'excuse me.' It's worse than France for pity's sake."

"You're such a snob, Tara."

"I can afford to be. And I can afford to get my eyes fixed too. When my eyes go, I'm either going to have them corrected or get the best pair of designer frames on the market."

"Good for you, Tara. Just remember, the road toward menopause is growing shorter and shorter for all of us. Even you."

"No lie," she says. "I intend to be the queen of plastic surgery in case you didn't already know that."

"You can fix the affects of alcoholism too."

"By stopping, right?"

"Right. And admitting you're powerless over it. I know that's the first step."

We reach the top of the peak where our houses are located. Three years earlier, we dubbed it, "Butt Buster Hill." On our first step over the crest, a pickup truck speeds past us. We hardly heard it coming. Instinctively, I grab Tara and pull her off the road. I recognize the truck. We both do. It's the teenager from across the street. He's just gotten his driver's license.

I shake my fist. What's he doing home at this time of day? Shouldn't he be in school? "I'm going to call his mother."

"I'd rather call the cops on that kid. I mean it, one of these days I will," says Tara.

We return to the road and reach Tara's brick driveway. "See ya," she sings as she opens the latch on her gate. "Thanks for the run. And the talk."

"So what do you think? Should I start calling you Tara S.?"

Tara doesn't respond.

I shower, dress and leave the house with wet hair. I considered working at home this morning, but one look at the piles my kids have left behind from two weeks of vacation, and all the Christmas decorations looking tired and ready for storage, made leaving home the only answer. I considered writing my column at the local coffee shop, but don't want to risk running into the fundraising groups and room mothers planning their latest efforts. Brandy calls them "the circle of hags." If you're not serving on their committees, some days you're not even worth a simple hello. Since my mother died, I'm avoiding all volunteer work and don't want to face the snub. So instead I drive up the hill to the office of *The Rattlesnake Times*. There's a community desk there for the freelancers, and hopefully it'll be available.

"What do you know about working in an office?" I hear Amanda's words at Sylvia's Christmas Dice Club echo in my head. Clearly that woman doesn't know a thing about me. How much do any of them know about what I do? Except for Sylvia, no one ever asks. I think I'm judged primarily for what I *don't* do. Because I don't work in a traditional nine-to-five job, is all my time at home considered free time? When did the world become so judgmental? Is this what feminism has accomplished?

I wonder if I should call Rush Limbaugh.

I reach the office, step inside, and smell coffee. Nodding to a few of the reporters, I wish a lot of "happy new years," and make my way to the break room to get some lousy, newspaper coffee. There isn't any half-and-half, only powdered creamer, so I decide to drink it black. The first awful sip makes me smile. I remember well how newsroom reporters and black coffee went together like police officers and doughnuts.

I place my briefcase on the floor and laptop on the desk. The moment my computer's ready, I call up the alcohol column I started last night.

"Screwdrivers?"

"Not the tools, you idiot. Vodka and orange juice. I raided their liquor cabinet."

I place my fingers in home-row position and think of my old friend, Brenda. I wonder if she still drinks…

"Bartlett!" Someone shouts my name and it snaps me to attention. I close my laptop and turn around. It's my editor. "What are you doing here?" he asks.

"Column. Writing."

"Come in here a minute," he says.

Oh brother. What does he want this time? I get up and place my briefcase on the chair, as though saving my spot, and make my way through the narrow aisles. The lighting is harsh and artificial. Scattered employees peek over their computers and their morning newspapers and watch me walk. I feel like a kid on the way to the principal's office.

His name is Chuck Fannin. I enter his corner office and he turns and walks to his desk. He immediately sits down. This man always sits in my presence. It's because of my height. I've got a good two or three inches on him and clearly, he finds me intimidating. "Hi. What's up, Chuck?"

"What's the topic this week?" he asks. He's not an unattractive man. In his mid-50s, he's in good shape and still has his hair. I focus on his thick, gray mustache. Who told him that looked good? "New Year's resolutions of Valley housewives?"

I sit down. "I'm writing about my first drunk."

"Your first drunk what?"

"I was sixteen. Screwdrivers. You?"

"Wild Irish Rose. Swiped it from my Aunt Lovely's flask."

"You have an aunt named 'Lovely'?"

"Had. She was from the South," he says. "So, where are you going with it?"

"I'm not sure yet. I think it's about taking the first step toward recovery."

"So it *is* about resolutions. You considering that route, are ya?"

"No." I run my fingers through my bangs. "No, it's not about me. It's a friend."

"A friend, huh? You sure about that?"

I get up. "It'll be in your 'in-box' by one. Judge me then." I take the first step out of Chuck's office and think about the bottle of wine I helped polish off last night after dinner.

I sit back down at the desk and open my computer.

Do you remember the first time you got drunk? I do. I was sixteen. It was at Brenda Peterson's house in Lake Oswego, Oregon, and it was the day before I began my junior year of high school. It was one of the best days of my life.

I lean back my head and look up into the fluorescent lights. I wonder. Maybe it *is* about me?

Chapter 6
February

It's four o'clock somewhere. And it certainly isn't happy hour. Four o'clock is the new witching hour in my house. It used to be between seven and eight p.m., when it was time to bathe the kids and get them to bed. Now it's the mark on the clock indicating it's time to get the kids ready for their afternoon activities.

I liked it better when the witching hour meant I was sending them to bed. At least I knew where they'd be and what they'd be doing for the next eight hours. No wonder middle-aged mothers can't sleep.

—Shonah Bartlett
From her column, *The Dice Club Chronicles*

Tara

I know without looking that it's four o'clock. The kids have eaten their snacks and quietly work at word problems and spelling packets in their bedrooms. The sounds of Ian's "hula hoe" scrape outside my door. While I've been shaping a new line of planters, he's been ridding the yard of weeds.

I examine my hands. They're most likely the same color as Ian's. Caliche red, like terra cotta. Dried clay embellishes the lines of my knuckles and coats the insides of my fingernails. They look like the hands of a grandmother.

It's just about time to clean up for the day. I reach for a small bowl containing a cornstarch mixture, and use a homemade brush made of chicken feathers to coat the newly formed clay. Cornstarch helps to keep the imprint tools from sticking. It's just one of many tips I learned from my mentor. He also told me about making my own brushes from feathers. Chlöe the Canadian from my Dice Club raises chickens. I get them from her.

Using cut pieces of PVC pipe, I etch subtle geometric designs into the elongated sides of the two prepared planters. It's a freestyle design, and at first glance it looks like the letter "G" swirling over and over and around the corners. "G, for gold." I envision gold flecking in the glaze.

Glancing up at the clock hanging on the wall behind the kiln, I whisper, "four-fifteen." I've felt every one of those fifteen minutes course through my veins. With each heartbeat, comes a pang.

Pang-*pang*. Yen-*yen*. Itch-*itch*. Urge-*urge*.

Some days are harder than others. Why today?

I take a deep breath and then carry the planters, one at a time, to the glazing table. My heartbeat is audible. Lowering my chin, I watch my chest rise and fall. Clay dust colors my skin like an uneven tan. I close my eyes and lick my dry lips.

God, I'd kill for a glass of wine.

Again, I ask, why today? Yesterday I was fine. Today the craving, yearning, longing …*thirsting* …is overpowering. It came on like a wicked desert wind, and swirls through every inch of me.

Should I? It's been, what? Fifteen days? Sixteen? That's more than two weeks. That's pretty good. Longer than my first attempt in January. February is a short month. I should be able to make it to the end, especially because we skipped another Dice Club. I was supposed to host, but I told Brandy and Sylvia I couldn't because the girls were sick.

I don't know if I could put on a Dice Club party without drinking.

I look at my calendar and squint. What's the date? My last drink was on Valentine's Day. Well, that's not exactly true. It was the day after. I stayed up well past midnight having a Valentine's party at the gallery. How did I get home that night? Was Ian even there? I do remember the Bloody Mary I sucked down at noon the next day when I finally rolled out of bed. The thin straw was like an IV attached to my pursed lips. I remember thinking the red tomato juice was like my last valentine. And the second one didn't really count. I was just finishing off what was in the shaker.

I smash the remaining unused clay into the giant lump stored inside a brittle plastic bag. Ian taps on the glass door and it startles me—makes me feel like I'm caught in the act of doing something wrong. "Hi, Babe," he sings.

His sweating, handsome face fills the doorway. "Ian, please don't sneak up on me like that."

He steps inside. "Sorry, Babe. Didn't mean to scare ya. What cha workin' on?"

"I'm just cleaning up." I roll the bag closed and tear a piece of duct tape to seal it.

"Get cha anything? Glass of merlot?" he asks.

I poke my index finger into the side of the bag, and press it forward until my nail cuts through the plastic. The cold, lifeless clay fills my nail and surrounds my fingertip. I grit my teeth. *Hasn't he noticed?*

"Tara?" He approaches me from behind and puts his dusty hands on my bare shoulders, and I can't help it. I flinch. Stray curls, which have escaped from my ponytail, coil around his warm touch. "Relax," he tells me. "Why so tense?"

My skin reacts like a Venus Fly Trap sucking in its prey. I wonder, what if he just moves his hands to my neck and squeezes? God! How I wish he would!

Ian uses his strong thumbs to massage the knots in my neck. I pull my finger from the clay and succumb to the physical comfort he provides. Slowly, I turn and face him. His hair is long. Too long. But I like it. His expression is soft. Sincere.

If I'm sure of anything, I'm sure my husband loves me.

A tremble shakes my stomach and moves up like a current, through my breasts and into my shoulders. I shiver as I search his eyes. Are the answers behind his beautiful glare?

Has it been long enough? Have I proved I can quit drinking if I want for long periods of time? Ten days is a lot. Double digits.

Ian frowns and loosens his grip. "Honey," he says, "are you okay?"

Chlöe

How did it get to be four o'clock already? I've got to get to school and pick up Roger Jr. from his study session. Can I leave Julie at home? Damn it! When a child wakes up with a fever and has to stay home from school, it ruins your day. And I had every minute of this day planned, including a four-hour stint at the clinic. My youngest, Julie, is home sick and I've lost all focus. I hope I don't lose my job. That would be brutal.

This day is shot. On Monday through Friday, I truly don't want my kids around after eight in the morning. During the few moments I have the house to myself this is my turf—my secret world. I've donated too much time scraping up oatmeal from the counters, changing shitty diapers, memorizing the Margaret Wise Brown literary collection, and overhearing the inane ditties of a giant purple dinosaur. I deserve this level of peace and quiet before I have to run all over town like a chicken in nursing shoes.

I'm not only a nurse, I've *earned* my degree in Ph.Mommy.

My children have been labeled "highly gifted." They rarely miss a day of school. So this is very unusual. Telling them they can't go to school is like a punishment. In fact, sometimes I use it as a threat if they dawdle in the morning instead of dressing, brushing their teeth, or getting their backpacks together. "If you can't pick out a pair of shoes in two minutes you can't go to school!" I don't care what anyone says. Threat psychology works.

I check on Julie, fast asleep. She's not the only one sick around here. One of my chickens is losing her feathers and hasn't laid anything in two weeks. And our oldest goat, a pygmy named Christopher Columbus, has something like a dozen kidney stones. I've got to leave them all behind and get to school to pick up Roger Jr. My middle child, Lisa, is still at Math Olympics. Going to school will take no more than fifteen minutes. It'll be okay to leave my five-year-old for a few minutes. Who will know, eh?

Once I get onto the paved section of the neighborhood, I roll over the neighborhood speed bumps, spotting a trail of pebble-sized goat pellets on the blacktop. When I walked Roger Jr. and Lisa to the bus this morning, I took the younger goats. I should have gotten back out here to brush aside the poop. This is as much of a cowtown as Calgary, but no one in the Rattlesnake Valley appreciates it as much as you'd think. Next week the rodeo comes to town and everyone around here goes to Disneyland. Or Hawaii. Heck, if only that were in *our* future. Not unless Roger gets a better job. The Electronic Hut just ain't cuttin' it!

The line of cars at the corner stop sign is longer than I expected at this time of day. I check off cars like an inventory: "Suburban. Suburban. Mercedes. Work truck. Hummer. Lexus." Big sigh. Why Roger took the Suburban to work today and left me with this farm truck, I'll never know. The Suburban is supposed to be my mom-mobile.

It takes five minutes to get to school. The parking lot is nearly empty and I pull my truck into a narrow parking space. I better stop in and see if Julie's teacher is still around.

Taking long strides toward the kindergarten classroom I think of my daughter's teacher, Mrs. Myers. Even the immunities she's built up from twenty-three years experience in the classroom, which one might think protects her like a coat of armor, aren't enough to keep her healthy among these germ-laden sickies. Fighting a losing battle, Mrs. Myers has sported a pale shade of green in her complexion since early November. Her hands are hot pink from scrubbing them sixteen times a day. The germs don't stop her from being loyal to her students, however. Like the Energizer Bunny of the teaching world, she comes to school each day and weathers the storm, going, going and going.

I poke my head inside the classroom and see Mrs. Myers sorting papers. I clear my throat and the teacher looks up and cocks her head like a puppy hearing a high-pitched tone. "Julie's still sick. She may be out for the rest of the week."

"Come on in," says Mrs. Myers.

Out of habit, I stomp my feet. I don't want stray manure still clinging to my worn boots to pollute the classroom. I step inside. The classroom is peaceful, without a hint of the chaos of hours recently spent sheltering eighteen five-year-olds. I pull my hair into a ponytail, twist it and tie it in a knot at the back of my neck. "Anything I can bring her? Coloring projects? Make-and-take books? I don't want her to fall behind."

"This is kindergarten," sighs Mrs. Myers. "She's a good student. Let her sleep. How's she doing?"

"Still has a fever. But she's okay, thanks. How are *you* doing?" I feel I cannot mask a sympathetic expression. It's the nurse in me.

Before she answers, the weary teacher looks left and right to see if anyone might be close enough to hear her response. "I feel like shit, thank you very much," she whispers.

Maybe I should bring her a surgical mask from the clinic. I tell her to "take care" and leave. Outside I release my breath, unaware that I'd been trying to hold it while inside the room.

Roger Jr. is waiting at the flagpole. "There you are. Geez. I've been waiting for fifteen minutes. I'm going to be late for soccer."

"Do you have any idea about the day I've had? I've got a sick child at home, Christopher Columbus looks like he's about to keel over, I've missed work and we can't afford to have me lose my job. We'll end up in the pogie. I've got to get you home and fed and in your soccer attire, which I'm not even sure is clean; your father is working late tonight and who do you think is going to do the grocery shopping and make dinner?"

"Geez, Mom," says Roger. "Take a pill already."

Take a pill? Where did he get that, the little hoser? I should ring his neck. What I really want is a drink. But who can drink when you have to run your kids all over town?

Through the rearview mirror on the drive home, I eye my son, who is strapped into the backseat. He's engrossed in a science book. Suddenly, the boy brings the book to his face, sneezes and wipes his nose with the back of his hand. His azure eyes, eyes so much like my own, look back at me in the mirror. "Please use a Kleenex, Sweetie," I say.

In this desert paradise there is rarely a cloud in the sky; however, a gray cloud of germs hangs over the school at all times. "They shouldn't call it the school year, but rather, the germ year," I tell him. "Be sure to wash your hands. With soap."

"Use a Kleenex. Use soap," he sings, mocking me. "That's all you ever say."

I punch the buttons on my radio, listen momentarily to a classical piece by Brahms, and then punch another button. I turn up the volume and hum along with The Judds. I listened only to classical music while pregnant with each of my three children. Listening to country music instead of classical feels like cheating on a test.

It can be utterly fatiguing being the parent of highly gifted children.

Rounding the last corner before heading down the dirt road to our place, I stretch my neck and am happy to see our rundown adobe blockhouse still standing—no fire trucks or child services vehicles. I turn off the ignition, relieved I've gotten away with my little motherly indiscretion.

We're greeted by the sound of more country music from the kitchen radio, chirping parakeets, and running water. Believing the water might be the irrigation system in the backyard, I look out the window.

Nothing.

I walk toward Julie's room, and as I reach for the door handle, I realize it's the sound of her vaporizer. Peeking inside the dark, damp room, a small, gray cat escapes and scampers past me. Julie is still asleep.

I make my way back to the kitchen and glance at the calendar. Each square is filled with a variety of inks, a different color for each child. Crap, it looks like I'll have to pick up Lisa today. My work doesn't end. "Homework tonight, Roger?"

"Did it at school. What's to eat around here?"

"Have an apple and get your socks out of the dryer. See if your uniform's in there. And can you text Lisa and tell her I'll be late picking her up from Math Olympics?"

"You do it," he shouts. "Aren't you supposed to drive the soccer carpool tonight?"

"Can't do it. Dad has the Suburban and I had to make other arrangements." These kids have no idea that my whole day is about making arrangements. I stand in the hallway for a moment, glancing at a wall full of family photos. They're growing up so fast. I catch a glimpse at my face in the hall mirror and it startles me. Pulling my hair from the knot at my neck I arrange it around my shoulders. Time for Clairol number ninety-seven. I lean forward and trace the half moon circles beneath my eyes. "I've got to get more sleep."

Better feed the animals before I get Lisa. I fill a travel mug with tap water and turn off the radio. Opening the back door, I'm met with alarming high-pitched screams. "Oh my stars!"

I grab the nearest pair of rubber boots, and before they're completely on, I run to the corral. The boots flop around my feet like loose fitting socks. Before I get to the chicken wire gate of the goat corral, I know what's wrong. It's Christopher Columbus. He's passing a kidney stone.

It's *not* a pretty sight.

Brandy

The back door slams and I drop the yellow onion I just pulled from the hanging copper basket next to the kitchen sink.

"It's sixteen-hundred. Eight bells!" calls the gravely voice of my father. An echo fills the room as he shuffles into the kitchen. Dressed in baggy, gray slacks and a thin white shirt, I look to his feet and see a tired pair of sheepskin slippers. "Eight bells, I said!"

"Eight bells and all is well?" It's a phrase I've heard all my life.

"For this shift maybe," he says. "I'm ready for my first dog shift. How about a shot for your old man?" He pulls a padded wooden stool from the bar counter and slowly lowers himself upon it.

"If you're looking for some prune juice we've got some in the sub-zero."

"Prune juice," he scoffs. "I'm not constipated. Why would I want prune juice?"

"Would you prefer buttermilk? We've got some of that too." I throw the dishtowel over my shoulder and walk across the room to retrieve a glass from the cabinet.

"Buttermilk! Prune juice. *Blech!*" he snorts. "Brandy Lynn I know you've got five children—six if you count your twin—but you had better realize that I am NOT one of them."

I use the towel from my shoulder to wipe my mouth. I'm afraid of what might come out. "Dad..."

"How about a beer? Levi's got some M.G.D. out in the garage fridge."

Little does he know that's not Levi's. It's left over from when I hosted Dice Club back in October. If memory serves, everyone was drinking hard stuff that night. Cosmopolitans—or whatever came out of Tara Shephard's car bar. How long does beer keep?

"Do you still keep that frozen mug in the freezer?"

"We never moved it," I tell him. I walk to the sub-zero and pull open the freezer drawer. My fingers sting with cold as I move around various packages and boxes of food. "There it is. Your frozen blue mug. It's been sitting here since the last time you visited."

"Was that last Christmas?"

"It was Fall. Remember you went to the kids' soccer games?"

"Soccer," he barks. "Back in my day we never played soccer. We played football. *American* football! And we didn't even use equipment. You should have seen the time I..."

"So. . ." I have to interrupt or this American football discussion will go on for fifteen minutes. And yes, I've heard it thirty-five times in my life. " ...Do you want that beer?"

"Hell yes, I want that beer. Be a good girl and go and get it for me. Will you?"

Big sigh. He's worse than the kids. I pull the mug from its icy grave beneath old bags of frozen peas and boxes of Costco *taquitos,* and place it on the counter in front of him. I want to tell him to get the beer himself. I even imagine myself saying: *What's wrong with your legs?* Funny, I would have verbalized this question to anyone but my father. Am I starting to feel sorry for him? I realize his life is growing more and more narrow, his pleasures diminishing.

Marching into the garage, I count how long he's been with us. Damn it all to hell. He's been here nearly two months. And I'm two months closer to my death.

The refrigerator is filled with an array of aluminum cans: Sprite, Thai Ice Tea, Minute Maid Lemonade, Diet Coke with lime, and Miller Genuine Draft. I reach in and grab a can of beer. It feels warm compared to the frozen mug. Rolling it in my palm, I examine the white logo letters and the golden sheen of the can. Staring at it for a while, long enough so that my vision blurs, a familiar feeling of regret overwhelms me once again. "I am a terrible daughter."

I return to the kitchen, stale beer in hand. "Here you go, Daddy. Want me to open it?"

"I've got it, Mommy."

"I'm Brandy, Dad. Not Mom."

"I *know* who you are," he croaks. "Brandy and Sandy. You're twins. I can't believe your mother gave birth to twins so late in life. It's probably what killed her you know."

"I'm pretty sure it was the cancer, Dad."

He pours the beer, and a look of obvious satisfaction and anticipation covers his face. My God, he's practically drooling. My skin bristles with each "glug" of the "glug-glug-glug" that fills the mug with bubbling, amber poison.

As the foam reaches the rim, he stretches out his wrinkled, hematoma-stained hand, and points past my head. "Get me a little salt out of that cabinet there. I don't know why you and Levi never put salt and pepper shakers on your table. Mommy always had them on the Lazy Susan. Remember that Lazy Susan? I think someone gave it to us for one of our wedding anniversaries."

"Yes, I remember the Lazy Susan, and that you like to sprinkle salt in your beer. Sandy does it too."

"Makes the head rise," he says, sprinkling fine white crystals into the glass. "See that? It's an old trick I learned back in New York City during the War. Did I ever tell you about the time we were on liberty and met a couple of characters we thought were girls?"

"Dad, please! We've heard this story a hundred times." I lower my voice to imitate his deep baritone and annunciate the punch line I've indeed heard too many times to count: "*And you know what I mean by fruit!*"

My father's denim blue eyes, a mirror of my own, grow big and he lifts his glass. "I guess you *have* heard that story before." He sips his beer, and white foam paints his upper lip. "We just couldn't believe they weren't women. There was a lot less of that sort of thing back in my day, you know, and these two were pretty attractive. When my buddy reached down and squeezed her leg, you should have seen his face when he grabbed a handful of fruit."

"And you know what I mean by fruit," we say together.

I can't help but laugh. I'll never forget the first time I heard that story. I hate to admit it, but it's still funny.

"Gimme a sip of that, Pops." I reach across the counter and grasp the beer. I have to see if it tastes stale. Frost covers the outside of the mug, and with my fingernail, I etch the letter "B" into the ice. Bringing the foamy head to my lips, I taste the salt and stick out my tongue. "Yuck! How can you drink this?"

He takes the mug. "It's the only thing you'll let me have," he says.

"Good point. I'll be right back."

I walk into the formal dining room and spy an upright wine cooler, which looks like the size of a small apartment building. I know there's something left in here. There's gotta be. I bend down, reach to the third shelf and pull out the sole bottle. Cradling it in my hands, I rock it like a baby. "La Crema Carneros Pinot Noir. Sonoma, 2002." It makes me smack my lips and reach for the corkscrew. "Happy hour starts early today."

Sylvia

I'm five minutes late for my four o'clock appointment. It isn't like me to be one minute late. For anything. But there was an accident at one of the busier intersections, and the traffic lights flashed with strobe alarm for the last two miles of my journey. I detest traveling anywhere near the Valley's busiest hospital. It's always a zoo.

At last reaching my destination, I jam the gearshift into park and fluff my hair with long painted fingers. I turn off the XM radio—tuned to the raunchy comedy channel—and then reach down, pressing the button that automatically raises the roof of my car. I couldn't resist having the top down on my milk white BMW on such a sunny, March day. Would I have ever been able to drive a convertible in March while in Lake Oswego, Oregon? Hell no! It would still be raining!

God, I love my life.

With keys in hand, a sapphire-encrusted "S" dangling from my keychain, I open the door and swing one leg to the pavement. Then I remember I'd stored my newest Kate Spade, a Kariba Zebra McCardel shoulder bag, on the floor of the backseat so the wind wouldn't blow out the contents. Reaching back, I grab it and admire the African motif. It complements my black leather, CAbi vest, DNKY jeans, white INC. mock turtleneck and chocolate suede Jimmy Choo Dragonfly pumps.

Surveying the parking lot, I do what I always do. I look for familiar cars. A silver Lexus catches my eye, as does a white Escalade parked in the handicapped space next to the front door of the building. I can't stand running into people I know when visiting the Rattlesnake Valley Plastic Surgery Center. Even though I only come here for a few harmless Botox injections, I don't want anyone to know how worried I am about my forehead. It's so ...vain!

Each year past forty has walked across my face with all the care of a child stomping through mud puddles. Honestly, keeping up appearances is completely exhausting!

Crossing the parking lot, out of the corner of my eye I spy a green, compact car. It's a Dodge Stratus and it stands out in the lot filled with expensive models like a weed in a flower garden. Zeroing in on the broken taillight, *umph!* It feels like I've been punched in the stomach.

"Oh my God!" What's Amanda Prince doing here?

I look left and then right. There are other doctor's offices clustered around the complex—dermatologists, podiatrists, chiropractors, optometrists, orthodontists—a real smorgasbord of medical care for individuals with limitless disposable income. What business could Amanda possibly have on this side of town? And, even more perplexing ...how much medical care does Richard's health plan cover for his employees?

I suddenly feel like a guilty thief biding time before the arrival of the police after an alarm had sounded. Better pick up the pace. Ouch! These shoes are not made for trotting. Regardless, I actually leap up the stairs to the lobby.

"Hello Mrs. Ostrander," says the doorman. He bows slightly at the waist and pulls open the glass door.

"How are you Luis?" I ask without making eye contact. If I don't look directly at him, it feels more like I'm not really here.

I'm slightly out of breath. Before going through the second set of doors, I step up to the building marquis, a gold-plated plaque with engraved black letters. "Welcome to the Rattlesnake Valley Medical Group," it reads. Scrolling down the list, I realize I've never before read the roster of doctors practicing within the walls of this building. Oh, wouldn't you know it! I recognize many as members of the organizations to which Richard and I belong. How could I forget? I found my Botox doctor through casual conversation at a cocktail party for... what was it for?

I push my fingers through my hair. It doesn't matter.

Now there's a name that's rather familiar: Dr. Melinda Charles-Lloyd, Psychiatric Care and Grief Counseling. I exhale and shift my weight. "I'll be damned."

I know this doctor—I can picture her bobbed hair and big-toothed smile at one of the many cocktail parties I attended prior to the holidays. I'm certain I passed on her card to Amanda. Could it be that Amanda finally made an appointment to talk to someone about the loss of her child?

I glance at my gold, diamond-studded Movado watch. "Four-ten." I *hate* being late! I reach into my bag for a tin of cinnamon flavored Altoids. Popping one in my mouth, I step inside the Plastic Surgeon's office.

"Hi Sylvia," says the receptionist. "He's waiting for you in Salon One."

"Thanks Ginny." I'm out of breath. "Sorry I'm late."

"No problem," she says. "This time of day we're always a little behind." She gets up from her chair. This girl is so thin, so perfect. I wonder how much work she's had done. He probably gives her a discount. "Can I do anything for you? You look a little ...stressed. You okay?"

"Excuse me?"

"I said, can I help you?"

"Oh, no. No. That's okay. I'm fine. I'm just a bit flustered because I'm late. The traffic lights were flashing. I think there was an accident or something."

"Happens every day," says Ginny. She rounds the corner and meets me on my side of the counter. "Let me take your, uh, jacket? I mean your vest. That's beautiful."

"Thanks. I just got it. One of my neighbors had a designer clothing sale at her home last week and she delivered it this morning." I take it off and hand it to Ginny. I should give it to her.

"It's as soft as butter," she says.

"Yes." She wants it too much. I think I'll keep it. At least for now.

"Here, follow me," she says. "Are you just having the usual today? Between the eyebrows? The forehead? I've got you scheduled for fifty units."

"I'm not sure. Lately it seems every time I come here and we diminish that terrible vertical line between my eyebrows, it looks better. But then the rest of my face looks like hell."

Ginny laughs. She opens the door to the exam room, "Salon One," and we step inside. "Have a seat," she says.

"You know what it's like? I feel the same way any time I remodel a room in my house. When I'm finished the new room looks good, but then the rest of the rooms look tired and in need of ...something."

"I do know what you mean." Ginny hangs my vest on a hook behind the door and looks at me.

I squint at her. "I mean, look at these crow's feet! And these smile lines around my mouth! I never noticed them until I started flattening out my forehead."

"You're not alone. Lots of people say that."

I don't like the idea of being like "lots of people."

"Talk to him when he comes in. I'm sure he'll be willing to do whatever you want, Sylvia. Maybe even some fillers around the mouth. He might have time today. But if not, you can always come back. He'll know what to do for you."

"Yes, I'm sure he will." A thousand bucks' worth, no doubt.

I grab a hand mirror from the table next to her, and focus on the lines around my mouth. Fillers, huh? I smile like I'm about to apply powdered blush, and then relax my cheeks and sigh. "Hopeless."

Ginny checks her watch. I check too. It's four-twenty. "I thought he was in here already," she says. "It'll only be another minute or so. In the meantime, how about a glass of wine? He just got back from Napa and brought some excellent chardonnays I think you'll enjoy."

I set down the mirror. "Why not? It's five o'clock somewhere."

"Isn't that saying supposed to be 'it's noon somewhere?' "

"Whatever. If I'm going to get more than my usual shots in the forehead you had better fill it to the rim."

Shonah

My son, Sammy, walks into the room and points at the clock. I'm shocked. "How'd it get to be four o'clock already? Are you even close to being finished with your homework?"

"Not really," he says.

"Your carpool is going to be here in less than twenty minutes and you better be ready or you'll miss soccer practice. Who's driving today? Is it Chlöe the Canadian or the Tasmanian Devil's mom?"

"No clue. I can't find my shin guards."

"Again with the shin guards! What the he ...heck am I going to do with you and these blessed shin guards?"

"I don't know," he says. "Just don't kick me, I guess."

"What about your homework? Please tell me I don't have to check math."

"It's fine, Mom. Dad can check it if you don't want to. It's pretty easy stuff."

"God, I hate math!"

"Really, Mom?" he asks sarcastically. "I don't think you've told me that ten times yet this week."

I look at my son and watch his big, black eyes blink several times like a series of exclamation marks. "Smartass." I say it under my breath.

"Don't swear, Mom."

"Don't edit me. I've already got one of those at work."

I open the refrigerator door and pull out a can of Peach Nectar, my new afternoon drink of choice since I gave up drinking wine on weekdays. It was pretty easy to do. Easier than I thought it would be. I open the can and bend the aluminum flip-tab back-and-forth, back-and-forth. The kids collect them for the Ronald McDonald house and I've become obsessed with the process, pulling can after can out of the recycling bin and decapitating them for the ever mounting pile. This can is particularly stubborn. With my index finger, I keep at it.

"Damn!" There goes my nail. "Damn it. Shit! This stupid thing broke my nail."

"Mom!" scolds Sammy. "Language!"

"Never-you-mind. Go get ready for soccer and leave me alone with my mouth."

He grabs the peach nectar and steals a sip. "There's your next column, Mom. Cleaning up your potty mouth when the kids are old enough to swear back at you."

I laugh. "Sweetie, they're just words. And you've been swearing since you could talk."

"Is that a fact?"

"Fact. I'll never forget the time when we were all riding in a car going out to dinner with some friends. It was five o'clock and I told you you'd have to miss your favorite TV shows."

" 'Dragon Tails' and 'Arthur?' "

"Yup. Good old P.B.S. You lived for those shows and it was a good thing because it was your daily television allotment and it gave me an hour to get dinner ready. Anyway, when I said you were missing them that night, you scrunched up your cute little face, slapped the front of your car seat, and said, 'oh, shit!' "

"I did?"

"Yes, and just like that. 'Oh, *shit!'* With perfect disappointment inflection."

"Well they say I'm gifted, you know."

"So gifted you can't keep track of your socks. Get out of here already, will you?"

I pour my drink into a glass and take a long, satisfying sip. It's ten minutes after four. Dan and Jonas will be home in an hour and I still haven't decided what to fix them for dinner. The kitchen is a mess. The dishwasher needs emptying and all of last night's pots and pans still sit in the sink unwashed. Better get to work. I roll up my sleeves, take off my rings and turn on the hot water. It always takes a minute to get hot enough for dish washing. Too long. I hate wasting water in the desert. It just seems wrong. Finally, steam emanates from the stream and I plug the drain. Pushing the soap dispenser four times, I swirl the water in the shape of an "S" and bring the bubbles to life.

Staring out the window at the mountains to the east, I scour the pots and pans and form a Calphalon mountain in the drying rack to the left of the sink. Meanwhile, Sammy emerges in his practice uniform, socks and all, and grabs himself a granola bar and an orange for a snack. I'll have to feed him when he returns at eight o'clock. Thank goodness, soccer is winding down for the season. It all depends on how well they do at the State Cup series.

There's a horn in the driveway. "Time!" I walk him to the front door and kiss him on the forehead. "Be good," he says.

"Brat." I shake my head, smile, and wave to the soccer mom on driving duty. It's Trudy. Trudy, whose son we call the "Tasmanian Devil," is on duty. I thought it was supposed to be Chlöe. Hmm. Her schedule must have gotten in the way again.

As I shut the front door, my phone rings and I race to it, checking the caller ID screen to make sure it doesn't say "TOLL FREE" or "UNKNOWN CALLER." I wait for the third ring before seeing "TARA SHEPHERD," and use my finger with the broken nail to push the talk button.

"Hello?"

"It's me," says Tara. "Busy?"

"Not really. What's happening?" Tara doesn't respond. I feel my brow furrow. "Are you there?"

"I'm here," Tara says. Her voice is shaky.

"What's wrong?" I sit down.

"I have a glass of wine in front of me and I'm about to drink it. It's merlot. Ian brought it to me and I swear it's taking every fiber of my being not to pour it down my throat."

"Tara, I…"

"Don't!" she says. "Don't say anything. About the wine I mean. Or about me drinking it. Just help me get to five o'clock, will you?"

"What happens at five?"

"Happy hour ends," she says. "At least it ends in my house. Between four and five is the worst. If I can just make it to five, I'll be okay."

"Okay." Can I do this? "So, what do you want to talk about?"

"Well for starters, I heard from my friend Ginny who works at the Plastic Surgery Center that Sylvia Ostrander comes in regularly for Botox treatments."

"She does?" I don't know why I say this. I'm absolutely aware of Sylvia's Botox addiction.

"For over a year now."

"Well, if anyone can afford it, it's Sylvia. We should all look as good as Sylvia. Oops, there's my 'call annoying.' Let me see who it is." The phone line clicks a second time. "It's Brandy. Want her to join us?"

"Sure," says Tara. "But don't say anything about the drinking, okay? She's the last person I want to have know about this."

"I won't." I push the "flash" button on my phone. "Hi Brandy. I've got Tara on the other line. Let's conference."

"Hi all," says Brandy after a short pause. "I thought I'd join you for a drink. My father is driving me insane. He keeps begging me for a shot of Jack Daniels and I finally broke down and gave him a beer."

"It's okay for him to drink beer?" I ask, cringing at the topic.

"It doesn't seem to affect him the way the hard stuff does," she says.

Tara remains silent. I think of the glass of wine in front of her. Could the same thing be true about her? Would a glass of wine be harmless?

"Hey guess what, Brandy?" I ask, "Tara just told me that Sylvia gets Botox."

"Duh!" says Brandy. "That's news? How'd you find out, Tara?"

"My friend who works at the Center told me."

"Well that's a breech of confidentiality if I've ever heard one," says Brandy.

My phone clicks. "Damn! I can't believe it. Call waiting again! My phone doesn't ring for hours and all of a sudden it's Grand Central."

"Who is it?"

I wait for a name to appear on the screen. "Oh my gosh, it's Sylvia."

"Ha!" laughs Brandy. "Her ears were burning. Must be all the Botox."

"I can't do a four-way. You two talk and I'll call you right back, Tara. Okay?"

"I'm free until five," Tara says.

Oh no. I told her I'd get her through to five. I bite my lip. I'll call her back in ten seconds. Again, I push the flash button. I had this phone for nearly two years before I learned how to use the flash button. "Hello?"

"Shonah? Tis I." Sylvia's voice, as always, is liquid and melodic. "You'll never guess whose car I saw parked in front of the medical complex outside a well-known grief counselor."

I dip my finger into the glass of peach nectar and suck the thick, sweet juice from my knuckle. I glance at the wall clock above the sink still filled with suds, and see that it's ten minutes until five. Sylvia is, no doubt, referring to Amanda. I want to hear this.

"Shonah are you there? Did you hear what I said?"

"Yes. Tell me."

Tara

I don't really have anything to say to Brandy. I can't talk to her about the wine in front of me. She won't understand. She asks me what I'm working on.

"Planters."

"Anything special? Anything I might like?"

"You don't like anything!"

"That's not true," protests Brandy. "I have two of your pieces. And you still owe me a Tony Soprano platter."

"A Tony Soprano platter? What are you talking about?"

"Don't you remember you promised you'd get me one that was used on the set? You told me the night of Sylvia's Christmas Dice Club.

I can't remember if it was before or after that bitch Amanda spilled wine in my lap."

I look at the clock. Five more minutes. I wish Shonah would call back. Just hearing the word "wine" come out of Brandy's mouth makes me focus back on the glass in front of me. I lick my lips, pull the glass toward me and lightly caress its long stem up-and-down between my thumb and forefinger. Brandy is still talking. Blabbering on about Amanda. I lower my nose. Sniffing in deeply, I let the robust red aroma fill me. Should I?

"Are you still there?" Brandy asks.

"You shouldn't be so mean about Amanda. Can't you at least try to put yourself in her shoes and empathize with her grief?"

"I'm a physical therapist in case you forgot." There's an edge to her voice. "I'm all about healing. I think . . ." Her voice momentarily drops out. "...work on it. Damn it. Just a minute, Tara. It's my call waiting beeping. Hold on."

The line goes dead. I press the phone closer to my ear, wondering if I'll hear anything of her on the line with another caller. Will it be Shonah? I can't hear anything. I grab the glass of wine, get up, and bring it to my slop sink.

"It's Chloë on the other line," says Brandy clicking back on the line. "She's got a sick goat."

"Good Lord!" I pour the wine into the sink. "Chickens and goats. As if she doesn't have enough to do. What's wrong with the goat?"

"Nothing a .22 in the wash can't cure," says Brandy.

"What?"

"Stock animals. It's how most of them go. At least it's how they go on a real ranch. Not that little Old McDonald farm Chloë Forrest has in her claptrap backyard. All her animals are pets. 4-H education. It's good for the kids, but in this case, not so good for the goat. I'm going to send Levi over there with a .22. He'll take care of it."

"You mean he's going to shoot it?" I put my hand to my stomach. Focusing on the red splash of the wine in the slop sink, I think I'm going to be sick. I don't want my mind to envision blood and splattered goat brains, but I can't help it.

"Princess Tara, you're so naïve," says Brandy. "I've got to go." She hangs up.

I pull the phone from my ear and look at it, as if it might explain Brandy Lynn to me. How can this woman call herself a healer? She doesn't have a compassionate bone in her body! If I told her how I feel right now, how I'm struggling ...I could scream! I want a drink so bad it physically hurts me. I pick up the freshly emptied wine glass and again hold it to my nose. Sniffing as deeply as possible, I fall back slightly, losing my balance.

Oh no. Oh …Lord! My stomach tightens and contracts. I can't control the rise of my insides. "Ugh!"

My slop sink now holds a layer of vomit. Quickly, I turn on the cold water and wash away the evidence of my sickness. I straighten, point an index finger to my temple—my own .22—and pull the trigger. *Pow!*

Nothing happens.

Chapter 7
A March Morning

Whenever my husband and I are on a road trip together, we have the habit of reading every sign we see out loud. Our boys do it now too. Another thing we often say when we spot a big beautiful home located just off the Interstate is, "Gee, do you think someone gave them that land?" On longer trips when there are prolonged silences between us, occasionally we'll pass a seedy neighborhood that makes me wonder what would have to happen to us in order to make it necessary to have to live in a place like that.

There's a philosophy in real estate that if you're tight on funds then you should try to find the worst house in the best neighborhood. I lived in "that house," in every neighborhood until I moved to the Rattlesnake Valley. Is there any such thing as the "worst house" in this desert oasis?

—Shonah Bartlett
From her column, *The Dice Club Chronicles*

Chlöe

My next door neighbor's dog, Bingo, is barking his fool head off. This thick, chocolate lab, which is the size of submarine, roars every morning like a foghorn before sunrise. Since we moved to the neighborhood, the barking has served as my wakeup call. Who needs an alarm when you've got Bingo? He's out there making noise even before the chickens.

But I've been up for hours. I haven't slept since we lost Christopher Columbus.

It's approaching midmorning. What's Bingo barking at this time? I bend the burgundy-colored blinds and peek out the kitchen window. There must be someone back there—an exterminator or a landscaper. Maybe the pool boy? Those people are always having something done in their yard. There's a constant stream of vehicles coming and going all day long. And with the number of times the UPS truck pulls into their driveway, either the woman of the house is having an affair with the deliveryman in brown shorts, or she's an eBay junkie. Clearly she has money to burn. Must be nice.

I let the blinds snap and then run a finger through the dust. I can't believe how quickly the desert dust amasses on these slats. It's because of our dirt road, but it's also probably all the delivery trucks stirring it up. There was never this much dust in Calgary.

A lot of things were different in Canada.

Back home I knew my neighbors. We were all on a first name basis. Here in the Rattlesnake Valley, the only reason I know our nearest neighbor's name is because it's printed on the Neighborhood Watch list. I call her "Elvira" because she looks a lot like that Halloween character with the long, black hair and R-rated cleavage. I gave her that moniker two Halloweens ago, which was the only time we'd ever come face-to-face.

I thought taking our three kids trick-or-treating would be a great way to finally meet the neighbors. God knows, not one of them had come by to welcome us to the neighborhood. Maybe it's because we're "foreigners." But what would anyone have against Canadians? We look just like everyone else, speak the same language. Is it because the trim on our house needs a fresh coat of paint? Maybe it's the long dirt road leading to our front door. Perhaps it's the lack of window treatments on our street-facing windows? The goat pellets on the street? Or maybe it's the maple leaf on the front of my car. These Americans have flags all over the place. What's wrong with a little support for *my* home and native land?

I had to take matters into my own hands, and I thought knocking on doors and asking for candy at Halloween seemed like an acceptable method. So, after the sun went down, we put candles in our pumpkins and a plastic caldron filled with Reese's Peanut Butter cups on the front porch, and set off. Our first stop was next door. The kids ran ahead and were already pushing the door chime for the third time when Roger and I reached the front porch of this stately, two-story manner. At last, an overhead chandelier switched on and the front door opened.

"Yes?" the woman asked. She was dressed in a sheer black negligee, had ghostly white skin and blood red lipstick. The kids' faces lit up. They thought it was an excellent costume. "How can I help you?"

"Trick or treat!" they sang.

"Oh. Is it Halloween? I didn't know it was today."

"It's easy to forget," joked my husband, Roger. "Especially because it falls on the same day EVERY year!"

Elvira parted her sanguine lips and exposed aspirin white teeth. She held up an extraordinarily long index finger and told the kids to wait while she dug up a treat. I wanted to gather the children and leave immediately, but Roger couldn't wait to see what she dredged up. Meanwhile, Bingo the dog growled and roared and it made the kids cover their ears against the racket. As they stood waiting for their treat, the garage door creaked open and they saw Elvira's partially clad buttocks sticking out of the backseat of her Lincoln Town Car.

I didn't like the look on my husband's face, or for that matter, Roger Jr.'s face either. Not one bit.

"Here you go! Here you go children," said Elvira as she trotted in pinpoint stilettos from the garage to her front porch. She carried a glass pickle jar filled with silver coins. "You can reach in here and grab a handful of change," she said. "I'd do it for you, but I just had my nails done."

She held up her hand and wiggled her fingers, exposing five painted black nails, each the length of a mesquite tree pod. To the frightened children, it looked like the clawed hand of a werewolf. My daughters, Julie and Lisa, wasted no time running down the driveway and toward the next house. Roger Jr., on the other hand, grasped his plastic candy-collecting pumpkin tightly, and with his free hand, reached in for the loot. He never took his eyes of Elvira's chest.

"What do you say?" I prompted.

"Thank you," the boy said flatly.

I forced a smile. "Thanks. We're the Forrests. We moved in next to you about eleven months ago." I took my husband's arm and we left.

Those were the only words I've ever spoken to Elvira.

I check my watch and confirm that I'm behind schedule. It's my day off from my part-time nursing job at the Rattlesnake Valley Orthopedic Clinic, and it's a good thing for two reasons: One, my back hurts from lifting too many heavy patients the day before and two, I'm hosting the Dice Club tonight and have a hundred things to do before picking up the kids from school. I want to get to school early so I can talk to the gifted teacher about a new reading list for my elder daughter, Lisa.

"Let's see. What's the most important thing?" I grab a piece of scrap paper and dig through an old coffee mug full of pens and pencils, looking for a pencil with a sharpened tip. There's rarely one here. Finally, after four failed attempts, I find a chewed Dixon-Ticonderoga Number Two stub, a leftover from the prize package I won at the back-to-school Dice Club. Seems like ages ago.

Why's my life going so fast, eh?

I write "#1" on the list, look up and put the pencil between my teeth. It takes only a moment before I realize the first thing I want to put on my list is the "B.H.T." Smiling and releasing the pencil from my toothy grip, I write the initials next to #1. The B.H.T. is my acronym for "Bargain Hunters Triangle." My three main stores are the K-Mart Super Center, Big Lots and Ross Dress For Less. Money is always tight and I've become an expert at finding good deals on everything from socks and underwear to generic foods and, of course, Nice 'N Easy number ninety-seven, my blonde-in-a-box indulgence.

I continue drawing up the list:

#2. Booze and frozen dinners for tonight

#3. Orthodontist treatment conference

#4. Get new mortgage papers notarized

#5. Dice Club gift ???

I add five more question marks after "Dice Club gift," and underline it three times. I chose the theme, *I Love Lucy* and yet I'm not sure what to get. I think I saw a Lucy and Desi lunch box at K-mart last week.

I haven't seen anyone in the Dice Club since Sylvia's Christmas party. Gee, I wonder if there was a party in February and I just never heard. Could they be trying to tell me something? None of them even called or sent a card when my goat died. Brandy must have told them. Gosh, what kind of friends are these women?

Again, the neighbor's dog barks and barks. "That's so bloody obnoxious!" I slam down my pencil and stomp to the back door. Stepping into my yard, I kick soccer balls, basketballs, volleyballs and tennis balls out of my way. Weeds are everywhere. I sigh at the mess, and the dog continues its rant. Placing my thumb and forefinger on my rolled tongue, I blow one sharp whistle, then cup my hands around my mouth and shout, "Bingo! Quiet!"

The dog barks back a noncompliant response. I have a good mind to call the police. Feeling futile, I kick away one more tennis ball, while the chickens gather around my feet. I pick up a pogo stick and lean it against the house, and go inside. I don't have time to deal with Bingo today. The door slams behind me and without looking, I reach back and turn the lock. When I look up, I'm shocked to see my husband standing in the kitchen.

"Roger! What are you doing here, eh?" He looks disheveled, and completely out of place. His white shirttail hangs over the top of his khaki Dockers and his tie is loose.

There is no response. Instead Roger drops his keychain on the counter next to my list and jams his hands into the side pockets of his pants. He lowers his double chin, and the sun pouring in from the south-facing windows reflects off his balding pate.

I step closer to him. "Honey? Is something wrong?"

"You betcha there's something wrong," he says. "I think you should sit down."

"Roger?"

He clears his throat. "Listen, Honey . . ."

"You're scaring me! Did something happen to . . . to one of the kids? Are the kids okay?"

"The kids are fine," he says. "At least I think they are. No, no, it's not the kids."

I reach out and grab his tie, pulling him toward me. "What is it?"

"I might as well just come right out and tell you."

Oh God. I focus on the pencil-thin mustache above his lip. He grew it shortly after we got married fourteen years ago. At the time it made him look older, more sophisticated. When had it started turning gray? I narrow my eyes and tuck a stray piece of hair behind my ear. The momentary silence between us makes the air tense. I see dust particles dancing in light streaks behind him.

"I . . . I," he stammers.

"What?! Just say it."

"I lost my job."

"No!" Oh my GAWD! We *will* end up in the pogie!

"Yes, I'm afraid so. Holiday sales weren't what they expected, and January was flat. I just found out we posted a loss in February. Three of us were let go. There's a severance," he adds quickly, "but it ain't much."

"But what about the refinancing? I was going to send off the papers today."

"I know. I'm more worried about the lease on that Suburban. We've still got two years on that thing."

I feel like I'm going to fall down. Instead, I lift myself upon the counter and allow my feet to kick the cabinets. "Holy moly and the orthodontist. I have a meeting in," I look at my watch, "less than an hour. Lisa's ready to have her braces put on."

I don't want to tell him how much I'll need to spend to put on this party tonight. Maybe I should make it a potluck and ask each woman to bring something. I could change the theme from *I Love Lucy* to "I Love Shipwreck Stew?"

Roger puts his hand to his forehead and squeezes his eyes closed. He turns away and walks to the refrigerator. Pulling out a carton of orange juice, he frowns and shakes it. "There's nothing left in here. Who put this back in the fridge?" He pitches the empty carton across the room and into the kitchen sink. I watch as a few stray drops fall to the floor in slow motion.

"I thought about this all the way home and I think, maybe it would be a good idea if we, um, if …We should sell the house," he says.

"Roger, no!" I jump to the floor.

"Just listen. The market is picking up right now and we can find something a lot cheaper. We can pay off this mortgage and the lease on the car and get into a situation we can afford."

"But we can't afford anything else in this neighborhood! We already have the crappiest little house in the Valley. I don't want to the take the kids out of the school district. Not now."

"Well, we may have to. But we'll get through this. In the meantime, how would you feel about increasing your hours at the clinic? I'm sure they'd like to have you full time. The pay and the benefits could be pretty good. Maybe even pay for the orthodontist?"

"No-o, Roger!" It was the whine of a child. I turn away from him and pace the room. "We talked about this. The kids need me. Their school! All the volunteer work I do there! You know it helps them. You know it's why they're so gifted."

"We need the money, Chlöe. And it would help take some of the pressure off of me."

A lump develops in my throat. I shake my head and thin, blonde tresses swing into my face. This can't be happening. There has to be another solution. A buzz begins at my temples. I fear a migraine coming on. Don't look into the light. The buzz grows in intensity. I dig my fingers into my scalp.

Just then, Bingo lets out another roar and Roger bangs his fist on the kitchen counter.

"BINGO!" we both yell. "SHUT *UP!*"

Our eyes meet and Roger's expression softens. He rubs his middle finger across his mustache and lets out a small chuckle. "Look at it this way, Chlöe," he says. "If we move, you no longer have to listen to that damn dog."

Suddenly I feel a passionate attachment to Bingo. I'm going to have to find a way to make ends meet so we don't have to move.

Shonah

I load my golf clubs into the back of my silver Land Cruiser. Our tee time is a mere eight minutes away, and I'll have to exceed the 45 miles-per-hour speed limit on Bellisimo Boulevard to get to the Club on time. I have no problem putting my pedal to the medal.

Spring is in full bloom in the Rattlesnake Valley. By late February, the frosty mornings ended and everyone labeled it a "mild winter." With an inability to go into full dormancy, this forced the citrus plants to flower early, and the air—particularly the air surrounding the lush links of the Valley Verde Golf Course—is sweet with the pungent perfume of orange blossoms. I step out of the car and take a deep breath. It's beautiful here.

I spot Tootsie Fennimore. I can't believe I'll be playing golf with a pro.

"Hey there, Sweet Pea," she says to me and kisses my cheek. She turns her head and sneezes. "I may sneeze through this entire round." She sniffles softly, politely, and takes off the bright red stocking of her driver. "Never could get used to that smell."

"I can't get used to Shonah's smell either," says Brandy strolling up to us like she owns the place.

"Not Shonah," laughs Tootsie. "The orange blossoms."

I flash Brandy my middle finger and she sticks out her tongue.

"That's good to know, Tootsie," says Brandy, walking up behind her. "Maybe I can give you a run for your money on the course today."

"Let's not worry about that. You should take Sylvia in your cart. I'll take Shonah. If we leave those two on their own, the guys behind us may get impatient." Tootsie nods to a foursome of men on the putting green in the distance, all wearing Bermuda shorts and big, flat hats. Two pretend they're not looking at her, while the other two can't take their eyes off her. No doubt, they *all* know who she is. "No offense, Shonah."

"Uh, none taken?" I'm feeling a bit picked on this morning.

"Do you think I give a shit about what the men think?" asks Brandy. "We pay our club fees just like they do."

Sylvia emerges from the clubhouse wearing a pair of powder blue shorts and a matching sun visor. She directs the young man carrying her clubs toward the carts next to Tootsie and Brandy. "Over here," calls Brandy. "You're with me today Sylvia."

"Oh terrific," she says. "Don't make fun of me or I swear I'll quit and just drive the cart."

"Or you can be our caddie," says Brandy.

"Don't worry, Sylvia. They're making fun of *me* today." I place my clubs on the cart and fiddle with the strap.

"You look very nice, Sylvia. Fresh and young," Tootsie comments. "Did you do something different?"

Brandy and I exchange a knowing look that says: *Fresh Botox.*

"No, nothing," says Sylvia. "Thank you, though. Just wait til you see my golf game!"

"Why don't you consider what we used to say in college? 'It's not how you play, it's how you look that counts!' " Tootsie winks at Sylvia, then pats the seat next to her for me to sit. We motor to the first tee.

Tootsie wastes no time. She steps near the tee and swings her club. Her backswing is slow, her follow-through seamless.

Brandy, a regular at the Club, watches and admires. "Yes, but some of us can play well *and* look good at the same time," she says, nodding at Tootsie.

Sylvia grabs a handful of tees from her bag and pokes them into the dashboard of the cart. "Why am I doing this? I suck at golf and am just going to hold you all back. You'll never want to play with me again. I should stick to my private lessons and stop embarrassing myself."

I retie my shoe. "Don't feel bad. I'm wearing new shoes. I don't know if my feet can take eighteen holes in them. Even if we're riding."

"Miss Shonah, my dear, you'll be just fine," says Tootsie. "Grab yer driver. We're up."

I check the GPS monitor in the cart and see that it's a 345-yard, par four hole. It will take everything I have in my bag, and hopefully I'll connect. I'm always nervous on the first tee because I feel so exposed. This morning, I'm particularly nervous since I haven't swung a club in three months *and* I'm playing with a retired pro. It's the first time I've played with Tootsie and I imagine she'll be gracious. Still, I don't want to look like a complete klutz. "You go first Tootsie, and show us how it's done."

Tootsie compresses the pale yellow golf ball on the sweet spot. *THWACK!* The ball accelerates straight out, a gentle rise, and then I lose it in the desert sky. Is that it? Falling lazily into the middle of the fairway? It travels a mile—or at least to a comfortable spot within pitching distance to the green.

"Good God!" remarks Sylvia. "You should be hitting from the men's tee!"

Tootsie puts her hand to her crotch. "As soon as I grow something right here, Darlin'," she says with a smile.

"How about a little Bingo, Bango, Bongo?" asks Brandy.

"Perfect," says Tootsie.

I take a practice swing. It feels good. "I'm in."

"What the heck is that? Bingo, Bango, Bunko?" asks Sylvia.

"No!" laughs Brandy. "Not Bunko, you goof. *Bongo*. It's a golf game we play for dimes."

"I can't compete with the likes of you!" says Sylvia.

"That's exactly the point," Tootsie says. "Just a second. Let Shonah drive and I'll explain."

I drive a hot pink ball into the fairway, a little to the right and just shy of a sand trap. Not too bad. At least I didn't miss.

Brandy is immediately on the tee, and with her back to us, she uses her left-handed driver to launch a shot that lands dead center. It isn't as long as Tootsie's drive, but it's a beautiful shot by anyone's standards.

"Very nice," says Tootsie. "What's yer handicap these days, Brandy?"

Brandy is reluctant to respond. "Fourteen. But it shouldn't be. I had a few really good back-to-back games and it lowered me just prior to a three-day tournament where I was terrible. I finished in tenth place."

Sylvia swings and misses. "Do I have to do this?" It takes her a total of three swings to hit the ball, and when she finally connects, the ball flies off to the right, skips over the cart path and out of bounds. "That's enough. I'll just take a drop up by the green. I need a couple holes to warm up."

"It's just a friendly game," says Tootsie. She depresses the foot pedal of the cart. "You watch, you'll probably clean up on the dots."

"Dots?" asks Sylvia. Her face mangles into confusion and she holds on tightly as Brandy takes off, following closely behind us.

"Sylvia is a hoot." Tootsie laughs and calls over her shoulder. "Bingo, Bango, Bongo awards dots, or points, for the first on the green, closest to the pin, and longest one-putt. You could walk off this course with at least a dollar in your pocket, girl!" The cart jerks forward and I hold onto my ball cap.

I hear Brandy over the buzz of the carts. "You could always use an extra dollar, right Sylvia?"

"Speaking of an extra dollar," says Sylvia as we drive slowly, looking for balls, "someone keeps holding out on putting in her five dollars into the Dice Club pot each month. I think I know who it is."

"Who?" asks Brandy.

"Chlöe."

"Really?"

"Well at Blanca's house she didn't show up until we were already opening the bag gifts, but that wasn't the only time we were short."

"It's five bucks,' says Brandy. "I'm sure it was just an oversight. Five bucks isn't going to break anyone."

"I don't know," Sylvia says. "Have you seen her house?"

Brandy cranes her neck looking for Sylvia's ball. They'll never find it up this far. She spots her own and buzzes forward. She grabs an iron and jumps out of the cart. We stop at my ball, about forty feet behind Brandy's.

Brandy is unconcerned that I'm hitting behind her. "I'm back here!" I call. "Can you wait a minute?" Tootsie is looking off into the distance, unconcerned with any of us.

"Oh, sorry," says Brandy. Then she turns to Sylvia. "I don't really want to look for your ball. Why don't you drop next to me?"

Gee, is that fair? Shouldn't she at least hit next to me?

"I think I'll just chip," says Sylvia. "My short game has always been pretty good." She eyes the foursome behind us, gathering on the tee and moving back-and-forth like impatient chickens. "Oh no. They're getting eager already."

I swing, and my shot is short of the green. It rolls lazily into a sand trap.

Within seconds, Brandy uses her five iron and pops the ball onto the green. "Bingo!" she cries, and pumps her fist. "This is one way to say I can compete with Tootsie Fennimore."

"I thought Bingo, Bango, Whatever was to help benefit Shonah and me," says Sylvia.

Brandy stores her club and bounces into the driver's seat. "You actually have to hit the ball in order to have any benefits. Now, to answer your question about Chlöe, no, I haven't seen her house. She's never hosted prior to tonight. Why is that?"

"If you saw her house, you'd know. Trust me, you might want to get a tetanus shot before you go over there."

"Geez, Sylvia," says Brandy. "What's up with you? That sounds more like something I'd say. Am I finally corrupting you?"

I can't hear Sylvia's response. Tootsie places her hand on my knee and squeezes. "I think Sylvia's out of sorts because of what happened with Amanda at her house. Think about it. We haven't had a Dice Club since."

We meet up again at Tootsie's ball. She gets out.

"I'm starting to wonder if this Dice Club is really working," says Sylvia. "We practically disbanded because of what happened at my house. And now Chlöe finally decides to host, and the idea of going there ...*ugh!*... and seeing Amanda's car in the parking lot outside the grief counselor's office ...it all just made me feel ...I don't know. Angry."

"Angry?" Brandy raises an eyebrow. "That makes NO sense. You *wanted* Amanda to get help."

"But what does that have to do with Chlöe?" I call. Tootsie looks at me, silently asking me to be quiet for her shot.

"Nothing. I don't know what I'm talking about." Sylvia shakes her head. Tootsie swings and puts it on the green. I want to applaud.

Brandy takes off and I hear Sylvia ask her to stop. "I'm going to use my pitching wedge," Sylvia says, and drops a snow white Titleist onto the sloping fairway. She positions herself over it, bounces slightly at the knees, pulls back the club to a quarter swing, and swings through the ball. It makes a satisfying sound and arches into the air, landing right next to the flag.

"Very good!" shouts Brandy. "Look how close it is to the hole. That has to be worth a 'bango.' I've already got the bingo by being first on the green."

"Sylvia put on her cap and came to the party," says Tootsie.

"At least I can do *that* right," said Sylvia.

I feel cheated.

We're on the green. We all look at each other and smile. It's a beautiful day. Tootsie sneezes twice and a big, black grackle perched on a dead branch of a eucalyptus tree lets out a squawk. "Are y'all going to Dice Club tonight?" asks Tootsie.

"Sure," Sylvia and I say together.

"Yes, of course I'll be there," laughs Brandy. "When have you known me to ever miss a party? After everything Sylvia's said about Chlöe's house, this is something I have to see."

Sylvia stamps her foot. "Would you stop?"

"I still haven't gotten my gift," says Tootsie.

I'm the farthest away from the hole, just inside the apron, after taking a couple swings to get out of the trap. I'm still a good sixty-five feet away from the pin. Brandy grabs the narrow rod of the flag. "Do you want this in or out?"

"Take it out, thanks." I squat behind the ball, close one eye and study the lie. I really don't know what I'm looking for other than a leaf or something halfway to the hole to help me aim in the right direction. I know I don't stand a chance of sinking it from so far out, although it would be nice to get a "dot" on the first hole so I, too, could feel I "put on my cap and came to the party." I square myself over the ball, look to the hole, look back at the ball—hole, ball, hole, ball—ease back my club and tap. "Go!" I know I didn't hit it hard enough.

"Louder!" cries Tootsie.

Brandy shakes her head in disappointment. "Gotta put some muscle into it, Shonah."

The ball stops a good fifteen feet shy. It's no "gimme" from there, and therefore I don't wait for anyone to say, "that's good." It wasn't.

"Who came up with the theme for this month?" asks Tootsie. "Am I supposed to go out and buy something with Lucy and Desi on it, or what?"

"*I Love Lucy*," says Sylvia. "Chlöe came up with it, of course."

"Yeah, but why *I Love Lucy*?" asks Tootsie, as she replaces her marker with her ball. She makes a wide circle around the hole, squats and studies her lie. Cocking her head left and then right, she rises and marches back to her ball. "We've been away from one another for so long we should call it something like 'Reunion Bunko.' "

Sylvia looks down the fairway and bristles at the four men standing with their hands on their hips and waiting for us. "Those jerks," she says. "Why are they always in such a rush?"

"They're not," says Tootsie.

"Ignore them," Brandy says. "We're fine."

Tootsie positions her feet, takes a step back and executes a practice putt.

"I was thinking about dressing up like Desi and bringing a set of bongo drums," I say.

"Hey, we could have called it 'Bingo, Bunko, Bongo!' " says Brandy.

Tootsie steps back and looks at her lie one more time.

"I was going to dress as Lucy," says Sylvia. "I can practice crying like her on this golf course today. *Waaaaaaaaaa!*"

"Be quiet while the pro makes her putt," scolds Brandy. "She's got a birdie on the line here."

"And a Bongo," says Tootsie as she taps the ball. Like the little engine that could, the pale yellow ball travels to the hole, peeks over the lip, and falls in. 'Yes!" says Tootsie. "The old gal still has it in her."

"You wish!" says Brandy.

"Brandy!" scolds Sylvia.

Brandy's jaw drops. "What?"

"It's okay," says Tootsie. "We're still in baby mode. It's okay to talk about it ya'll. I'm not taking my temperature anymore or calling up Michael in the middle of the day to meet me somewhere and get it on. So don't you worry about it. C'mon ladies. Let's put in the rest of these putts and move it along."

In Brandy's usual quick fashion, she taps the putt and it speeds past the hole and falls off to the left. "Whoops," she says. "So much for my birdie. I'll be lucky to save par on this one."

"I'd be more concerned about saving face if I were her," Sylvia says to me.

I make my putt for a seven on the hole and Sylvia steps up and taps in her "gimme." This time Brandy studies her lie, and after a series of practice swings, sinks the putt and happily takes her par. To celebrate, she replaces the flag and then poses momentarily in front of it with her hands on her hips, mirroring the stances of the men following us.

"It's going to be a long day fellas," she cries. "You'd better get used to it." She salutes them and walks off the green.

Chapter 8
A March Afternoon

What is it about the seeming anonymity of the Internet that gives us license to lose our tact? Since I started writing this column, my mailbox has been filled with commentators.

I'm happy to report that most of the emails are supportive, and I particularly like when readers share their own stories about some of the topics I cover. But then there's the occasional anonymous email that someone is compelled to send, which feels like someone giving me the finger on the road from behind the steel cage of an SUV.

I wonder, would the writer be that obnoxious in person?

—Shonah Bartlett
From her column, *The Dice Club Chronicles*

Cyberspace
TO: Sylvia Ostrander, TaraShephardPottery, Brandy Lynn, Amanda Prince, SBartlett, Blanca.Midnight, LPGATootsie, CanadianForrest
FROM: CanadianForrest
SUBJECT: Dice Club!!!

Hello Ladies,
Just a reminder about tonight's gathering at my house. Please try to be here by 6:30. I'm serving dinner at 7 and I want to start rolling by 7:45 at the latest. Remember I've got three kids to get to school in the morning and a million things to do, including going in early to the clinic to see about getting some extra hours. (Long story, I'll tell you later.) The theme is *I Love Lucy*. Use your imagination for the gift. P.S. The entire evening will be in black and white. I haven't heard from anyone

saying she can't make it. (Sylvia, have you?) I know most of you haven't
been here before so let me know if you need directions. BTW: Do you
think it would be possible to ask you all to BYOB?
Chlöe

TO: CanadianForrest
FROM: TaraShephardPottery
SUBJECT: RE: Dice Club!!!

Am I rude by asking what dinner will be ....? I'm choosing my
outfit.

TO: TaraShephardPottery
FROM: CanadianForrest
SUBJECT: RE: RE: Dice Club!!!

You kill me!

TO: Sylvia Ostrander, TaraShephardPottery, Brandy Lynn, Amanda
Prince, SBartlett, Blanca.Midnight, LPGATootsie, CanadianForrest
FROM: Brandy Lynn
SUBJECT: RE: Dice Club!!!

BYOB? You're kidding, right?

TO: CanadianForrest
FROM: TaraShephardPottery
SUBJECT: Food

And that means..............or are you not sure yet? I hear your [sic] a
wonderful cook. I have not had a morsel of food today............maybe
I am just hungry.

TO: TaraShephardPottery
FROM: CanadianForrest
SUBJECT: RE: Food

You're lying. No one has ever called me a wonderful cook. In fact, tonight you're all getting Swanson's Frozen TV dinners and we're eating on pop-up trays in front of the television. I'm just too busy today to cook. Does this help with your wardrobe selection? Brandy is giving me grief about BYOB, but I need the help. Roger just lost his job.

TO: CanadianForrest
FROM: Sylvia Ostrander
SUBJECT: RE: Dice Club!!!
Chlöe, do you realize you sent this message to Amanda? She quit. Remember?
—Sylvia

TO: Sylvia Ostrander
FROM: CanadianForrest
SUBJECT: RE: RE: Dice Club!!!
Oops! No, I didn't realize Amanda quit. I just used the group email list I had in my file. What should I do?

TO: Sylvia Ostrander, TaraShephardPottery, Brandy Lynn, Amanda Prince, SBartlett, Blanca.Midnight, LPGATootsie, CanadianForrest
FROM: Brandy Lynn
SUBJECT: BYOB
Hey Chlöe, I just thought of something. Thank God my dad is leaving tonight. I could bring what's left of his beer to your party. Is beer what you mean by the last B in BYOB? I could bring some Burgundy too if you like. I'm a red drinker. Maybe Sylvia still has those bottles of "Bitch." That's another B for ya!

TO: CanadianForrest
FROM: Blanca.Midnight
SUBJECT: RE: Dice Club!!!
I'm happy to bring some bottles for you. I still have some leftover from Leather and Lace Bunko back in November. I can also bring a plate of food. Let me know, *mi'ja*. Love, Blanca.

TO: Blanca.Midnight
FROM: CanadianForrest
SUBJECT: RE: RE: Dice Club!!!
If you want to bring a food tray, that would be great. You're a doll. Whatever bottles you could bring would help. Roger lost his job today and aside from that I still have a million things to do. I think I have to use a coffee table in the living room because I really don't have the space. Do you think anyone will mind? I don't. I better get back to my errands. See you tonight.
Chlöe

TO: CanadianForrest
FROM: SBartlett
SUBJECT: RE: Dice Club!!!
Hi Chlöe. Looking forward to it. Tootsie doesn't usually check her email. (Have you ever gotten a message from her?) I golfed with her today, though, and she said she was coming. See you tonight at 6:30 sharp!
Shonah

TO: CanadianForrest
FROM: Sylvia Ostrander
SUBJECT: Amanda
Well, it's too late now that you've sent it. Don't worry about it. If Amanda shows, she shows. BTW: She may have finally started getting some counseling. Lord knows I gave her a hundred cards of different grief counselors and maybe when she finally snapped at my house that night, it was the equivalent of rock bottom.
—S

TO: Sylvia Ostrander
FROM: CanadianForrest
SUBJECT: RE: Amanda
I'll be sure to have an extra TV dinner just in case. I'm praying for Amanda. I know I'd go crazy if something happened to one of my kids. Heaven forbid and knock wood!!! Signing off. I've got a million things to do!!!!!

TO: CanadianForrest
FROM: Sylvia Ostrander
SUBJECT: RE: RE: Amanda
You're not seriously serving TV dinners. Are you?
—S

TO: SBartlett
FROM: TaraShephardPottery
SUBJECT: Tonight's Dice Club
Shonah, I told Chlöe I was coming. Even that I was planning my outfit.
But I've been thinking about it and I'm not sure I want to go to Dice
Club tonight. I've managed to stop drinking for nearly five weeks and
if I go, it might send me over the edge. I think not having Dice Club
to go to for the past two months has been the reason why I'm able to
keep from drinking.
Love,
Tara

TO: TaraShephardPottery
FROM: SBartlett
SUBJECT: RE: Tonight's Dice Club
Tara, I'm not drinking either. We can both not drink together. Please
come tonight. I'll drive.
XOX,
Shonah

TO: SBartlett
FROM: TaraShephardPottery
SUBJECT: RE: RE: Tonight's Dice Club
I'll think about it. Call you later.
Love,
Tara

TO: Sylvia Ostrander, Brandy Lynn
FROM: SBartlett
SUBJECT: Tara
Hi you two. Tara needs our help. She didn't really want to discuss this

(so please don't say anything to her), but she stopped drinking and has managed to stay sober for a pretty long period this time. She's afraid to come to Dice Club because of the booze. I told her I wouldn't drink tonight. I think we really need to support her on this.
XOX,
Shonah

TO: SBartlett, Brandy Lynn
FROM: Sylvia Ostrander
SUBJECT: RE: Tara
Of course we'll support her. This is what friends are for.
—S

TO: Sylvia Ostrander, TaraShephardPottery, Brandy Lynn, Amanda Prince, SBartlett, Blanca.Midnight, LPGATootsie, CanadianForrest
FROM: Brandy Lynn
SUBJECT: RE: Tara
Tara's drinking problem is just that. Tara's drinking problem. I'm glad this sloppy drunk has found the strength to give it up, (it's about time) but it doesn't mean we have to as well. Remember one of our rules when we formed this club? "No drink counters!" I think she should

Brandy

My phone rings and it startles me. Before reaching across my desk for the telephone, I push a key on my computer to save my email. I've got a good rant going to Shonah and I don't want to lose it. The *whooshing* sound of a paper airplane—the signal of sent email—sounds just as the phone rings a second time. "Damn it! I didn't finish that." I pick up the portable phone and press the "talk" button. "Hello?"

"It's me," says the familiar voice of my twin, Sandy. "I've made arrangements to take Dad to the airport tonight."

"Good. It's about time you pitched in."

"I know, I know. I'll be home at five-thirty. I'm helping a buddy paint his rental unit today. Can you make sure Dad's packed and ready to go?"

"We'll see, Sandy. I've got my elbow dislocation patient I have to run to the office to see because I just got off the golf course. And I've got Dice Club tonight for the first time in ages."

"You and your Dice Club. What do you women actually do at these meetings?"

"Wouldn't you like to know?"

"So, do you all sit around bashing men and burning bras?"

I sigh. "Jesus H. Christ. What decade do you live in anyway?"

"I don't know, Bran, you've managed to bring the topic of male bashing into the twenty-first century. I used to think having a twin sister gave me some insight into how the female mind worked. But lately, you're going off in a direction I sure as hell don't understand."

"Blame Dad," I look at my watch. I've got fifteen minutes before I have to be out the door and still need to iron my shirt and clean up the breakfast dishes left by the kids. "By the way, it's a party, not a meeting, and it's at Chlöe the Canadian's house. From what I heard, I'll bet it could use a coat of paint. A real dive."

"Tempting," he says laughing. "Do your friends know how you talk about them behind their backs?"

"Just telling it like it is, brother."

"That's my sister."

My phone emits a high-pitched tone. "My call-waiting is going off. Listen, don't worry. I'll have Dad ready. I've had him packed for days. It's like, 'don't let the door hit you in the ass on the way out,' if you know what I mean."

"Get your call," he says, and hangs up.

I listen for the dial tone, click the "off" button, and wait for the phone to ring. As soon as it does, I answer. "Hello?"

"Brandy, are you a complete imbecile?"

"Who is this?"

"It's Shonah. You sent that last email to Tara! To everyone! How could you do that? And it wasn't even finished."

"Oh, crap!" I move the mouse next to my computer to light up the screen and click on the "sent mail" folder. Spying the last sent piece of mail in the "TO" column, I click on "Sylvia Ostrander." The message immediately fills the screen. "To Sylvia Ostrander, TaraShephardPottery…" My eyes move through the extended list of the Dice Club,

"…oh no!" Scrolling through the record of my "sent mail," it looks like I addressed the entire group to all the messages I sent today. Damn cyberspace! Damn it to hell! I let out a deep breath and drop my chin. My head throbs and I can't help but shake it back-and-forth so that my hair falls into a curtain, covering my eyes.

"Oh no is right," says Shonah. "What's wrong with you? I suggested Tara needs our help and you go and write this to the entire group? And you sent it to her? Is there a way to unsend it?"

"God, I don't know. Is there? Why did I click on the group address?"

My heart pounds heavily inside my chest and I feel my body temperature rising. "I was just thinking about ...wait a minute." My mind goes
into fast-forward motion. "If we have the same server, which let me
see . . ." I straighten, and double-check Tara's full email address. "We
don't. Shit! I didn't mean to send it to her. I didn't mean to send it
at all. My phone rang—*stupid* Sandy—and I accidentally hit the send
key." I bite my lip.

"Yeah, I've done that too," says Shonah. "But I've never sent something like this. It's so hurtful, Brandy. She asked me not to discuss it
with you guys. She's going to think the entire Dice Club has been talking behind her back."

"We DO talk behind her back. Please! The tits alone have been a
topic of many a conversation. We talk about everybody. Sylvia's Botox?
Tootsie's infertility? Chlöe's..."

"I don't care about that," interrupts Shonah. "Boob jobs, babies, and
Botox are fair game."

"And booze isn't?"

"No, it isn't. Even so, people aren't supposed to KNOW what you
say about them behind their backs. That's why it's called 'behind your
back.' "

As Shonah speaks, I reread my unfinished message. "Oh, it's not that
bad. Maybe Tara doesn't have to see it. Can you call her husband and
ask him to delete it? Or better yet, can you run next door?"

"Are you out of your mind?" Shonah is incredulous. "I'm not going
to do either. Besides, if I know Ian, he won't erase it. And Brandy, it *is*
bad. It's not only insensitive, it's mean—especially because you sent
it to everyone. What did you expect to accomplish?"

I feel a lump form in my throat. It's like unexpectedly swallowing
a big round piece of hard-candy, a sour ball. Tears form in my eyes.
"You're right," I say softly. "I told you, I didn't mean to send it all. Oh
my God, I'm such a bitch."

"Yeah, you are," Shonah says flatly. "I mean, we all know you've
been under a lot of strain with your dad there, and I think we've been
pretty supportive."

The soft blonde hairs on the back of my neck prickle. I reach for
the top of my computer screen and slam it closed. A vision of my
white-haired, weary-faced father fills my mind. I think of the nights of
my youth when our mother was still alive and our father sloshed his
way through another meal, recounting embellished tales of his days at
sea. And how he ridiculed my older sisters and my mother of being too
"female" to offer anything useful to society. Wiping away these fleeting

thoughts as I've done so many times before, I think of how I had never even come close to sharing with my so-called friends what it was like to be on the receiving end of my father's physical abuses.

"Brandy," says Shonah, "Tara is... "

"A sloppy drunk," I blurt out, interrupting her. "You're the one who told me her daughter once discovered her passed out in her own puke."

"What?" gasps Shonah. "That wasn't gossip. It was..."

"Gossip! Gossip? Who gives a crap? Don't think I don't know what it's like to grow up in an alcoholic house. My old man was a mean drunk, but at least he was functional."

"I don't believe you, Brandy. You're not a mean drunk. You're just plain mean. I'm not only mad at you for not being supportive of Tara, I'm mad that she's going to think Sylvia and I and the rest of the Club don't support her either. For your information, I haven't had a drink in over a month. Not that you'd notice anything about anyone else besides yourself."

"What's that supposed to mean?"

"I think you know what it means. Did you ever stop to think why Amanda spilled that glass of wine in your lap? Really, Brandy, do you have any clue what it means to be supportive of your friends?"

"What does Amanda Prince have to do with this?"

An uncomfortable silence grows between us. I hear Shonah take a deep breath. But I speak before she can say anything. "You told me yourself you thought Amanda was completely out of line at Christmas Dice Club. Are you now saying I deserved it?"

"No, no," says Shonah. "I'm not saying that. I don't think you deserved it. You were just an easy target for her that night. Everyone isn't as strong as you. Not everyone gets your sense of humor."

"Man, Shonah. Are you sure you want to go down this path?"

"What path? The path leading to a stronger friendship? The path of honesty? Of understanding? Of ...forgiveness? Man, Brandy! I told you, I'm pissed. And right now I'm on a pissed off path. Sometimes we all have to face the ugly truth."

"Oh that's rich coming from you, Shonah. You and that column of yours where all day long you sit back and write about us, judging from your high-and-mighty throne."

"I'm not judging."

"You'd like to believe that. But it's a real invasion of privacy. And as for Tara, I mean, good for you that you can choose not to drink to support your friend, but for an alcoholic it's a much bigger decision. Are you going to write about that too?"

"Wait a minute," starts Shonah. "How did this get turned on me? I've written about alcohol and my feelings toward it without giving away. . ."

"No, you wait and let me finish saying what I was going to write in that email. I'm glad Tara is coming to grips with her problem. Really, I am. But sooner or later she's going to learn that it's a world bathed in alcohol. It's everywhere. Including Dice Club. If she can't be around it than she shouldn't come."

"Oh, I'm pretty sure she won't after she reads that email from you."

"Good. Let *me* be the bad guy. I've spent enough years at Al-anon meetings to know that in dealing with alcoholics you've got to put on your armor. They—and all their enablers—don't like to have their faces rubbed in it. But trust me, if they actually go into recovery and work the twelve steps, they'll make an inventory. They'll realize how their drinking has affected the people around them."

"What has Tara ever done to you?"

"Besides make a complete ass of herself nearly every time I've been with her in the past three years? And there you are always taking care of her. Always driving her home. Uh, can you say 'enabler?' "

"God, Brandy! I can't believe how judgmental you are."

"Right. I forgot you were perfect."

"Stop it," Shonah says. "This is getting ridiculous. We're friends, Brandy. I'd like to think we were close friends. But I'm close with Tara, too, and right now she needs my support. She's working at this thing. It's not enabling her to just let her know we're on her side."

"I AM on her side!"

From the corner of my eye, I see the time on my watch. How did I think I could actually take four hours today and spend it on the god-damn golf course. It wasn't even worth it. Tootsie beat me by twenty strokes.

I open my computer again and when it pops to life, I confirm I'll be late for my elbow dislocation. "I've got to go, Shonah. Listen, we can talk this through another time. I'm sorry about what I did. I really didn't mean to include Tara on that email. It was some kind of Freudian slip, I guess. A high-tech one."

"I'm beginning to hate email," Shonah says.

"Tell me about it." I push the "off" button on my phone. Two more messages had beeped into my "in box" while Shonah was reading me the riot act. They'll have to remain unread for now. I still need to iron my shirt. And the dishes will have to wait.

Sylvia

A dial tone blares from my phone and I pull it away from my face. Brandy is not picking up. What a fool! How could she send out the email to everyone in the group? It had to be an accident.

I *knew* someday she'd say or do something to cause a real hurt or a real problem. She made Amanda so mad she spilled a drink in her lap! And now …God knows how Tara is going to respond to being called a "sloppy drunk!"

Those golf shoes really hurt my feet. I shouldn't have tried to play the entire course. What a disaster.

I look at my phone, not knowing what to do. I wonder if Tara has read the email and if there's a way to prevent her from doing so if she hasn't. Should I call her? Should I call Shonah? Yes, that's it. Shonah can run next door and make sure Tara's okay. I dial her number.

"C'mon," I moan, shaking the phone as it rings, the way I sometimes jiggle the toilet handle after a flush, hoping to encourage a response. After the third ring, she finally answers and I speak before she can say hello. "It's Sylvia. Did you read Brandy's email?"

"What was she thinking?" cries Shonah. "I just got off the phone with her."

"Who, Brandy? Or Tara?"

"Brandy. We had a fight about it."

"Really?"

"I called her an imbecile and she accused me of thinking I was perfect."

"Oh boy." I can only sigh. Glad it wasn't me. I move to the mirror in my powder room, lean forward and furrow my brow. Looks like the Botox is holding up. I test my smile. The lines around my mouth are getting deeper. Maybe I should try the Restylane. Or there's something called Perlane now too. Shonah's talking but I'm not listening.

"…I've always said I didn't want to get on Brandy's bad side. Now I know why," I hear her say.

I flip off the light and walk into the hall. "I wouldn't worry about it. Brandy's a very smart woman. I'm sure she knows she made a mistake and she'll make it right. If anyone understands alcoholism, it's Brandy. Her mother was even worse than her father."

"Really? I didn't know that."

I stop dead in my tracks. "Oh God, you didn't hear it from me." *Damn!* "How do I get myself involved with these things?"

"It doesn't matter," says Shonah. "This is about Tara and how we can support her. Offering my support—whether it's not drinking around her or just listening to her—is the least I can do for her. I'm not sure I would have begun facing my own issues with alcohol if it weren't for her."

I pass my well-stocked wine refrigerator. I don't want to think about my issues with alcohol. But Tara definitely has a problem. "Maybe we should have another Betty Ford Bunko. A real rehab one this time."

"I hear ya, sister. Listen, I gotta go. I'm going to call Tara and make sure she's okay. See you tonight?"

"If anyone's still going. Should I give Chlöe a call?"

"No. Don't tell her about all this. She doesn't need to know."

"I won't. God, with the way this day's been going, the only one who will show up is Amanda. Those group list emails went to her too."

"They did?" asks Shonah. "I was so caught up in the letter going to Tara, I didn't see that."

My golf shoes are sitting next to the front door. "Hey by the way, did you have fun on the golf course?"

"No. I hate golf. And I have a real problem with how much water they use to keep the course green. This is the desert!"

I kick off my shoes. "Maybe you should move back to Oregon."

"Maybe."

"Bye for now."

I walk to the kitchen and place the phone back in the cradle. Walking toward my bedroom, I wonder. What should I wear to Dice Club tonight?

Tara
TO: CanadianForrest
FROM: TaraShephardPottery
SUBJECT: RE: Dice Club!!!
Chlöe, I can't make it tonight. Something came up. Sorry for the late notice.

I pull down the "Sign Off" menu, click and release. "Goodbye," says the familiar voice of the AOL cyber man. I flip my hands, palms up, and study my quivering fingers. The shaking comes and goes.

Turning in the swivel chair, I get up and slowly walk down the narrow hall from the den to the kitchen. My kitchen is an ever-changing palette of color—as metamorphic as a gallery. The tiled walls behind the sink and countertops portray the rich hues of a serape. All bright, happy reds, blues, purples, oranges, yellows—a Mexican fiesta was on my mind as I painted and fired each tile and then placed them on the walls without guides. Grout lines vary in size and shards of shiny glass and a treasure of crystals and gemstones punctuate the mosaic design. While creating it, I was mesmerized by my own artistic palette—a drunken artist, hallucinating in vivid color, and distracting me from knowing when it was time for the party to be over.

My thoughts stagnate. I squint against the sunrays pouring into the room. They reflect off the stainless steel refrigerator and dishwasher, a recent remodeling expense when I decided to change from black-faced appliances.

In the middle of the room, I stop. Arrested. I feel like I'm in a spotlight, a harsh glare magnifying every feature. I glance left, and then right, a feral cat sensing a predator. Struggling to focus, I can't make out the time on the clock. The black hands look like shadows. I know my kids are in school. Who knows where Ian is? Did he say he was going out? I try hard to imagine his whereabouts, but no answer comes. I don't know. Yet there is something I do know, and it's both painfully obvious and delightfully clear.

I know I'm alone. No husband. No kids. No ...friends.

Turning around, I spy the half-size cabinet doors above the two-tiered, stainless-steel-faced oven. I approach, reach, and slide my fingers through the handles from the outside in, so that my fingertips momentarily touch. Then, with the strength I might have used to pull open the iron doors of an old church, I expose the collection of dark bottles.

My bare heels lift off the floor, and I feel the pressure at the base of my toes. There are old, smudged bottles of red wine—probably vinegar by now—sticky brown bottles of Baileys and Kahlua. I push them aside, and take comfort in the clanking sound of glass against glass. A half-full bottle of Rose's Lime, a sickening shade of green, looks pitiful, like the runt of the litter. I push it aside as well. Lowering myself to my heels, I step back.

It's not in here.

I can't waste my time with anything but a full strength dose. Not after all these weeks. Diagnosis: Drunk. Dosage: Absolut. It must be in the freezer. The studio freezer.

I turn my back on the traitorous cabinet, leaving the doors open like a pile of dirt collected by the broom but not swept into the dustpan. Evidence. I'm a sloppy criminal failing to cover the clues leading to my ultimate prosecution. I return to the narrow hallway, and pass the large double doors of our front entry. I pass the den, the powder room, and the hallway leading to the girls' wing. I near the door made of mesquite planks and wrought iron—the door of my sanctuary. My studio. And just as I reach for the latch, the doorbell sounds.

"Bing-*bong*!" A classic tone. My hand freezes on the hand-forged latch. Alamo, the dog, lets out one low, annoyed bark. Caught.

The doorbell sounds again and the dog releases another Pavlovian response. I don't have to answer the door. Let whomever it is think I'm either not home or working in my studio. I am, after all, on the way to my studio. I can get away with this. Alamo will never tell.

Disengaging the latch, I pull open the door. The welcoming, earthy aroma of my art envelops me. Guiding the door closed, I switch on the light, and let out a deep exhale. "Safe." My gaze is like a dagger, aiming straight for the dorm-sized refrigerator stationed under the back counter like a safe. I march toward it, pull open the door—no combination necessary—and squat.

"What?" My heart rate increases. "Where is it?"

The wire rack is barren. It's not even very cold. "Where IS it?" Did I drink it? Did I remove it or stash it somewhere else? Did someone take it? Ian? I pivot toward the accordion door in the opposite corner of the room. It encloses the storage cabinet where I store smocks, aprons, tarps and clean-up rags. Across the room in no time, I push open the door and the accordion folds snap against the metal doorframe. I'm feeling frantic. I pull open the top drawer of a paint-stained, wooden bureau. Rummaging, looking only for the buried treasure—a silver flask I had once slipped inside the garter belt I wore as a Halloween costume when dressed as Marilyn Monroe—"Sugar"—in *Some Like It Hot*. It's not there.

"Damn it!" Such obstacles.

I push the top drawer closed and open the one beneath it. Strike two.

One drawer left. I pull out the third drawer and as soon as I reach in, I feel it. It's smooth and slightly cold to the touch. What a relief. Wasting no time, I grasp the flask and see it as a miniature version of my kitchen appliances. Unscrewing the cap, I lower my nose to the small, round opening. The potency alerts my senses with all the power of smelling salts.

The flask is at my lips. I press toward it, as though meeting a lover for a long-awaited first kiss. I feel my neck arching back. My eyes are closed, and my lips suckle the spout. Hot, searing liquid spills past my teeth, soaks my tongue and blazes its way down my craving throat.

I don't taste. I feel.

I feel an eruption of sweat tingle the spot on my head where my hair meets my brow. I feel the carnal, single-mindedness of a dragon in dry dock and searching for its moat. Each second of the swallowing supplies a feeling of both satiation and yearning.

It's a powerful, potent cocktail.

My eyes open. A boiling pressure inflames my nose. The feeling travels through my sinuses and stings the whites of my eyes. They glaze over and I imagine them turning crimson. But tears do not spill down my warming cheeks. Not yet. Instead, the toxic fluid slowly seeps down my throat. It knows the route into my system—a familiar and well-traveled path. Vodka, like lighter fluid, ignites the fire in my belly.

My head, at once heavy, comes forward, chin to chest. The colors around me blend and swirl. They go from rich, harsh pigments to softer, demure pastels. Aah. I'm medicated. Relieved. It's my chemotherapy.

Bang! Bang! Bang! Urgent pounding at the studio door fills the room.

The flask slips from my fingers and hits the concrete floor with a low-pitched thud. I squat to retrieve it—to stash it once again. Putting my hand atop the square container, envisioning it as an IV bag, in a quick movement, it slides forward and causes me to fall upon my chest. My knees give way and I ram my forehead into the wall supporting the accordion door. The sharp tracks of the jamb slice into me. The pain is acute and immediate. Lightening strikes behind my eyes, like too many flashbulbs on a pageant runway.

Again there's banging on the door. "Tara, I know you're in there. Open up!"

The voice from the outside is muffled. But I recognize it. I bring my hand to my brow and wince. "Ow!" There's bound to be a bruise.

"Tara! I can see you. Let me in," calls the voice.

The room has gone dark. The colors have disappeared. I blink. Is someone shining a flashlight in my face? What happened?

I look toward the door. The pounding has stopped. Barring the hum from the empty refrigerator, the room is quiet. Slowly rising to my knees, I'm face-to-face with the narrow wall next to the accordion door. I cock my head to the right and lean forward, studying the pencil marks hashing across the wall from floor to ceiling. My throat tightens as the pencil marks fill me with memories. I trace the recorded heights of my children, from nineteen inches, to twenty-eight inches, to thirty-two to thirty-seven. The numbers are made by various tones of lead, and in some cases, ink. Some are smudged. Those toward the middle of the wall are in a different, more juvenile hand. When had the girls taken over this annual chore? Now engrossed with the wall chart of the girls' heights, I lift myself like a hatchling, shedding a rough, broken, and once protective shell. Reaching up, I grow tall. At full height

I find my own name, "—TARA, 1999." It was the year Ian had built the new studio. Towering above that, "—IAN, 1999." Crowning the height chronicle of my immediate family in Ian's familiar, boxy hand it reads, "Shephard I-Q Scale." Then next to his name, "Genius Level." It makes me smile. Ian can always make me smile.

Where is he?

I sense someone in the room and turn around to see a tall, dark shadow standing in front of the door. As motionless as a statue, I realize at once it's not my husband.

"How did you get in here?"

"Key," says Shonah, holding up a small, blue key. "You gave it to me. Remember?"

I look away and move toward a stool at the workbench. "What do you want?"

"I …I," stammers Shonah, no doubt taken aback by my snarling tone. I turn to see her shift her weight. Her eyes move to the floor where I catch her looking at the flask. She looks back at me and gasps. "I wanted to see if you were okay."

"Why wouldn't I be okay?"

Shonah steps toward me. "Tara, for heaven's sake. You're bleeding!"

"It's nothing." I lift my hand to the wound on my forehead. With a quick wipe, I lower my fingers and examine them. The blood is a healthy shade of red.

"It doesn't look like nothing. Let me get you a clean cloth."

"No!" Oh God, I'm shouting. "You've done enough for me today I should think."

"Oh," says Shonah. "I see. Obviously you got that email. Listen, I…"

"You what? You wanted to tell me what a loyal and trustworthy friend you are? Tell me how much you support me?"

Shonah halts as though I'd pointed a gun at her. "Well, yes, I…"

"Bullshit, Shonah! Bull *SHIT!* I asked you not to talk about this with Sylvia and Brandy and clearly you couldn't keep yourself from sharing this juicy little story."

"Tara, it's not like that."

"No? No-o. It's not like that. Why don't you tell me what it is like? Huh, Shonah? The great, know-it-all guru of life in the suburbs!"

Shonah

Didn't I just hear the same words from Brandy?

"...Oh that's rich coming from you. You and that column of yours where all day long you sit back and write about us, judging from your high-and-mighty throne..."

Brandy's harsh tone echoes in my head. Is this the line on me? The name they call me behind my back? The proverbial light bulb zaps me like a laser beam. Of course it is. And why should it surprise me? We all talked about one another. Why should I be immune?

Quickly, I begin an inventory. I recall a recent conversation about Sylvia's Botox injections and about Blanca Midnight's underwear ads. Chlöe has too many goats and a hovel of a house. Tootsie has a freakish fetish for wrapping paper.

As for Tara, everyone in the group recognizes her drinking problem. She's made it impossible for us not to be concerned. And that's all I am. Concerned. My concern is the reason I'm here. My eyes return to the flask on the floor. "You're drinking again, aren't you?"

"Yeah, so what? You should love that," Tara says. Rising, she reaches for a large plastic bag filled with wet clay. Perching on her stool, her painted toes like talons clutching the bottom rung, she clasps the top of the bag and heaves it toward her with a grunt. She rolls down the sides of the bag and plunges her fist into the clay. "Go and report it to your friends. Better yet, why don't you write about in your column?"

She opens her fist, stretching her fingers into the substance she knows so well. It's the substance over which she has absolute power to mold into the creations inside her head.

She looks at me. "That's right. *Your* friends. Let them all take pleasure in my weakness. Just like you do every single time you sit down and write your convoluted versions of our pathetic lives."

Schadenfreude. I purse my lips and feel my teeth grind together. Shifting my weight, I consider the feeling of being accused of taking pleasure in another's misery. "You're wrong, Tara. That's not the case."

"Am I?"

"I've never thought of my friends' lives as pathetic. Never." I shake my head, but Tara doesn't see me. She continues digging into the gray, lifeless clay.

"Don't deny it, Shonah. I'll bet ya'll just love it that things are going wrong for the group LUSH! I know what everyone says about me. I know you're jealous of my looks and my success. Ya'll just wish you had a husband as attentive as mine! That's right. I *know* it. You may think I'm stupid, but I know what's going on. I know more than you think.

I don't have some highbrow advanced degree in English Literature or Journalism or even Art bloody History, but I've earned my success through hard work and talent. And I've had to deal with jealous, petty bitches my entire life. You're just one more, Shonah Bartlett. As far as I'm concerned you and the entire Dice Club can go fuck yourselves!"

"Tara!" My God, I've never heard her talk like this. What's happening? The walls are closing in on me and a buzz begins inside my head. I lift my fingers to my forehead and push away my stick-straight bangs, and run my finger between twin vertical lines dividing my brows like double exclamation points. "You're mistaken," I tell her. "Sadly, sadly mistaken. I *am* your friend, Tara. I care about you as much as I care about anyone in my life that I love."

I reach out to her and feel a warm tear cascade down my cheek. I don't wipe it away. With another step, I stop the moment Tara looks up. The tissue around her cut has swollen and turned purple. Her face is twisted with anger.

"Don't touch me," she says. "Please, just leave me alone. I don't want you here."

I sigh. "Oh Tara, I know what you've been going through, and whether or not you believe me, I'm trying to find a way to support you. I'm going to keep trying, no matter how hard you make it. No matter how much you might try to push me away."

"Keep telling yourself that, Shonah," Tara says. She releases the clay, returning the unformed blob she has been kneading between her fingers to the mother lode, and rolls the bag closed. She puts her feet on the floor, stands and turns her back to me, now only three feet from her. Without turning she says, "I think you are a traitor in every sense and that no one's personal business is safe with you. I think you should...I think you should ...just get *out!*"

"What?"

It's so unfair. So utterly unreasonable.

Tara is clearly not well. She's suffering and she's blaming, and she's going to need my support even more. I will her to look me in the face. But she won't. She's as stoic as a sentry, smoldering like a candle that has just been extinguished.

I have no choice. I turn and quietly leave.

Tara

The studio door closes, and I turn in time to see the tall, dark figure of my neighbor—and former friend—walk away. Turning again, I look on the floor near the accordion door, and spot my precious flask sparkling in the sunlight. It's like the wink of a trusted friend.

I walk toward it, scoop it from the floor, and devour the last drops of salvation.

Shonah

My usual long strides are shortened. Putting one foot in front of the other, I watch the white, meshed toes of my Nike running shoes propel me forward. Caribbean blue pool water sparkles beside me, ground-hovering purple lantana lines the flagstone path. I reach the back gate leading out of Tara's lush oasis. Turning around, I survey the landscaping. It's the yard of an artist. Fuchsia, tissue-paper thin blooms of bougainvillea and bubblegum pink oleander flowers cover the tall, stucco walls. Purple, suggesting royalty and opulence, is the dominant color. It's the same color as Tara's forehead wound.

Before opening the gate, I reach out and pluck a cluster of oleander, a loose pompon of color. I throw it over my shoulder. "This is poisonous." Tara surrounds herself with poison.

I step through the gate, and with extra force pull the door closed with a slam. Opening lines for a column travel through my brain like the running tape across the bottom of a television newscast:

"Is there anything that defines unfairness more than the feeling of injustice?"

"Got an alcoholic in your life? Put on your armor."

"How many emails does it take to ruin a friendship?"

"Hi, my name's Shonah and I'm an ...I'm a ..."

"I'm a what?" I ask the enormous, multi-armed saguaro residing on the property line between our houses. One thorny arm protrudes upward from the sturdy trunk. It reaches high, like a waiter carrying a tray overhead. Next month, the cactus flowers will bloom, and the white clusters atop this "arm" will resemble a plate of cauliflower.

Will I ever stop living my life according to lead sentences?

A pack of coyotes howls and yaps like a band of Indians in an old, western movie. It sounds like there's a dozen—perhaps fighting over a mole or a jackrabbit—but there are probably only three or four. Their voices fall and rise in sharp octaves. It's a familiar sound, which I once thought haunting and sinister. Now, after so many years in the desert, the reverberation is musical and comforting, and as predictable as a sunset.

I kick the gravel road, a little more forcefully with each step. Pebbles scatter in sharp directions and golf ball-sized stones roll in my wake. Small clouds of dust emerge like exhaust from an engine picking up steam, releasing energy.

Reaching the gate to my backyard I kick it. Hard. "This is so unfair!"

Stepping inside, I walk past a scrappy, green Palo Verde tree and through the garden of voluntary prickly pears, massive cactus clusters with faces the size of ping pong paddles. I reach the *ramada* next to our pool and look at the padded chair. I'm too wound up to sit. Pacing back-and-forth, a faint yet rhythmic squeak escapes from my left shoe.

The howls of the coyotes simmer and my mind is filled with images of Tara. I remember the first time I met her. It was at a Labor Day party, put on by one of our neighbors. Dan and I had just moved into our home, and both boys were still in diapers. Our youngest was still on the boob. I was in the kitchen and feeling awkward because I didn't know anyone. So, I offered to help the lady of the house, JoEllen Merritt, get the food on the buffet tables.

"Here," said JoEllen, a woman in late middle age with frosted, helmet-head hair and a square jaw. She handed over wooden salad spoons and I noticed her French polish and her oversized diamond rings. "Why don't you dress and toss this salad. That would help."

"Simple enough," I said. I grabbed the wooden spoons and peeked into the attached family room where the men had gathered in front of the television set. They were watching a sporting event of some kind, citing newspaper sport's page statistics, and drinking beer. My baby lay quietly in a bouncy chair at the foot of the sofa next to Dan. Sammy, my elder son, was in the corner constructing primary-colored buildings with oversized Lego blocks. Satisfied with everyone's safety, I poured the oil and vinegar mixture atop the leafy greens and plunged the wooden tools into the bowl. Gingerly, so that I didn't spill anything on the counter, I mixed together the ingredients.

"Give me those!" said a high-pitched voice from out of nowhere. Before I could turn to see who was attached to the voice, the salad spoons were torn from my hands and a hip bump pushed me aside. "Hasn't anyone ever shown you how to toss a salad?"

Stunned, I stepped back and stared at the most beautiful head of red hair I had ever seen. It flowed over the woman's shoulders, hanging nearly into the salad bowl, and moved like a prom dress—swooshing back-and-forth—as this woman with the ear-piercing southern accent, this salad spoon stealer, wildly tossed lettuce leaves. Drops of oil flew from the bowl, spattering like bacon grease in a hot frying pan. Saturated lettuce leaves spilled to the counter.

"This is how ya do it!" said the woman, laughing, almost maniacally.

"That's Tara Shephard," whispered JoEllen. "She lives next door to you." JoEllen used her hand to mime a drink pouring into her mouth.

"Aah, I see," was all I managed to say. Hearing a crash in the family room, I turned and witnessed Sammy destroying the Lego building he had just created. Happily, he fell upon the spilled toys. I shook my head and smiled, and then spied the tossed salad covering half the area of the countertop, just like so many forsaken Lego blocks. Abandoning the project, Tara had moved to the bar where a tall, balding man stared at her predominant cleavage. She waited as he turned the martini shaker from side to side. Tara swiveled her hips and looked up at him like an expectant child waiting for praise.

"She's some kind of ex-beauty queen. Keep your husband away from her. And by the way, can you say 'boob job?' "

"Really? How can you tell?"

"Girl, what color is the sky in your world? I can spot 'em a mile away. Especially in this Valley." She took a step back and examined my ample chest. "Yours look real. But then again, you're nursing, aren't you? You're in for sag city when that chapter of your life ends. Trust me. I nursed three. All off spending their trust funds by now, God bless 'em. I know women your age. You'll be taking the name of her plastic surgeon in no time."

I frowned and adjusted my bra strap. I will not, I thought.

I looked back toward the bar and was surprised to see Tara staring directly at me. I remember shifting my weight, and cocking my eyebrow as I watched the ex-beauty queen flash a winning smile. She winked at me.

I will always remember that wink and how it made me feel. Somehow, that wink made me feel …chosen. And at that moment, I decided I liked Tara Shephard.

We started running together the next morning.

Finally, I sit down and release a regretful sigh. The trilling of a hummingbird makes me snap my head to the right. It's like the sound of someone saying, *"Pssst! Over here. I've something to tell you!"* I spot the tiny bird, and hold my breath while watching it hover over a hot pink penstimmon flower. It pokes its narrow beak into the tubular blossom, moving back-and-forth—in-and-out—like a crafter performing needlepoint. Its wings are invisible, flapping at the speed of light. Its colors are marvelous—metallic green and blue—glazed pottery more beautiful than anything Tara could ever create.

I blink and the tiny bird darts off. "Pssst!" What was it trying to tell me?

Left staring into the azure sky, the humming bird becomes a fleeting memory. I look past my own garden wall and see the orange tiled rooftop of Tara's studio, a place I once thought of as the house of my best friend. It brings a frown. Now it feels like enemy territory.

"What are we? A couple of sixth graders?" We are middle-aged women, and yet we're fighting like middle schoolers.

But alcoholism isn't exactly a middle school problem.

I scratch my head as another opening line comes to me: *"Friend-ship. Is it worth it?"*

Like a champagne cork popping from a bottle, I shoot out of my chair and hurry inside, where I sit down in front of my computer.

Chapter 9
A March Evening

When it comes to lessons of friendship, I can't help but think back to the sixth grade. It was a pivotal year for me, when I moved from a private, parochial school to a public school. It was the year I learned a few important lessons regarding girl-to-girl relationships.

Thirty-five years have gone by and much to my surprise, today I learned the lessons of sixth grade didn't end with an elementary school diploma. Today I learned that some girls—and I may be one of them—never really get out of the sixth grade. It's just that our problems are no longer about A: acne and B: boyfriends.

They're more about A: addiction and B: bunko.

—Shonah Bartlett
From her column, *The Dice Club Chronicles*

Brandy

I almost didn't come to Dice Club tonight. But I knew I had to. We haven't met since Christmas Dice Club at Sylvia's and I don't want the group to disband. But so far only Sylvia and I have shown up and Chlöe's getting impatient. Maybe they've gotten lost trying to find this little dump in the back corner of the Valley. It looked like an exclusive subdivision until I turned off on the dirt road that leads to Chlöe's place. Thinking it was an alley or a utility road, I almost missed the turn.

This house is very compartmentalized. Low ceilings make it feel even smaller than it is. There's a root beer like stain on the drywall next to a cloudy skylight and the distinct odor of animal in the air. Cat piss I think. It's downright assaulting. Honestly, my stables smell better than this. Now I know why she hasn't volunteered to host in the past.

"Where is everyone?" asks our hostess. She looks at her watch for the fourth time in five minutes. "I was pretty clear in my email that I wanted to start rolling by seven o'clock. Doesn't anyone have a respect for schedules? We should have been eating twenty minutes ago!"

"Maybe the TV dinners turned them off," I suggest, trying to avoid getting blamed for people not showing up.

"Well, we all know why Tara isn't here," says Sylvia. She scowls at me.

I mirror her scowl, which I'm totally sick of, and warn, "Don't start."

"What?" asks Chlöe, "Did I miss something?"

I try to respond but Sylvia speaks first. "Didn't you see the email Brandy accidentally sent to the group?"

"No," answers Chlöe. "I got one from Tara asking me what dinner would be so she could plan her outfit, and Blanca Midnight said she'd bring bottles leftover from Leather and Lace Bunko. Then I had to switch off line and immediately go out and buy my gift for the bag, along with two new pairs of soccer socks—you know, Roger Jr. is on the traveling team with Shonah's son and he goes through them like mad since the coach never takes him out of the game. They're kicking butt heading into State Cup at the end of this month. Then I had to put in an appearance at the clinic—as if I really had time today. I'm thinking of going full time there, but stopped at Valley General to put in an application. I have a friend who works there and she's always talking to me about switching over to the hospital instead of the clinic. You guys know Janice Wasserman, don't you? She's a substitute nurse at the school like me. Anyway, the pay's better. I don't know how I'm going to manage getting everything done if I have to put in forty hours. Or if they make me do twelve hour shifts? That wouldn't be good. If only Roger hadn't lost his job. I might not have a choice. Anyway, what were we talking *aboot*?"

I'm not listening.

Chlöe finally takes a breath and pulls chili pepper-covered oven mitts from her hands. She tests the temperature of the foil atop one of the TV dinners.

"Did you say something about Janice Wasserman?" I ask, again happy to keep the subject off Tara's drinking problem and the accidental email. I know it's only a matter of time before everyone will have read the email and I'll officially be labeled the club's heartless bitch. I know Janice from Valley Verde Golf Club. Talk about a bitch.

Chlöe is busy with the foil and she doesn't respond to my question. I sip my wine and check my watch. Dad's probably on the plane by now. Sandy came through and managed to get him to the airport. No doubt my old man's charming Jack Daniels after Jack Daniels out of the first class flight attendant. He'll be lucky to make it home from the airport. *Christ!* Bring on the guilt. It stabs me just below the belly button. I pat the pocket of my jeans, feeling for my cell phone. Whom can I call to meet him at the airport? Is it Burbank or LAX? Orange County? I don't even know and I'm sure Sandy didn't think to make home transport arrangements. Sandy can't admit our father's an alcoholic—a ticking time bomb just looking for the right Molotov cocktail to cause an explosion. But that's Sandy. I've always believed a good chunk of my twin brother's ability to care about others disappeared on the day our father left us in the Rattlesnake Valley with our aunt and uncle. Getting him to drive to the airport was an enormous accomplishment.

Think, Brandy. Whom do you know in So-Cal? Is Dad's next door neighbor still alive? What's her name? Thelma? Moira? Something with a soft *a* at the end.

Images of the people in my life flash through my mind like a slide show: Levi on his horse; the kids with their hands out like tiny birds lifting their beaks for mother's nourishment; my dad begging for a drink; my brother dropping piles of dirty laundry in every corner; Shonah calling me an imbecile; Tara passed out in puke; the sinister look on Amanda Prince's face when she spilled wine in my lap; my ailing patients at the physical therapy clinic.

Then there's the disapproving face of Sylvia Ostrander staring right at me.

I look from her disapproving face to Chlöe's perpetually disappointed face. They distort like images in carnival mirrors. The Canadian looks a little like my elbow dislocation patient—another bottled blonde with a schedule-spewing affliction. Six weeks earlier she was thrown from her horse, and this afternoon she accused me of being a dominatrix. It's clear she needs surgery; however, she refuses to believe it. She insists that every other injury she'd experienced had been cured by physical therapy, and asked what was wrong with me that I couldn't make everything right? "I don't suppose it makes any difference to you that your body chemistry has changed since your last injury," I said to her. "You're fifty-five years old—not exactly a spring chicken." The woman snatched her elbow from my clutches, stepped into her dusty cowboy boots, and stomped out of the room.

Each day I work at the clinic I come face-to-face with chronic pain, and my patients' systematic expectations for a cure. Their eyes portray the hate they feel for the rigorous workouts I put them through, and yet their occasional smiles signify hope. But mostly they pass on their hate—as though I'm the cause of their injuries. I put them through the paces, forcing them to walk or to bend—to put on their own necklaces and tie up their own ponytails. "One foot in front of the other," I command day after day. "Walk!"

Everyone in my life—my family, my patients, my friends—they may think I'm a heartless bitch; but they're the ones who've sucked the heart right out of me.

I hear my name spoken with the same tone a principal uses to admonish a naughty student. "Bran-dee… " It's Sylvia snapping me out of my head.

"What!" I turn and face her. "I don't know anything. Do we have to talk about this?"

"Talk about what?" asks Blanca Midnight as she enters the room, her high heels clacking on the Saltillo tile. She carries a food tray the size of a snow saucer, places it in the middle of the island counter, and pulls away a green cellophane wrapper. "*Voila!*" she says and curtsies. She's wearing a red wig, has on a 1950s-style tailored dress, black with white polka dots, tight at the waist with a glistening patent leather belt and a flared skirt. A black Lucille Ball. Good Christ, she's as tall as a skyscraper. I don't know how she made it through the low arch in the hallway. The ceilings are so low here, the top of her wig practically scrapes the ceiling.

"*Looocy*, you got some *splainin'* to do," I say.

"No," says Sylvia. "*You* do, Brandy."

Tootsie

"Finally!" The yapping of my dogs is a telltale sign. And from my bathroom I feel the pressure difference in the house when the garage door opens. I know my husband is home at last. It's the moment I've been waiting for. I look down at Trixie and Teddie. "It's about time he got here!" They dance around my ankles.

I swear that man is always late. And tonight of all nights. I had to hold in my news all day, which was nearly impossible on the golf course with my ladies, Miss Shonah, Miss Sylvia and Brandy Lynn. I told them I was going to Dice Club tonight, but I'm not sure I'll want to be apart from Michael.

Quickly, I run my fingers through my hair and use an eyelash curler to bring my lashes to attention. Throwing the curling contraption into my makeup drawer, I slam it shut. I take a last look at the pregnancy stick, straighten it, and check one more time to assure myself of the plus sign. It's there. *"Yes!"*

I can't help it. I run from the room and the dogs chase after me, barking.

"What are you still doing here?" asks Michael as he emerges through the door. He carries the evening newspaper under one arm and a brown bag of groceries in the other. "I thought you'd be at Dice Club, but your car's still in the garage. This is the night, right? Thursday?"

"Darlin', where have you been?" I'm breathless, and the sight of my handsome husband, a tall man with square shoulders and chiseled facial features, nearly takes my feet out from under me. He's wearing a dark blue suit and what he calls his red power tie, which means he must have been in meetings. Perhaps his last meeting had run late.

Michael heads for the kitchen. The dogs yap incessantly. "Quiet, you two! *Git* to your crate!" They obey at once and plod with their bellies to the floor toward the dual crates in our Arizona room.

Michael sighs heavily and sets down the grocery bag on our granite countertop. "Boy oh boy, I'm sorry I'm late, Sweetie." He grabs the newspaper with his free hand and tosses it onto the table. "There was an accident on Bellisimo Boulevard. Traffic's backed up all the way to the bridge and I've been stuck in it."

"Bellisimo Boulevard? Where?"

"Not that far from here. Did you hear sirens?"

"I didn't. I've been inside. Oh my. Hope it's no one we know. Did you recognize anyone?"

"Looked like an SUV and some kind of coupe. The coupe definitely lost that fight. Oh, and I think there was a pickup too. Hard to tell which cars were actually involved." He pulls out a plastic bag with two small onions from the grocery bag. "You wouldn't believe the commotion. I swear this Valley is planned terribly for traffic flow. When the Boulevard goes down to a two-lane road it becomes the only way for residents to get in and out. If something like this happens it's total gridlock. I really ought to talk to the transportation commission. We've gotta do something."

"You go git-em, Big Daddy." I lift to my toes and kiss his rough cheek. It's a seven o'clock shadow.

Unloading the remains of his grocery bag, he moves between the counter and the refrigerator with purpose. "I bought some eggs. Was thinking about making an omelet for dinner since I thought you'd be out. I've been craving a Denver omelet all day."

"You mean supper, of course."

"Supper, dinner. Whatever. I've always liked breakfast for an evening meal. I only do it when you go out. And why, dear girl, aren't you out? Those bunko babes have got to be well into their first round by now."

"Well ...I was waiting for *you*!"

Michael places a gallon of milk in the refrigerator and turns around. I've positioned myself right behind him. He smiles, reaches out, and grabs my waist. "Don't you look fetching tonight, Mrs. Fennimore."

"Thank you kindly, Mr. Fennimore." I bat my freshly curled eyelashes and feel myself blush—just like a proper Southern Belle. "You know, my darling, soon I'm going to have to start calling you by another name."

"Oh, really? What name would that be?"

"How does Daddy sound to you?"

Michael gasps and releases his grasp. "Tootsie," he says, smiling. "Are you saying ...are you...?"

"Yes, Michael. I'm saying we're expecting." I let out a little yelp—a foreign tone, which I think is something that might actually be coming from the baby. "C'mon I'll show you the plus sign." I clutch his elbow and lead him down the hall, past my special trophy room. "Except for match play, it's one time in my life when seeing a plus sign on a score card is a good thing. I've been climbing the walls waiting for you to come home so I could show you this."

"Does Dr. Jefferson know?" he asks. "Did you see her today?"

"No, not yet. I was golfing with the girls. But Honey, I have a really good feeling about this one."

We reach the bathroom and I grab the good news and show it to Michael. A smile lights his face. He pulls me back to him, scoops me off the floor, and holds me like a groom carrying his bride over the threshold. Kissing me deeply, he lets me up for air and then beams. "I can't believe it, Tootsie. This is the best news I've had in ...in a long time. Hell! In my life! *Woo-hoo!*"

This is exactly how I pictured it would be. "Michael, put me down!"

"Are you feeling okay?"

"I'm fine. Except for your rough face scratcin' my skin, if things get any better I'll have to hire someone to help me enjoy it."

Blanca

I'm glad I brought the food tray. I could have brought more. There's a wonderful deli with prepared takeout trays right next to Tara's gallery, where I spent most of the afternoon. Poor Chlöe. I had no idea

It's Not Your Mother's Bridge Club   151

she lived in such squalor. This reminds me of my *primo's* place down in Mexico. I use a toothpick and pluck a chunk of white cheese from the tray and put it on my tongue.

"Blanca, did you see that email Brandy sent?" asks Sylvia.

"For heaven's sake, *what* email?" asks Chlöe.

I look around the room before answering. "I saw it. Not surprised to see Tara isn't here. But where's Shonah? I wonder if she got caught in the same traffic that held me up."

Sylvia flashes an evil eye at her girl, Brandy. I swear those two are like an old married couple. They fight as much as David and I ever did. "I talked to Shonah this afternoon," Sylvia says. "She didn't say anything about not coming. But she did say she had some words with you, Brandy Lynn."

I have the urge to cross myself. *In the name of the father, the son and the holy...*

"Hardly *anyone* is here," whines Chlöe. She holds up her index finger and starts going around the room, pointing to each woman like a Lacrosse coach counting a roster. "One, two, three, four ...Tootsie's not here. We have enough for one table. How's that supposed to work?"

"We golfed with Tootsie this morning," says Brandy. "She said she was coming."

I laugh and fluff up my fake hair. Hope this wig stays on through the night. "She's always late. But I should talk, right? I was late because like I said, traffic was really, really bad, *mi'jas.* I think there was an accident or something. I thought I heard sirens."

"For awhile there I thought Amanda Prince might show up since I didn't know she quit—no one tells me anything—and I didn't delete her name from the group email list," says Chlöe. "I didn't even consider getting a sub. I guess if we're just missing one we can use a ghost?"

"Amanda is as spooky as a ghost," says Brandy. "Scares the hell out of me!"

That girl doesn't stop. She's starting to make me mad. *"¡Por Díos!* Seems to me you have to take quinine these days to be immune from Brandy's comments."

"What did she say?" asks Brandy, narrowing her eyes. "Quinine? Blanca Midnight—or whatever your name is—quit speaking Spanish, won't you? Didn't anyone ever tell you this is America? Are you even legal?"

"You got a problem with me speaking Spanish?"

"Stop it," says Sylvia. "Of course she's legal. She was married to David Fernglen, remember? Blanca, no one has a problem with you speaking

Spanish. I speak it to my cleaning ladies all the time. I like the practice. But what are you talking about ...quinine?"

I let the cleaning lady comment pass, and even the lame defense of my immigration status. I know Sylvia well enough to know she didn't mean to be offensive. I think it's the liberal white community that raises most of the stink about being politically incorrect—not we people of color, who are so accustomed to real racial slurs we know one when we hear one. Shonah probably would've had a heart attack right here in this low-ceiling kitchen if she heard what Sylvia and Brandy just said. And not that it's anyone's business, but I was born right here in the U.S.A. Am I legal? That Brandy! ¡Cabrona! I think she *always* means to be offensive. She's completely insecure. Hates everything—especially herself.

I narrow my eyes at her. "Do you know anything about malaria, Brandy?"

"No, Blanca. I don't travel in Third World countries."

"Of course you don't. Well, quinine is a drug you take prior to and while you're in places like Africa, or where mosquitoes carry the obnoxious little parasites. It works for most people, but some who spend prolonged periods there get it anyway. It's one of those infectious diseases that stays in your system and can rear its *cabeza fea* if your immunity is weak. I think my ex is suffering from it right now from his recent trip."

I can't help but smile, pleased with the idea of my ex suffering from malarial symptoms.

Brandy looks at Sylvia and Chloë, no doubt to see if either has a clue as to what I'm talking about. They all look lost.

"What the hell, Blanca? Are you comparing me to your asshole husband?"

"Ex!" I must correct her. "Chloë, *mi'ja*, where's your corkscrew? I've got a nice bottle of red."

Brandy tenses. "Are you going to pour it on me or something?"

"Oh Blanca, please don't pour wine on Brandy," says Chloë. "What's this about malaria?"

I adjust my red wig and point at Brandy. "You Brandy, should learn to be more supportive of your Dice Club ladies. That email you sent really crossed the line."

Chloë sighs and moves around the aluminum TV dinners like she's dealing out cards. "Can't we just forget about it now and eat this food before it gets cold?"

Brandy pushes her tray aside. "This isn't food, Chloë," she says, and reaches for a ham roll. She brings it to her mouth. "*This* is food!" She wiggles the roll in the air like a miniature pennant. "There's enough here to feed us and that severely gifted brood of yours for a week. You should be grateful to our African-Mexican, Red-Headed Witch Doctor over there. Or is it Mexican African-American? I'm so confused." She bites the roll like an animal taking a chunk out of something.

"Hey," says Chlöe. "I'm sorry I didn't have time to cook. If you guys had any idea how busy I am on a daily basis you wouldn't begrudge me my TV dinners. Besides, I thought TV dinners for an *I Love Lucy* theme was cute. So, joke's on me, right?"

"I'll eat one," Sylvia says. She reaches across the table, pulls a tray toward her and lifts the foil. "I used to eat these as a kid whenever my parents went out on their Friday night dates and I got to stay up late and watch *Love American Style* on TV. I lived for the mashed potatoes. Got any butter?"

Brandy looks like she's going to be sick. I can almost read her mind from the look she gives Chlöe. It's funny for Chlöe not to realize that to know her is to know how busy she is on a daily basis. Her busy schedule is all she ever talks about.

I finish the wine in my glass. I'll bet my teeth have taken on a garish, cabernet hue. Red teeth, red lips, red hair. I move to where Chlöe's placed the bottles and refill my glass. Brandy follows me. Sylvia sets down her fork. "You're not getting out of this, Brandy Lynn," she says with a mouth full of processed potatoes.

"Getting out of what?" asks Chlöe. "*Now* what the hell are we talking about? Brandy, are you determined to ruin my party?"

Brandy grabs the bottle of red from my hand. "Oh for crying out loud!" she cries, and tips the bottle toward her glass. "I made a mistake today. Okay? Chlöe, if you had stayed online long enough you would have seen it by now. It was a stupid, bad mistake and I'm a terrible, rotten person. There! Are you happy Sylvia? Blanca?" She shoves the bottle back at me, takes a sip, and then walks back to the kitchen table.

"Oh God, Brandy. Calm down. It's not the end of the world," says Sylvia. "Shonah sent Brandy and me an email saying she was concerned about Tara. Tara stopped drinking and was afraid to come to Dice Club because it might make her fall off the wagon."

"Tara? Really? When did she stop?" asks Chlöe.

Sylvia shrugs. "I have no idea. I'm just going by what Shonah told me."

"It's about time," says Chlöe. "You all have to admit it was a problem for her."

"See?" says Brandy with a look of smug satisfaction. "Jesus Christ! All this should be directed at Tara, not me!"

I can't help but cross myself again. "It doesn't matter when she stopped. Only that she stopped. I noticed her cutting back at my house, you know, the night Tootsie put on the thong?"

"Well that sure wasn't the case at my house the following month," adds Sylvia. "Shonah had to drive her home and come back the next day for her own car."

"So much for no drink-counters at Dice Club," Brandy says into her glass.

"What did you say, Brandy?" asks Chlöe.

"Nothing. Not a thing, Chlöe. Why don't you tell us more about your busy day?"

"Brandy!" scolds Sylvia.

"Shut up already, Sylvia! I'm sick of you treating me like a child all the time!"

Time to end this. "That's okay, *mi'jas*. Brandy just likes to tell it like it is, which is exactly what she did in that email. She's like that mosquito. Always buzzing around, biting, spreading the infection."

"You can say that again," remarks Chlöe.

"Oh please, Chlöe!" barks Brandy. "Sometimes it's a wonder we can get you stop telling us *aboot* every detail of your day. Talk about an annoying buzzing mosquito!"

She just can't stop. She just tells it like it is, no matter who might get hurt. "Brandy, every time Chlöe opens her mouth you either ridicule her or cut her off."

"That's not true," she protests.

"Yes, it is," says Sylvia. She looks down at her hands. They are wrapped around a wine glass, which looks as big as a goldfish bowl. "I do it too," she says. "We all do."

"Wait just a cotton pickin' minute," Chlöe says. "If this is about to turn into a scene like the one at Sylvia's house, I'm telling you right now, eh, I'm putting a stop to it. For Pete's sakes, I have stock animals that behave better than all of you!"

I knew I smelled animals. "Sheep, right?"

"Uh, goats, actually," Chlöe says. "We raise pygmy goats."

"Yes that's right, pygmy goats," says Brandy. "One had kidney stones. Levi came and helped her take care of it."

"My husband has kidney stones!" remarks Sylvia.

"So does Levi."

I haven't the vaguest idea what a kidney stone is. "If it's a bad thing, I sure hope my ex-husband has them along with his malaria."

"Christopher Columbus had them," says Chlöe.

Now Christopher Columbus I do know. "He discovered America, yes?" It was like shouting out the answer to a multiplication flash card, and a way to prove my official residence. "I know that much, *mi'ja*." I slap Chlöe a high five. "And he was originally from Italy, right? What was *his* immigration status?"

"We're not talking about the explorer, Blanca," Chlöe says with a smile. "Christopher Columbus was my goat."

"Was?"

"I'm afraid he…" She drops her head. "He went to the Great Goat Beyond."

Chlöe

Everyone laughs. Including me. I use a swizzle stick to stir my drink and daintily sip it. All eyes are on me. It's the first time I've taken center stage among this group and surprisingly, I like the feeling. Meanwhile, Brandy looks relieved.

I'm really fond of all the women in the Dice Club. But—and this would probably come as a big surprise to her, I'm especially fond of Brandy. I can't help but stare at her and admire the healthy glow of her cheeks, her silky, blonde hair and penetrating blue eyes. No one looks better in denim than this woman—particularly when she offsets her look with silver and turquoise jewelry. Brandy moves with the greatest of ease. She can enter any room and at once feel comfortable. She's got a quick wit and absolute confidence. Brandy is everything I'm not.

She meets my gaze. "What?" she asks.

"Nothing." I take in a forkful of the waxy carrot and green bean mixture from my TV dinner. It's awful.

"I can understand why Tara didn't show up," Blanca says to Brandy. "Your email wasn't the most gentle thing in the world, but I will admit you didn't say anything that wasn't true. Tara's so high profile in this Valley that the entire town talks about her antics. I've had patrons in her own gallery ask me about her, and even my kids' teachers have expressed concern for her behavior at various school or school related functions."

"Me too," says Sylvia.

So have I.

Blanca continues. "Sooner or later she's going to have to own up to her behavior and hopefully she'll choose to heal. Look at Amanda. Didn't Sylvia say she finally started getting some counseling? Would she have done it if it weren't for this club?"

"I said I saw her car outside a counselor's office. I just assumed," says Sylvia. "I haven't set foot in my husband's office since the incident at my Dice Club. And it's not like I can call her."

I take a cheese cube from Blanca's tray. "What I want to know is why Shonah isn't here."

"She was really pissed at me for sending the email," Brandy says.

This stupid email just keeps coming up. Now I'm completely frustrated. "Will someone please tell me what the email said? Or should I go check?"

Sylvia raises her hand and explains. "After Shonah sent one about her concern for Tara, I wrote her back and said, of course we'd support her. But Brandy over there didn't express the same, shall I say, support? Oh damn!" she says suddenly. "My cell phone is buzzing." She pulls it from her purse, checks the caller ID, ignores it and sets it on the table.

"No, I guess I didn't offer the same kind of support," says Brandy. "First of all, I didn't mean to send it. A phone call came in and I accidentally hit the send key. Chlöe, you're not the only one with a busy schedule. I had to arrange to get my father to the airport today. Anyway, for some reason I can't figure out, I addressed it to the group email. All of you have it. It said I thought it was about time Tara dealt with her drinking problem. But what I wanted to say is that it doesn't mean the rest of us have to stop drinking too. If she feels she can't be around us anymore, that's her choice. I don't think I'm being unsupportive if I keep drinking a glass or two of wine on Dice Club night."

We all simultaneously set down our drinks. A small, clear-glass forest of alcohol vessels glisten on the table like twinkling stars.

"But that still doesn't explain why Shonah isn't here," says Blanca. "And where's Tootsie?"

"I can guess why Shonah didn't come," Brandy says.

"Did you send her an email too?" asks Blanca. "Did you call her husband an 'asshole' too?"

"Blanca Midnight," says Brandy flatly, "I don't think there's a woman in this room who doesn't think your husband is an asshole. I've heard you call him a lot worse."

"*Sí, mi'ja*," says Blanca. "But he's *my* husband. I mean my ex-husband, of course. I have a right."

Brandy nods, licks her finger and runs it around the rim of her wine glass. "Shonah and I had a fight."

I shake my head in disbelief. "No way. A fight? I thought you, Shonah, Sylvia, and Tara were all tied at the hip. It seems to me like none of you even goes to the bathroom without consulting one another."

Sylvia, in the middle of a sip when she hears my comment, spits chardonnay from her mouth. It sprays in a fine mist from her lips and onto the food tray. "Oh my God!" she says, and slightly chokes. She sets down her glass, grabs the table with both hands and knocks her jewel-encased cell phone to the floor.

I race to her side. "Are you okay? Can I get you a glass of water?"

"So much for my food tray," says Blanca. "You couldn't have aimed in another direction?"

Sylvia's face reddens and her eyes fill with tears. She stoops to the floor and picks up her cell phone, and then places it back on the table while I fill a glass with tap water. "I'm sorry Chlöe. Blanca, about your food …oh my God, I'm so embarrassed. It's just that when Chlöe said we were tied at the hip I couldn't help it. We're *not* tied at the hip!"

I place the water in front of Sylvia and reach for her cell phone. Opening it, I press a button and display the contact list. "Brandy home. Brandy cell. Brandy work. Shonah home. Shonah cell. Shonah office. Tara home. Tara cell. Tara gallery." I look up at the group. "They're all right here. Shall I go on?"

"What does that prove?" asks Brandy. "I'm sure her daughter is on there too, along with her husband's mobile and office numbers. So what?"

I feel I've proved my point. "The first three dedicated to the top table of your Dice Club?"

She grabs the phone from me and pushes aside the glass of water. "That's because Brandy programmed it for me one day when the four of us were at lunch. She put in her numbers, and then Shonah's and Tara's. I put in the rest. For heaven's sake, Chlöe, what's your point?"

I take back the phone and continue scrolling down the list. "I'll bet *I'm* not in here. Let's see, uh, nope! I don't see anyone else from the Dice Club."

Sylvia grabs her phone from my hands and stuffs it into her back pocket. "Am I on *your* contact list, Chlöe?"

"I don't have a cell phone."

"With your schedule? I don't believe it," says Brandy. "You sure seem to know how to use one."

"My kids have them. Roger Jr. and Lisa. We bought them because they got straight A's three full years in a row. That's twelve quarters of report cards."

"Well, whatever!" Sylvia says, clearly flustered. "If you think you people are my only friends you're nuts! I mean seriously, Chlöe, when have you or I ever had a phone conversation or gotten together for lunch? And who says we have to? Do we all have to be all things to all people?"

"I'd be willing to bet that I'm not on anyone's list. When it comes to all of you, sometimes I feel like I'm back in high school. Sylvia, you and Brandy are the queen bees, picking and choosing the ones you want to be in the Club. I know I am definitely *not* one of the cool kids. I can't help it I can't afford to have a house as nice as yours, and serve my Dice Club elaborate meals. I can't even afford these stupid TV dinners now that Roger's lost his job. And we're probably going to have to move!"

"*Uno momento por favor,*" says Blanca. "*Mi'ja*, Chlöe, let's not do this. Not now. Not here. There's four of us here. Is anyone interested in playing bunko, or what?"

"No!" rings a chorus of voices.

Amanda

I check the printed MapQuest directions in the passenger seat next to me, squint and make my way into the dark neighborhood. I've never been here and it feels oddly different than the other neighborhoods in the Valley. I wonder if I have the right directions.

Trying to make out my pencil scratches, I take the first left and go past a big house lit up like a shopping mall. Turning right on the next street, I wind around a corner and into a cul-de-sac. Dead end. I have to back up and turn around.

I go another block then turn on a dirt road. There's a yellow caution sign reading "Children at Play." This must be it. My tires crunch the rocky, potholed surface. Hope I don't get a flat. Going down to the end, I find there aren't a lot of cars. "One, two, three," I count. Could this be the right place? Holy man! *My* house is nicer than this. Pulling into the driveway, I park behind a white Suburban decorated with two purple and teal bumper stickers reading, "My Child is an Honor Student at Rattlesnake Valley Elementary School." It has to be Chlöe Forrest's vehicle. I've always preferred the bumper sticker reading, "My kid beat up your honor student!" I wonder which kind of student Sean would have turned out to be.

Putting the car in park, I get out and let the door fall closed. Probably should lock it up. Smoothing my hair, I take a deep breath and make my way up the uneven bricks of the walkway leading to the adobe home. A dim light hangs in the entryway and the air smells of manure. Kids' toys are all over the place and a potted barrel cactus looks like it could use a good watering.

What am I doing here? Do I really want to face the Dice Club after what happened?

With another deep breath, I make a fist and knock on the front door.

Ian Shephard

I don't like the look of all the brake lights in front of me. Is there some kind of parade? Rodeo was last month, wasn't it? Besides, there wouldn't be anything at this time of night. And on a …what day of the week is it anyway? A Thursday?

At a full stop in my white, Chevy pickup, I stick my head out the window and try to get a read on what's going on. The line of red lights snakes ahead for miles.

"This is bullshit." Turning the steering wheel sharply to the left, I edge the truck into the lane for oncoming traffic. Nothing is coming. I use the dirt shoulder, kick up a cloud of dust and make a U-turn, now heading south. There's a dirt utility road a quarter mile back. Using it will get me home quicker.

I just want to get home as quickly as possible. It's Tara's night out and the girls will probably be with the babysitter, which means the house will be quiet. And mine. These days I look forward to my time alone, particularly since Tara's been so difficult to live with lately. She's grown so moody that I never know what'll hit me when I walk in the door.

Seeing the unmarked road ahead on the right, I turn without using my blinker. Flipping on the brights, the truck becomes like a carnival ride as I bounce and jiggle on the uneven surface. It reminds me of the turn my marriage has recently taken.

For the first time in twelve years of marriage, I've looked for reasons to get out of the house. Today I left just after lunch when Tara was busy in her studio. I spent the afternoon with Sandy Lynn, the brother of one of Tara's Dice Club friends. We helped a mutual friend paint one of his rental apartments. Painting isn't my favorite kind of manual labor, I prefer finish carpentry, but my buddy paid twenty-five bucks an hour. It was too hard to resist. And I have some investment opportunities in mind for the spare cash.

I can't wait to get home to my computer to see how my stocks did today. I heard on the radio that the market was up by almost a hundred points.

Turning off the dirt road, I find one more shortcut through an empty lot leading to the road that gets me to our subdivision. Sure comes in handy to know some of the Valley's more useful utility roads. Too bad for those left sitting on Bellisimo Boulevard.

I reach our driveway and find the gate left open. Huh? That's weird. Steering my truck down our long driveway, which meanders to the back of the house, I reach to the ceiling to press the garage door button.

Brake.

Even more weird. The garage door is open and the lights are on. Our Land Cruiser is still here, but Tara's car, a Mercedes coupe, is gone. Why would she leave the door and gate open? That's not like her.

"Hmm." She must be off to Dice Club.

Getting out of the truck, I step down to the pavement of the garage floor and slam the door. There's a twelve-pack of Bud in the back of my truck. I grab it and then reach for the garage door button, but before I can touch it the door to the house swings open.

"Daddy, Daddy!" cry both girls, "Mommy's not here!"

"Girls! What are you doing here? Nicole, did Mom let you baby-sit tonight?"

"Mom's gone!" says Nicole. A piece of red hair is in her mouth.

"I know. Her car's gone. She's at Dice Club tonight, right?"

"We don't know, Dad!" they say while jumping up and down.

I set down the beer and squat. The two girls, little replicas of their mother, are dressed in long, white nightgowns. They pounce upon my knees and throw their arms around my neck. "Nicki, are you in charge or is the babysitter here? Who do you have tonight? Lara or Erica?"

"Noooooooooooo!" they cry. "Nobody. Nobody's here. We told you! Mommy's not here!"

"What?"

I rise with both girls still clinging to me. Guiding their bare feet to the tiled floor we walk toward the kitchen. The first thing I see is a sink full of dirty dishes. Turning, I spot the open cabinet doors. The open liquor cabinet doors. With the girls clutching my legs, I walk to the cabinet and peer up.

It's empty. It's as bare as a cave where you could shout your name and hear an echo.

"Oh no."

"What, Daddy? Where's Mommy?"

"I don't know, girls. Give me just a minute. Nicole, take your sister into the family room."

"Noooooo!" they both whine. "Dad, we're hungry!"

I can't deal with that right now. I walk to the opposite end of the house toward Tara's studio, my work boots noisily stomping. The girls follow. Stepping into her private sanctuary, I knowingly feel for the light switch and flip it. I'm unprepared for what I see.

"Holy shit!"

"Daddy!" the girls scold. "You're not supposed to say that bad word."

"Stay here, little ones." I use my hand to hold them back. There are white paint stains on my fingers. I feel Nicole pressing against me and I tell her to take her sister to her room. They shouldn't see this. Nicole nods and guides Gabrielle away from the studio.

I close the door behind me and move inside tentatively. My foot crunches broken glass. Sniffing the stale air, a mixture of clay and spirits, at once I feel the power of all my wife's secrets.

Sylvia

This party is a bust. Almost as bad as mine. No one is showing up. Wait a minute. What was that? "Did you hear a knock?"

"Who knocks?" asks Blanca.

"You mean who's *there*," Brandy says.

Chlöe shrugs. "What are you talking about, eh?"

"Knock, knock joke," says Brandy. "You know, 'knock-knock-who's-there?' "

"No, *mi'ja*. I mean who knocks? I didn't knock when I came in," says Blanca. "Don't we know each other well enough by now that we can walk right in? I mean, we're expected. Right?"

Brandy and I exchange a look. I believe I can guess who it is.

Chlöe walks toward the front door. *"Shhhh!"* She tries to silence us. There it is again—another knock. We follow her and watch as she stands on her toes, placing both hands on either side of the peephole. "Oh my GAWD!" she shrieks. "I've really cooked it this time, eh?" She turns and faces us. "You won't believe it."

"Yes we will," Brandy and I say together.

"It's probably Tootsie," offers Blanca. "Late as usual but with a fabulously wrapped present."

"It's not Shonah, is it?" asks Brandy.

"You're all wrong," says Chlöe with a broad smile. "I bet *she'll* eat one of my TV dinners."

She pulls open the front door, and, of course, there she is. Amanda.

I shift my weight and narrow my eyes. She looks smaller somehow, and better dressed—in tight jeans and a black leather jacket. My God, she's actually had her hair styled and highlighted. If I didn't know any better, I'd say it's my exact style. *Eww.* That's little creepy.

There's a collective gasp among the other ladies.

Amanda reddens slightly and takes a deep breath. I notice she doesn't look in my direction. Not even close. "Thank you for inviting me, Chlöe," she says. "I always thought you were the nicest person in this Club. Okay if I come in?"

She's right. Chlöe did invite her. It was an accident, but she was definitely invited. We all step back as Chlöe opens the door as wide as it can open. There's no need to tell Amanda that the invitation had been a mistake. "Come in Amanda. Come in. Are ya hungry? There's lots of food," says Chlöe.

"Hi Amanda," says Blanca. "I brought food from the deli next to the gallery."

"This is a surprise, Amanda." It just falls from my mouth. Amanda takes a couple steps into the hallway and turns her back to me. "We haven't seen you since..."

"Since she dumped wine in my lap," says Brandy. "I thought you quit."

I send Brandy daggers through my eyes and mouth the words, "shut up!"

"Hello, Brandy," says Amanda. "Did the stain come out of your jeans?"

"Never washed 'em," answers Brandy. "I hung them in my hall closet and renamed it the Hall of Shame."

"Really?" asks Chlöe.

"No, not really, Chlöe" says Brandy. "Yes, Amanda. The stain came out. How about *your* stain? The stain on your heart? Rumor has it you've been seeing a shrink."

Oh my God! I may just throw this wine in Brandy's face if she doesn't shut up now! I squeeze the bowl of the glass and I feel my whole body fill with tension. There's a scream welling up in me and I can't hold it back.

Crash! An explosion of glass fills my hand. I suck in my breath, while tiny shards of crystal fall to the ground like snowflakes, and lay there glistening in a small puddle of chardonnay. Wine drips down my wrist and onto my jeans as I let go of the stem. What's left of the goblet darts to the floor. Another crash.

Everyone looks at me with big eyes.

"Oh!" I can't help but gasp.

"I'll get a rag," Chlöe says.

"*¡Díos Mío!* Where's your Dust-buster?" asks Blanca.

With a rag in one hand, Chlöe approaches me, and with her other hand, mechanically points to the hanging mini-vac in the corner. "Sylvia, your finger's bleeding. Come with me."

I look down. She's right. There's blood. Lots of blood. "Oh... my."

"Wait," says Amanda. "Let me take care of this." She takes off her jacket and folds it over her arm. With her free hand she lifts my bleeding finger. "Sylvia," she says. "I'll help you. It's the least I can do."

"The least you can...?"

"Are you sure, Amanda?" asks Chlöe. "You do realize I'm a nurse?"

Amanda ignores Chlöe and tosses her coat on a chair. I start to speak—to tell her that I'd rather Chlöe help me. But Amanda cuts me off. "*Shhh.* Be calm," she says. "Chlöe? The bathroom?"

Again, Chlöe points.

Amanda takes my arm. "Listen Sylvia, I owe you an apology."

"What about me?" calls Brandy. "Do you owe me an apology too?"

Amanda looks over her shoulder as we start down the narrow hallway leading to the bathroom. "I'll get to you, Brandy. You can wait. Chlöe, do you have a first aid kit nearby?"

"It's above the refrigerator. Let me grab a stool."

I stop and pull back my hand from Amanda's grasp. "I don't know what's wrong with me tonight. Five minutes ago I spit wine all over the food tray and now I've spilled it all over the floor."

"You're about to spill blood on the floor if you don't get that finger wrapped. Is that what you want?" asks Amanda. She again grabs me by the elbow and leads me down the hall. "Don't you think we need to talk?"

I see Chlöe climb the stool and pull out the first aid kit. "Give me that," says Brandy. "I'll take it to them."

I hear the familiar roar of a hand vacuum as we turn into the bathroom.

Brandy is close behind us and hands the first aid kit to Amanda. "Here. Take this," she says. "Sylvia, if you think you're going to be too handicapped to throw dice, let us know. I'm gonna go call Tootsie and see what's keeping her."

Tootsie

Is that my phone? I'm lying next to Michael and we're naked. I couldn't wait to make love with him for the first time knowing our child was there, snuggled between our warm bodies—the bodies that created him. Her? Oh! What a delightful mystery!

The phone continues ringing, buried under my clothes somewhere across the room. Slowly, I open my eyes in the dark room, and am momentarily lost.

"You should get that," moans Michael. "Might be your Dice Club friends. Don't you want to go to the party? Go and tell them the good news?"

"Right now all I care about is that you know."

The phone keeps ringing. "Maybe it's your mother," Michael says. "You don't want to withhold this good news from Ronnie Vermillion Thompson, do you?"

"Good news indeed," I laugh. "She'll love knowing I'm pregnant. But that she'll be a grandmother? Not sure how she'll take that!" Reluctantly, I get up. The ringing grows louder, more urgent. "All right already!" I race to the phone and pull it from the chair where I'd left it. "I'm here!" Flipping it open, "Hello?"

"Did you forget it was Dice Club night?" asks Brandy. "We talked about it on the first green. Remember that long come-backer putt I sunk to save par?"

"Oh, no. No, Brandy. I thought you were my mother."

"Nope."

"I didn't forget about Dice Club. I'm coming. At least I think I'm coming." I raise my eyebrows at Michael and he nods. "I'm running late. Michael just got home and I guess I dozed off. My goodness, I didn't realize how tired I was." I put my hand to my forehead and swoon. "*Gee whillickers.* I suddenly feel like I was hit by a bus."

"Maybe you're pregnant," says Brandy.

I move my hand from forehead to tummy. "How on earth did you know?"

Shonah

The aftermath of another brilliant Sonoran Sunset paints my office walls with a melon alpenglow. I get lost wallowing in the wistful hue. By six o'clock, when I still hadn't showered or wrapped the Desi and Lucy metal poster I planned to bring to Dice Club tonight, I knew I wouldn't go to Chlöe's party.

I whiled away the rest of the afternoon locked in my office, typing nonsense into my computer. I didn't answer the phone. Nor did I respond to the knocks on my door, which alternated between the light taps of my boys and the hardened fist of my husband. They know better. They know not to disturb me when I'm writing.

At least that's what I was trying to do.

My column, usually an easy writing exercise that flows from my brain to my fingertips as though I'm having a conversation with a trusted friend, just isn't happening. Filled with the new knowledge of what my friends really think of me, I've frozen with fear and self-doubt. The voices of Tara and Brandy echo in my head. *The great know-it-all-guru of life in the suburbs...you sit down and write your convoluted versions of our pathetic lives...* The words blare like city sirens, horns in traffic, planes flying overhead in search of a landing strip. They're all I can hear.

Little more than a rat in a maze, I start a paragraph with one of my many opening lines, follow a corridor trying to compose a theme, but a paragraph too far and I hit the wall. No cheese reward. No reward of any kind. Tara is next door drinking and I can't help but feel partly responsible. Should I write about that?

"I can't." Tara would only accuse me of thinking I was perfect, or that I was writing about her pathetic life only to make myself look good. Right now she's blaming me for everything.

Again there's a knock at the door. "Mom!" It's my Jonas. His voice is high and pure, more like a young girl than a boy. More knocking. "Mo-om!" I can't stand the two-syllable version of the word "mom." Annoyed, I lift my fingers and they hover over the keyboard like claws. "Dad said to tell you we're leaving."

"Good. Have a nice dinner."

"Aren't you going out?" he asks.

"No."

"But isn't it your Dice Club night? I thought you loved your Dice Club night, Mom."

"I do," I say. "I mean, I did."

"Huh?"

"Nothing, Honey."

I consider getting up, opening the door and kissing his innocent cheek. But don't. I don't want him to see the look on my face, and the hurt and anger that are no doubt seeping through my pores.

"Bye, Mom," he calls. Then after a second, "Love you."

"I love you too." My voice is a soft whisper. I don't know if he heard me. I can't stand that. He needs to hear me. I race to the door, open it and call out. "Jonas!"

I hear his soft-soled tennis shoes make their way back to me. "Hi, Mom," he says sweetly.

"Love you too, kiddo." He hugs me, turns, and runs off.

Returning to my office, I relax into my chair and gaze at the dim light of the computer screen. In the garage, the car horn toots twice. He's coming, Dan. Just give him a second. What's the rush? I touch the keyboard and the screen brightens, showing me a lot of gray type on a white background. I can't even remember what I wrote. "Whatever this is," I say to no one, "I'm going to finish it. Even if it takes the rest of the night."

I take off my glasses, lean back in my chair and adjust my eyes to reread my notes.

I sit here alone in my office, watching the clock, completely aware that my Dice Club is meeting tonight. It's the last place I want to be right now. And yet, I don't want to be here either.

"No! I don't want to be here!" I call to the walls. I lean forward in my chair, putting my elbows on the desk. Big sigh. "This isn't about anyone else's pathetic life but my own." The great know-it-all guru of life in the suburbs strikes again.

The phone stands on the left side of my desk, a silent sentry. Should I pick it up and call Tara? Will she be there? Or did she go to the Dice Club in spite of Brandy's email? What if she drank all afternoon? Would she be capable of driving to Chlöe's house?

I pick up the phone. Perhaps Ian will answer. I'll express my concern to him. Maybe talk about having some kind of intervention.

I wonder what her forehead looks like. Ian will see it. He'll realize it's time to get her into some kind of program.

I've got to get *someone* to help me deal with Tara!

I put down the phone. I'm still not ready. Standing, I pull up the tight black shirt over my head and free my pushed up breasts from the confines of an expensive black bra. I throw both the shirt and the bra to the floor and next add the rest of my clothes to the pile. Naked, I walk outside, cross the yard to the pool area and lift the cover to the hot tub. The sterile smell of bromine greets me and rising steam from the swirling water beckons my entry. I step inside and gradually lower myself into the bath. Steam clouds swarm past my face and rise above my head.

It doesn't take long to adapt to the warmth. I lean back and marvel at the cloudless night sky. All remains of the earlier sunset have disappeared and stars have just begun to share their faint twinkles. I'm glad I didn't go to Chlöe's. At the very least, I've saved myself a headache from the clamor.

I wonder if the Dice Club will even survive. Will we stay together in spite of all the recent upheaval? Will we all be friends for life? Or will these women become passing acquaintances, mere names on a list for holiday greeting cards? With the exception of Sylvia, whom

I've known since childhood, the rest of the women have only been in my life since I moved to the Rattlesnake Valley. I met Tara during my first month in town and Sylvia introduced me to Brandy when both boys were still in car seats. My social circle truly blossomed, however, once the boys started school. That's when volunteer committees and fundraisers, ice cream social Fridays and soccer Saturdays covered my calendar. I'm pretty sure I've served on at least one planning committee with a majority of the women in the Club.

Pulling my hands from the water, I study my fingertips. How did they wrinkle up so quickly? Better get out before I have a full-blown hot flash. I stand and look at my long, wet limbs glistening in the backyard lights. Stepping over the edge of the tub and down the small set of wooden steps, I like the idea of no boys around to see me—to see me parade across the yard in all my naked glory, my unleashed breasts hanging to my bellybutton.

Just as I open the iron gate leading out of the pool area, I hear the familiar sound of Tara's studio door slam. My head snaps in that direction. "Tara?"

No response.

I run to my bedroom door, rush inside and grab a pale pink robe from the footboard of my bed. I put it on and head back outside, careful not to let the door slam behind me. I creep toward the wall separating our property from the Shephards'. Tiptoeing, I leap from flagstone to flagstone, around the ground cactus and gravel landscaping, and when I get to the concrete barrier, I place my swollen hands on top, peering over my wall and past Tara's.

An enormous shadow moves around Tara's yard like a ghost. "Is that you?"

No answer.

"Tara!"

"No. It's not Tara, It's me. Ian. Is that you, Shonah?"

"Yeah, it's me. Is Tara home?"

"What? I can't hear you."

"I asked you if Tara was there."

"No," he says. "She's at Dice Club. I just came home and found the girls here alone."

"What? What do you mean they were alone? Is she letting Nicole baby-sit now?"

"Shonah, I'm not sure what's going on. Tara's car is gone and her studio is …well, it looks like a war zone."

"A war zone?" I think back to our argument hours earlier. The studio had looked like it always looked. Tidy. Colorful. What happened after I left? My heart starts to pound. I shiver, even though I'm not cold. Warm droplets run down my face, drip to my shoulders, and are soaked up by my thick robe. Squinting, I visualize the silver flask lying on Tara's studio floor. It sparkles in my memory as vividly as the stars overhead.

Something deep inside tells me that Tara is in trouble.

"I'm coming over, Ian. Just give me a minute to throw on some clothes."

Amanda

Sylvia Ostrander and I stand beside a small porcelain sink in the tight confines of what must be Chlöe's children's bathroom. The room smells of moldy towels. A plain, toothpaste speckled mirror reflects us. Sylvia and I are the same height, and now we both have chestnut hair with copper highlights, a cropped cut gently framing the face. The stylist did a good job imitating the photo of Sylvia I brought to the salon. "Make my hair look like this," I had said.

Miracles do happen. But now I see that's where the similarities end.

Sylvia has on a tight, red sweater. The low, wide neckline shows off her delicate collarbones and is the perfect backdrop for her newest piece of jewelry, a vintage turquoise, squash blossom necklace. It, of course, was a gift from her husband, my boss, Richard Ostrander. As usual he dispatched me to the specialty shop to pick it up. The sweater falls gently over the top of her blue jeans, crisp with iron creases from thigh to toe. A pair of brown leather mules, designed like cowboy boots, completes the Southwestern casual look.

I look like the before picture. I'm wearing a plain, brown V-neck sweater, no jewelry, faded jeans and tennis shoes. I easily outweigh Sylvia by fifty pounds. "Hold your hand under the sink for a minute. I'll get some toilet paper and you can…"

"No," says Sylvia. "Hold off on the toilet paper. She has disposable hand towels here. I'll wrap it in one until it's ready for a Band-aid."

"I should have realized mere toilet paper wouldn't be good enough for you. Don't you know these towels came from Big Lots? I saw them there for eighty-nine cents."

Sylvia pulls her wounded hand from the running water and clutches the edge of the sink. She turns and looks me in the eyes for the first time since I arrived. "Why do you DO that?" she asks.

"Do what?"

Except for the gushing sound of running water, it's silent. I notice my heart rate increases and the pounding echoes in my head. I look down. Is the beating visible through my shirt?

"Do *what?*" I ask again.

Sylvia turns off the faucet and grabs a Big Lots towel. "Amanda," she says, "you have no idea how incredibly mean to me you are, do you? Didn't you say something about an apology? Is this how you're apologizing, by being mean?"

"Mean to you? Mean to *YOU?*" I can't help but throw back my head. "Huh! That's rich." I move to the toilet paper dispenser and pull. The paper rolls out quickly, like a streamer, and hits the floor. I tear it and wad the strip into a tight ball. "Here!" I throw the wad into the sink. "Honestly, Sylvia. From the minute we met you always made me feel as though I wasn't good enough to wipe your ass. But boy oh boy I sure have kissed it a number of times. Nice necklace by the way. Any idea where it came from?"

Sylvia puts her injured hand to her neck, fingering the sharp silver edges of the exquisite jewelry piece, and the other hand through her hair. "What are you talking about?"

I take a deep breath. She has no idea what I go through for her and Richard. It triggers my anger. Yes, there's the trigger. This is what Dr. Charles-Lloyd advised me to notice. "Notice the triggers as they come up and then control the behavior." I pick up another Big Lots towel, hand it to her, and let out my breath. "I'm a paralegal, Sylvia. A trained paralegal. I took night classes for a long time. I worked all day and did legal research and writing at night. I graduated top in my class. And I'm good. I'm the best in the office and Richard knows it."

"Everyone knows it," says Sylvia. "Richard always..."

"Richard always has me doing his menial crap. His Xeroxing. His errands. His trips to the Indian museum to pick up expensive pieces of jewelry for his little *wifey!* I should be writing legal briefs, Sylvia, not running around doing gopher jobs."

"Amanda, this isn't my fault," says Sylvia with a sigh. "Look..."

"No Sylvia, you look. Take a good look at me. Consider ME!"

A vice-grip clamps on my temples. Sylvia looks down to avoid my intense glare. We both see her crimson blood penetrating the flowered, pastel hand towel, spreading like an ink stain. Sylvia removes the towel and examines her hand. The cut at the base of her index finger, white around the edges and pink in the center, is in the shape of a pout.

"You may need stitches, Sylvia."

"Oh God, no! There's no way I want to spend the rest of the evening in an emergency room. Who can I call? I know a dozen doctors who might be willing to stitch me."

A drop of blood emerges, spilling from the wound like a tear. Sylvia reaches for the cold-water handle and again turns on the water. She takes a gauze pad from the first aid kit and busies herself with the wound. She can't do it. She can't take one minute to consider me. "I knew it. I knew you couldn't think of anyone but yourself."

"You know something Amanda," says Sylvia, "you're right. I *can't* do this. I can't do anything for you. I can't increase your salary or get Richard to change your job description. I can't buy you expensive clothes or an expensive car or expensive jewelry. I can't tell you how to behave at Dice Club parties and I can't defend your actions. Not anymore. I'm done. Finished!" She closes the cold-water valve and reaches for another towel. Wrapping it around the wound, she turns and looks directly into my face and exhales deeply.

"When your son died," she says calmly, "I was there for you in the only way I knew how to be. God knows our hearts genuinely went out to you and Manny, and at the same time, our biggest fears came to the surface. I don't know what I'd do if anything ever happened to my daughter. I don't know how I would get through that."

She puts her hand on my shoulder. "Amanda, I know you're grieving. I know you're hurting and angry. You're depressed and, I don't know, beside yourself with grief. We all understand this and we're doing the best we can to help you get on with your life. But this is all we—or I should say I—this is all *I* can do for you. But you need to know that there's only so much of your hostility I can take. I just never know what you want from me!" Sylvia shifts her weight and takes a deep breath. "Amanda," she says, "I can't bring back your son."

"I know you can't bring back my son. Don't you think I know that?"

Sylvia tightens her grip and I try to shake her off. "Listen to me. Just listen to me. Don't tell me you understand what I'm going through. No one knows what I'm going through!" My voice escalates and it feels like it's echoing in the small bathroom. "No one! Not even Manny." I feel my eyes fill.

Sylvia raises her injured hand, still wrapped in a towel, and places it on my other shoulder. "I thought you started seeing a counselor," she says. "Dr. Melinda-something?"

"Charles-Lloyd. How do you know that? How does everyone know I'm seeing a shrink?"

"I saw your car outside her office. She works in the same building as my ...as my . . ." Sylvia rolls her eyes and drops her hands. "As my plastic fucking surgeon. Okay?"

What did she say? My eyes suddenly feel like they're going to pop from my face. I blink twice, dispatching pent up tears and then slowly, my lips tighten and stretch into a smile. "Plastic surgeon, huh? Well, well, well. I guess we all have our little secrets."

"Oh, don't wet your pants. It's just a little Botox. Never mind about that. *You* could use a little Botox yourself. We were talking about the grief counseling. You are seeing her, aren't you?"

Nodding, I reach for the toilet paper and use it to blow my nose. "How's it going?"

"It's going. I mean, *I'm* going. Three times a week."

"Three times? That seems like a lot."

"Yup. It is." I throw the toilet paper into the toilet and flush. "Every time I pull into that parking lot, I walk up the stairs and think to myself, this is it. This week I'm going to narrow it down to two times. Or even one time. Then within fifteen minutes of being in her office, I know I'm going to be there on Wednesday and then again on Friday."

"Does that mean she's helping?" asks Sylvia.

"Yes, she's helping. She's helping a lot. Sometimes I wish I would've started seeing her sooner. But I just wasn't ready. And I resented it each time you or someone else suggested counseling. It was like you were telling me I wasn't grieving in the right way. And besides, I felt if I started to talk to someone about it, then I had to believe that it truly happened."

"Oh, Amanda," Sylvia says. "I'm so sorry. Really, I am."

"I know you are. That's what I wanted to talk to you about. I didn't intend to be mean to you. Ever. I meant to thank you."

Someone pounds on the door and we both jump. "Hey you two," says Brandy. "You gonna spend all night in there? Amanda, we're starting to think you have a thing for bathrooms!"

We look at one another and smile through a shared sigh.

"She's one of a kind, that one," I say.

"Thank heavens!" Sylvia says, and she puts her arms around me and hugs me.

Brandy

I'm standing outside the bathroom door waiting for Amanda and Sylvia to kiss and make up. I knock again. "I've got a scathingly brilliant idea for bunko tonight."

"I believe the scathingly part," says Sylvia as she emerges arm-in-arm with Amanda.

"But brilliant?" chimes in Amanda.

Chlöe walks toward us wearing the expression of a nurse, a serious combination of intelligence and TLC. "Amanda, how's the patient?"

"I think she'll live," she says. "But you should probably have a quick look to see if she needs stitches."

"I *don't* need stitches," moans Sylvia. "Please tell me I don't need stitches."

Chlöe takes Sylvia's hand, lifts the gauze pad and furrows her Canadian brow. "*Looocy*, if I've *tole* you once, I've *tole* you a *thousan'* times. You won't get into show business."

"Okay?" laughs Sylvia. "And the verdict is?"

"You're fine. Let me put a butterfly on it and you'll be all set." She actually has one in her pocket, whips it out and slaps it on Sylvia's cut like a short order cook slapping a piece of bread on top of a sandwich. She tells her to use tape to keep the gauze in place and purses her lips in approval. "Hey, let's play bunko. Brandy, what's your idea?"

"Okay, since it looks like there'll only be six of us, we should all just play at one table." I look at my watch. "Toot-toot-Tootsie will be here any minute. We can start a ghost card for her and mark nothing on it. She wins too much anyway."

"That sounds like a plan," says Chlöe.

"Fine," says Sylvia. "I'll try not to spill anything. Speaking of which, may I have another glass? I don't think the one I was using will work."

Blanca pops out of her chair. "I'll get it for you *mi'ja*. Glass of white, right? *Blanca?*"

Amanda tosses a five-dollar bill on the table. "Here's my five bucks. I'm in."

I didn't think Amanda came to play. I wonder if she'll say anything to me. "Gee Amanda, I don't know if we have a policy for letting back in members who've quit."

"Are you kidding?" asks Amanda.

I take Amanda's hand. "Of course I'm kidding." Doesn't anyone realize that I'm always kidding? I lean over and whisper in Amanda's ear. "I'm glad you came." I mean it. I am glad she came. I'm all about healing. And we could all use some healing. Now that my father has left, I might even be able to see straight again.

"My therapist told me it would be a good idea to come to Dice Club," Amanda says. She looks beyond my shoulder and addresses all the women, now gathered around Chlöe's dining room table. "Yes everyone. It's true. I'm seeing a shrink."

A shrink, huh? I can't resist. "You do look like you've lost some weight."

"Buzz off all ready. Will you Brandy?" says Amanda with a laugh.

"You bet!" I kiss Amanda's cheek. "Welcome back!"

"You know," whispers Amanda in return, "you're not as tough as you think you are. But don't worry. Your secret is safe with me."

I step back. What? Raising an eyebrow, I study Amanda for a moment. She does look good. It's like she shed some kind of skin—the angry armor she's been wearing since Sean's death. I see that same metamorphosis in my patients all the time.

Isn't it amazing what we can accomplish when we're willing to do the work?

Amanda notices me looking at her and winks. Okay. Now she's getting a little creepy. I mean, it's not like I'm ready to be her best friend or anything. Besides, what secret does she think she's keeping safe? What the hell is she talking about? Now that she's in psychotherapy she's qualified to analyze me? I don't think so. Besides, I don't have any secrets.

But, *ha!* I sure know someone who does. Where is Tootsie anyway? She should be here by now.

I'd better get this party started before I spill the beans about Tootsie. I know she wants to tell the group herself that she's finally pregnant. "Someone ring the bell and let's roll. Let's go! Ones!" I throw the dice and they splay on the table in a wide triangle. "Nothing! Who's next?" I swat the dice to my left.

"No need for a bell," say's Chlöe. "It's every woman for herself. Take the dice, Blanca Midnight. You're next."

Blanca scoops up the dice, rolls and searches for non-existent ones. "*Waaaaaaaa!*" she cries in her best Lucille Ball impersonation. She passes them left. "Amanda, it's you. Show us your stuff."

Amanda picks up the dice, shakes them in her hands like beans inside a maraca and lets them fall to the table. "One!' she cries. She scoops them again and rolls. "Two, three!" One more roll. "Nope! Three, total. Next!" She marks three tallies on her scorecard and pushes the dice to her left.

Sylvia grabs the dice, extends her wrapped finger and dramatically drops them to the table. Slowly, almost lifelessly, they roll toward one of the three vacant chairs at the table. We all crane our necks to see the roll. Three ones. "BUNKO!"

Tootsie

A quick shower revives me, and I throw on a hot pink sheath and a pair of cute matching sandals. Michael is flipping his omelet when I emerge, ready to catch the girls for a few rounds of bunko. I want to tell them myself about the baby before Brandy Lynn blurts it out. I'm not sure if that woman is capable of keeping anything inside. She's got tongue enough for ten rows of teeth!

Kissing Michael on the cheek, he takes a moment to place his hand on my stomach. "Have fun," he says. "The traffic should be cleared up by now, but be prepared just in case. Don't forget your cell phone."

"Good idea." I make a U-turn and head back to my bedroom where I'd left the phone. I'm not real confident about finding Chlöe's house, and need to program in her number just in case I get lost. I grab the phone and stop at my special room where my laptop is. There's a list of the Dice Club's names and numbers in a file on my desktop. Jogging the mouse, it takes a moment for the screen to light up. I easily locate the file and punch the numbers of Chlöe's home phone into my directory. *Ping!* An alert sounds, and I see there are thirty-six email messages waiting for me. I should really check my mailbox more often.

There's one from Chlöe ...details, details, Dice Club details ...several from Brandy, I'll skip those for now, and, lookey here, three from someone who thinks I should enlarge my penis. Okay, that's enough of that noise. No wonder I don't bother to check my mail.

"Okay m' darlin', I'm off." I show Michael my cell phone and stash it in my handbag. "Don't walk me to the door. Just enjoy your supper."

"Dinner."

"Whatever. I won't be late."

I lower myself into my stylish, two-door Lexus and know my time behind the wheel of this hot little car will be short-lived. I'm going to need something with a backseat when the baby comes. There'll be a lot of things I need.

I'm simply giddy at the idea of finally being a mother!

Driving through the neighborhood, I take note of each house and consider the children living there. Will our child have any neighborhood playmates? There aren't a whole lot of young families in this expensive subdivision. Heavens to Betsy, I'll probably be the oldest mother in the Mommy and Me group.

Reaching the stop sign, I turn left on Bellisimo Boulevard and immediately face a barrage of red taillights. I roll down the window and am met with the smell of burning flares. Flashing amber lights make the atmosphere surreal, like something out of an alien movie. This is, no doubt, the accident Michael was talking about. My goodness, it must be really bad to still have all this action. I come to a stop, taking my place in line to be waved ahead by the policeman on duty. Looking left, I see the mangled wreckage of a small car loaded on a flatbed tow truck. I squint, trying to make out the color. What a mess. It's light, silver I think. I inch forward. Looks like a small Mercedes. But oh! The front end is shaped like a horseshoe. It must have smashed into that big pole over there. Wait a minute. I recognize that car. It looks like…

"Oh, sweet Jesus!"

Tara

Am I dreaming? Who is this woman? Is it …is she …? She looks like me. She has red hair and clay-stained hands. I don't know. Are my boobs really that big? She's in my studio and she's holding bottle after bottle to her lips in quick motion—as if they're empty and she's trying to get the last drops. Liquid seeps from the corners of her mouth. Good heavens, what is she doing? One at a time, she violently throws each empty bottle against the wall. *Smash!* I hear the explosions. They ring in my head. Glass shards spray about the room like fireworks.

The woman doesn't duck. She allows the shards to hit her—lets madness etch her skin.

Smash! A dark green wine bottle hits the door. It's the door her friend used to walk out on her. "This one's for Shonah!" she shouts. *Smash!* A tiny Rose's Lime bottle spews green goop over newly formed clay pots, like a new brand of glaze. "That's for Brandy!" she cries. She throws back her head and drinks from a dark bottle of Kahlua, and this time, a stream of brown liquid seeps down her chin like an alcohol worm. The woman, her red hair coiling like Medusa's snakes, uses both hands to send the bottle crashing at her feet. "That's for Ian!"

She falls to the ground and releases a hiccough. "You bastard!" she cries. "Where *are* you?"

The redheaded woman picks up a clear, triangle-shaped shard and holds it to the light. Turning it, the glass reflects a rainbow of colors. Aurora Borealis. The Northern Lights. It was the one thing she remembered about her daddy. He had promised her that one day he would take her to see them. It didn't happen. I know that didn't happen. I focus on the rainbow shard as it gets closer and closer to her pale, smooth forearm. The image goes gray as she presses the glass into her skin. Dragging it toward her elbow, her eyes grow as she watches the crimson blood bubble up in a thin, perfect line. "He's the bastard!" she cries, letting go of the cutting tool.

The woman gets up quickly, plants her bare feet in a sea of broken glass and lets her head fall forward. Licking her dry, cracked lips, she craves one thing. More vodka.

The tiger is out of its cage, and only vodka can tame it. There's no stopping the thirst.

Bleeding and besotted, the figure has become a shadow. The only color is her hair. And her blood. She steps into a pair of flip-flops and tears a set of keys from a hook next to the garage door. She pulls open the door of a small car, slumps into the low leather seat, and inserts the key into the ignition. Touching the garage door opener above the rearview mirror, she leaves a garish blood streak on the soft gray ceiling upholstery.

"Damn!" she cries, snarling at the paramecium-shaped stain.

I feel an even greater sense of recognition. I know how this woman feels about her car. *My* car. My Mercedes. I never allow my daughters to ride in it, knowing they'll leave messy desert footprints on the carpets and candy wrappers in the creases of the seats. Each month I have it meticulously detailed—whether it needs it or not. And I can never walk by it without beaming, telling myself that it belongs to *me*. To Tara Shephard, the little gal from the oil fields of Texas. I could have easily ended up trailer trash. But I didn't. I had MADE it! I own that car free and clear, and by God, I deserve it. M-E-R-C-E-D-E-S! It spells M-O-N-E-Y as far as I'm concerned and it's better than a tiara on my head. It's the crowning touch to who I've become.

I hear the engine rumble and watch in my dream as the redheaded woman tears out of the driveway. She doesn't close the garage door. She turns onto the street and leaves the front gate wide open. I see the Kwik Mart down the road, even though I know it's a mile away. The woman drives slowly out of the subdivision grimacing when the bottom of her car scrapes over the second speed bump. Reaching the community gate, she waits for it to open, pulls ahead and fails to look for oncoming traffic before zooming out to the main street. She turns to the east, heading toward Bellisimo Boulevard. Behind her, the sun has begun its colorful descent into night.

At the Kwik Mart, the parking lot is filled with work trucks—painters, carpenters, landscapers—all the tradesmen heading inside for their giant sodas and forty-ouncers of beer. Unable to find a parking space, I watch the Mercedes, as out of place as a Junior Leaguer at a hoedown, pull to the side of the building. The woman grabs her Jackie-O sunglasses from the glove compartment and pulls down her sleeves to cover her bare, bleeding arms. She steps out of the car and goes inside the store.

The door triggers an electronic tone. Through the snowy television monitor, I see five heads gathered in the back of the store next to the refrigerated shelves turn and look. The tradesmen watch as she approaches the counter.

"Do you have Absolut back there?" she asks the clerk.

"In airline bottles," he answers in a dull monotone.

"What do you have in pints?"

He studies her a moment, noting a garish gash on her forehead, as red as her hair. The woman crosses her arms and shifts her weight. He's young, brown-skinned, a ball cap sits backward upon his head. The woman flips her hair and manages a smile. "You wanna see my I.D?" she asks.

He frowns, shakes his head and turns. He reaches for the bottles, lined up like soldiers on the shelf behind him. "You want a pint, you say?"

Her flip-flop goes up and down. "Preferably today." She's tapping her foot, terribly impatient. "What is that? Smirnoff?" she asks. "Gads, rot gut. It'll have to do. Make it two." She slaps a twenty on the counter and watches as he reaches for the second bottle, and then places them in a brown paper bag. She doesn't wait for her change.

The woman clutches the bag to her chest and quickly walks to her car, waiting for her on the side of the building like a conspirator. She closes herself inside, opens the first bottle and fills her waiting mouth.

Color returns to her skin. The snakes slither out of her hair and the beautiful apricot tresses become smooth and shiny.

I feel a burning in my throat. *Where am I?* Again, everything fades to…am I dreaming? Or am I *remembering?*

"Ma'am? *Ma'am!*" The voice is urgent. Male.

There's a sharp pain in my ribcage.

The redheaded woman squeezes closed her eyes, takes a breath, and tips the bottle into her mouth. She does it again. And again. With each sip there are more colors inside my head. It's like the tiles in my kitchen. Or a Peter Max painting. I watch as the woman drinks until she empties the bottle. Tossing it onto the passenger seat, she starts the engine and turns on the radio. Animated voices of drive time D.J.s fill the car. "It's rush hour," says one.

A smile forms on the woman's glistening, alcohol saturated lips. "More like happy hour," she says with a maniacal laugh. She lets out a deep, satisfied breath, backs up, and abruptly throws the gearshift into drive. She pulls the Mercedes onto Bellisimo Boulevard, and instantly blinded, faces the sun—one on one.

Everything momentarily turns white and I hear her scream. "I can't see," she cries. *"Oh my..."*

Chapter 10
Late Night in March

The driver would have no memory of the westbound white, Chevy Tahoe that couldn't stop quickly enough to avoid clipping the right rear of her tiny car, pushing it left into oncoming traffic. A dark blue, Ford Taurus, heading east, had no chance to avoid the silver Mercedes, ultimately sending it into a steel utility pole.

—Shonah Bartlett
From her column, *The Dice Club Chronicles*

Sylvia

I've got two bunkos on my scorecard so far, and may be tonight's big winner. That's amazing. I never win. Too bad there are only five of us here. I'd like everyone to help me celebrate this momentous occasion. We've just finished rolling for sixes in the first round and take a break. There's still been no word from our missing players, Tootsie, Shonah and Tara.

There's enough wine in the last bottle of chardonnay to fill my glass halfway. I hold it to the light, spotting miniscule pieces of cork. Cheap wine. I'm going to have a hangover whether or not I drink this. These days it doesn't take much more than two or three glasses to wake me up in the middle of the night and make me feel like crap for hours. "You know what? I'm going to call Shonah's cell."

"I'm telling you, she's not going to show up here tonight," says Brandy.

"We'll see." My jewel-cased cell phone is still where Chlöe left it after taking me to task about my contact list. Flipping it open, I punch 2 from that very list and scroll to Shonah's cell number. I wait for one ring. Then a second. And a third. It rings four times before activating her voice mail. Shifting my weight as Shonah's son, Jonas, recites her "not available to take your call" message in his sweet little voice, at last I hear the *beep*.

"Shonah, it's Sylvia. Where are you? Are you stuck in that traffic jam? We heard there might be an accident near your neighborhood. Tootsie was supposed to be here about an hour ago and I'm getting worried. And we haven't heard from Tara either. Have you? Call me as soon as you get this message. Okay?"

I push the off button and the small, electronic tone sounds like an exclamation point. Staring momentarily at the one-inch photo screen, a picture of my smiling teen-aged daughter with a mouth full of braces, I hope she's in her room doing homework. Richard promised he'd check her math. Geometry is killing her, poor kid.

Again I press the number 2 and the contact list reappears, replacing my daughter's photo. Scrolling down, I move the cursor to "Tara Cell" and send. Bringing the phone to my ear, I listen to endless rings. "Brother!" I click off before the voice mail recording. The last thing I want to hear is her long message complete with website address and gallery hours. No one self-promotes more fervently than Tara Shephard.

"Neither Shonah nor Tara answered," I announce to the girls, still gathered around the solitary bunko table. "Should I call Tootsie again? I'm getting worried."

"They're fine," says Brandy. "It's really very simple. Tara's not here because she's pissed at me for sending that email. Shonah's pissed for the same reason. They're probably together talking trash about me. And Tootsie's most likely …oh, I better not say anything about Tootsie." She clasps her hand over her mouth.

"Brandy!" I can't help but roll my eyes. "You exhaust me!"

"I saw that email you sent, Brandy," says Amanda. "And just so you guys know, I realize I wasn't actually invited to this party. It looks like some of you didn't take me off the group list. I know because I still get those inane forwards you all send around in circles."

"I never read them," says Chlöe. "I don't have time. And no one told me you quit the group. Say, are we going to start another round?"

"I *like* those forwards," says Blanca. "It's the only worthwhile email I get!"

I bite my lip, believing I only send around the *truly* funny forwards. I examine my scorecard and go over the tallies with my pencil. Two bunkos in the first round. This is huge! I set down the card and drum my fingers on the table. Knowing there's a car accident nearby is eating at me. I can't help it. The Rattlesnake Valley is just too damn small and I worry about everything. I know practically everyone in town. "Blanca, did you see the accident?"

"Did I see it happen?" she asks and shakes her head. "No, no. Just dealt with the traffic filtering off Bellisimo Boulevard."

"So it happened before Tootsie left the house, right? Brandy, what time did you talk to her?"

"What are you, a detective? Tootsie's fine. She's more than fine and I spoke with her well after Blanca got here. Sylvia, if you're really worried why don't we turn on the news? Chlöe, where's your television? Wait. Do you let your children watch television?"

"Of course we have a…" Chlöe is cut off by the sound of her ringing phone.

Chlöe

"It's probably just one of my kids wanting to know if the coast is clear. Excuse me, I'll be right back." The phone rings again and I reach for it and push the TALK button. "Forrest residence, this is Chlöe Forrest, R.N."

"It's Tootsie."

"Tootsie!" I say it loud enough for everyone to hear. They all look up with beseeching eyes.

"Listen," she says, "I've been stuck in the worst traffic jam I've ever seen in the Valley. I don't know how long it's been since I left the house. I pulled over, though, because I'm trying to get more information."

"What's going on?" asks Sylvia.

"Is she coming?" Brandy asks.

"*Shhh!* Just a minute!" I tell them to pipe down and return to the phone. "Tootsie, hold up. The girls are worried about the accident we're hearing about."

"I'm worried too," she says. "Like I said, I'm trying to find out what happened. I heard there was some kind of SUV, which I didn't see. But what I did see on one of those tow trucks that doesn't drag it, you know? It was like on the back of a …a what-do-you-call-it…?"

"A flat bed?"

"Yes! Why couldn't I think of that?" Tootsie seems to be losing her breath a little bit.

"Tootsie, are you all right?"

"I'm sorry, I don't want to jump to any conclusions, but by any chance is Tara there?"

I take a deep breath and look at all the women who've now gathered closely around me. "No, Tara's not here." Sylvia moves toward me, bending in to try and hear Tootsie through the phone. Amanda and Blanca follow.

"What! *What!*," demands Sylvia.

I hold up my index finger and shake it, as if telling a child to wait a minute. "Tootsie, what kind of car was on the flatbed?"

"Silver," she says. "I think it was a Mercedes. A little one. You know, one like…"

I slam my hand down on the table. Brandy, the only one still seated, looks up. Everyone else looks at me and their eyes dart back-and-forth at one another. A panicked moment of shared fear passes between us. "Silver Mercedes," I say.

A resounding chorus calls out: "Tara!"

Shonah

I take off my robe and throw it on my unmade bed. On the weight machine I haven't used in a week, my blue jeans lie across it like cobwebs. Holding them in the air, I take note of the heavy creases at the knees and hip joints. Flapping them with a snap, I judge them sufficient for an emergency. "This *is* an emergency," I tell myself with an admonishing tone. How can I be thinking of what I have on? Suddenly, the numbers 9-1-1 come to mind. They're like numbers on a chalkboard in a math class. I was always so bad at math. Where does Sammy get his ability with numbers?

My heart races. I step into my dirty jeans without bothering to put on panties, and forgo the bra, choosing a clean T-shirt. It's white, old. Has a faded yellow album cover photo of Neil Young's *Come's A Time* on the front. I slip into my Birkenstocks, grab a watch from the nightstand and, as though trained to do so, note the time. "Eight-oh-one."

I check my wallet for cash—one, two, ten, twenty, forty—enough—remove the bills, fold and stuff them in my back pocket. Grasping my keys, I lock the front door behind me and run next door, holding my forearm below my breasts to keep them from bouncing. I don't run the length of our driveway, but instead, cut through the raw desert between our homes. It's still too early in the season for snakes.

Should I have left a note for Dan and the boys?

I reach the property line dividing our territories. Seeing the garage door open, I enter. There are two cars, Ian's pickup truck and Tara's Land Cruiser—her kid-mobile, as she calls it. The gap where Tara's Mercedes is usually parked, between the two monstrous vehicles, looks like a missing tooth.

I call out. "Ian? Girls?" There's no response.

Without knocking, I step inside the house and the girls run toward me. "Mrs. B, Mrs. B!" they cry. "Where's Mommy?"

I stoop and hug them to me. "Oh, Sweeties, it's okay. Everything's okay. You know you could have come over to my house if you were afraid. Don't you know that?"

"We're scared," says Gabrielle. "Daddy's in Mommy's studio. He won't let us in."

"No, no. It's all right. I just talked to him outside." I stand up and take their small hands in mine. As a threesome we head down the hall toward Tara's studio, and just as we make it past the kitchen, Ian slides open the glass door leading to the patio and steps inside. He's holding a phone in his hand.

"The Verde County Sheriff's Office just called," he says. "I have to go. Shonah, can you stay with the girls?"

"What?"

He holds up his hands and indicates with his eyes that he doesn't want to elaborate in front of the children. This is one of those moments when even at my age, I'm shocked into the realization that I'm one of the adults in the room. My heart lurches to my throat and I can barely speak. "Of course, Ian," I manage. I pull the girls to me. Without realizing I've done it until they squirm, I've covered their eyes with my hands and their ears with my elbows.

"What happened?" I mouth the question with great exaggeration.

"There's been an accident," he whispers. I read his lips, having a hard time focusing on anything but the eggshell paint speckles on his forearms and the blood red accent wall behind him. I turn my attention to his eyes, expectantly waiting for him to continue.

"Tara's in the emergency room," he says. He grabs his keys from the kitchen counter and darts past us.

"Daddy, where are you going?" cry the girls. They break from my clutch and chase Ian, who is determined to make his way to the garage door.

He stops and looks over his shoulder. "Stay with Mrs. Bartlett, girls. Daddy will be right back. Everything's okay."

Ian Shephard raises his eyebrows, looks past his redheaded daughters, and looks me in the eyes. The calm expression he had evoked for them morphs into something more like Edvand Munch's painting, *The Scream*. He drops to his knees and pulls the girls to him, holding them in a tight hug. They whimper like puppies. Quickly, he gets up, turns, and closes the door behind him.

The girls grab my legs.

"Shit!"

I feel a squeeze on my left side. "You said a bad word, Mrs. Bartlett," Gabrielle says in a tiny voice.

"Yes, Sweetie, I certainly did." Are all children born editors?

I think the best thing to do is to get Tara's daughters to bed. Although they have separate rooms, I tuck them in together, and then sit in a rocking chair and read a chapter of *Anne of Green Gables.* They're both asleep after four pages.

Kissing them on their foreheads, I breathe in their sweet smells and my eyes fill with tears. They look so much like Tara. I close the shutters and turn off the light next to their bed. My throat tightens and I silently pray. "Please God …please let their mother be okay."

As quietly as possible, I leave the room and close the door behind me.

Amanda

All the women are buzzing around like bees in an upset hive. I've become the silent observer in the room, unsure of my place. Chlöe's still on the phone, Blanca's shoving ham rolls into her mouth like she's beefing up before a period of hibernation, Sylvia's rubbing her hands around her empty wine glass and may very well break another one, and Brandy refuses to believe Tootsie has seen Tara's car. "Oh come on everyone!" she says. "There are hundreds of silver Mercedes around here. Why would you all think it was Tara?"

"Well she's not here is she?" mumbles Blanca.

Chlöe speaks into the phone. "Tootsie, did you see the driver?" She pauses a moment and relates Tootsie's response. "No, just the airbag." Another pause. "No ambulance, only the tow truck. It's gone now." Chlöe pulls the phone from her ear and looks at it. "My call waiting. Not getting a reading on the caller I.D."

"Take it," shouts Sylvia.

Chlöe nods. "Tootsie, I'll call you back." She pushes a button. "Hello? …yes? Yes, Ian." She covers the mouthpiece. "It's Ian Shephard." She speaks into the phone again. "Yes, yes, I'm hosting Dice Club… what? Wait, *what?* Oh …no… No!"

"It *was* Tara's car!" Sylvia yells. "I knew it!"

Chlöe grips the edge of the table. She holds her fingers to her lips and takes a deep breath. "Shonah's there with the girls? …She said what? …Okay… it's good that you called. I know people at Valley General. Ian, please drive carefully…I know. Okay. Thanks for calling. Yes, okay. I will. Bye."

Calmly, she pushes the off button. "I don't have details, but Tara was in an accident and Ian's on his way to Valley General Hospital. Shonah's staying with the girls. I think she could use some support right now."

"Who needs support? Do you mean Tara or Shonah?" asks Sylvia.

"I mean Shonah. Tara's in the best hands she can be in right now and may very well need surgery. There's probably not a lot anyone can do right this minute except sit with Ian while he waits."

Blanca swallows her mouthful of food and pulls the garish red wig from her head. "What else did he say, *mi'ja?*"

"Shonah told him they'd had a fight. And she said Tara was drinking."

"Who had a fight? Tara and Ian or Tara and Shonah?" asks Brandy.

Chlöe returns her phone to the cradle on the wall. "Shonah."

Brandy shakes her head and leaves the room. She grabs her jacket and her purse and fishes inside for her car keys. "I'm going to the hospital," she says. "Anyone want to drive with me?"

"Wait a minute, Brandy," says Sylvia. "Chlöe, do you have any idea if she's going to be okay?"

"I told you everything I know," she says. "I can try calling my friend, Janice Wasserman, to see if she's on duty tonight at the hospital."

"You're friends with her?" asks Brandy.

"Duh Brandy! She introduced me to you," Chlöe says flatly. "We talked about her earlier tonight."

"We did?"

"Don't you remember how jealous she was when you asked me to be a part of this Dice Club instead of her?"

"Oh yeah," concedes Brandy.

"You see? I told you no one listens to me," says Chlöe with a dramatic sigh.

"Okay, who cares?" says Sylvia. "Okay, okay, okay." She falls back heavily in a chair. "I'm hyperventilating. I think I might have to breathe into a paper bag for a minute."

"I'll get you one!" says Chlöe.

"Wait up, Brandy," says Blanca. "I'll go with you. We'll take my new car. I parked behind you anyway and blocked your's in."

"Let me come too," says Chlöe. She hands me a small brown bag and I give it to Sylvia. "Can I use someone's cell phone on the way to call the hospital?"

I put my hand on Sylvia's shoulder as she holds the bag to her mouth and breathes. She looks up at me and removes the bag. "Amanda, do you think you can drive me to the hospital? I don't know what's wrong with me this evening, but I've been shaky since I got here and I shouldn't drive."

I take the bag from Sylvia and tug her elbow. "Come with me for a second." Sylvia gets up slowly and I lead her away from the rest of the women, who are gathering their things and getting ready to leave.

"What is it?" she asks.

My voice is a whisper. "Sylvia, I can't go to that hospital."

"Amanda, I…"

"I haven't been to Valley General since …since he died there. I'm just not ready. Please tell me you understand."

"Of course I understand, Amanda. It's okay," she says. "I'm sorry." She brings the bag back to her mouth, inhales and exhales, filling the bag like a balloon. Her eyes grow with the next inhale and her face distorts comically as she breathes in and out of the bag. I can't help but snort and smile.

Sylvia is clearly offended. "What?"

"Nothing. It's just that …oh, never mind." What I want to say is that it's an enormous relief to see Sylvia no longer seems to be that one hundred percent together woman I've always thought her to be. "You know something Sylvia, it was a big enough step coming here tonight and facing the likes of all of you. I survived that. But I don't think I'm ready to tackle the hospital and all of those feelings any time soon."

"I completely understand," she says. "Don't worry. I'll get a ride with Blanca and the rest of them. I hate to leave my car here at this …this, uh, place. But someone will bring me back here tomorrow."

"Tell you what. Why don't I go over to Tara's and sit with the girls? That way Shonah can go to the hospital and be with the rest of you. She and Tara are such close friends."

"That's a lovely idea, Amanda," says Sylvia. "I'm sure Shonah will appreciate that."

Tootsie

I think the best thing to do is turn around and go to Tara's house. If Tara's home, then I've worried for nothing. I can be there in five minutes rather than staying out in this mess. I pull a U-turn and drive toward Tara and Shonah's subdivision. Oh good golly, do I know their gate code?

Pulling beyond the stately pillars guarding their posh neighborhood like sentries, I spot taillights. Excellent. It's a resident. I'll just sneak in behind this Beamer. Curving left, I climb a steep hill and wind around to, what is it? The second left? Yessireebob, it is.

"Damn it!" Tara has a gate too and it's closed. I park on the street and walk around the gate, starting down the long driveway to her front door. It's like walking to a department store for pity's sake. There must be a hundred lit saguaros in this front yard. Goodness, it's beautiful.

Halfway there, my cell phone rings. It must be Chlöe calling me back. I look at the number, but don't recognize it.

Shonah

Ian promised he'd call. He's been gone twenty minutes, however, it seems a lot longer. I'm pacing like a cat in a cage. I don't know what to do with myself. Opening the refrigerator, the only thing in it is a twelve-pack of Budweiser, some condiments and various faded vegetables in the crisper drawer. Doesn't anyone in this house shop for groceries? I grab a bag of baby carrots and let the door fall closed.

I pull a carrot from the bag and run it under the faucet. "A war zone." Ian had said her studio looked like a war zone. The words replay in my head again and again. Man oh man, what should I do? Should I call the hospital? The police? Dan and the boys will be home any minute. I should call him first and let him know I'm here.

Shit. Forgot my cell phone.

I use Tara's landline and call. No answer. I wait for the beep. "Dan, I'm next door looking after the girls. Call over here when you get this."

Hanging up, I crunch the carrot between my teeth and tentatively walk toward the studio, imagining it taped off with yellow crime-scene tape. If I go inside, will I be tampering with the evidence? My heart pounds harder at the idea. Maybe I *should* try to hide the evidence. Tara might be charged with something. I pick up the pace and then abruptly stop. Wait a minute. No one said the accident was Tara's fault. It could've been the other guy's fault. Yes, that's a distinct possibility. Maybe it wasn't her fault.

Reaching the studio, I lift the iron latch and push open the door with my foot. It emits an eerie creak, like the door of a dungeon. I stick my head into the dark room and can't help but close my eyes, afraid of what I might see.

Bing-*Bong!* The doorbell sounds. The dog barks and I jump back. "Holy mother!" It must be Dan. Or …oh no! What if it's the police? I better hurry. Trotting to the front door, again holding my breasts in place, I want to get to it before the bell rings again and the girls wake up. Who could it be? The police? Two uniformed officers coming to deliver the bad news? To ask where Tara had been drinking this afternoon? In my brief steps to the front door, I compose answers to a potential police interrogation. *"No officer, I didn't see Tara drinking."*

I should have never left her alone with that flask.

Turning the door handle, I press my nose to the cloudy glass bricks surrounding the door. I can't see a thing, not even a shadow. Why doesn't Tara have a peephole? Does she open her door to just anyone? Oh, that's right. She has the gate. Pulling the door open a crack, I don't find uniformed officers on the stoop. "Tootsie!" I pull the door completely open. "What are you doing here?"

Tootsie extends both arms and grabs me around the waist. "Come here," she says, drawing me to her. "Amanda Prince just called me. She's on her way here from Chlöe's house to take over your babysitting duties. I'm going to drive you to the hospital."

I lower my head and rest it on Tootsie's shoulder. My long arms wrap around her fully, and I can't help but marvel at the smallness of my friend. "Your hair is wet."

"Yes, it is."

I release Tootsie and step back. "Weren't you at Dice Club?"

"Uh, no," she says, and a smile forms.

"What is it?"

"Oh Shonah," she says, "the Lord sure works in mysterious ways. I've just received the best news of my life and at the same time Tara's in the hospital fighting to stay alive."

"How do you know that? What do you mean she's fighting to stay alive? Did you talk to someone?" I hold my index fingers to my temples and feel the urge to pace. "All I know is that she's been in an accident. Ian went flying out of here and he said he'd call me but he hasn't."

"Oh, Honey," Tootsie says, reaching for my hand to stop me from my dizzying gate. "I'm sorry. I shouldn't have said that. I'm not entirely certain of her condition, but Michael was very late getting home, which is why I wasn't at Dice Club. He said the backup getting into our little ole section of town was incredible. Then, well, I tried to get to Chlöe's and I couldn't get past the aftermath of the wreckage. I saw a silver Mercedes just down the road apiece. It was totaled."

"Oh ...my ...G-g-g..." I melt to the tile floor. My knees hit with a one-two thud and my palms slap the surface with a loud clap.

Tootsie drops down to me. "Shonah, I'm so sorry. Let it out, Sweetie. Just let it out. You've got to get it out of your system and then be strong. We don't truly know anything yet and you need to have faith. Are her girls in bed?"

I nod.

"Good. They've never met Amanda and I don't want them to be afraid. She can be a scary ole broad when she gets that cross look on her face."

What did she say? Wait a minute, now I'm confused. "Did you say Amanda Prince is coming here? What did …how did…?"

"Apparently she was at Dice Club tonight. She said the rest of the group went to the hospital, but she didn't want to go. Couldn't face it."

I immediately understand why. It must be a terribly scary place. "Her son."

"Yes," says Tootsie. "I'm sure that's it."

Fresh tears fill my eyes. The lump in my throat is so strong, I can hardly speak. Swallowing, I use the back of my hand to wipe away the tears. "I don't know how anyone lives through the death of a loved one. And the death of a child? That has to be the worst!"

"Yes," says Tootsie. "I'm sure it is."

"And now …now these little girls might lose their mother? I tell you, Tootsie, that's the scariest thing about having kids. You love them so much, and you worry constantly that something might not only happen to one of them, but also to you! I know how badly you want a baby, but sometimes I think you're better off than the rest of us. They can age you dramatically because of all the worrying."

Tootsie stands up and places her hands on her belly. "I'm pregnant, Shonah."

It takes a moment to digest what she has said. "What?"

"I'm pregnant. Found out today."

"You *are*?"

Tootsie enthusiastically nods and smiles.

"You're kidding me!" I get to my feet. "Oh Tootsie! This is such good news." I clasp her hands and squeeze. "Do you have a due date?"

"Well, I'm not really sure, but I think it'll be sometime in late September? I haven't told anyone yet except for Michael, of course, and I was goin' nuts waiting for him to come home. Then once he did get home and I gave him the good news, well…" She blushes. "Let's just say I couldn't immediately go runnin' off to play bunko."

"A little Bingo, Bango, Bongo in the bedroom?"

"You're bad!" says Tootsie with a laugh. "Anyway, that's why my hair's wet. I jumped in the shower and thought I could make it to Chlöe's. And then all this happened."

I glance at the wall clock. "You know, Dan and the boys should be home by now. He must not have checked the messages. I'm going to call again. If he doesn't answer, let me run over there and leave him a note."

"Doesn't he have a cell phone?"

"Dan?" I can't help but snort, and then reach for a tissue to blow my nose. "The man still operates like it's 1980."

Brandy

Blanca Midnight checks to make sure I'm strapped in before putting the gearshift into Drive. Her Range Rover is less than a week old and it still has that new car aroma. She must be selling a lot of paintings to afford this beast. Driving out of Chlöe's end of the *barrio*, Blanca looks like she has a driver-of-a-new-car attitude—nervous and still unsure of all its features. "The lights go on automatically, but I don't know where to find the brights," she says.

"Blanca, didn't you read the manual?"

"Are you serious? Who reads those things?" She's returned the red wig to her head, and piled high atop her head, it brushes against the ceiling. She's added black, cat-eye glasses to her ensemble. She looks at me. "I only wear these when I drive at night," she says, using her index finger to push them up her nose.

Sylvia and Chlöe sit silently in back. We turn onto the paved road leading out of the neighborhood and I press my nose to the passenger side window, marveling at the enormous estates we pass. They all have expertly positioned up-lights highlighting giant saguaros and specialty palms. It's like watching an episode of *Lifestyles of the Rich and Famous*. Chlöe the Canadian's place must have been someone's barn—or caretaker quarters. Something! It sure doesn't match the rest of what's around here.

"Rats!" says Blanca. "I should have brought the food tray. Who knows how long we'll all have to wait at the hospital."

Visualizing the food tray covered with Sylvia's saliva, I'm glad it was left behind.

"Brandy, would you dig my cell phone out of my purse? I don't like to talk on the phone when I drive, particularly when I'm still nervous about driving this new monster-sized vehicle. Chlöe, why don't you use it to call your friend at the hospital."

I reach for her purse. "Blanca, you look like something out of the B-52s."

"Shut up, Brandy," she says.

That's the second time tonight someone has told me to shut up. I mimic her. "Shut up, Brandy."

"*Mi'ja*, don't be so touchy. We know you're upset about Tara. We're all upset. Look at it this way, you didn't make Tara start drinking again."

"Why would I think that?" No one in this car knows how many Al-anon meetings I've been to in my life. I dig inside her enormous purse. "Don't preach to me, Blanca. I've been around that block too many times. Where the hell is your cell phone?"

"Front pocket. And I don't mean to preach to you. I don't know what I'm talking about anyway." She slows and then brings the car to a stop at the stop sign. "I turn right to get to Valley General, don't I?"

"Yes," responds everyone in the car.

"Just pay attention to Brandy. She'll tell you which way to go," says Sylvia. "She likes to tell everyone where to go."

I locate Blanca's cell phone and turn around. "Why don't you go to hell, Sylvia?"

"Oh, *that's* it," says Blanca, turning the car toward the hospital. "You and Sylvia kill me. You're always bickering just like an old married couple."

I avoid Sylvia's eyes and throw the phone in Chlöe's lap. "Yeah, so what if we are? Most of the time I'm just kidding. It's Sylvia who's so critical. She just eggs me on." I face forward again. "But sometimes, like tonight, it really bothers me. It's been a tough day. Scratch that. It's been tough for weeks. Did you know my father finally left today?"

Blanca reaches a stoplight, comes to a full stop, and looks at me over her glasses. "No, I didn't know that. I don't know much of anything about you, Brandy. You don't offer a lot of personal information. At least not to me."

"Well, what's to know?" I turn away and once again look out the window. The streets seem barren. Everyone is either still stuck in that traffic jam or inside in front of their televisions watching *ER*. Imagine that! Here we are on our way to the real ER. I wonder if there'll be a doctor as cute as George Clooney. Is he even still on that show? Damn, erase the thought. "Let's just think about Tara right now and get to the hospital. Make another right at the next light."

Ian Shephard

"Sir, I understand you're upset but I'm going to have to ask you again to calm down and lower your voice." The admittance nurse pushes a clipboard at me for the second time. "The best thing you can do for your wife right now is to fill out these forms and give us the information we need regarding her medical history."

"This is bullshit! I get a call telling me she's been brought to the emergency room and I'm not going to fill out a goddamn thing until you tell me where she is."

"I'll handle this," says a husky, dark-haired woman in a short gray coat. A stethoscope hangs loosely around her neck. "You're Ian Shephard, aren't you?"

"Do I know you?"

Stethoscope woman holds out her hand. "My name is Janice Wasserman. I'm a nurse-practitioner. Our kids go to the same school. Some-times I sub as the school nurse." She stops talking. Does she expect me to say something? Talk about the weather. What the hell? I've never seen her before in my life. "I know your wife," she says.

I take her waiting hand in mine. "You know Tara? Have you seen her? Treated her? Will you *please* tell me where she is? Is she okay?" I release the handshake and bring both paint-stained hands to my scalp and clutch my hair.

The woman puts a thick arm around my shoulders and walks me away from the counter and toward the waiting room chairs. She's built like a brick shithouse, this one. "Come with me," she says. "I need you to sit down."

I don't want to sit down. I shrug her arm off my shoulders and plant my work boots firmly into the shining, white tile floor. "Just tell me. Right here, right now. I can't stand the weight of this. Is she…is she…?" My knees buckle and Janice Wasserman reaches out and grabs me under the arms. I accidentally pull the stethoscope off her neck.

Sylvia

Blanca is driving so slowly. I wonder if it's the new car or if she's had too many glasses of wine. I really only saw her with one glass of red. But then again, I'm no drink counter and clearly my mind was elsewhere tonight. I was a wreck. "Boy, if I knew how this day was going to turn out when I woke up this morning I might not have got-ten out of bed."

"I felt that way too when my husband came home and told me he lost his job," says Chlöe.

I turn to her. "He did?"

"Oh, I guess you didn't hear me say that earlier," says Chlöe. "Figures. You never listen to anything I say."

"What!?"

"Oh, come on now," says Brandy in the front seat. "You keep saying that but it's not true, Chlöe."

"Yes it is," says Chlöe. "I don't know why you people even have me in this Club. I'm not like you. I can't keep up with any of you. My house isn't even big enough to host a Dice Club. It's no wonder why hardly anyone showed up. And now we're probably going to have to sell it, cause I don't think I can make enough to afford the mortgage. Even if I go full time."

"Chlöe…" I reach for her hand.

"No, never mind," she says, brushing me away. "Don't say anything.

It's something you couldn't possibly understand. I mean, just look at the difference between us. I can't afford to live in one of your guest-houses, for pity's sake. And everyday I work my fingers to the bone. I never have a minute just to relax like all of you!"

Blanca abruptly hits the brake and we all fall forward into our seat belts. "Now wait just a damn minute," she says. "That's not fair."

Brandy slugs her in the arm. "Holy shit, Blanca. There doesn't need to be another car accident tonight."

"I'm a single mother, Chlöe," says Blanca. "That means no husband here to help me. Ever. He's always off in some Godforsaken Third World country helping out everyone but his own kids, while I work two jobs and try to keep painting in my spare time. So don't you sit there feeling sorry for yourself in my car telling me how busy you are and crying poor, poor, poor me. I've paid a pretty damn high price for this so-called lifestyle and frankly, you can have it. I'd give it all up for a happy marriage. For a man who treated me right and didn't leave me here in the desert to rot like some kind of animal carcass!" Blanca grips the steering wheel and swallows hard.

"I only meant…" starts Chlöe.

Blanca slowly moves the car forward again. Good thing no other cars were behind us. "*Díos mío*, Chlöe, if I have to hear one more time about every friggin' detail of your schedule, I'm going to …I'm going …hell, I don't know what I'm going do. But let me just tell you this, *mi'ja*. You say no one ever listens to you? Maybe they would if you weren't talking all the time."

Good Lord, I've never heard Blanca let it out like this. She's usually always so happy. This situation with Tara is freaking everyone out! I pull on my seat belt strap to loosen it and stare out the window. Tears burn my eyes. We shouldn't be fighting right now. We should be thinking about Tara. Poor Tara. And her little girls. This can't be happening. *It just can't.* I press my forehead to the glass and it feels cool against my forehead. Please God, please. I'll do anything to help her. Just don't let her die. Don't let her leave those girls without a mother. Let her be okay. Please, just let her be okay. I swear I'll be a better person. I'll start going to church again. I'll pray more. I'll be kinder. Just please! *Please, let her live!*

Blanca

We sit at a red light waiting for it to change. I have a headache from yelling at Chlöe. I feel terrible. I don't know what came over me. Why is it taking so long to get there? The drive from Chlöe's to the hospital is less than fifteen miles, but the distance seems twice that far and the stoplights twice as long.

After my outburst it's awkwardly quiet in the car. I think everyone is worried sick. Chlöe hasn't been able to reach her friend, Janet Washerwoman—or something like that—at the hospital. I just hope Tara wasn't drunk driving. I know she's been making an effort to stay sober. She's been really clearheaded and lively lately at the gallery, and her latest line of planters with the golden undertones has been selling like crazy. One was recently seen on television at a garden party on one of those real housewife reality shows. Tara was so happy she nearly burst out of her bra!

I break the silence. "You know Tara's been doing really well lately with her work. And she didn't drink anything at my Dice Club back in November."

"I noticed that too," says Chlöe. "The no drinking thing. It was kind of hard not to because her behavior was so ...so..."

"Normal?"

"Yes, Blanca," says Chlöe with a small laugh. "I guess you can say that."

The sign for the emergency entrance jumps out at me. It's hard to miss the white letters on a bright red background. "Here's the emergency entrance. I can drop you all off and park if you like."

"No," says Sylvia. "Let's go in together."

Ian Shephard

"One of your wife's legs was crushed, with possible damage to the femoral artery. She has three cracked ribs, a collapsed lung and a ruptured spleen," says Janice Wasserman. "She suffered heavy blood loss and further, there looks to be some head trauma. We don't have a neurosurgeon on call tonight and we don't want to MedEvac her up to Phoenix. Right now she's stable but unconscious, and the doctors don't feel comfortable transporting her. The next forty-eight hours are crucial."

I feel my eyes growing bigger and bigger and my chin drawing a little higher with each injury listed. It's like taking punches to the jaw. "Just tell me if she's going to make it."

"She was in good physical shape going into this, but like I said, the next forty-eight hours will tell us everything."

"Isn't there a doctor I can talk to?"

"The doctors are working on her right now, Mr. Shephard. We're doing everything we can. But I'm afraid that's not all."

"There's *more?* My God! What more can there be?"

"Her blood alcohol level was point-two-four."

I don't know what this means. I shift my weight. "Two, four… Uh, is that …bad?"

"It's three times the legal limit in this state."

"Three times? *THREE* times?" I don't believe it. How did they find that out so quickly? I shake my head in disbelief. It's not possible. Tara hasn't been drinking *anything* lately. She's refused my offers of wine in the late afternoon and cocktails before dinner. She said it was her New Year's resolution not to drink as much. "There has to be some kind of mistake."

Janice Wasserman looks past me and her black, severely arched eyebrows lift. I follow her gaze and see two uniformed deputies walk authoritatively through the automatic doors. I quickly turn my attention back to the nurse. She nods at them and her voice takes on a formal tone. "The sheriff's deputies will talk to you, Mr. Shephard."

"Wait a minute, wait a minute! What are you telling me? Are you saying this was, what, a D.U.I? They'll take away her license—not let her drive for a year or something?"

"Others are being treated," she says, backing up as though suddenly I've got some kind of infectious disease. "You're going to have to speak to the deputies."

Did she say others?

I watch two sets of khaki legs stride toward me and hear the faint squeaks of their leather shoes and gun holsters. The sounds magnify in strength with each step. "This can't be happening." The nurse is still backing up and I step forward and grab her white sleeve. "What do you mean there are others? Others in the accident? How many? Are they here?"

"There were some superficial seat belt burns and abrasions from the airbags," she says softly. "They're still inside. But…" She pauses.

I yank on her sleeve and she frowns. "But what? Tell me!"

The deputies step between us. "Are you Mr. Shephard? Mr. Ian Shepard?" asks the taller of the two.

Before I can respond, Brandy, Sandy Lynn's unmistakable twin sister, dressed in denim and with her hands on her hips, followed by Tara's employee, Blanca Midnight Fernglen, who is the blackest version of Lucille Ball to ever walk the earth, burst into the admittance area. "Don't say anything to them, Ian," says Brandy. "Here's my cell phone. Call Sylvia's husband, Richard Ostrander. He's the best lawyer in town." She places the phone in my hand. "It's number four on my contact list." She turns her attention to the nurse-practitioner. "Hello Janice," she says. "Chlöe said you might be on duty. She tried calling you about ten minutes ago to get information about Tara."

"Brandy Lynn?" says Janice with a note of hostility. "I should've known you might be a part of this. Is there anyone you *don't* know in this Valley?"

"How is she?" Brandy asks.

"I've just explained it all to her husband, and he needs to sign those papers." She looks to Brandy's right and eyes Blanca, slowly scanning up from her high-heeled shoes, through the black and white dress, past the lipstick, and to the top of her red wig. "Aren't you Blanca Fernglen?"

Blanca nods.

"What are you supposed to be?"

"It's Dice Club night," Blanca says. "*I Love Lucy* theme."

"Oh yes, the infamous Dice Club. Isn't that what you ladies call your bunko group?" asks Janice. "I've heard about your drunko bunko group. It's the talk of the Valley Verde Golf Club."

I look at the deputies. Their eyebrows shoot up.

Two more women walk through the front doors. "She wasn't at Dice Club," calls out a blonde with a bad dye job. "It was at my house. Tara wasn't there."

"Hello Chlöe," says the nurse. "Listen, I've got to get back."

"Wait Janice," cries Brandy. "Is that all you can tell us?"

"I'm sorry. I have to see to another patient. Brandy, go over those papers with him," she says pointing at me. "She's a good one to have on your side, Mr. Shephard," moving her finger from me to Brandy. "Sharp as a tack. Just needs to slow down her swing."

Brandy clearly drags out the words "fuck you" under her breath and then calls after the nurse. "Another patient from the accident?"

Janice Wasserman doesn't answer. She disappears behind the double doors.

"Mr. Shephard," says one of the deputies, "it's really not necessary to call an attorney. You're not under arrest. No one is. We just want to ask you a couple questions."

The four women, Brandy Lynn, Sylvia Ostrander, Blanca Fernglen and the blonde whose name I can't put my finger on, gather round me, closing me off from the police officers like a protective barrier. I look past them and speak to the deputies. "Look officers. I don't know squat. I came home from work and my wife was out. I thought she was at her Dice Club. These are her bunko friends."

"What are bunko friends?" asks the short deputy.

"It's just a game we play," says the blonde. "A dice game your wives probably play. Haven't you heard of it? You have four to a table and you start rolling for…"

"Not now, Chlöe," says Brandy. "Why don't you go see if you can get Janice Wasserman to give us more information about Tara? At least pull some strings to get Ian in to see her."

"See?" says the blonde, Chlöe, to the others. "I told you no one ever listens to me." She skulks away toward the admittance desk.

Chlöe

I don't think I know anyone besides Janice who works here, and she seemed a little cold. Where does she get off calling us the "drunko bunko" group? What a bitch! So we have a drink or two. Last time I checked it was legal in this country, and not everyone drinks like Tara! And she was definitely rude to Brandy. What did she mean, slow down her swing? It must have something to do with golf. I think Janice is a big shot at the local golf club.

I reach the granite counter of the admittance window and peer through the sliding glass windows, disturbingly covered with finger-prints. Heck, I know my house is no sterile zone, but isn't this the Valley's most prestigious hospital? No one's here. Sliding open the panel, I lean in my head and look around. They must all be with the patients. That's strange. You'd think they'd have a bigger staff. Hmm. I wonder how much these nurses are paid. Looks like they could use my expertise, and if I get a job here we just might be able to keep the house. I wonder if Janice would give me a reference.

Casually walking to the admittance door, I push it open. I step inside and squint at the harsh lighting. The familiar antiseptic smell of the many hospitals in which I've worked during my career fills my senses. Rounding the corner, I see a man and a boy sitting in chairs outside a curtained area. Another man in turquoise scrubs brushes past me and the room bursts to life. Action, noise, people. Where did they all come from?

Focusing on the Harry Potter heads of the man and the boy as they slump forward in their chairs, I notice the boy has a bandage on his forehead and the man wears a neck brace. I wonder if they were in the accident. I approach them and clear my throat. "Excuse me?"

They look up at the same time and stare at me with twin expressions.

My mouth falls open. "Oh my Gawd!"

Amanda

Shonah greets me at Tara's front door with an awkward embrace. She sniffs the air. "Have you quit smoking?" she asks.

I point to my shoulder. "I'm wearing the patch. It helps. Three weeks tomorrow."

"Good for you. Good to see you, Amanda." Her movements grow even more awkward and jerky. "Thanks for coming. I can't stand not knowing what's going on with Tara."

"I'm afraid I can't tell you anything."

"Tell me anything? Oh. You mean about Tara?" Shonah quickly waves her hand in front of her face. Clearly, she's not wearing a bra and there are moth holes in her faded Tee-shirt. Her cheeks are flushed, and her hair short, freshly cropped like a boy out of a barbershop. Like Sean. Wow, I never noticed. "Tootsie's here," she says. "She's gonna take me to the hospital."

Something inside me melts as Shonah leads me into Tara's colorful kitchen and I see Tootsie Fennimore taking her purse from the counter and putting it on her shoulder. There's a noticeable change in Tootsie too. Something's different.

"Uh, hi Tootsie." I cock my head. What is it? Her hair's wet for one thing. No, that's not it. It's her boobs. And there's a glow.

"Hi Amanda," she says, cutting off my thoughts.

It hits me. "Are you pregnant?"

Tootsie's mouth falls open. She shakes her head and closes her eyes. "Darn that Brandy Lynn. She just had to let the cat out of the bag, didn't she?"

I shake my head. "Brandy Lynn? No, she didn't say anything. You are, aren't you! I can tell by looking at you."

"Are you kidding?" asks Tootsie. "How on God's green earth is that possible?"

"It's true," says Shonah. "Isn't it wonderful?"

"Well I knew you were trying, Tootsie. And yes, it's wonderful. Really good news. I'm happy for you. I mean it."

"Thanks, Amanda."

I nod and walk toward her. We share a brief, graceless embrace. "You know, come to think of it, Brandy did hint around about you having a secret, but she honestly didn't say anything about you being pregnant."

"You told Brandy?" asks Shonah. "I thought you said Michael was the only one who knew. Did she know on the golf course today?"

"No," says Tootsie. "I didn't tell her. She guessed over the phone when she called from Chlöe's to see what was keeping me. Honestly, if Amanda could tell just by looking at me, Brandy probably knew it when she saw me on the course. She's kind of spooky, that one, the way she's so quick to know everything all the time. Besides, doesn't she have, like, a dozen kids?"

"Five," says Shonah. "Gave birth to three. Whatever! It's great news and everyone will know soon enough."

Tootsie holds out her hands in front of her midsection indicating a pregnant belly and smiles. Shonah holds out her hands in front of her chest indicating enormous mommy boobs. "Someone might even write about it in the Sport's section," Shonah says. "Local retired golf pro finally gets knocked up!"

"Stop it!" says Tootsie with a laugh. "Miss Shonah, don't you be telling any of your newspaper people a thing. I've got to be careful and make sure it takes. At least let me get through the first trimester and out of the danger zone. I'm not the sweet young thing I once was!"

They should get going. "You two ready? Anything special I need to know about the girls?"

"They're sound asleep," says Shonah, frowning as she snaps back into the reality of Tara's accident. "I can't believe this is happening. I don't know how long we'll be, Amanda. Does it matter?"

"I'll call in sick tomorrow. I'm sure Richard Ostrander, Mr. High-Powered Attorney At Law, will understand."

"Tootsie," says Shonah, "I just want to run next door. I'll cut through the yards, go in and leave a note for Dan. Pick me up?"

"You bet," says Tootsie. "And you should probably put on a bra, sister."

Chlöe

What are *they* doing here?

Shonah Bartlett's son from the soccer team, Sammy, a decent mid-fielder, is sitting with his father, Dan. Sammy goes to school with Roger Jr., and is in my carpool. He elbows his father and points at me. "It's Nurse Chlöe," he says. "She works at our school sometimes. Gives us fluoride, which I *hate.*" He practically spits the word "hate."

Dan squeezes his son's knee. "*Shhhh,*" he scolds.

I motion toward Sammy. "He's right. I'm Chlöe Forrest. I'm Shonah's friend. I mean, she's in my Dice Club—or, er, I'm in *her* Club. Whatever. And I drive the carpool. Soccer mom. Guilty! What happened to you?"

Sammy looks away while Dan stares at me dumbly. He opens his mouth and I wait for his answer. Nothing comes. Is it possible he doesn't recognize me from the sidelines?

I take a step forward and lean over. He may be in shock. "Are you okay?"

"I …I never saw it coming," he stammers. "I was just minding my own business, driving out of the valley on Bellisimo Boulevard. I was taking the boys to dinner as I always do on Dice Club night and …and the son-of-a-bitch just slammed right into us." His chin drops to his chest and he throws his arm around the boy's shoulder.

"Ow, Dad," cries the boy. "That hurts! It's where the seat belt cut me. Can't we just go home? Where's Jonas?"

That's right. The little one. "Where *is* Jonas? I know him. He's in the gifted program with my daughter, Lisa."

"No he isn't," says Sammy in an ornery tone. "It's me who's in it with Roger. Lisa's a year older than Jonas. You probably just see him with my mom at soccer."

"That's right. Of course. I'm sorry."

Dan looks up at me. "Do you know where Shonah is?"

I shake my head. "No, sorry I don't."

"She said she wasn't going to Dice Club tonight. Something about a fight with Tara and Brandy? I tried calling both the house and her cell, but she didn't answer. I can't imagine where else she might go."

"Oh wait a minute. I know where she is. I forgot she went over to Tara's place when Ian had to …oh no!" My hand flies to my mouth. I shouldn't say anything else before I can find out what's going on. I'm not even sure Dan's listening to me. I've seen that distant, spaced out and in-shock expression too many times. "Dan, Shonah's fine. Do you know anything about your other son?"

"My other son? Jonas. Yes. He was in the front seat. I shouldn't have let him sit there but he begged me! I swear, I never saw it coming!"

I place my hands on both their shoulders. Bending at the waist I use the most soothing nurse voice I can muster. "It's going to be okay. Do you hear me? Nurse Chlöe is going to get to the bottom of this. You just stay here and I'll be right back."

I march at a quick pace and the heels of my shoes—not my normal, soft-soled nursing shoes—clack on the high-polished tile. Stopping at the first door, I pull it open. Supply room. "Damn!" Moving forward, I open the next door and two sets of surprised eyes look up at me. One is a female nurse, who squeezes the ball of a blood pressure monitor. It's wrapped around the thick arm of a Hispanic man with a black eye and a bleeding facial wound.

"Can I help you with something?" asks the nurse tending to him.

"Yes, I'm an R.N. I'm looking for a patient named Bartlett. I think he was in a car accident?"

"Yeah, the kid," says the nurse. "Down the hall on the left. You've got to go to the pediatric unit. But ma'am…"

I don't wait for her to finish her sentence. I let the door fall closed behind me and follow the nurse's directions, turning left and bursting through another set of double doors. The noise level increases. I hear voices, far too many voices. I hear the sounds of a code team coming from behind the first, blue curtain. They stop me in my tracks.

"Clear!" directs a male voice.

I hear a jolt of electricity shoot from the defibrillator paddles.

I hear the high-pitched death tone of the flat line.

"Come on!" I hear the same male voice command.

I hear the collective sigh of the medical team.

"One more time," someone yells. "Clear."

And then a jolt.

Again, the flat line tone. Time slows. It's like a dream, and I hear a thin, yet stoic voice pronounce the time of death.

I hear my own heartbeat pound through every joint of my body.

"Ma'am," I hear. "You're not supposed to be here."

I hear it all, and I realize what's happened.

I can't move.

"Ma'am?" It's another nurse dressed in salmon scrubs and carrying a clipboard.

I bring my hands to my face and can't stop the flood of tears from spilling over my fingers. With the steady sound of the flat line buzzing in my brain and the words "time of death" ringing in my ears, all I know is that I don't want to be a part of the world that is about to change so drastically for my friends.

I back up, turn, and go through another set of doors. Turning left, then right, I look around, lost. I don't know where I'm going. I clutch at my hair on either side of my part and all I can think of is that I have to get out of here!

I stop and try to get my bearings. Which way did I come in?

Suddenly, something touches my leg.

"Nurse Chlöe? Is that you?"

I let go of my hair and turn to the voice coming from my left. It's a small voice, weak. Where's it coming from? I look to my right and then again to the left. All I see are empty corridors and too much sterile white. Again, I feel something touching my leg. Finally I look down.

"I didn't know you worked here."

Shonah

My house is quiet and dark. I press my palms to the wall, feeling for the light switch. Finding it, my eyes instantly go for the clock above the kitchen sink. "Damn it!" What business does Daniel Bartlett have keeping the boys out past their bedtime? They both have spelling tests in the morning and we have to deliver Jonas' science fair project to the school. It's an elaborate report on global warming, and the first science project he did completely on his own.

I'm so proud of him. Usually he lets Sammy do all the work.

I race to my bedroom, grab a clean bra and whip off the Neil Young shirt. I smell like the hot tub. Giving my underarms quick wipes of deodorant, I go inside my closet and select a plain, black pullover. Checking my teeth—fine—I run my fingers through my still damp hair and rush for the front door. Closing it behind me, the name "Tara" forms on my lips.

"Please let her be okay," I whisper as I jog through the courtyard and toward Tootsie's waiting vehicle.

I step inside Tootsie's car and she heads down the driveway. "Please let her be okay. Please let her be okay. Please… " I repeat these words over and over as we make our way to the hospital.

"It's good that you're praying," says Tootsie.

"It's more like begging. Who am I begging? God? I don't know. Is this praying? Is this what prayer is?"

"Yes, Darlin'. It certainly is."

Heat courses through my veins, and by the time we reach Bellisimo Boulevard where the only signs of a traffic accident are flare ashes and a utility truck next to a pole, heat transforms into anger. It doesn't feel like the warmth of God. A line of sweat forms on my upper lip. I wipe it away and my thoughts turn to Hell. "This is hellish! It's not like God, it's like the Devil had a hand in this. I mean, I stood there today and listened to the angry words spewing out of Tara's mouth. She said some pretty mean things to me. It's like she just needed an excuse to start drinking again. And I let her do it. *I let her do it!*" I slap my hands on the dashboard and it startles Tootsie.

She gasps. "Shonah, calm down. This isn't going to do anyone any good. Take a sip of water." She hands me a bottle of Evian.

I take it and unscrew the top. "I'm sorry. You're right. Of course, you're right. I'm sorry." I take two deep swallows of water.

We drive the rest of the way in silence until Tootsie slows at the entrance to the hospital. "Okay, we're here," she says. "Let me just find a place to park and we'll take a few deep breaths and calmly walk inside. Okay?"

"Okay."

Tootsie

I take Shonah's arm and we walk toward the large, double glass doors of the hospital. The word "EMERGENCY" shines in plain white letters with an alarming red background. We step on the carpet and the doors fly open with a *whoosh!*

Shonah takes another swallow of water. While her head is back, I squeeze her arm and bring us to a stop. Slowly, a cluster of women standing in the middle of the room turns in unison, responding to the sound of the opening doors. I see the faces of the Dice Club.

Sylvia Ostrander.

Brandy Lynn.

Blanca Midnight Fernglen.

Chlöe Forrest.

Sylvia breaks from the cluster first and walks to us. "We came as soon as we learned it was Tara," she says. "And now ...now, Sweetie, I'm so sorry."

"I know," says Shonah. "Me, too. Tara is really lucky to have so many good friends. She's sure going to need them when she sobers up and faces a drunk driving charge, which I'm assuming is the case. And she *is* going to come through this. I know it. She is."

I give Shonah's arm another squeeze and look at Brandy Lynn, who is shaking her head back-and-forth. All the women exchange concerned looks with one another. Chlöe is crying. What do they know? *Did Tara ...did she ...is she ...is she going to make it?*

"Where's Ian?" Shonah asks and glances around the room at the mostly empty chairs. She scans the rows, as though looking for letters in a word search puzzle, and then her eyes come to a stop when she sees the faces of ..."What the ...?" she utters.

I see them at the same time and a jolt of recognition punches me in the stomach.

Shonah drops her water bottle, shakes loose my grip, and walks to them.

I follow her.

"Dan?" she asks weakly. "What are you do . . .ing ...here?" She reaches for her son, who jumps from his chair and throws his one free arm around her. His other is in a sling.

"Mom!" he cries. "Oh, Mommy."

Holding her son with her right hand, Shonah touches his sling with her left index finger and then reaches for Dan, placing her hand on his bruised face. He's wearing a whiplash collar, and his expression is one of terror. He opens his mouth. But he can't speak.

"Dan?"

We all rush to this family, and as we do the escalating roar of an approaching train fills my head. And heat—heat as powerful as the sun—burns through all my protective layers of logic and knowledge, of feigned strength and a cool demeanor.

I believe I'm going to vomit.

Brandy

I put my arm around Shonah's waist. Sylvia stands at her other side. She looks at me, then Sylvia, and then back again at me. "What's going on, Brandy? Where's Jonas?" she asks. "Where's my son?"

Putting my free hand on Sammy's head, I know I have to be the one to tell her. "Shonah, they were in the accident."

"The accident?" she asks. "The accident?" she asks again. She bends at the waist and tries to shake free the touches of Sylvia, Sammy and me. Sammy won't move. He buries his face in her chest, like a rooting babe seeking comfort and nourishment. She places her hand atop his head, on top of mine. "Oh my God," she says.

She breaks free and grabs her husband's hand. He looks at her, his obsidian eyes filled with tears, and then squeezes them closed. His face crumbles.

"I never saw it coming," he says.

Chapter 11
April

Attention ladies: That heat you feel? The kind that comes in a flash and fills you with an invisible hot liquid that turns your skin pink and releases liquid above the lip in the area you recently had waxed? You know what I'm talking about.

Everything around you momentarily has an aura of a painted Hollywood set, like the mountains surrounding our Valley on the rare cloudy day. Your heart beats faster, your knees get weak and at any second, you think you're going to lose your latté.

Well, I've got good news. It's not you getting old. It's the globe.

My son's recent science fair project on Global Warming has led me to the conclusion that it's not a drop in estrogen levels affecting my hypothalamus, but rather, it's a rise in carbon dioxide levels collecting in the atmosphere and trapping the sun's heat that's causing both the planet and me to warm up.

—Shonah Bartlett
From her column *The Dice Club Chronicles*

Tara

"Jonas!" I'm screaming and no one can here me. "Jonas, where are you?"

I can't move. I'm flat on my back. A brownish, then orange light creeps through the cracks of my eyes and I must fight to open them. They feel glued shut.

Is it hot in here, or is it just me? I'm dry. I need fluids. Am I dreaming?

My hand, as it reaches toward my face, feels like it holds a lead weight. With effort I pull it up and touch the sharp crust in the corners of my eyes. Tension pulls at my temples, an all-encompassing pain penetrates my skull. Have I been drugged? There's a soft, cotton bandage on my forehead and my leg is elevated, wrapped and hanging from a cord.

Where am I?

I try to raise my head. I can't. What's that noise? There's a steady beeping of, what is that? A heart monitor?

Oh, no. Is it mine? Where the hell am I?

The pace of the beeping quickens. It's so darn hot in here!

I hear a voice. Where's it coming from?

"Honey? Tara, are you awake?"

Another voice. "Mama?"

And a third. "Mommy's waking up!"

Finally opening both eyes, I cringe at the harsh white light and squeeze them closed before willing them open once again. "Ian? Is that you?" I can't see around my leg. "Girls?"

"It's us," says Ian. He comes into view as he nears my bedside. I feel him clutch the rail. Both girls follow him, slowly. Shyly. "We're here. We're right here."

"Ian!" A picture of him is fully developed inside my head. His sandy hair is long, too long as usual, and his skin is tanned. He could be a movie star. Matthew Mc-what's-his-name's twin brother. And he's mine. But is it Ian? I can't bring the figure before me into focus. "Ian, tell me that's you. Where have you been?"

"I'm right here. I've been right here the entire time."

My head throbs. I grimace against the pain. "What entire time? What happened?"

"You had an accident, Honey," he says. "You don't remember?"

"An ...acci ...an accident?" The heart monitor quickens. I see the girls' small hands squeeze the blue denim of their daddy's legs.

"Mommy, you've been sleeping for almost three months," says Gabrielle.

"Not months, stupid," says Nicole. "Weeks."

"That's what I meant," my little one says. "We didn't think you were ever going to wake up."

"Yeah, we had to eat McDonald's. Daddy ordered pickles on my hamburger," says Nicole. "I *hate* pickles!"

I try to sit up, using my hands to lift my heavy torso. My head pounds and pounds. Ian grabs pillows and adjusts them behind my back. "Don't try to do anything too quickly," he says. "You had a nasty gash to the forehead. A dozen stitches and one hell of a concussion."

"Stitches? A concu…? Wait a minute!"

"Honey, you need to calm down."

"What happened to the other drivers? The passengers? What about Jonas?"

"Jonas Bartlett?" he asks.

"Jonas?" asks her elder daughter. "You were just calling his name."

"He's yucky," squeaks Gabrielle.

"Yes, Jonas Bartlett." Again, I cringe at the pain in my head. "I keep hearing his name. I think I've been dreaming about him."

"It was just…" starts Ian.

"Where's Shonah?" Tears flood my eyes.

My daughters, Nicole and Gabrielle, like twin mirrors of the child I was, both pout. Their eyes fill and as they dig their small fingers into Ian's legs, tears fall down their rosy, pink cheeks.

"Shonah's in the waiting room," says Ian, raking his fingers through our daughters' long, tangled hair. "At least she was the last time I checked. Practically your entire Dice Club has been coming in shifts since you were brought in. Your friend from the gallery, the hot Mexican model, keeps feeding everyone. She's got enough trays of food out there to feed the entire staff."

"Blanca's here?"

"Yes, of course, Blanca Midnight," he says.

"And Amanda keeps trying to braid our hair," says Nicole. "She's been staying at our house, Mommy."

Amanda? Amanda Prince. What the …? Gabrielle leans toward me and whispers, "I don't like her. She has a mean face."

I pet her loose, stringy hair and close my eyes. "I need to see Shonah."

Shonah

"She's awake," says Ian as he enters the waiting room. Brandy and I are the only ones here. "Shonah, she's asking for you."

"For me?"

"Yes."

"Maybe she wants to go jogging," says Brandy. "Here, take these." She hands me a bouquet of stargazer lilies.

"Okay, Brandy. Thanks. Hey, I meant to ask you, how did you know they're Tara's favorites?"

"I know a thing or two about a thing or two," she says. "Listen, I have to run to meet my ten o'clock elbow. Call me later."

I kiss her cheek and watch as she whips around her silky blonde hair and strides out the door. That woman exudes sheer confidence. If she ever found a way to package and sell it, it would have to come with a warning label. We have long since forgiven one another for the hurtful things we said after the email incident. Fate had a hand in helping us put things into perspective.

Ian points down the hall to the room where Tara's been in and out of consciousness since the night of the accident. I nod at him and walk to her room. Tentatively peeking inside, she appears to be asleep. She looks beautiful. Her strawberry tresses are splayed across the starchy, white pillowcase, while she hugs another pillow to her chest. It's covered with a 600-thread count case, printed with tiny pink rosebuds on a tea-stained background.

I set down the flowers next to two other flower arrangements. The Dice Club has been decorating her room and making it feel more like home. Pulling up a chair, I sit next to Tara's bed and reach for her hand. I shake my head. "I hear you're asking for me?"

Tara opens her eyes. She blinks, adjusting to the light. Turning her head, she focuses on me. "Hi," she says. "Is that you?"

"I'm here, Tara."

"Shonah."

"Yes. Right here."

"How can you be here? How can you stand to be here? After what I've done?"

"Tara, don't. It's okay. We're okay. I forgive you. Really, I do. You weren't in your right mind. I knew it then and I know it now."

"But..."

"But nothing. How's your head?"

"My head hurts."

"I told you that was a pretty bad cut you had even before you were crazy enough to get behind the wheel. How you thought you could drive anywhere is just insane." I've said all these things to her already. Whether or not this time she's conscious enough to take it in, I don't know, but there seems to be a brighter light behind her green eyes, so I continue. "They cited you with a D.U.I. You realize you caused traffic to be backed up for an hour? People were pissed. And your blood-alcohol was outrageously high. Point two-four-something."

She mouths the words, "Point two-four?"

"The legal limit is point oh-eight, *mi'ja*."

"*Mi'ja?* That's right!" says Tara. "Blanca! I saw her. Blanca Midnight saw it. She saw it all from the gallery. No wait. It was Chlöe. I distinctly remember hearing her voice—that Canadian accent telling me everything. Everything she heard."

What is she talking about? "I don't know about Blanca and Chlöe, but unfortunately for you, a lot of people saw it. You're gonna have to pay the deductible on Dan's Tahoe, you know. And there was another car too. Not to mention the power pole, Tara. You knocked out electricity to the entire subdivision next to ours'. Your Mercedes is totaled."

"But what about... Wait a minute, Shonah. Didn't they tell you?"

"Tell me what?"

"Oh, God! I'm so confused." Tara brings her hands to her eyes and rubs them. "Please tell me this is all just a terrible nightmare."

"It *is* a nightmare. You're lucky to be alive! It could've been a lot worse. You've destroyed both our cars. You're facing charges. You're gonna lose your driver's license, and I'm gonna be stuck hauling your kids all over town to their dance classes and piano lessons and whatever else you've got them signed up for. It's already been in the paper. Everyone knows."

"But Shonah..."

"But nothing. You're going to have to go into rehab. We're all just waiting to see if you choose Bellisimo Vista or Betty Ford. Betty Ford is the odds on favorite. In fact, I think Chlöe's banking on it. She's trying to not lose her house. Even got a job working here in the pediatrics unit. Since she started last week she has stopped in to see you every day."

"Chlöe Forrest?"

"Yes, of course Chlöe Forrest. Do you know anyone else by the name of Chlöe? But anyway, Sylvia knows the manager of Vista. Maybe she can get you a discount."

"Wait a minute, Shonah." Tara tries to lift herself. She struggles and I reach out to help her. She knits her brow and stares at me intently with watery green eyes. "Why are you being so flip?"

"*I'm* being flip? Tara, I'm just laying it on the line for you. I should really hate you right now for everything you said and everything you did. You smashed into my FAMILY! They were innocently going out to dinner like they always do on Dice Club night. And I didn't even go to Dice Club! The seat belt practically dislocated Sammy's shoulder. Dan took an airbag to the face and couldn't breathe right for a week. And Jonas..."

"Jonas!" she cries. "*That's* what Chlöe told me. It was about Jonas. I heard her! Shonah, I'm so sorry."

"Sorry? Yes, sorry. I'm sure you are." I turn and walk away from her. I pick up Brandy's bundle of stargazer lilies and breathe in the potent, sweet aroma. It reminds me of the honeysuckle nights of my youth— my life before driver's licenses. Before deadlines. Before heartbreaks. Before children. Before a life filled with complicated relationships.

How does Tara expect me to react? How does anyone expect me to behave after this? To start a war? Hold a grudge forever?

The lilies are intoxicating. I set them down and see yellow lily dust has stained my fingers. I turn and face the widow, peering through the blinds at the majestic mountains surrounding our Valley. It's already pushing a hundred degrees. Local television meteorologists are having contests, giving viewers the opportunity to guess what day will post the first triple digit day. Everyone's talking about global warming.

Still looking out the window marveling at the desert landscape in all its April glory, I take a deep breath. "You want to know about Jonas?"

I turn and face Tara's frantic green-eyed stare.

"Well, Jonas is great," I tell her. "I couldn't be more proud of him. His project won first place in the Science Fair."

Chapter 12
May

From the editor: Shonah Bartlett is on hiatus for the summer. Her column, *The Dice Club Chronicles*, will return in September.

Brandy

Second place in the Valley Verde Golf Club Women's championship is nothing to sneeze at. If only I hadn't finished behind my archrival, Janice Wasserman. I tried to get Tootsie Fennimore out on the links prior to the tournament to benefit from her professional tips, but now that she's pregnant, she doesn't want to do anything but sit at home with her feet up and load up on folic acid and a balanced diet. Can't say I blame her. This may be her only shot and she's not going to do anything to upset that apple cart.

It's Saturday and I'm traveling to the Coast by plane. I cleared my calendar and left my husband, Levi, and my twin brother, Sandy, in charge of the ranch and the kids. Last week I informed my partners at the physical therapy clinic that I was taking a leave of absence. "I don't know when I'll be back," I had said. "Could be a week."

Could be a summer.

My father needs me. After leaving the Rattlesnake Valley in March, he phoned each day complaining of his many ailments and ranting about the hired help. He's convinced his housekeeper spends all her time making long distance calls on his phone and eating his food. "She goes to the grocery store three times a week—sometimes four—and I'm sure she's just meeting her friends for doughnuts and coffee down at the *Starbutts* place on the corner."

"It's not butts, Dad," I told him. "It's bucks. Star-*Bucks*. And they don't have doughnuts."

"Does it matter what the hell it's called?" he barked back. "For all the money she says she spends on food, there's never anything in the fridge when I go to make myself a sandwich." His complaints didn't end with the housekeeper. The nurse who comes in weekly to take his blood pressure and monitor his medications is "an incompetent boob," who he suspects steals from him. He rants whenever her name comes up. "The price of prescriptions can't be that high!"

There's no question my father is deteriorating. Each year past eighty, his physical condition spirals downward in fast-forward motion. Man, he's such a mean old cuss. Why do the mean ones live on and on? Just to make our lives miserable?

The only one in the family with any medical training—not to mention money—it makes sense for me to be the one to arrange for extended in-home care for him. With little discussion, Levi gave his approval. I gotta say, it's one way he's an understanding spouse. Not that we have much left of a marriage, but Levi and I do have an understanding where our extended families are concerned. On a daily basis, we know how not to get in one another's way. And one thing that would definitely get in the way of the silent peace that exists between us would be my father's permanent residence in the guesthouse. It's enough that my brother once moved in "on a temporary basis." Eight years later he's as permanent on property as the broken down John Deere tractor basking in weeds behind the corral. And about as useful.

In spite of the volatile relationship I have with my father—his dogmatism, my obstinacy—I am, perhaps, the only one of his children to whom he'll listen. I've grown to accept it's because we're so much alike.

Flying in first class, the front row, I finish my cabernet just as the flight attendants latch the door, complete their cross check, and sit facing me. I wave my glass. "I'll take another as soon as we're wheels up." That'll be just enough to get me through my detestation of flying.

The two young women, one a blonde Barbie doll, the other her redhaired cousin, Midge, sit on their hands, nod and smile. "Of course," they say in unison.

Placing my Bose Acoustic Noise Cancelling headphones on my ears, I plug into the armrest and allow Celine Dion's *My Heart Will Go On* to flood into my brain. The easy listening channel. I can use a little easy listening. Closing my eyes and letting my head fall back against the cushioned chair, I sink into the reality that I'm temporarily free from my life—my children, my husband, my brother, my patients, my friends. Too bad the flight is only an hour. All I have to look forward to is the biggest of my burdens, my father.

After everything that's happened with Tara and the Dice Club, I think getting out of town is a really good idea. The emotional trauma—the not knowing—and facing the possibility of losing my friend, particularly because some felt I helped stimulate Tara's bender by sending that email, was too much. Granted I didn't pour the drinks into Tara's mouth, but you could say I dangled the bottle in front of her. I could have been more supportive.

Alcoholism. It can really ruin a good time. Maybe I'll forgo that second glass.

Tara was lucky. Things could have turned out a lot worse. During her last days in the hospital, when she was still confused and falling in and out of unconsciousness, she confided in me that when she blacked out she had experienced a terrible nightmare. A nightmare that included massive consumption of vodka purchased at the "skanky little Kwik Mart" down the road from her house, a place into which she normally wouldn't dream of setting her high-heeled feet. What she had a hard time understanding is that it wasn't a dream. Her accident occurred as she pulled out of the driveway of this convenience store.

"It was terrible," she had said. "Everyone was here in the hospital. Everyone knew. Except for Shonah. No one could tell her. No one."

"Tell her what?" I had asked. "About her family having a terrible accident and wrecking their car because of you? Or about you falling off the wagon? Shonah was the one who witnessed it first hand in your studio that afternoon."

Tara wouldn't say everything about what she had dreamed. But she said she kept hearing Chlöe's voice. Now why didn't that surprise me? Everyone who has the slightest acquaintance with Chlöe the Canadian hears her voice incessantly. But I found out that on the night of the accident when Chlöe went into the emergency room, she overheard the code team pronounce someone's time of death. She thought she was in the pediatric wing, and she thought it was Jonas Bartlett. Poor Chlöe believed she'd have to go out to the waiting room and tell everyone this terrible, terrible news. She started stumbling around the place trying to find her way out, and whom does she find? Jonas Bartlett, very much alive.

Jonas was riding in the front seat when the accident happened. The airbag went off at something like a hundred miles per hour and knocked him unconscious. He came to after a short spell, but they had to keep him overnight for observation. Dan Bartlett was a mess. He was beside himself with guilt for allowing his ten-year-old to ride in the front seat and Shonah read him the riot act. Huh! As if that woman has never made a mistake.

Damn, I wonder how it feels to be perfect.

I'm still amazed at how the Bartlett family forgave Tara for what she did. Would I be able to do that? I try to wrap my mind around this for a moment, and then quickly erase the thought. I can't bring myself to imagine any of my children harmed in any way.

Meanwhile, the high-powered attorney, Richard Ostrander, settled the case against Tara, which revoked her driver's license for one year and made her responsible for property damage to the power company. She paid the insurance deductibles on the other cars involved and the emergency treatment for the Bartletts. Her detox wasn't too dramatic and primarily took place when she was unconscious, never knowing the Librium was going into her system.

"The punishment I put upon myself was more than enough to rehab me," she told Sylvia, Shonah, and me as we joined Ian in escorting her to Betty Ford. "I promise to come back a new woman, and I'll never touch another drop of vodka as long as I live." Then she flashed that winning smile and rolled away in a wheelchair, a haze of apricot hair.

I haven't told anyone, but I made a vow to myself to do everything I can to support her. It's the least I can do.

Tootsie hosted the next Dice Club and we called it "Breathalyzer Bunko." Trust me, no drunk driving came out of that party. Drunko bunko my ass! I ought to beat Janice Wasserman over the head with a nine iron. She has no idea how much we've always looked out for one another. We may not be drink counters, but we certainly know how to monitor who is and who is not capable of getting behind the wheel. By the way, I brought the party favors to Tootsie's house, the newest Breathalyzer on the market. It has a keychain attachment and I got them for forty dollars apiece on an eBay Dutch auction.

"Welcome to John Wayne Airport in beautiful Orange County, California, where the local time is three forty-five," says the Barbie flight attendant. "For those of you with connecting flights please check the monitors just inside the gate area. If the O.C. is your final destination, we hope you have a pleasant stay. Meanwhile we ask that you please stay seated with your seat belts fastened until the captain brings the aircraft to a complete stop and turns off the fasten seat belts sign."

The plane jolts to a halt and I grab my roller suitcase from the overhead bin. I'm first off the plane. Stepping into a crowded waiting area, a sea of tired faces look at me blankly. Gone are the days of excited smiles and expectant eyes, when family members and friends waited at the gate to be the first to welcome you home, or whisk you away toward what were sure to be happy and fun-filled vacation hours. Now the people at the gate are plugged into iPods, laptops, BlackBerries and cell phones, and merely idle away minutes awaiting announcements from the equally bored ground crew, who let them know it's their turn to walk through the accordion and onto the plane.

Pulling my suitcase behind me, I walk with the Saturday crowd—mostly families with one parent pushing an overloaded stroller and the other chasing after a three-year-old. I glance at the shops filled with colorful souvenirs reminding me where I am. "The O.C." screams at me from the front of every type of garment ever made.

The line for the ladies room snakes out a wide opening and into the corridor. Just past it, the opening to the men's room is as barren as a cave. Women take so much more time with everything.

Striding past the security area, I see three people standing with their arms outstretched while uniformed agents wave wands over their bodies. Others sit replacing their shoes and threading their belts through their pants. I can't help but chuckle at the strange choreography of modern air travel.

"Welcome home, Miss," says a uniformed black man seated in a director's chair. "From that smile it looks like you're happy to be here."

Startled, I slow my pace and curb my smile, changing my expression to a frown. Is this guy talking to me?

"Don't worry, Miss," he says. "Your secret is safe with me."

"What did you just say to me?"

"Nothing, Miss. Have a nice stay." He smiles a brilliant white smile.

I focus on his teeth. *Your secret is safe with me.* I repeat these words to myself. It's the voice of Amanda Prince I hear inside my head. It's what she said to me on the night she showed up at Chlöe's Dice Club—on the night of Tara's accident.

"Thank you," I say absently.

Lowering my eyes, I head toward the escalator, planning to make my way to the taxi stand. I'll be at Dad's place in time to do a little grocery shopping and prepare him a nice dinner. Corn beef and cabbage. It's his favorite and it's what he expects of me.

"Well there she is," says a familiar, gravely voice. "The best thing I ever did."

I look up. Standing just to the right of the escalator with both hands perched atop a gnarled, chest-high walking stick is my father. A yellowed smile surrounded by gray stubble lights his face. His eyes sparkle like light sapphire crystals as he tips his white admiral's cap.

"Dad?"

"Ahoy there, Brandy Lynn," he says, stretching out an arm. "Thought I'd take a ride out here and surprise you. And from the look on your face I can see that I did."

I move toward his outstretched arm and feel his strong fingers burrow into my shoulder. As he pulls me close and holds me, the polarized feelings I have for this man—my father, Daddy—crash inside my skull and rumble like an earthquake.

"Thank you for coming, Sweetie," he whispers in my ear. "I'm so glad you're here."

"Dad." His grip is tight. Utterly secure. I feel locked inside it. Locked inside as the battle between love and hate roars, waging war inside my brain and threatening to fill my eyes with tears. I feel myself start to squirm and long to detach.

"Detach with love." It's a distant, silent voice—another Al-anon slogan, one I've never quite mastered. It's only easy to detach when he isn't right in front of me. I've worked hard to set my limits, to define through a bold exterior what I would and wouldn't tolerate from the people in my life. With everyone else, it's easy. But with my father?

Maybe that's my true secret.

Patting his bony back, I harden in self-defense. He's too thin. I'll add ice cream and chocolate chip cookies to the grocery list. Maybe a six-pack of M.G.D.

Finally, he releases me. "I can't believe you came all the way here, Dad. I was just thinking that no one ever comes to the airport anymore to greet arriving passengers. I miss that."

"The only thing I miss these days besides Mommy is you," he says. "How long can you stay?"

I take a step back and wipe my eyes with an index finger. "I don't know, Dad. I don't know." Unzipping my purse, I reach inside for a tissue. "Let's just take it one day at a time. Okay?"

The old man nods and looks at his watch. "Whoop!" he says. "Whatta ya know? It's four bells."

"Four bells and all is well?"

"Now that you're here. Let's say we take a taxi to the nearest happy hour and have ourselves a belt."

"Daddy, you're impossible." I use the tissue to dab at my eyes and then give my nose a quick blow. Balling up the tissue, I stuff it inside my purse and while zipping it closed, spy the keychain-sized Breathalyzer safely tucked inside. Looking up at my dad, his fuzzy gray eyebrows arched in expectation, it occurs to me that I may never again have the need to use a Breathalyzer.

Chapter 13
September

While the first thing anyone learns about the game of bunko is that it's as easy as counting to six, perhaps the last thing anyone learns is that it dates back to the 1800s. Some believe the original game, Eight-Dice Cloth, came from England, however, today's bunko got its start during the Gold Rush in the city of San Francisco. Bunko, derived from the Spanish card game banco, *also has ties to the street corner rip off known as "Three Card Monte."*

Gold Rush-era bunko included both dice and cards, and took over gambling houses or Bunko Parlors. Soon, the term "bunko" became synonymous with "swindle" or "fraud," and was the new moniker for any game resembling a scam.

In the last half of the nineteenth century, bunko gained respectability and play worked its way eastward, across the plains and to New York. Soon, the dice-only version was a popular parlor game. Then during Prohibition, bunko had a relapse, and once again found its way into illicit gambling halls and speakeasies that cropped up in the Midwest. In the city of Chicago in particular, the notorious Bunko Squad regularly performed raids on bunko parlors.

—Shonah Bartlett
From her column, *The Dice Club Chronicles*

Sylvia

I'm using a new brush to apply blush to the apple of my cheek. Relaxing my makeup application smile, I bite my lower lip and consider what lipstick might look best with my pale yellow camisole. I have a conference with my daughter's "Area Studies" teacher. Why the girl has chosen to focus an entire semester on China, of all places, is incomprehensible. "Our national debt is, like, eight trillion dollars, Mother," she had said haughtily. "And China, like, practically owns us. We should know as much about *them* as possible. Next semester? I'm taking Mandarin lessons. There's a night course downtown, and I'll have my driver's license by then."

She gets it from Richard.

I don't know why the teacher called me in for a conference. I wonder what he looks like. He sounded young on the phone. Is he Asian? What do Asians sound like? I cock my head, first to the right, then left, and run my fingers through my hair. Something that feels a lot like excitement stirs inside me.

Rifling through my lipstick drawer, the tubes and pencils rolling like tools in a disorganized junk drawer, I make a mental note to organize my makeup. Dissatisfied with my choices, I close the drawer and place my hands on my hips. Pivoting, I face the long corridor leading to the compartmentalized storage areas of my closet. Walking past the shoes, the suits, and the warm temperature jackets, I turn at the warm temperature tops section. Neatly folded and stacked along the left wall are my camisoles, arranged in a pastel rainbow. Pink, apricot, lemon—I smack my lips. Pulling the lemon one from the stack, I flap it open and examine it. Perfect.

"Hon?" calls Richard from outside the closet entrance. "You in there?"

"Back here. Tops. Warm weather."

"C'mere a minute," he says. "I've got something to show you."

"Be right there." I put on the camisole, adjust my bra and thong straps, and sashay, hips first, to the closet entrance. It's my model walk. Blanca Midnight's got nothing on me!

"Close your eyes," says Richard.

"Close my eyes? What?"

"Just do it, Almost-Birthday-Girl."

"Richard, my birthday isn't until October! Are you trying to age me prematurely?" I refuse to close my eyes, and trot to the opening where Richard stands wearing nothing but a grin. His hands are behind his back and his penis stands straight out, pointing at me.

"You had better have something behind your back, Mister, cause I'm not putting out unless there's jewelry involved. And even then, you'll have to wait. I've got a meeting this morning and I'm not showering again."

Richard's smile doesn't fade. He's been so much more relaxed since his big case, the Turner case, is over and he won. "I said close your eyes."

"Okay, okay!" I succumb to his command and lower my lids. "But I'm really not ready to celebrate being another year older. I can't believe I'm going to be forty-six. That officially puts me in my late forties."

"That's mid-forties, and you're still just a sweet young thing," he says. I peek and see him pull his right hand from behind his back. He's putting something on his ...Oh my God! My eyes pop open. Richard has placed a necklace on his penis and it hangs like a small, sparkling noose. "Funny you should mention the number forty-six," he says with a chuckle.

"It's such a nothing number. Who cares after forty?"

"I care," he says. "Go ahead. Grab it."

"You mean the necklace, right?"

His inky black eyebrows dance toward his silver hairline. I try to frown, but my forehead stopped moving a long time ago. Taking the necklace into my hand, I gasp at the weight of it and hear Richard's penis *thwack* against his taught belly. "Richard! What did you do? Diamonds!"

"Designed by Marco Vincente," he says proudly. "There's forty-six. Count them if you like."

"Oh, my! It weighs a ton." I hold the stunning necklace to my throat and lean to the right, trying to see it in the mirror past Richard's broad, naked shoulder. "This is overwhelming. Where on earth am I going to wear it?"

"O-oh," he sings, "I don't know. Why not wear it to the next Dice Club and make those gals green with envy?"

That makes me laugh. "Darling, they're not the envious types. They're my friends."

Oh no. Suddenly it dawns on me. I lower the necklace and grasp Richard's wrist. "Please tell me you didn't have Amanda Prince pick out this necklace."

"What?"

"She told me. It was a few months back—back when she first returned to the Dice Club—that she was more like your personal shopper than your paralegal."

Richard places his hand on my waist. With the other, he uses his index finger to latch onto my thong strap. He pulls me close and buries his face in the crux of my neck. I feel his hardness against me and it prickles my skin. "I didn't," he whispers with warm breath. "I ordered this six months ago and asked him to have it ready before your birthday. It came in early and I couldn't stand to hold onto it for a whole month."

I put my arms around him. "Oh, Sweetheart. I'm sorry. I didn't mean ...I mean, ever since Amanda started therapy she's been working through her grief and things are finally good between us. I don't want to give her any reason to be..."

"Don't," he says, interrupting and pulling back. "Amanda loves you. I love you. *Everyone* loves you, Sylvia. You are a beautiful, kind, and generous woman. Happy birthday."

A chill travels down my spine and my sinuses pinch. I breathe in and gently close my eyes. Opening them, my vision blurred by tears, I exhale. I'm not sure I can speak. My muscles go limp looking at my handsome, loving husband standing before me vulnerable and naked. How lucky am I? How lucky am I to have this wonderful man in my life?

Thank you, God. Thank you for my life.

"Richard, it's a beautiful necklace. Will you help me put it on?"

"Of course," he says, taking the diamonds from me. He positions me in front of him and we both face the mirror. A handsome couple, we smile at our reflections.

"You better remember this when your real birthday comes along, so you're not expecting something else."

I laugh. "Uh, right." I know it's only the beginning of a very long birthday celebration. "You know something, Richard, I better get this in the safe. I can't let your daughter see it."

"What do you mean *my* daughter? You had something to do with creating that charming creature too, you know."

"Yes, but I'm not the one who talked her into taking Chinese lessons. I wipe a tear from my eye, careful not to smudge my mascara, and then reach behind my neck to unclasp the necklace. I let it dangle on the edges of my index fingers. "Show her this thing and she may sell it to try and pay back some of the national debt."

Leaving Richard behind in the shower, I follow the coffee aroma lure to our gourmet kitchen. I fill a cup, lightly blow into it and sip. Needs cream. Walking toward the subzero, I spot the newspaper on the counter unopened. "Ah, Shonah's column should be in here today."

Setting down my cup, I pick up the paper, and while working off the rubber band, Shonah's one-inch-by-one-inch, grainy newspaper photo comes to mind. It's great to have her back home. She and her boys were gone for the summer, staying with her widowed dad in Lake Oswego, which is just down the road from my own childhood home.

With Brandy away in Long Beach caring for her father, Tara in rehab, and the Dice Club taking its usual summer hiatus, it's been a lonely, hot summer in the Rattlesnake Valley.

Between trips to Cabo and St. Vincent, I've thought of my Dice Club friends often. Some of us got together to celebrate Chlöe's promotion to head nurse at the hospital, and Blanca Midnight had a very successful opening at the swanky Desert Artisans gallery, selling six paintings on the first night. My thoughts often drifted to Shonah in our hometown. I wished I were at the Lake with her. It's when Oregon is at its best because the sun finally comes out and stays. But my childhood home has long since sold. Last I heard it was worth over a million dollars. All the lakefront homes are—even those we once considered cottages.

Shonah and the boys left the Rattlesnake Valley on a high note. Jonas had taken his science fair project on global warming all the way to the State Finals where he received top honors. It was wonderful to see her and Dan learn the meaning of the phrase "bursting with pride."

How easily we live vicariously through our children.

I sit down at the kitchen table. Flipping newspaper pages, I hesitate when noticing a half-page, four-color ad for my plastic surgeon. I wonder when my next Botox appointment is. With my right hand, I feel for indentations between my eyebrows and continue turning pages with my left. Finally I spot Shonah's photo and use my palms to flatten the page. Turning them up, I scowl at the ink stains turning my skin gray. "Cheap piece of shit." Why doesn't she write for a different publication? I get up, walk to the sink and wash my hands.

"Mom, are you ready to go?"

I didn't hear my daughter enter the room since I was silently singing the second round of "Happy Birthday to You" while washing my hands. It's something I've done ever since I saw a segment on the *Today Show* about germs and how long one should spend lathering.

"Mom! I asked if you were, like, ready to go."

I turn off the faucet and look over my shoulder at my daughter. Her dark blonde hair is tied in ponytails and she has on a white collared shirt and a striped tie, obviously taken from Richard's closet.

"I don't want to be late for school," she says. "And you shouldn't keep Mr. Young waiting."

"Oh sure, Honey. I'm sorry, I didn't realize the time." I reach for a paper towel. Did she say Mr. Young? I knew there was something young about him. I'm worried I might have newspaper ink on my face. "Honey, how's my face?"

She's moved to the kitchen table and is hovering over the open newspaper. "Rubber Baby Buggy Bunko?" She rolls her eyes. "Your friends are weird, Mom."

"Perhaps. But none of them would think of wearing ponytails along with their father's power tie." I grin and reach for my car keys hanging on a cabinet hook next to the sink. Grabbing the jewel-encrusted "S" on my keychain, I wrap my fingers around the keys and move toward my daughter, glancing down at Shonah's headline, which is indeed, "Rubber Baby Buggy Bunko." I'll have to read it later. "Trust me, Sweetie, that headline is perfect for what our Dice Club is going through right now."

"It's gross, Mom. Tootsie Fennimore is, like, the oldest pregnant person ever. Why would anyone her age want to have a baby?"

"Not *a* baby, my darling. Babies."

Tara

Dressed in red shorts, a white tank top and running shoes, I hope Shonah notices without me having to ask that I'm interested in resuming our morning workout. Not yet ready to run, I do need to walk. Rehab may have saved my life, but when trading in pints of vodka for pints of Cherry Garcia and Chubby Hubby, I've packed on some pounds. According to my scale, twenty.

I need Shonah and I to get back to where we were before that day— before that terrible day when in the aftermath I believed I had killed her son. I'll never be able to express to her the shame and regret, the utter feeling of loss I have often imagined to be on a par with the way Amanda Prince feels about the loss of her child. I did my best to make amends with her and Dan during step nine of my program. And they were gracious. Their forgiveness has meant so much to me. But it seems to have come too easily. As a result I continue to beat myself up over it and I haven't been able to look either one of them in the face.

Oh, how I want things to get back to normal!

Taking a deep breath, I use my newly French-polished index finger to push the doorbell. It was silly to indulge in this manicure. I'll ruin it as soon as I set foot in my studio and open a bag of clay. I hug the newspaper to my chest like a protective shield and the door opens.

"Hi Mrs. Shephard."

I gasp for air, completely unprepared to see the beautiful, ivory-skinned boy before me. His dark hair hangs loosely just to the top of the gold wires of his John Lennon glasses. His smile exposes a full set of silver braces. Jonas. It's the first time I've seen him since the accident. Still hugging the newspaper, I feel the fake French tips dig into my exposed arms.

"What's the matter?" asks the boy. "My mom's here. She's just in the bathroom, I think. Probably doing the crossword puzzle."

"Nothing's wrong. I'm just surprised—actually happy—to see you. That's all. I never got to apologize for..."

"It's okay, Mrs. Shephard. It was just the airbag. Figures it was the one time my dad let me ride in the front seat. He'll never do *that* again. I'll be strapped in back for the rest of my life!"

I can't help but smile. "You're really growing up, aren't you?"

"I guess."

"Uh, wait a minute. Shouldn't you be on the bus?"

"I'm in middle school now, Mrs. S," he says proudly. "Later bus."

I should have known. It's just that my girls haven't been taking the bus. Ian has been driving them to school on his way to work. He's gotten a job as a project manager with Tootsie's husband, Michael Fennimore's, commercial construction company. They're working on a development about an hour south of the Rattlesnake Valley, and he's away from home so often that he wants to spend as much time as he can with the girls. They've become an inseparable trio. The girls now go to him first for all their questions—all their bumps and bruises. I have to work my way back into their life.

Jonas gestures toward the blue bag in my arms. "That Mom's paper?"

I laugh uncomfortably, caught in my insecurity. "Oh, this? Yes, yes it is. I picked it up at the end of the driveway."

"They switched the publication day to Thursday. I'll take it. Mom's column is in there today. First one since we got back from Oregon. I told her she should write a how-I-spent-my-summer-vacation essay, but she told me that was a shit idea. Her words. Not mine. Told me to stick to science and leave the writing to her."

I hand him the paper and smile. That's familiar. "I think I heard about that. I mean, your science project. What was it again?"

"Global warming," he says. "Uh, thanks. Say, you wanna come in? She should be out in a minute. I'd knock on her door but she'd probably kill me."

She'd probably kill me. Kill me. **Kill me**...

"Mrs. S.?"

I feel my head shaking as the words "kill me" reverberate like an echo across a wide lake.

"No? I mean, I could knock. She wouldn't really kill me, you know."

"No, I know she wouldn't k-kill you. Of course not. Listen, never mind. Why don't you just tell her I'll see her tonight at Tootsie's baby shower. Okay?"

"Yeah, how 'bout that? Mom says she's having twins. Calls 'em 'Roll' and 'Pop.' You know, like Tootsie Roll and Tootsie Pop?" His voice surprisingly lifts an octave when he says the word "pop" and it makes him laugh. It's an innocent, jubilant laugh.

What a beautiful child. Thank God he's alive.

"Have you seen her, Mrs. S.?"

"Seen who?"

"Tootsie Fennimore. Have you seen her?"

I shake my head.

"She's huge! I think she's got at least three in there. Anyway, I gotta run and catch my bus. I'll tell Mom you came by. She says you're all having a Rubber Baby Buggy Bunko party tonight. That's cool."

"Yes. It's cool. Very cool."

The door closes and I turn, focusing on the long, asphalt driveway before me. I have one hundred and eighty days, my six-months chip. Slowly making my way back home, I wonder, can I bring myself to face everyone again? And can I do it without taking a drink?

Shonah

With yesterday's newspaper under my arm and reading glasses perched on my nose, I emerge from the bathroom a new woman. Glad to be back in the weekday routine, I breathe in the quiet atmosphere of my home. The boys are off to school, Dan has a morning full of meetings, and I have an easy writing assignment to tackle. My editor asked me to write a column about the history of the game of bunko. He said his wife, a prestigious neurosurgeon, has been invited to join a bunko group in their exclusive Foothills neighborhood, and wants to know a little bit more about this game before she responds. It's hard to imagine anyone being that cerebral about whether or not to play the game of bunko—neurosurgeon or not.

I think *he* just wants to know. Men are often lurkers outside of their women's bunko groups. I told him the topic wouldn't be a problem. In fact, the opening line presented itself the minute he asked:

While the first thing anyone learns about the game of bunko is that it's as easy as counting to six, perhaps the last thing anyone learns is that it dates back to the 1800s.

Glancing at my kitchen calendar, the household diary of all activities, I take note of soccer practices after school and Tootsie's baby shower tonight. Just like last year's first party of the season, I'm the host. The difference this year is that I'm not the least bit frantic. I've hired a caterer, and a cleaning team is coming this afternoon to de-bug my home. I still have to wrap the gift, however. Tootsie might not know a thing about being a mother—yet—but she does know about gift-wrapping. Most of us in the Dice Club spent more time laboring over the proper packaging than on deciding what to give this first-time mommy.

She's going to be really surprised. I'm giddy with the thought.

I pour orange juice into a glass, lock the front door, and walk to my office, where I find *The Rattlesnake Times* sitting on my chair. A yellow sticky note is attached to it.

Tara delivered this. Said to tell you she came by. C-ya after school. XOX, Jonas.

That was nice. She must have come by while I was in the bathroom.

I pull the paper from my chair, sit down and open it to my column. "Rubber Baby Buggy Bunko." I read aloud. Can't help but laugh through my nose.

Then it hits me. "Oh shit!" Quickly, I close the paper. If Tootsie reads this, she'll know what the Dice Club is up to tonight. They'll label me the spoiler! I eye the phone. My first instinct is to call Sylvia. No, Brandy—she'll know what to do, or at least give an honest opinion. Damn, why didn't I think to call Michael Fennimore to have him keep Tootsie from seeing the column before the shower?

Wait a minute. I set down the phone and switch on the computer. "Get over yourself, Shonah!" As if all my friends race to open the newspaper to see what I have to say! "I'm sure." Tootsie, pregnant with twins, surely has a lot of other things on her mind.

Clearing my own mind, I wait for the computer to finish its warm-up routine and then click on my word processing program and read through my piece on the history of bunko.

...In the city of Chicago in particular, the notorious Bunko Squad regularly performed raids on bunko parlors.

I lift my fingers from the keyboard. The Dice Club is like a bunko squad. Each month, we truly do raid one another's homes, kick out the men and the kids, and fill it with too much noise. I've read that seven million American women play the game of bunko, and it's deemed a legitimate form of entertainment in suburban developments across America. They're even playing it in the Foothills!

There's even an Association dedicated to this dice game, which was chartered in 1996, and it claims to be "dedicated to the organization, preservation, promotion and expansion" of bunko. The Association credits the return to "traditional family values" for the bunko explosion of the 1980s.

Again I stop and give thought to the phrase "traditional family values." Hmm. Would Tara agree that her Dice Club nights of the past had anything to do with a return to traditional family values? Dice Club night, if anything, is a night to *escape* traditional family values. Having mommy connect with her gal pals by releasing her from the role of Sisyphus housewife or working mother to cavort with a group of women—potentially wild, well-on-their-way-to-tossing-600-threadcount-sheets-to-the-desert-wind women—is not a family value. I lean back in my chair and wonder. "What kind of value is it?"

There's only one way to find out. I grab the yellow sticky note from the newspaper and push back my chair. Where did I leave my running shoes?

Tara

It's another warm day and the studio is awash with mid-morning light. Full of energy, I voraciously attack a mound of wet clay. It feels cool and soothing on my hands. Perched atop a stool, wearing a red apron over my running shorts and sleeveless top, it takes no time to ruin my manicure, and for streaks of dried clay to decorate my limbs and cheeks like war paint. I feel a creative frenzy coming on. Time for a new, exclusive line of Tara Shephard platters. The Rehab Line. Or something.

I have a lot of catching up to do.

I realize I may be trying to replace alcoholism with workaholism, but at least I do it with a clear head. And it will only mean one thing:

profit. I've let down my family by spending so much time away, and now I'll work the rest of my life making it up to them.

The artist inside me is soothing. I look around the studio. I'm happy here. Defined. A soft, yearning ballad, James Blunt, pours from the surround-sound speakers. With my hands occupied, I lower my elbow to the remote control, turning up the volume.

You're beautiful. You're beautiful it's true.

I think I hear a faint knocking on the studio door, but let it pass, singing with the music. A second later there's a pounding. Definitely someone here. I yell over the music. "It's open." Looking up from the clay, I see my friend enter the room. A flashback, a hot jab of memory, fills me. I pull my hands from the clay and grab my knees, covering them with the cold, gray substance. It dries at once, crazing upon my skin like damaged molds as I place my bare feet on the floor and stand up. I reach for the remote and turn down the music.

"I heard you came by," says Shonah. "Jonas left a note."

"Jonas, yes." I rub my palms against my apron. "I can't tell you how good it was to see him."

"Yeah? Well? He's a great kid," Shonah looks around the room. I look with her. Everything is organized. Neat. She rubs her nervous fingers through her bangs. "Looks like you're back to work. I didn't mean to interrupt, but I was wondering if maybe you'd like to start working out again? How's your leg?"

"Oh, right. That's why I came by. I wanted to know if *you* were interested. My leg is much better. I'd have to go slow, but I've just gotta do *something*. Look at me. I've completely blimped out!"

"Tara," she says, "I don't think I've ever seen you look better. You look, uh, healthy!"

I snort. "You mean fat!"

"No!"

"It's okay. I know it. But, yes. Yes, I'd love to go with you. Can you sit down for a minute first while I clean up?"

"Are you sure? I mean, it looks like you're in the middle of this."

"Oh, it doesn't matter. This is more important. There's something I have to tell you anyway, and I just have to get it off my chest." We both look at her large breasts. "You know it's funny? I've gained twenty pounds and it's all in my butt. These bad boys have stayed exactly the same." I turn and walk to the sink, plunging my hands in cool water trapped there where my tools are soaking.

Shonah laughs and follows me to the sink. "Is that what you wanted to tell me?"

"What? No." Turning on the faucet, I rinse my hands then reach for a clean rag. "It's about that day. You know, that day here in the studio and the things I said to you."

She shakes her head, protesting. "It's not important, Tara."

"It *is* important. It's important to me, and it's part of the program. The steps."

"Is this the one where you make amends?" asks Shonah. "Cause listen, as far as we're concerned you already did that. You don't have to make any apologies to me. Really, it's not necessary."

"Shonah, just hold up a second. It's not that. It's part of step five that I don't feel I've really completed. It's about admitting the true nature of our wrongs, or something like that. It's about the accident."

"Tara, I told you…"

"It's about your son. Jonas."

"My son? Tara, I told you it was minor."

"Not for me. I've been living with this horrible thing since I woke up in the hospital and I haven't been able to tell you. And it's stupid, really, because today when I saw him …I mean, when he answered your door, it hit me."

"What hit you?"

"It hit me that …It. Didn't. Really. Happen."

"Tara, I don't know what you're talking about but you're actually starting to scare me."

I grab her wrist, pull her to the stool in front of the workbench, and motion for her to sit. "When I was in the coma, I must have been going in an out of consciousness. I kept seeing Chlöe Forrest standing there. I could actually see her black roots! Those horrible one-inch roots. Then all of a sudden, everything I knew to be good and clear and right just disappeared."

"Chlöe *was* there," says Shonah. "We were all there."

"I know. It's like I saw ya'll through the whole thing. I saw the entire Dice Club."

"Tara, what does this have to do with Jonas?"

I take deep breath. I have to say it. "I thought it was him. I mean, I thought …I thought the one on the table with the flat line that Chlöe told me about, the one they pronounced dead …I thought it was your son and that I had killed him because I was blind drunk behind the wheel."

Shonah stands up and puts her hands on my shoulders. "Stop."

I close my eyes and drop my head. "I know it didn't happen. But it could have."

"It didn't."

"I know I'm being ridiculous holding onto this guilt. This all-encompassing guilt. But it was so real." I take another deep breath and then spew out the words. "I couldn't get it out of my head that I'd done it. And that you'd never speak to me again, and that I'd be in jail, and my kids would have to come see me wearing that ugly orange jumpsuit—I look terrible in orange. And that they'd forever have to live with the fact that their mother was a drunk murderer and..."

"Stop it!" shouts Shonah. "Just stop it right now or I swear I'll slap you."

"You should! I know I said some awful, hurtful things to you. And I know you were just trying to help." I feel my eyes glaze over. "I'm sorry, Shonah. I'm truly very, very sorry."

She puts her hand behind my head, grasping a handful of hair, and pulls me forward. It actually hurts me. Good. I want her to hurt me. "*Shhh,*" she says. "It's okay."

Stroking my hair she holds me like a mother holds a child and does her best to soothe me. "Why, Shonah? How can you be so understanding?"

"It's the most valuable thing I have to offer you, Tara," she says.

I look up into her kind, calm face and she smiles at me.

"It's the gift of my friendship."

Epilogue
Rubber Baby Buggy Bunko Shower

I haven't attended a baby shower in a hundred years. And the last time I hosted one it was still a cute party game to guess the measurement of the pregnant girl's tummy. Aside from the games, our discussions at these showers included things like the debate over breast milk vs. formula or disposal diapers vs. cloth.

A forty-something Dice Club friend of mine is about to give birth for the first time and tonight I'm hosting a shower for her. Because all our Dice Club parties are themed, we've dubbed it "Rubber Baby Buggy Bunko." Our debate while planning this shower has had nothing to do with diapers or formula, but rather, it's been about the question, how late is too late in life to have a baby? Some of my friends, for example, wonder how long will older parents be around to raise these late-in-life babies and, even more importantly, will they have the energy?

When it comes to my friend I know these aren't concerns. She, in fact, may have been the first person to utter the slogan, "forty is the new thirty." And it's ridiculous to think that she'll be doing any of this on her own.

Which brings me to another recent debate the Dice Club had when Hillary Clinton was still running for the White House. It was over the premise of her book, It Takes A Village. *With this book, she made the African proverb, "it takes a village to raise a child" the basis of her thesis about raising a new generation of strong, purposeful young adults. Most of the people in the room thought her book was a platform for socialism and other ultra liberal concepts they'd never accept. I, on the other hand, sided with Hillary on this one, that it does indeed take occasional input from a grandparent, a neighbor, a teacher or a friend to lend a hand. Anyone who's ever done carpool duty can't disagree. Parenting—good parenting—is hard work. We could all use a little help from time to time.*

In the past year, my Dice Club has learned to ban together as a supportive group of friends in ways we never expected. And because of this, our pregnant friend will have so much help with her new bundles of joy—yes she's having twins—she'll think she hired a staff.

Clearly, in her case, it doesn't take a village. It takes a Dice Club.

—Shonah Bartlett
From her column *The Dice Club Chronicles*

Tootsie

The room, a well-appointed living area in southern Arizona, has all the elements of a bunko party. But it isn't. It's a baby shower. I sit in an oversized chair, an upholstered throne some call a "mother-daughter chair"—a place where I might lovingly nurse my first born children and later read aloud *Good Night Moon* and *Charlotte's Web*. A half-empty punch bowl and picked over dessert trays are in the background, and seven women surround me, filling the warm air with high-pitched laughter and enthusiastic reaction to each gift I open.

My name is Tootsie Fennimore, and I'm forty-one years-old. I'm a first-time mother carrying twins, and I fill this big-ass chair. After a long battle with infertility, I'm so happy about my pregnancy and the support of my loving friends, that I've vowed to make each member of the Snake Eyes Dice Club an honorary godmother.

Some feel the term *grandmother* might be more appropriate; however, my mother, the dignified Veronica Vermillion Thompson, would never hear of that. She'll be the one and only grandmother of these children.

As usual I was running late and was the last to arrive. All the women stood in front of a massive pile of the best-wrapped gifts anyone has ever seen, and from what they tell me, they couldn't wait to yell "Surprise!" when I walked into the room.

I wasn't surprised, though, and I didn't even fake it. I told them I'd known about it for days.

"For days?" asked Shonah. "You mean it wasn't my column that gave it away?"

"Oh, I saw the column all right, Darlin'," I told her. "Very cute. Didn't make me feel old at all!" I rested my hands atop my enormous belly and nodded my head up and down, indicating yes. "Truly, Shonah, has it really been that many years since you last attended a baby shower?"

"Tootsie," said Shonah, "I didn't mean…"

"Oh, I'm just kiddin' with ya, sister. I loved the article. I've already cut it out and put it in my babies' scrapbook."

Sylvia

After my meeting with Mr. Young, my daughter's exceptionally good-looking and flirty Area Studies teacher, I took a long cold shower, and chose my sexier, black silk camisole for the evening. Tonight I wear it along with a pair of low-slung blue jeans and my new diamond necklace.

I admit I was the one who told Tootsie about the surprise shower. "You can all blame me."

"That's right, she did tell me," says Tootsie, surveying the dropped jaws around the room. "And thank the good Lord she did. Had I walked in and heard ya'll shout like that, I might have given birth right there in Shonah's front hallway."

"I'm a nurse," says Chlöe. "Head nurse at the hospital, in fact. I'd be able to deliver your babies."

"I could've boiled the water," Brandy says. "Or used tongs as forceps."

"I had a C-section," says Amanda.

"So did I," calls out Tara. "You think I could-a had *one* of them naturally. But no! I have to do everything the hard way."

"Well I'm the mother of five," says Brandy. "Even though I didn't give birth to all of them, if anyone can juggle multiple children it's me. And Tootsie, I'd bet my youngest that you're carrying more than two. I think there's a litter in there. You're HUGE!"

"Shut up, Brandy," sings everyone in unison.

Brandy smiles mischievously and then licks her middle finger and marks the air with an invisible one.

Blanca Midnight reaches out and puts her hand on Tootsie's belly. "You're not all that big *mi'ja*. You should have seen me with my first. But I did it the old fashioned way. I huffed and I puffed and blew that *nene* out!"

"Would that be the same *nene* who saw my very sad naked self the night you made me model a thong?" asks Tootsie.

"Yes, *mija*. But he was a lot smaller twelve years ago."

"So was she," says Brandy, again licking her finger, stroking the air and tallying imaginary points.

Shonah links her arm in Brandy's. "I've missed you," she says. "Brandy, you are one of a kind."

"No she's not," says Tara. "She's a twin!"

Shonah

I sit at Tootsie's feet and record each gift opened by the guest of honor. Knowing Tootsie will appreciate it I make detailed notes about the gift-wrap next to each item.

After nearly an hour of opening gifts and passing them around the room for all to admire, I record the last of them:

Sylvia: New Mother's Deluxe Spa Package. White basket, yellow cellophane wrap with two white bunny bows.

Blanca: Double layette. One white. One mint green. Rainbow tissue paper, yellow ribbons.

"There's only one more," says Tara. She raises her eyebrows and nods in the direction of a giant box filling the corner of the room. It's the size of a clothes dyer and covered in newspaper. All heads turn and stare at it.

"You wanna bring me that big one, Brandy?" asks Tootsie. "I think a strong gal like you can lift it." She winks at me.

"That's from me," calls out Amanda.

Brandy rises, happy to accept the challenge. She approaches the box, squats and wraps her tanned, toned arms around its middle. "What is it?" Grunting, she lifts and straightens with ease. "Damn! It's a lot lighter than I thought it would be." She carries it to Tootsie and places it at her feet.

"I know my wrap job sucks," says Amanda. "Don't judge me, okay? Costco didn't have any stork paper and I had to resort to the colored ad pages of the Sunday paper."

"This is more like the Olympics of gift giving rather than gift wrapping," says Tootsie. "Seems I've fallen in with the right group of mothers."

"That's us," says Brandy. "Nothin' but a bunch of mother f... "

"Don't you DARE say it," says Sylvia.

Tootsie tears the paper in sections, like peeling a banana, and exposes the large black letters identifying the contents. "Diapers!" she squeals. "A mountain of newborn-size disposable diapers. This should last me a while, hey?"

"You'll go through those in no time!"

"Good Lord! Diapers!"

"I hardly remember changing diapers."

"Seems I spent half my life up to my elbows in those damn things."

"That's one thing I DO NOT miss."

"Oooh, that's such an itty-bitty size."

"They grow up so fast."

"You're going to use disposables?" asks Chlöe.

The entire room goes silent and everyone turns their heads toward Chlöe Forrest.

"What?" she asks innocently, holding up her hands. "You rich American women don't realize the problem *aboot* disposable diapers in the landfills? I mean, I know it takes a little more time to use the pins or the cover-ups and then wash and dry them and all, but I managed with all three of my kids, in spite of always having to work and do all the household chores like cooking and cleaning and shopping and..."

"Somebody stop her," says Blanca. "Somebody stop her right now before it's too late and I put my hands around her neck."

Tara, sitting next to Chlöe, drapes her arm around Chlöe's shoulders and pulls her close. "It's okay, Chlöe. We all love you." And then she cups her hand around Chlöe's ear and whispers, "I used cloth diapers too."

"Well, I claim to be this big environmentalist, but I used disposables too," I offer. "Even on the one who educated the Rattlesnake Valley about the evils of Global Warming. No one is allowed to tell him that. Do you hear me?"

"You can make it up to the environment in another way," says Sylvia. "Start a recycling program in your neighborhood."

"A diaper recycling program?" asks Chlöe.

Brandy looks at her, cocks her head and frowns. "Is she fucking serious or what?"

Chlöe

"Well that's the last of them," says Shonah, rising. "Should I break out the cake?"

Blanca and Tara go to work picking up discarded wrapping paper and collecting used plates and glasses. I ask Shonah if I can see the list of gifts. She hands it to me and I sit on the arm of Tootsie's chair, reading over who brought what gifts to the shower.

Suddenly, I feel a tight squeeze on my shoulder. I turn my head and meet Tootsie's penetrating gaze. I never realized it before, but she has two different colored eyes. The left is as blue and watery as the Caribbean Sea, and the right one is green, like an emerald jewel. And right now it has all the intensity of a frightened cat. "What's the matter?"

Tootsie tightens her lock on my shoulder and a deep vertical crease appears between her mismatched eyes. That's a labor pain if I've ever seen one. "Tootsie, how many weeks along are you?"

Tootsie purses her lips and blows out in short puffs.

"Oh, baby," says Sylvia, witnessing the action.

"Babies," I correct. I move my hand to Tootsie's knee. "How many weeks?"

"Thirty-seven," she says.

"Term for twins is thirty-eight. That's what they told you, right?"

"She's right," says Shonah. "My sister has twins. Okay, nobody panic. Tootsie, I want you to breathe."

"What's happening?" asks Blanca.

"Should I boil water?" Sylvia asks.

Tootsie relaxes and smiles. She takes my hand into hers. "I'm fine," she says. "Just a little Braxton-Hicks, I guess."

"That's false labor," I announce. "It's when…"

"We KNOW what it is, Chlöe," everyone says at the same time.

Blanca

Tootsie's pain seems to have gone away. I bring her a piece of cake, and Chlöe brings her a cup of juice. The rest of the Dice Club busies themselves by cleaning up the remains of the party.

Amanda Prince eats the last bite of cake and places her empty paper plate in the trash. From the kitchen, she looks at Tootsie holding court like a queen, big as the room. I approach her. "You okay, *mi'ja?*"

"Yes, never better," she says, nodding at Tootsie. "Just look at her over there. Her flushed cheeks and happy smile exude life. How lucky she is. How lucky she is to be at the beginning of life. The start of it all."

Amanda takes one last sip of her juice, throws away the cup, and approaches Tootsie.

"Tootsie," she says softly, "I know we don't know each other all that well, but, I …I just wanted to tell you…"

All at once, Tootsie's eyes close and her face crumples into a roadmap of deep, agonizing lines. She drops her cup, spilling juice into her lap. "Ach!" she cries.

I rush to her side. "Just breath, *mi'ja*. Just like they say in the birthing classes. I tell you, it really works." Everyone starts calling out instructions. Too many mothers.

"Blow out in short puffs."

"It really helps."

"He-He-He-Whooooooooo!"

"Oh my God," says Shonah, spying the wet juice stain in Tootsie's lap. "Did her water break?"

Tootsie closes her eyes, blows out her breath in short puffs as directed, and clutches my and Amanda's hands as though she were holding on for her life.

"That was really close to the last one," says Sylvia.

"It's probably not time yet," Chloe says, "but to be on the safe side, I think we should get her to the hospital. I'll get her right in and call the doc."

"I think that's a good idea," says Tootsie, releasing her grasp and moving her hands to the chair arms in an attempt to stand. "Will someone call Michael?"

"What car should we take?" asks Tara. "Anyone bring something big?"

"I've got the new Tahoe," says Shonah.

"Range Rover," I offer.

"I drove the Suburban. She can lie down in the backseat," offers Chloe. "Haven't lost the house or the car, all thanks to Valley General Hospital."

Amanda

"I've got Manny's van. There's a bed back there. She'll be comfortable and some of you can sit with her. I'll drive to the hospital."

Sylvia turns to me and raises her eyebrows. She mouths the words, "Are you sure?"

I nod. "Yes, I'm sure. It's time. It's time to go back to that hospital and this time, to celebrate life." I take a deep breath, look at Tootsie and smile. "I can't think of a better way to do it."

"Neither can I," says Tootsie.

I kiss her cheek. "What do you say? Ready?"

"Of course, Amanda," she says. "Thank you. But let's get this ball rolling. These little darlins' might not wait."

Tara

Amanda and Blanca each take an arm and escort Tootsie toward the door. Sylvia grabs Tootsie's purse and follows. I open the door for them and they step through it as a unit. Tootsie stops, turns, and sees the happy and hopeful expressions of all her friends. "Wish me luck," she says.

"Good luck, Tootsie. We'll be right behind you."

"I'm calling the hospital," yells Chlöe.

I close the door and those of us who remain gather our things and prepare to make our way to the hospital, just as I know they did the night they came to look after me.

Shonah, who pushes her bangs from her forehead, looks at me from across the room and gives me a reassuring smile. "Chlöe," she says pointing toward the kitchen, "the phone's over there."

I realize, of course, it's a much different atmosphere than that dreadful night.

How grateful I am to have these women in my life here in the Rattlesnake Valley. They've made me feel like I belong. They are my steel tumbleweeds.

Brandy

There are only four of us left. Tara, Shonah, Chlöe the Canadian, and me. I'm not getting stuck cleaning up this mess. Quickly I grab three baby bottles, jump on top of the diaper box, and begin juggling the bottles. I get the rhythm and sing at the top of my lungs:

"Toot, Toot, Tootsie, goodbye...Toot, Tootsie, don't cry..."

They all watch as I complete my performance. Tara's smiling, Chlöe's spewing her schedule for the next three days, and Shonah's shaking her head.

I manage to get through the first verse of my made up song before I drop one of the bottles. Not bad, not bad. I always was a decent juggler. Learned how to do it at the sorority by using lemons from the tree in the backyard.

In spite of themselves, the girls applaud. So, I jump down off the box, bow at the waist, straighten, then place my middle finger in my mouth and once again, make a tally in the air. "We had better get to that hospital before Tootsie Roll and Tootsie Pop make their debut, don't you think?"

They nod their heads, grab their purses, and we head for the door.

It's going to be another long night for the Snake Eyes Dice Club.

Acknowledgements

The women in the bunko group of which I've been a part for several years inspired the characters in this book. They willingly provided their "porn names" when I requested them, and each month proved to me that real life is far more funny than any fiction I could create. I know a few may be nervous that I've broken the rule of "what happens at bunko stays at bunko," but they should rest easy when they meet the characters of the Snake Eyes Dice Club, all products of my imagination. To all of you, past and present, I offer my respect and thanks for allowing me to be a part of your lives. I love you, ladies.

Thanks to Ric Bollinger, Sligo Literary Agency, McKenna Publishing Group, and to Leslie Parker.

Thanks to Mike for taking care of the kids on the first Thursday of the month for Bunko Night, (and the first Wednesday for Book Club) and for all your input. Thanks to readers Karen Gardner, John Leary, Diana Methot, Melinda Bollinger, Selah Cooper-Holl, Wendy Chestnut, Kirk Ort, Stephanie Chelly, Jerry Travis, Hope Hollenbeck, Aury Wellington, Greg Crites, and many other reader/reviewers on thenextbigwriter. com, where I published the original version of this manuscript a few years ago. Thanks also to Anne and Dan Beaver. When you get to the Epilogue, you'll know why.

Printed in the United States
141124LV00003B/97/P

9 781932 172300